La Mariage

Le Mariage

Diane Johnson

Chatto & Windus
LONDON

Published by Chatto & Windus 2000

First published in the United States in 2000
by Dutton, a member of Penguin Putnam Inc.

2 4 6 8 10 9 7 5 3 1

First published in Great Britain in 2000 by
Chatto & Windus
Random House, 20 Vauxhall Bridge Road,
London SW1V 2SA

Random House Australia (Pty) Limited
20 Alfred Street, Milsons Point, Sydney,
New South Wales 2061, Australia

Random House New Zealand Limited
18 Poland Road, Glenfield,
Auckland 10, New Zealand

Random House (Pty) Limited
Endulini, 5A Jubilee Road, Parktown 2193, South Africa

The Random House Group Limited Reg. No. 954009
www.randomhouse.co.uk

A CIP catalogue record for this book
is available from the British Library

ISBN 0701169702

Papers used by Random House are natural,
recyclable products made from wood grown in sustainable forests;
the manufacturing processes conform to the environmental
regulations of the country of origin

Printed and bound in Great Britain by
Mackays of Chatham plc

To the memory of
Alice Adams and
William Abrahams

What the artist calls good, the object of all his playful pains, his life-and-death jesting, is nothing less than a parable of the right and the good, a representation of all human striving after perfection.

—Thomas Mann, *Homage to Kafka*

Le Mariage

1

Clara

It was widely agreed among the other Americans in Paris that Clara Holly had the ideal life here, and people also agreed that if her good fortune had distanced her slightly from the normal lot of Americans, even from human beings generally, it hadn't made a monster of her as often seems to happen to women in her category—beautiful, rich, well married, far from her Oregon beginnings. Sometimes women in this category, married to Europeans, are seen to acquire unplaceable mid-Atlantic accents and a certain amnesia about being American except for eight weeks spent on Martha's Vineyard every summer.

"And sometimes fortunate people can come to feel that they have earned their good fortune," remarked the princess Sternholz, née Dorothy Minor from Cincinnati, of Clara, though she liked her.

Clara Holly remembered her roots, yet would rather not, and almost never went back to the U.S. When in Paris she belonged very much to the American world that exists like a specialized form in a complex ecosystem, dependent on its hosts but apart from them, extending mossily from the Marais to Neuilly, the stodgy suburb to the northwest, and into the delightful countryside between Saint-Cloud and Versailles—so Marie Antoinette in its pretension to wildness, nature, and simplicity.

Clara and her husband Serge Cray, the renowned if now somewhat reclusive director, live out there, near the village of Etang-la-Reine, in a château of exceptional beauty that had once briefly belonged to Madame du Barry. This was a decrepit structure that had somehow escaped the notice of the ministry of such things, fallen into further decay, briefly become a bed-and-breakfast, and been bought by a newly rich Russian who sold its *boiseries* and *cheminées*—its panelling and fireplaces. After Serge Cray bought it, he directed the refurbishment, using studio carpenters and props from his costume film *Queen Caroline*, and Clara had thrown herself into restoring the gardens, going into Paris only a couple of times a week to shop or see an art show or go to a party.

Clara was always planning to go back to Oregon—her widowed mother lived in Lake Oswego, to whom she spoke almost daily—but somehow she didn't go more than every year or two. This was partly because of Cray, who could not go to America because of some income tax matter, a running battle with the IRS that did not quite warrant extradition.

Cray had some view that she would be held hostage. The idea of her going always threw him into one of his fits of gloom. He was Polish to his boots, though after the age of twelve he had been raised in Chicago. It wasn't so much her absence he would mind—they got lost in their rooms and corridors and saw little of each other—it was that America could attach a piece of his property: Clara.

Whether it could or couldn't, Clara respected his fears. They tallied with her own, which over the years had grown exaggerated from reading American newspaper accounts of violence, handguns, road accidents, and crime.

Now thirty-two, Clara had been married for a dozen years, but hadn't acted since that first film, when she met Serge, and when she gained a little bit of cult fame for a daring dance scene. In truth, her dancing had not been as memorable as her nubile beauty, just out of her teens, black curls and a voluptuousness that was close to plumpness. She became thinner with marriage and motherhood. Lars, their eleven-year-old son, was at school in England, to Clara's distress and over her objections, it being Cray's view that English education was superior to French for a boy with Lars's handicap. Mrs. Holly, Lars's ailing grandmother, agreed it was a shame to send a child so young off without his mother, and in her opinion Clara wasn't happy; but the husband was overbearing, as these film people are. Mrs. Holly would say all this to her caregiver Cristal. "There's nine hours' time difference between here and France," Mrs. Holly would always add, it being so odd to think of Clara all the way on the other side of the world where it was dark when the sun shone in Oregon.

Clara was controversial in the American community. The natural suspicion people are apt to feel of above-average beauty was allayed by her apparent modesty and intelligence. A certain loftiness was attributed to shyness, so that people could almost forget about how she looked. Some felt sorry for her because of Lars, deaf from birth, and of how she must miss him, while others remarked that into each life some rain must fall. Yet there was also the fact, undeniable, that the possessors of good fortune tend to take it for granted and then to expect it, and Clara was no exception. In her own view, she may have felt she had mysteriously earned her looks, wealth, and good fortune by the conscious exercise of virtue.

2
Tim

The night the American journalist Thomas Ackroyd Nolinger met the former actress Clara Holly in Paris—without, he says, special presentiment at the time—he had by coincidence been talking about Serge Cray that very morning in Amsterdam in connection with an interesting crime. Nolinger, European stringer for the American conservative newsmagazine *Reliance* (and also, using his initials TAN, for the liberal monthly *Concern*; he was more or less untroubled by the ideological contradiction), contributor to the English literary magazine *The Weekly*, occasional reviewer for the *TLS*, film buff, restaurant critic, and would-be novelist, had been sitting in the Café Prolle in Amsterdam reading through the pile of stuff his helpful magistrate friend Cees had brought him, and noticed something that touched on Clara, or actually her husband, little suspecting he'd be meeting her later the same day.

The crime that interested Nolinger was the theft of a valuable medieval manuscript from the Morgan Library in New York. Though far away, it connected surprisingly to his own life when he read, in the list Cees gave him of prominent collectors of incunabula and illustrated manuscripts, not only the well-known name of Serge Cray, the reclusive director, but the names of a couple of people he had actually met in Frankfurt. These were people the criminals might be expected to try to sell their stolen loot to.

The list of manuscript collectors had been compiled by Interpol, with the cooperation of the International Booksellers Association, from auction catalogues and records of private sales. None of the people on the list had ever been associated with stolen material, Cees explained, and they were not suspected in the recent theft, but all would be contacted by Interpol and made aware of the disappearance of the Driad Apocalypse should it be offered for sale to any of them. "The Americans have some reason to think the manuscript will be sold in Europe," said Cees. "That's why the list concentrates on European collectors."

Tim went to Amsterdam from time to time to be filled in like this, smoke some grass, have a few beers with Cees, and gather such information as was floating around formally or informally about Belgian sex rings, Luxembourgian assassination plots, hardening Swiss drug enforcement policies, art thefts, terrorist smuggling attempts. Tim had nothing special to do with any of this—he was not a crime reporter and didn't plan an exposé—but he still made the train journey from Paris every few months to hear Cees's stories. One of these days he would do something with them for *Reliance*, if he could find an American angle. *Reliance* always liked hearing how much more corrupt and criminal Europe was than America, though they didn't like hearing how much better the trains were. *Reliance* regarded trains as crypto-communist, requiring as they did state subsidies.

Regarding crime in general, theories floated vaguely in Tim's mind, solid enough to make a little essay: criminal conspiracy as a way of imposing order on the random materials of the chaotic world. Crime required focus, as did perversion; in that sense both represented Order. The psychological *soulagements* of crime—what was the English word for *soulagement*? He often lost words, which hurtled unrecoverably into some slot between his English and his French, a great disadvantage for someone who made his living writing.

Tim was half American, half Belgian on his mother's side and was called Tim instead of Tom by everyone but his mother. He had kept the pale tow-colored hair of childhood, and was one of those large pink-cheeked rugby-player types, unsuited by his European education for fitting into either culture, and more good-natured than his size would suggest. He was a journalist ostensibly, a wanderer, a dreamer perhaps. And perhaps slightly older than he appeared, which raised the possibility of a lost half-decade somewhere behind him.

Tim had known Cees a long time. They had met at prep school in Switzerland, Cees then a skinny curly-headed cynic, now something of a law-and-order zealot, and much fatter. From what anyone knew, Tim's father had been an American representative of a hotel and car-rental chain, stationed in Europe. The family moved a lot, from London to Istanbul, so Tim mostly attended Swiss boarding schools. His American aunts had referred to this as being "sent away" but he himself had seen it as adventure. His Belgian mother looked on the separations from her son as normal though painful, a form of sacrifice exacted from herself, sacrifice being the nature of life. Tim always spoke with great affection of his mother, inadvertently giving the impression she was dead, though she lived in Michigan.

Always looking for stories, his only means of supporting the rather *mondaine* Paris life he led, Tim resolved to figure out a way of getting an interview with Serge Cray about his collection of ancient manuscripts and incunabula—an approach to Cray he had never seen tried. People were mostly interested in his films, or at the outside his personality, and not especially in his old books. Collecting as a logical extension of the role of *auteur*? Filmmaking as a form of collecting, in the sense that it was an accretion of images and ideas? Tim got out his notebook and wrote these notions down, since he suspected they were too flimsy to stick in his mind, like many of his ideas.

A young man given to irony and no illusions, in one sense he was a generic young man, for there are always dozens of Americans like him in Paris, clinging to the rather precarious livelihoods they have managed to score, for the pleasure of being there or because they have burnt their bridges and have no idea how to go back home now that they have let the moment go by for getting their MBAs or internships at their hometown radio stations or newspapers or lesser Condé Nast publications. But there was something extra about Tim Nolinger, something more than just the patina of a Swiss boarding school.

"The FBI is coming here," Cees said. "That is a little bit rare. It is hard to see why it is of concern to them—a stolen manuscript from a private American library. Not a federal thing. They usually hand art theft on to the art people at Interpol."

"It might be a federal crime. American laws are complicated—state lines, jurisdictions. I went to an American law school for a year," Tim said. "No Japanese or Arabs on this list of collectors, I notice."

"I often forget you're an American," Cees said.

"Only half. But which half, I am asked, head or heart? Top or bottom?" Tim laughed, and took his leave. It was a question he didn't himself know the answer to, he'd been in Europe so long.

Having promised his French fiancée to turn up at a soiree in Paris, he had booked a plane at sixteen o'clock from Schiphol, which would get him back to France just in time to languish in the traffic at the nightmare rush hour.

Idea for a piece: the terrible traffic in Paris? It was a wonder more people weren't killed. Deploring French traffic was not just rhetorical; their most important people were run over in traffic— Roland Barthes, and the head of Cartier, who stepped out of his shop on the Place Vendôme. Death in traffic a tradition going back at least as far as the husband of Madame Curie, mown down by a horsecab, his mind on his wife's infidelity.

3

Anne-Sophie

The agreeable Tim Nolinger was the future son-in-law of the well-known French novelist Estelle d'Argel (*Les Fruits*; *Doric, Ionian*; *Plusieurs Fois*), engaged to her daughter Anne-Sophie. What a misfit the two of them, Estelle and Anne-Sophie. Her daughter's fiancé did not quite please the worldly and practical Estelle, who had greater ambitions for Anne-Sophie, had hoped for a count or a promising politician, or a future Academician, or at the least a sports figure—if from a respectable sport like tennis. Or at least someone French. Tim did play tennis, of course, but only as a form of recreation.

Anne-Sophie, a concern to her mother, was the American community's ideal young Frenchwoman, trim, confident, flirtatious, cheerful, enterprising, with her little shop. After attending *Sciences-Po*, she might have assisted a government minister or become an *attaché de presse* at a publishing house, but drifted instead into dealing in horsey artifacts, a hobby since girlhood. Anne-Sophie's stand, Cheval-Art, formerly belonged to a Monsieur Lavalle who, as he aged, spent less and less time there and over the years had pretty much turned the business over to Anne-Sophie, especially the bookkeeping and the buying; he would come in occasionally on Monday afternoons to take a turn at the stand. Their association had begun when she was still at school, and hung about, little by little betraying a knowledge, remarkable in a *jeune fille*, of Niderviller horse figurines and antique tack. At first her mother had mistrusted Monsieur Lavalle's intentions regarding Anne-Sophie, but she needn't have, for Lavalle was altogether *gay*.

Anne-Sophie, at home in her small apartment on the rue Saint-Dominique, was preparing to bathe. Rosy and compact, her breasts the little pink-tipped breasts of a Boucher nymph, she brought to mind a particular picture in the Musée du Luxembourg. Nipples just peeking out of the suds. Perhaps a polished toe surfacing at the faucet end. Anne-Sophie lined up the stuff she used for her elaborate baths: bath oil, soap, shampoo, rinse, *crème de gommage*, razor, pumice.

But tonight she felt too devastated, and at the same time excited, to unscrew the tops and embark on the long, absorbing ritual which might lull her mind into a sense of the ordinary after the shocking events of the day. These she wanted to keep a keen memory of, for Tim, when she met him at the princess's party. His journalist instincts would prompt questions she wanted to be able to answer. She had noticed everything, she thought, in case Tim should ask something specific, like "What was the guy wearing?" Gray shirt, blue knitted gilet, blue knitted tie soaked in blood! When it came to Tim Nolinger, Anne-Sophie had a Frenchwoman's sense of vocation—but she was also an expert in hunting prints and a very good businesswoman.

Anne-Sophie had from her novelist mother Estelle two versions of maternal lore on how to lead life. On the one hand were the lessons of the real life Anne-Sophie saw being lived by her mother and father, her brother and herself; on the other was the general philosophy she found expressed in Estelle's works, which represented a reality at once more sophisticated, more cynical, and more exacting. For instance, the comtesse Ribemont in *Against the Tide* says, "Never make a man feel guilty," whereas at home, her mother had often ignored the countess's principles by snapping at her husband, "You might have called, I've been frantic," or "Where have you been?"

Of the two, Anne-Sophie had concluded that the countess was probably right. There had been nothing really wrong between her parents, just a certain detachment Anne-Sophie found disappointing. Daily life could be led more beautifully, more passionately; Anne-Sophie had therefore patterned her behavior and beliefs on things her mother had written. "Pay attention to the *petits soins*," Madame Godchaud, the worldly grandmother in *Plusieurs Fois* by Estelle d'Argel, tells her granddaughter who is about to be married. The little details of grooming. That meant obsessive depilation and having dainty lingerie. So Anne-Sophie was careful of the *petits soins* both by nature and by the study of her mother's works, whereas in life Estelle had never mentioned such things, beyond the usual admonitions about clean underwear.

Patterning yourself after books can make you seem rather literal-minded, unable to figure things out for yourself, so Anne-Sophie was taken by some people to be too literal-minded. And someone interested in horses, in the common mind, was bound to be earthy and simple—a girl cannot be both horsey and flighty. So Anne-Sophie was misunderstood as a sensible outdoorsy girl, when in fact she also had a yearning for luxe and frivolity.

She clamped her mirror between her knees to keep it out of the suds and worked on her eyebrows, but her mind wasn't on them. She was thinking of the gruesome sight she had seen that day in the flea market.

The reception was at the undeniably grand rooms of an elderly American, the princess Dorothy Minor Sternholz, married to Blaise. Sternholz was not a French prince, of course, but something more easterly, perhaps Lithuanian or Czech, his a flimsy, distant title more imposed on him than claimed. (The French love titles, their revolutions notwithstanding. For that matter, Americans do too.) Blaise Sternholz the prince, the publisher of a sporting newspaper and a member of the International Olympic Committee, had been raised in the Sixteenth Arrondissement and had never been to Lithuania. Dorothy was a permanent fixture among Americans in the City of Light, and had notable art works acquired during a period before her marriage when, on the evidence of a number of paintings she posed for, she appears to have known quite a few French artists quite well.

The American community in Paris was something of a world unto itself. Americans there had their charities, their futile long-distance involvement in American politics, their periodic attempts to disseminate American wisdom, thought, and literature to France as in the days of Tom Paine, their English-language cooking classes, their music, their American Church and American Cathedral, their knot of French friends, their effusive celebrations of the slightly has-been American celebrities who turned up here, their embassy presided over by someone amusing sometimes—the new ambassador being viewed warily after the radiant hospitality of the last one—and the special store where they could buy their peanut butter and popcorn. Perhaps there were no natural contradictions between the French landscape and the Americans who inhabited it so diffidently, but it often seemed that Americans would do well to stay out of what they did not understand. Or was it they who brought the harm?

Arriving at Dorothy's party before Tim, Anne-Sophie embraced the Americans of her parents' age assembled there. Everyone kissed her in the French fashion. Especially intent kisses from Olivia Pace's elderly husband, the rich Robert Pace, did not escape her, nor his squeeze of her hand; he was what the French call a *vieux beau*.

Dorothy crossed to give her the usual two kisses. The princess's affection for Anne-Sophie stemmed in part from fellow feeling. Whereas Anne-Sophie's real mother was so unlike Anne-Sophie that she had never understood her, Dorothy did. Anne-Sophie's interest in horses put her in mind of her own interest in sports, and she often remembered the sense of unfeminine deviance and marginality that went with it, though Anne-Sophie was French femininity itself. Dorothy prided herself on being a great expert on French attitudes and culture, knowledge largely gleaned from her husband, whom she had met as a member of the U.S. Olympic rifle team forty years before.

Anne-Sophie raised her delightful chin, slightly dimpled like a child's, and gazed around the room for people more amusing to talk to. Disappointment. The usual suspects, and no other French people except the hopeless Madame Wallingforth. With despair she scanned the pretty rooms in deep salmon pink, curtained in green, candelabra of French vermeil, oil paintings of American subjects, especially barns and *petits bateaux*, large sofas in lime green, growly Anglo voices, that tall red-eyed anthropologist, and the pretty secretary or whatever she was, about whom, always, many rumors, the usual drab professor in bow tie and the plump wife—was this a reception for one of the bow ties, a famous economist or historian, was that it?—someone who had written a book, another book, about France? *Zut,* they produced them endlessly, anglophones and their books. Even Tim threatened to write one.

"Your reprehensible Tim telephoned to say he'll be late," Dorothy told her. "He's stuck in a taxi from the airport."

"*Tant mieux,* I'll have revenge then before he gets here." Anne-Sophie laughed and made a beeline for the good-looking black actor Sam Strait.

4

What Anne-Sophie Saw

When Tim eventually found himself as promised in these same high, vast pink rooms, their long windows festooned in green damask and thickly glazed against the heavy traffic on the rue du Bac, his heart sank at the boredom in prospect. His own set was raffish and motley, not usually American, and—from journalists to gym teachers—not always people he expected Anne-Sophie to like. She on the other hand had a collection of *bon-chic-bon-genre* young women (and men) she had been at school with, well-brought-up Parisians strayed into disparate walks of life by now, and also the occasional holdover from her horsey period, old riding teachers and stable managers, universally dull.

The spindly chairs were arranged in the French way around the edges of the room, as at dancing school. On none of these could he immediately see Anne-Sophie, but she was someone who would be dancing, not sitting. This was not a dance, of course, just a benefit cocktail party for the American Library—was that it? Or a book party. He couldn't remember. In their gabardines and worsted blazers, the mostly American guests looked like forlorn time-travelers in the grandiose eighteenth-century space.

Americans weren't popular this season, or rather, even less popular than usual. The U.S. was embarked on a rescue mission in the Balkans that was seen by the French as a barely submerged drive for world domination. One of the few French guests, Madame Wallingforth, pointed this out to Tim as soon as he came in.

Though he was not often in the U.S., he explained to Madame Wallingforth, he knew in his bones that it wasn't desire for conquest but its opposite that made his countrymen behave as they did. "Americans want to make everything shipshape so we can be let alone—like a man who has to shave before he can read the paper."

Madame Wallingforth sniffed. "Americans have colonial designs and always have had."

Except that he'd said he'd meet Anne-Sophie here, he'd have cancelled. He had no particular interest in Professor Hoff, Froff, whatever his name was, had had lunch with the aged and sociable princess very recently, and would have liked to go to his computer to research a couple of angles in the matter of the Morgan Library theft.

But he soon saw it was serendipity that had brought him. There was Serge Cray's woman (wife or mistress?)—exactly the person to approach about getting to meet Cray. Clara Holly, instantly recognizable if you had seen her one movie, could be a dozen years ago, with its memorable dance. Clara Holly, first standing somewhat hesitantly in the doorway, clearly thinking she might not come in, then making for one of the little gilt chairs. She sat down and made some adjustment to her shoe.

She was older than the exquisite girl of *Swan Dinner* but had not really changed, except in the way movie actors always seem changed in the flesh, to smaller, older, with normal human variations of skin tone or errors of dress. He moved closer and presented himself—or introduced himself, as Americans say, though it would seem rather risqué to say in French.

"*Bonjour,* Clara," Dorothy was saying. "I didn't think you were coming."

"I wasn't, but then since I'd come into town anyway . . ."

"Are you staying for dinner afterward?" They did their cheek kisses.

"I suppose, why not? Your dinners are always so delicious," Clara agreed. "Why you exert yourself on the food I can't imagine, since you know people would come for the booze anyway."

"I'm Tim Nolinger," Tim said. "Miss Holly, may I just speak to you for two seconds?"

This obsequious but intrusive approach was a mistake, because she sensed a journalist or a fan, and her smile congealed professionally. "Of course, hello," she said, putting out her hand.

Tim admitted to being a journalist, recited his credentials in hopes that one from the potpourri would appeal to her. European stringer for the American conservative newsmagazine *Reliance*, etc. He did not add film buff, restaurant critic, and the rest, but went straight to the point, her husband's collection and the Amsterdam police list.

Clara Holly seemed relieved not to be being asked personal questions about herself, or about Cray, and relaxed a little. Tim thought her powerfully good-looking, early to middle thirties, and the only imperfections he could see were two tiny pocks on her forehead. Having predetermined that she was bound to be either one of the two things, haughty or elfin, that actresses always were, he put her down for haughty and failed to register something more intelligent and satirical as well. So much for his newsman's instinct.

"You could come out and talk to Serge," she agreed. "He loves to show off his documents." Tim doubted that—Serge Cray did not have the reputation of a garrulous *collectionneur*. But he seized on the invitation, pleased at the success of his gambit. Then she dashed any sense of intimacy or special favor by telling him to call Cray's business office.

"The people there have his schedule and can give you directions if he says yes." She smiled again and escaped him.

Eventually he spotted Anne-Sophie, who, true to form, had now found the three other French people in the room and was knotted with them in one corner, talking furtively, defying her promise to persevere with the English-speakers in order to combat and conquer her anxieties about her English, although it was perfectly good.

The French people who turned up at these American occasions were usually compromised by some circumstance of their lives: they had worked for American companies, or had spent a year of childhood in an English-speaking country, or were Protestant, which always gave them a slight air of illegitimacy. He didn't join them, but caught Anne-Sophie's eye across the room; she sent an air kiss. He thought, as he always did, how much he liked her looks (she was like him a pale blonde), her blooming skin, her slightly pop-eyed and shiny look of Fragonard, Watteau—but tonight she also had a rattled, stunned quality that made her big eyes wider than usual.

By eight-thirty the drinks crowd had begun to drift off, and those who had been invited to stay to dinner were led downstairs, where a long refectory table had been set for a score of favored guests. Madame *la princesse* was magisterially hospitable—so

American that way. Tim believed his own presence was owing to Anne-Sophie, for she was popular with certain rich Americans, with her good English, her reliable taste in sporting prints and equestrian memorabilia, and, through a school friend, her good connections to one of the couture houses. In fact, he was prized in his own right, for his cheerful good manners and good looks, but not quite as much as when he had not been engaged. The princess poured him a scotch, with a gesture that suggested she expected him to take it to the table, American style. Estelle d'Argel sometimes thought Tim might drink a little too much. Anne-Sophie thought of this as typically Anglo-Saxon.

The stricture against seating a couple together did not apply until they had been married for six months, so Tim and Anne-Sophie were seated together, and during dinner Anne-Sophie kept giving him anguished, significant nudges behind the low, rather prematurely Christmasy centerpiece—it was late October—as if she were unendurably brimming with news. The other dinner guests included Clara Holly, on Tim's side of the table where he couldn't embarrass her further by staring, as he probably would have done. The others avoided staring at her, looked anywhere but at her. She must have a lonely view of the world, he thought. The others were several people who could be counted on for big donations, some *Herald Tribune* people, and a British sculptor Tim sometimes played tennis with.

After the soup (*homard aux morilles*), when the subject turned to the affairs of the day, and when she sensed the moment an audience was hers, Anne-Sophie d'Argel said, "*Moi? Pas grand-chose.* A man was murdered at my feet today, that is all. His throat was cut and I nearly walked in his blood."

This, of course, had the desired effect. The company stopped talking and waited for an amplification of her extraordinary statement. She could see in Tim's smile approving surprise at her narrative restraint, to have saved such a dramatic tidbit with such forbearance all the way through the aperitifs and first course.

"Yes," she said. "I was in my stand, my boutique in the Marché Paul Bert."

"She has an antique shop in the flea market," said someone.

"Yes, on the theme of the *cheval*," she explained parenthetically. "Hunting prints, the old Hermès saddles, chandeliers made out of horseshoes, anything equestrian—sometimes quite funny. But the man, Monsieur Boudherbe, in the next *allée*. First I heard the explosive clatter of a metal shutter, as if in raising it he had suddenly let it crash like a guillotine. Then the screams. *Zut,* the screams . . ."

The screams did come back to her with appalling vividness. She would hear them for months. She had not called the police, she had alerted Raoul Pécuchet (Directoire furniture) on the other side of her. He had looked in on Boudherbe, then rushed to use her telephone, then they had taken the police to where Boudherbe lay. "His throat cut, and two Americans standing over him, their faces white as Limoges."

She answered the questions of the dinner guests as best she could. Had the Americans done it? Had they been arrested? She did not think so, nor had she learned their names. Was there a motive? Is the flea market in general a dangerous place?

Talking about it was helping her manage the lurid memory of the sticky blood. She was not awfully pleased when Clara Holly said, "Well, how bizarre, I think I know something about this," and quickly drew the attention of the company to herself.

"It's just a funny coincidence," Clara said. "A woman called me this morning, from my hometown, in need of help, and it was—must have been—one of the Americans you saw. She was at the flea market and saw the murder."

She told the story.

Anne-Sophie could not read Tim's expression, but she noted the rapt expressions on the faces of other men. Clara did not seem to strike them as assertive and unfeminine.

5

La Virtue

This was the same day Clara Holly got two calls from Oregon, and it seemed to her that two phone calls from Oregon in one day were too powerful an assault, too much interruption to the rather ritualized graciousness of the French life she led here. She felt rather sorry for herself, which was unusual. "What a nuisance. Well, at least," she remarked brightly to her husband Serge, "self-pity has the merit that it is apt to be sincere."

She had been out gathering the late asters and lingering toma-toes from her garden—lady of leisure amid her emblems of order. There were tomato worms lurking beneath the withering stems, to be sure. Among the things that were worrying her: her elderly mother, Serge's artistic funk (which had now lasted nine years), the departure of her young son Lars to England to school, the begin-ning of the hunting season, and an ennui that had lately weighed on her, partly, she knew, because of the situation in Oregon she couldn't do anything about. She was ordinarily energetic, had mas-tered French subjunctives, had read all of Gertrude Jekyll, under-stood the preparation of *foie gras frais*.

Then, today, the weekly phone call from Cristal in Oregon, a day early, ranting and tearful as always. Today it was that her mother's dog Lady had been hit by a car, and wasn't dead but would cost four thousand dollars in vet's bills, or should they have her put down?

"I love your mom but I can't take this anymore, it's not right to dump all these cares on me all the time," Cristal was whining as usual. Clara could always imagine her drying her tears the instant she got off the phone. Or else she was really on this thin edge, a really unstable person, in which case Clara ought to find someone else to care for her mother. Nothing was simple.

"Try to save her," Clara said. Yes, of course she would send the money. Of course save Lady—silly, adorable one-eyed Border collie. Clara wasn't sure if her mother really noticed the dog anymore, this effort was for Cristal, and for Lady herself, of course. She asked to speak to her mother, but of course Mrs. Holly was in bed.

Nothing easier to predict than that Serge would agree to the four thousand dollars for the vet. She didn't bother to ask him. His passionate concern for animals was well known, was taken by certain critics and viewers to be the index of his lack of concern for humans, his essential coldness, this in turn explaining the perfection of his films. Clara understood the underlying assumption here, that humaneness excludes perfectionism, but she did not agree that these opposites applied to her husband Serge Cray.

Who was still, ten o'clock, reading at the breakfast table. Most days he was up at seven, busying himself in his office. In his mind, Cray was working. He was an artist and therefore was always working. But the darker and more complex his vision became, the more the means of its expression eluded him. He was not comfortable writing, for one thing, and therefore had to depend on writers, who were always problematic. Political difficulties impeded progress—the chaos in Russia, for example, when plans for an historical film (*Rasputin*, the story so rich in metaphorical power for today) had been well advanced. Increasingly exigent voices at Monday Brothers studio he found rattling—not the infinitely trustful and trustworthy voice of Woly, Wolford Bierman, but others behind Woly.

Today Serge was reading *The Man Without Qualities* at the kitchen table. He had been reading it on and off for years, as long as she had known him. Thirteen years.

"Lady was hit?" He looked up. Clara could see him imagining the screech of wheels, the dog's scream, the moaning animal's shuddering limbs. His imagination was vivid, visual, explicit, his face expressive, his scowls like thunder itself, his tender empathy with the animal kingdom showing in his strange eyes.

"Spinal operations would be needed and so on," she said, herself passionately fond of Lady, whom Mother had brought home as a puppy, maybe as a sort of substitute daughter, just when Clara had been given the great chance, was going off to France to be in a movie.

Then the other call, about noon, was also from an Oregonian, a young woman, Delia, "you-don't-know-me-but," but Delia was calling from Paris, sounding hysterical. Clara was used to getting phone calls from other Americans. They were always a nuisance, and they had always got her phone number from her mother. They would identify themselves as friends of her family, or her third-grade teacher, and their passports had been stolen on the way in from the airport, or perhaps she could suggest some restaurants/exhibitions/where to get the best exchange rate? Unspoken would be their hope of getting a glimpse of her fabled château and/or the reclusive Cray.

This call had several of the expected ingredients. Delia's folks, the Sadlers, did live down the road from Clara's mother in Lake Oswego, Oregon, and Delia's passport had been stolen. But Delia Sadler's third trouble had startled Clara—that the poor young woman had been involved that morning in a gruesome murder in the *marché aux puces*—all these things happening to her since she arrived in France the day before.

Her passport stolen, that standby among the troubles being experienced by Americans who telephoned her, was easy to deal with. Less so was Delia's incoherent story about some guy she was traveling with, and someone she didn't know with his throat cut, and the French police. Clara could hear that the girl was in trouble, panicked and demanding, though it wasn't clear what Clara was meant to do about it. Go and see her, of course, in some hotel near the Gare du Nord—the police had told Delia not to leave the premises—and talk to the police in the French language.

Clara said she remembered the Sadlers. "You must be younger? Frank was the one in my class."

"He's the oldest. I'm twenty-four," Delia said, and she sighed desperately. She was staying in the Hôtel Le Mistral, in the Eighteenth Arrondissement. Clara said that as she was coming into Paris anyway, she would stop by to see her and help if she could. The girl was trying to sound brave and resourceful. She was scared, obviously, and grateful to have someone she knew to talk to.

"You don't know her?" Serge had asked Clara as she left. "Nice of you to look after her." He was thinking that Clara, though acerbic, was thoughtful of others; that she had a good character, for someone so photogenic; and, regretfully, that her character did not interest him really. Docility and stability (not that she had them, it was just the category she occupied for him) had the defect that they were uninteresting and unobjectifiable, there was nothing visual, and no conflict. They were like potatoes or celery. Good character could not be the subject of a film, for instance, or even a book.

"I know the family," Clara said. "They live on the road down from Mother."

"Don't get mixed up in it," Serge said. "Don't give your name," he said. Sometimes he found Clara was too trusting—too, if you like, Oregonian.

She widened her eyes, those remarkable eyes that might have been her fame, very oversized eyes, gray with a luminosity he sometimes didn't like, as if she were on the point of tears. Their expression now could mean "okay, I won't," or else "there you go again being paranoid."

"I'll call you later," she said.

In the train Clara thought of Delia's story. She felt a distinct reservation about becoming involved with this girl, this problem. In principle she was happy to help out, and also she had a number of other errands, and a party to go to later, so to stop in at the Hôtel Le Mistral was not putting herself out much. But perhaps, regarding helping others, one had a saturation point that her mother and Cristal had already soaked up for today.

She tried to be good. Lately goodness had been on her mind. It was not insinuated there by a sense of guilt. Guilt hadn't been emphasized in her family. Instead she had been encouraged to be good on principle, because it was right to give back something to an imperfect world that had unaccountably been good to her. But this was always somewhat hard to keep in mind.

Also, what was meant by goodness had changed or evolved. In childhood it had meant obedience; in high school it meant chastity. Now in her thirties it meant charity and helpfulness to others. Her resolutions increased with her fortunes, but she had to admit she herself had not grown in virtue that she could feel, so that when she had a bona fide, not too taxing opportunity to help another, she took it, and would go into Paris to help any fellow American like a shot. She also had strong feelings about being an excellent wife, her chosen career, and so worthwhile in her present circumstances.

And of course she liked going into Paris—does personal enjoyment dissolve the virtue somehow? Etang-la-Reine was generic posh and might be anywhere, whereas Paris, with its fluted lamp-posts trimmed in gold and its lacy iron balconies, was *French* and always reminded her that she truly was living in this delightful exile.

Probably, Serge had a kind of real virtue. He contributed large sums to various political causes, though he was vague about what they were. Clara hoped they weren't the ones that ended up helping the IRA, those truly wicked people who, though white and English-speaking, behaved as if they came from the third world.

She looked up the address, an unfamiliar part of Paris, and took a taxi from the station through a busy, narrow street behind the Gare du Nord peopled with a brightly draped population of Africans and Algerians to the Hôtel Le Mistral, grotty and formica-fronted, with a little placard in the window advertising the prices, without *douche*, with *douche*, WC *commune*, WC *privée*. When she asked at the desk for Mademoiselle Sadler, a young woman got up from a plaid chair in the small orange and mirrored lobby and approached, limping badly. Listing like a ship, in fact. Delia Sadler—a tiny, delicate person, as if the vigor of the Sadler line had petered out when it got to her. Pale shadowed skin, wispy, disheveled, curly reddish brown hair, little wire glasses. Of course, people always looked their worst for a couple of days after getting off planes. Yet she had a Sadler look Clara recognized. She had the same look her brothers and sisters had, in this smaller format, same cow-brown eyes and Jersey-colored hair, though Frank and the others were husky, large people. She smiled tentatively.

Clara liked seeing familiar faces and all they brought back of nostalgic memories, watching Frank at Oswego Lakers football games in high school and so on. Had he been the center or an end? Mrs. Sadler had been revered for her habit of giving out, at Halloween, whole Snickers bars. Seeing people from Lake Oswego intensified Clara's pleasure in being out of there.

"I'm Delia," the girl said. Delia had never actually seen Clara's movie. There had just been the one and then Clara had married and dropped out. Yet she was familiar-looking, just as Clara recognized Delia's Sadlerness.

They shook hands. Clara suggested they go have a coffee and Delia could tell her what was going on. She was surprised to note the severity of Delia's limp. She had never heard the Sadlers had a handicapped child. Perhaps a recent accident?

"It's my defective hip," said Delia, making Clara blush that the girl could have read her exact thought as she was having it. "I'll have to get a plastic one eventually, but they want to wait as long as possible because of my age, because they only last so long before you have to do them over."

Except for this confidence, the girl said little, seemed bound in a carapace of fear. Clara tried to draw her out. "How do you like France?" she asked, ridiculously, when they had been served in the cafe next to the hotel. Delia was putting a lot of sugar in her coffee, and staring at it. Then she did look up.

"It's just great. I get my things ripped off yesterday the minute I arrive, I spend the rest of my whole first day in a passport office, and my second day I see a man with his throat cut."

"I'm sorry." Clara laughed at her own stupid question, and sounded as if she was laughing at the comedy of a man with his throat cut. "Please tell me all about it."

When she had, Clara wasn't sure she believed her. There was just something the young woman seemed to be holding back.

6

Delia's Story

D elia told Clara her tale.

"Our plane got in about seven yesterday morning. But I felt okay, alert. I'd had some sleep on the plane, I didn't feel too bad. Even so, I must have been out of it, because I have no idea when it could have happened. That my passport was stolen. I suppose it was on the train coming in from the airport. But no one bumped me or anything suspicious. At first I thought I'd left it in the taxi, but Gabriel—my business associate, the man I came over with—paid the taxi, so I wouldn't have got my wallet out then. But it was gone all the same, all the credit cards, and my passport.

"The blood. That was what I can't get out of my mind, and the dead, staring eyes."

So that first day, Friday—yesterday—she had to spend applying for a new passport instead of having a look around Paris. The trip was planned as kind of a fast business trip, but she had hoped to work in daily visits to the Louvre, and instead she spent the whole day at the American consulate. "Gabriel—I don't know what he did. He went to the Louvre, I guess. Then he came for me at the consulate, and we had dinner."

Also gone were her Oregon driver's license, dealer's license, swimming-pool membership card. She should have left that stuff at home. Such thoughts as this added to her anxiety about the problems now facing her—no money, quasi-imprisonment in this hotel, and the memory of the black blood and dead staring eyes of the murder victim.

"Luckily I could cancel the credit cards, I had the numbers in my Filofax. But they won't send your Visa card to anywhere but your permanent address. Isn't that stupid? What do they expect you to do?"

"So then, this morning?" Clara Holly's voice was the voice of an actress playing a role of kindly encouragement.

Delia and her companion Gabriel had agreed they would start out early this morning, by flashlight. They had separate rooms. She was awake and dressed, waiting for his knock. She heard him come along the corridor and whisper, "Delia? Ready?" She opened the door quietly, so as not to disturb people still sleeping, and stepped outside. A soft mood of dazzled love had for the moment softened her vexation over the passport. She and Gabriel had spent part of the night together, beginning with talking intensely, and finally making love. For the first time! But she didn't mention that part to Clara Holly.

Gabriel Biller—maps, prints, and drawings. Delia explained to Clara how she had come to Paris on business with Gabriel, and how together they had crept out in the cold dawn, really cold, walking up the rue Duhesme to the flea market.

"We can get some coffee in the lobby, they have it ready early. A lot of dealers stay at this hotel," Gabriel had told her. He had smiled at her. He too must have been thinking of the intimate passages of lovemaking that had swept them along in the night. He had a smile of unusually convincing sweetness and beauty. Delia had been hoping for months for something like that to happen, though she hadn't put her desire to herself quite so specifically. Handsome Gabriel, with a moronic live-in girlfriend back in Oregon, and now he was Delia's lover too, if only for now on this sudden trip. She didn't say this to Clara.

Gabriel and she were the only Americans staying in the hotel, Gabriel not really American but maybe some kind of Slav. There was a sort of mystery there. Though he had lived in Oregon since high school, and claimed to be nearly as much a stranger as she in Paris, he seemed to know Paris. Maybe it was because he came to Europe every year for the art fair in Maastricht.

Heart's desires—coming to Europe, getting off with Gabriel— must be paid for, certainly, but she had not thought the price would be this high. She didn't tell her feelings for Gabriel to Clara Holly— so what if Clara was married to the great director Serge Cray, big deal. What was she doing with her life, anyway? Nothing you heard about in Lake Oswego.

*   *   *

The flea market had not been what she expected. It was a limit-less city of forlorn or, rarely, sumptuous objects, and all of them in-congruous in the early morning, with the rattle of corrugated iron shutters being rolled up and the scrape of tables and chairs being moved into the alleys, and dealers shouting to each other, and the smell of croissants and coffee. She had never seen in actuality this rather ridiculous gold and black French furniture, or so many marble statues or dismembered marble mantels or so many plinths, seen by just walking by, and crystal chandeliers glittering though it was morning, and cracked urns, peeling rocking horses, doorknobs.

Gabriel had the address of a certain warehouse where his con-tact, a Frenchman, was waiting on some matter of business Gabriel had described but rather vaguely. Something he was selling. He had a map of the area. They were looking for the Passage de Sains. Street of health? Sanity? Delia walked along with him, as amazed as on an Oz road by the richness of things, the exuberance of the dealers, the general tarnish, heavy smoking this early in the morning, and staggering prices.

She herself would be buying antique linens and green pottery. She kept only to those. Her niche, stall, shop, at the Sweet Home Antiques Barn in Sweet Home, Oregon, was like a little garden of lace and flowers and illustrations from old children's books. She (and her partner Sara Towne) sold stacks of folded napkins tied in bundles, and long lisle stockings, sunbonnets and green pitchers and plates shaped like leaves. Visions of a sweeter, simpler world to come.

As they walked, her eyes took in the things she would come back for, green faience platters, tablecloths draped over screens. Her heart had lifted at all this abundance, and the prospect of ad-venture, never mind having been duped and stolen from yesterday, just as many people had warned when they heard she was going to France.

They found their way easily with the map, through a neighbor-hood of African stalls selling cloth, mud-caked masks, and modern carvings. Did one lovely object, some real talisman, exist among them? Delia would have stopped to look, but Gabriel walked on. Was he that sort of man, who walked ahead and expected the woman to keep up, and without looking back to see if she was? Did the sidewalk habits of men bear any relation to their behavior in bed? She was embarrassed at this inadvertent thought, but—what a good idea the trip had been, all opening out before her, the future, the profusion of beautiful things in the world. Never mind his dumb live-in girlfriend SuAnn, with her ancient VW van and her hag mother, Cristal, always bringing in little bits of junk to palm off for a couple of dollars.

The place they were looking for was shut. A scatter of handbills lay at the door, the corrugated shutters over the windows were fast. She didn't understand quite why Gabriel found this so upsetting.

"Shit," he said several times, and walked back and forth and around the corner, looking for something or someone. Then he had tried the door, and it opened, surprising him so that he lurched to the inside, catching himself on the jamb. He pushed the door wider open and stepped into a cavernous warehouse space stacked with furniture and cartons. Delia stepped in after him. In the dim early light, it was a magic cavern, a backstage, a magician's attic. Pictures in broken gilt frames and furniture were stacked along the walls to teetering heights, draped with padded cloths. Pieces of faded fresco suggested windows, vistas beyond, a palm tree made of tin grew from a box in the corner, a herd of heads of antlered animals were hung along the rafters. This mysterious world suggested all the places Delia had never been.

"Hello," Gabriel said, looking around. "*Allô?*"

They must have both seen at the same moment, in the corner beside the palm, the legs sticking out from under the quilted packing cloth, and the blood soaking it. She hadn't screamed, she didn't think, wasn't a screamer. Instead they were drawn toward this unnatural sight, reluctant to look and drawn toward it both, perhaps a person still alive. They would have to move the cloth. Gabriel would have to move it. Like a pair of dancers they moved together slowly toward the legs, the blood.

But he had stopped, catching her arm, and looked around them. Of course he was right, what if someone was still in here?

"I need to look around. He had some money for me."

"Shouldn't we call the police?"

"No, this is too complicated. I don't even know how to call them. I'll just look for it. Nobody knows we're here."

27

She didn't think the man could still be alive, there was something strange about the way the legs were flopped that could not belong to a living man. There was too much blood. And yet.

And yet, it was too late to search or to escape either. As they eased backward to the door, they could hear the crowd of excited French voices approaching behind them in the street, the door opened, and two policemen came in in their round box hats, staring balefully at Delia and Gabriel cowering together amid the debris of chairs and rolled-up rugs. Other people pushed in behind, a man in a blue apron, a well-dressed blond woman, another who could be her younger sister, and a tiny Arab man.

"Shit," Gabriel said. Delia sensed his impulse, the stiffening of his body for flight, and the simultaneous recognition that they were trapped at the scene of a French murder under the gaze of gathering police agents. Delia did not feel a sense of personal danger; for herself it was not as bad as the theft of her passport. When something awful has happened but not to you, it gives you a free feeling. But Gabriel was white and shaking.

Gabriel indicated the corpse's feet—for it must be a corpse—and said to the police, *"Nous sommes des Etats Unis,"* surprising Delia. It was one thing to say to a waiter, as they had last night, *"Oui, merci,"* and another to speak to a purpose in a moment of crisis in the French language. One of the newcomers pulled the bloody canvas the rest of the way off of the corpse, and it stared up at Delia, glittering pupil-less eyes, contorted mouth, black blood still flowing from the throat. For a second the room lurched around her.

" 'For the second angel dumped his cup into the sea, and the sea became like the blood of a dead man,' " Delia said to Clara. "You know, the Apocalypse, it felt like the Apocalypse." But Clara had never read the details of the Apocalypse.

Delia could gather from the gestures and gasps that the dead man was someone most of the people there knew, the proprietor of the shop, and that no one had heard anything amiss, and that then the younger blond woman—she in the Chanel-like suit, polished nails, smoking like a chimney—had called someone else who had come to look. When the police indicated Delia and Gabriel, heads shook, they had not been seen around, were doubtless telling the truth, whatever Gabriel was telling in his French; Delia couldn't understand, she just sensed he was believed. Heads nodded. The attitude of the police did not seem unduly suspicious of them. Twelve or fifteen people, counting the policemen, nodding with chagrined regret at this example of mortality and violence in a corner of their safe, comprehensible world.

"They told us not to leave the hotel, so okay," Delia said to Clara. She sighed a heavy, jet-lagged sigh. "I haven't. Gabriel said he was going to change money, and he hasn't come back yet. But he hasn't, like, left."

In the end there wasn't really much Clara could do. She gave Delia a few hundred francs and told the woman at the desk that she should look after her and that Clara would be paying.

"Your name, madame?"

Clara remembered that Serge had said not to give her name. "Mrs. Camus," she said. "Mrs. Albert Camus."

"Gabriel will be back, obviously," Clara assured Delia. "He isn't going to leave you alone, he probably just went about his business, or to make calls. He speaks French, you say, so he's not at a loss."

Delia Sadler did not seem convinced of this, but of course anyone would seem still troubled who had gone through two such terrible days.

"Now she's sort of a prisoner, but at the hotel, and she hasn't got a passport," Clara told the assembled company. She hoped someone would have a constructive idea about this. Could she herself, for example, go pick up the passport at the consulate and take it to Delia? Might the consulate send it over if they understood that Delia was under orders from the French police to stay put? Though not of course a suspect? Various people made suggestions.

"Poor Monsieur Boudherbe, with whom I used to dine every Saturday noon," said Anne-Sophie, plaintively, eclipsed, such a pretty girl, not used to being eclipsed. It did not escape Anne-Sophie that the Americans, inured to violence and blood, on account of television and the conditions of their society, seemed to feel sorrier for the girl stuck at her hotel than for the murdered man. Even Tim appeared to be absorbed in this tale told by Clara Holly, whom Anne-Sophie had heard used to be some sort of actress. Anne-Sophie had met her once before, here. Now that Anne-Sophie noticed, Tim was watching Clara Holly intently. She could see Clara was or had been good-looking enough, but she could take better care of herself; her skin was slightly rough, as if she worked in the garden, and she had had acne or smallpox, had the tiniest scars, the kind of thing they cover up on the screen. Yet Anne-Sophie could see that Tim was struck by Clara's beauty.

Professor Hoff, as these professors were apt to do, used the events as a point of departure for his cultural theories. The two Americans, if they had not actually committed the murders, were bound to be under suspicion because of French attitudes about America, and in fact had probably done it, some sort of drug deal, which the French had to become less naive about. They could not be complacent about the strength of their cultural values, as surely their own behavior in the Second World War or the recent events in Kosovo would have shown them. The sooner their own flaws were faced—it was now practically too late—the sooner a healing social consensus with which to combat the National Front, the right-wing political threat gaining support for its Nazi values and hatred of Algerians— . . . Anne-Sophie stopped listening.

7

Dernier Train

Going back to Etang-la-Reine on the last train, Clara felt quite pleased with herself. For one thing, she'd been helpful to Delia, fellow Oregonian, and life affords so few occasions for self-congratulation. She liked to be able to help, and when it was sort of a nuisance, she was the more glad to do it. She sometimes felt the need to earn her good fortune, but she lacked opportunities. When they had moved to Etang-la-Reine, she had tried to do modest good works in the neighborhood, donating old clothes or library books, but her efforts always went slightly awry. Eventually she realized that unlike the country people around Lake Oswego, around Etang-la-Reine the people were all well off, with professional lives in Paris.

In the train thinking of Oregon, picturing the weedy ditches along Kendall Road, the goldenrod and blackberry bramble, and tiny daisies and bleuets—no, *bleuet* was the French word. In exile you lose the English names for birds and flowers. Robin redbreast. Mums. She thought of the wild hedges of thorn and camellia. She thought of how her mother let her lawn go dry in summer, to save water—really to save it growing, so as not to have to cut it, to spare the racket of the mowers and the expense of the yard boy.

She could picture the Sadler house farther along the road, a bungalow with blue eaves and rooms added on at the side, set well back from the road. Were there a lot of Sadlers? Frank the one in her class, and JoAnne in the class behind. Mrs. Sadler always toiling on the borders of the lawn, green all summer. As with most expatriates, the longer she was away, the more curious, even precious these morsels of memory became.

Now Cristal, mother's caretaker—Cristal had explained that the correct word was caregiver—wanting to keep the lawn green, wanting extra money to pay the yard person, probably her cousin or some other member of her hapless family. Clara had sent the money, of course, just as she had now sent the four thousand for the vet, it didn't matter to Serge.

She thought about Lady, the dog, poor thing, at least she could be saved.

She didn't think much about the murder Delia Sadler had spoken of. It seemed improbable, even imaginary. The wildflowers of Kendall Road were more present to her mind. For her the pleasure was to think of Oregon. Though she didn't in the least want to leave France, her husband, her home, she liked to think of it. Seeing the Sadler face was a little like going back to Oregon. I should go back, she thought, as she always did after talking to her mother.

"Go later," Serge would often say, but it wasn't so simple. Her home was in France now, and in truth, Oregon was always boring and dusty, with nothing to do but walk out to the barn and look at the old harnesses. She didn't have any friends in Lake Oswego anymore. Take walks with Lars, and scratch her ankles in the bramble, and watch Oprah with her mother, and all she could ever stand was a week of this.

Sometimes she thought: He wants me to go. He likes to have the place to himself, though it's vast and we're hardly stepping on each other. He believes I look at him as if to ask what he's working on, whereas I do not ask, and he is always working on something. If only he would do something. Maybe if I were out of the way. . . .

But when she proposed a trip, he always said no, don't go, which suited her exactly.

She took a taxi from the station. Her house stood against the winter moon like a dark castle, no lights on in the courtyard. When she was not in the house (the French would call it a château, but she couldn't bring herself to), she thought of it as it had been when they first saw it, empty and despoiled, its shutters flapping, rats' nests and pigeon droppings on the stairs—and on the plaster of the walls, in red chalk, little sketches of flowers and festoons done by the eighteenth-century craftsmen, to be executed by the carvers of the boiseries.

It was those little drawings she had fallen in love with, loved that glimpse into the orderly and homely workings of the builders of old. Though the place had belonged to Madame du Barry, who had her head cut off in the revolution, her ghost had long since been exorcized, if ever it walked there. Clara could never find anything of her in the bricks and falling plaster. Then the studio carpenters had swarmed over the place, painters, the art director—so exactly like a set was it, to the Hollywood workers at least. The opulent scale seemed normal to them; to her it had seemed overwhelming, at first.

She saw an orange Mercedes stretch in her forecourt as they pulled in. She remembered that people from the studio in Los Angeles were going to visit him today. As she came into the house, she heard voices from the kitchen, Serge's and others. Hollywood visitors seemed to come more often lately, as the interval between his films extended, and his silence became more and more expensive for them. These delegations were headed by his friend Woly Bierman, a short, jokey man who always wore blue jeans, white shirt, gold chain, in the manner of the studio executives of the seventies, rather than the Japanese-style dark suits worn by his younger colleagues. There were always three or four of these with Woly.

Woly came out into the hall with Serge when they heard Clara, and embraced her. He wore strong American cologne. "Hello, gorgeous." Though she was used to Woly's jocularity, he seemed relatively somber tonight, perhaps sobered by bad studio numbers. She went back into the kitchen with them. Serge had been sitting with them in the kitchen, drinking coffee, talking about anything but film—California gossip, the declining state of things in America, cars. The housekeeper, Senhora Alvares, had nobly stayed up, and had brought out some of the gingerbread Clara always ordered from the American store on the rue de Grenelle. She retired promptly, once she was sure Clara had noticed this exceptional late help.

The conversation was elliptical, cursory, to do with whatever they had been talking about—it could have been the plot of a film. Mostly they just went on in an insincere way praising the gingerbread, as if she were a woman susceptible to praise of her housekeeping. She told them goodnight and went upstairs.

She was used to film people around, she even liked some of them. But she also began to have a feeling of fear and invasion, of petulant malaise. Had it started earlier, with Delia's call, or before that with the news from Cristal? She didn't ask herself if it had anything to do with Delia Sadler's gruesome story. She thought it had to do with the men with Woly, or Woly himself. And Serge.

Serge liked these visits from California, did not feel them as reproaches, though he knew they were intended that way: When may we expect your next film? Disguised as gossip: "Remember when Ray Stark used to wear those lime green jumpsuits?" "It's like trying to get Bob Towne on the phone." Serge, who had only spent two years in California, liked the inside talk. It reminded him of Poland and Chicago, sitting in cafes under tinted enlargements of Marie Sklodowska Curie and Konrad Korzeniowski. They would all sit up till two, then the Californians would drive back to wherever they were staying in Paris, probably the Intercontinental. Their voices kept her awake. Sometime later she heard a car, heard Serge come up, walk by her room. She did not expect him to come in, and he did not.

Though it was autumn, she tugged open the long window of her bedroom, liking the cold air. Someone was still down there, smoking on the parterre. In the morning there would be cigarette butts in the pots of basil by the kitchen windows.

Woly, smoking in the dark, standing there alone, saw her looking down.

"Come down, Clara, would you, for a minute?"

She hesitated, went downstairs in her robe and stood in the kitchen doorway. Woly didn't look at her, really, but through her, staring behind her at the gray shapes of things in the thin moonlight.

"Is he making progress, any, do you think? Do you have a sense of it? What's he really doing?"

"He doesn't have a script, if that's what you mean. I'm sure he told you that. His ideas—I think he's very involved in something," she said, irritated, and loyal to Serge. "He's always working."

"There's some high-level discontent," he said. "He costs a lot."

"Drive carefully, going back. Will you be all right?" she said, turning aside this invitation to discuss what he knew anyway.

"Yeah, I have a driver," he said.

Back in her room, she called Mother. One A.M. in France was a good time to get them in Oregon, four in the afternoon. But she only got the answering machine: "Cynthia Holly's residence, Cristal speaking. We can't come to the phone right now. . . ." Clara imagined they were at the vet's with Lady.

Cristal wasn't answering the phone because she was out digging in the garden. Digging a grave for Lady. Who was dead, of course. The four thousand dollars already in the mail, she hoped. She thought they probably wouldn't ask to see the vet's bill. Deal with that when the time came, and maybe the time would never come. Digging in the orchard, bits of damp leaf sticking to her ankles, ants and spiders, rotten nuts, tears streaming, bitter sobs for Lady, and for her own life, and Life.

8

Sunday Morning

Anne-Sophie felt the illogic of her wish to be in her shop instead of home having a leisurely breakfast with Tim, but she prepared to go to work, as every Sunday morning. The fear was in a way worse now, the morning after. "I'm going. *Je m'en vais*. It must be faced. It is necessary to get right back on the horse," she said, and could see from his expression that Tim didn't know what she was talking about. Then he understood. He could not imagine Anne-Sophie as the kind of girl to whom shocks and bloody visions could happen; it was so far from his view of her that he had almost forgotten, or expected that she had forgotten, the bloody corpse of Monsieur Boudherbe. She was disappointed at his lack of solicitude this morning, he suddenly realized from her pretty pout.

Tim had spent the night (for they only half lived together—he had held on to his apartment to use as an office), but he was the least communicative of humans in the mornings until he'd read all the papers, and anyway people can't share shock and bloody visions if they haven't had them themselves. "Everything will be the same as usual this morning," he said. "That's the thing about accidents and gore, someone cleans them up and they're gone."

She hoped not entirely gone. Though being at the flea market would remind her of the grisly sight of yesterday, she would find there her colleagues who had seen it too. There were things to be discussed, recollections to be augmented, fleshed out by other accounts. One could not *tout voir* in one instant of shocked perception, eyes immediately averting from the sticky slash across his throat. Some might have taken in his shoes, a detail of the room that she had missed.

"You have never seen anything like the dead body of Monsieur Boudherbe," Anne-Sophie insisted. Yes, she would much prefer being, today, with the others who'd been through it, better than discussing it with a blasé journalist skeptic. She wondered about the two Americans, about whether they were in jail. Indeed, the company of others whose souls now contained this knowledge of mortality was preferable to any blithe and insincere commiseration she might receive from those who hadn't seen it, especially Tim. She'd been offended, a little, by how the people at Dorothy Minor's had taken it in stride, failing to insist she go away for a week to Evian or Quiberon, failing to imagine she might now have nightmares for the rest of her life. Americans, she had read, had such things as "grief counselors," who probably didn't really help but whose presence would at least dignify the ordeal you'd been through. She was generally very pro-American.

"I'll come with you as far as the Gare du Nord. I want to interview the two American witnesses," Tim said, sensing that she didn't particularly want him to go with her. Also, the Americans might have a tale to tell. "She said it was a Hôtel Le Mistral?"

Ordinarily Anne-Sophie would have called her mother the next day to gossip about the princess's party, but she was still too scared and distracted to phone. She expected, also, to be disappointed in her mother's response. Instead, it was the princess who called Estelle d'Argel to talk over the party, as was their custom, for though Estelle never liked to come to these American things, she liked to hear about them. She had the dim view of human character natural to her and to novelists in general, and Dorothy had the dim view (perhaps natural to rich people) that the world was fuller of sponges and social climbers and the fickle than perhaps it is, and they both enjoyed reviewing social occasions from these points of view.

They were old friends, though generally Estelle did not socialize with Americans. Like most novelists, she was a bourgeoise with moderate habits and intemperate views on many subjects, in her case especially Anglo-Saxons. Her principal dislike was the English, but she did not have much good to say of Americans either, exceptions made for the princess, Dorothy Minor Sternholz, perhaps the art collector Ames Everett, and Tim Nolinger to an extent. Could her mother's aversion to Americans be why Anne-Sophie had taken up with one? Estelle found Tim presentable, goodlooking, if too much like an Englishman, and she privately thought his well-muscled body and what appeared to be wholesome sensuality might be somewhat lost on Anne-Sophie. *Dommage.*

She also appreciated his attempts to tell funny stories about things encountered in his line of journalism; and when his American father, a hotel man, came to Paris, he took them all to dinner somewhere nice like Lasserre. Also, Tim was good-natured, was well enough educated (Swarthmore), and had some of the advantages of being American (cheerfulness) without altogether seeming one. The downside was, he didn't have money, and it seemed to her that he was a little too old to be just now settling down, as if there were something in his past—for he must be in his late thirties. But perhaps she was out of touch with the chronology of success.

"I noticed that Tim found Clara Holly very attractive," remarked Dorothy, who liked Clara. Did she mean that Anne-Sophie should be forewarned? "She is attractive, of course."

"Oh, he probably won't take up with other women until after they're married," said Estelle, but she took the warning. A little red flag positioned itself in her mind to wave at the mention of the name Clara Holly, possible threat. Why else would Dorothy even have said such a thing concerning her dear Anne-Sophie? As an intellectual and a novelist, Estelle was naturally also a person of unusual pessimism, even malice, qualities that had worsened with age, so that though her old friends took on faith a good heart, new acquaintances were startled, even appalled, at the things she said. Her novels, of course, retained the characteristic mixture of earthy sensuality and astute judgments about human nature that had made her reputation. But she was always baffled about Anne-Sophie.

"Anne-Sophie is so rebellious," Estelle had often said to the princess, "but if I approve of her high spirits I must expect rebellion. Rebellion and high spirits go together." To others it seemed that Anne-Sophie was docility itself, too much so. But people expected rebellion would break out one day, and perhaps it was this her mother sensed too. In the meantime Anne-Sophie had smoothly surmounted the expected hurdles of life—had got her own apartment, boutique, a cat, had dated, at some unspecified point lost her virginity, all of these transitions without ostentation and without confiding in her mother, to whom, eventually, she introduced Tim and announced her engagement. So now here was Anne-Sophie, tamely getting married at last to an extremely presentable fellow.

For a child of a family of intellectuals and professionals, Anne-Sophie's commercial streak was something of a mystery, not altogether admired by Estelle—it was at once too practical and too small-time. With her looks, Anne-Sophie could have had amazing sexual adventures, not that Estelle would have encouraged them, but she would have tolerated more flamboyance on Anne-Sophie's part. Would have preferred it. So Estelle was pessimistic about Anne-Sophie. How had she happened to have a horsey child who kept a shop, and in the flea market, at that; why at age thirty hadn't Anne-Sophie married, why must she now settle for a penniless journalist? Estelle could not be expected to relinquish a natural parental dream of Anne-Sophie getting married, grandchildren and the rest of it, and was cautiously jubilant—against her nature—when Anne-Sophie got engaged. But she could have wished the fiancé to be more solvent, entirely French, and to have attended a *grande école*.

"*J'imagine,* at your age, you'll have to take fertility drugs, triplets *alors, quelle horreur,*" Estelle had said when Anne-Sophie told her mother that she planned to marry.

"People over thirty have babies all the time, *Maman,*" Anne-Sophie said, "with very few cases of triplets."

"In any case, I hope you'll wait till after the wedding. . . ."

Dorothy and Estelle passed to the subject of Anne-Sophie's bad experience in the flea market the day before. Dorothy was surprised to learn that Anne-Sophie had not told her mother about it. Estelle was not surprised, but she was concerned for the state of Anne-Sophie's psyche.

"They say the memory of something like that gets worse with time. She's still in shock," said Estelle. "It'll come back in aftershocks for a long time."

"Post-traumatic stress syndrome," said Dorothy, who kept up with American medicine.

At her flea market stall, Anne-Sophie hardly remembered having rolled down her shutter yesterday after the murder, and now she was almost scared to roll it up again, half expecting to find another body on the floor inside, or some other new gruesome sight, suite of the terrors afoot in the *marché aux puces*. As she was unlocking, some people, buyers or tourists, came across the *allée* to wait for her to do it, waiting to come in, buyers in the ordinary way, unaware of the mortal drama there yesterday, yet she almost felt afraid of them too. They were English people, by their clothes.

"We got your name," the woman said. "A friend of ours bought some Stubbs prints?"

"Oh, yes, *je me souviens,*" Anne-Sophie assured them. "Very nice condition, they did well. Just one minute here." She pushed the shutter up all the way and fastened the rod. The day had begun. Across the sawdust-covered lane, Monsieur Boudherbe's large depot stood open, and police were going in and out. Anne-Sophie could see the activity clearly from her desk at the rear of her space, but something held her back from approaching the open door and looking in. Monsieur Boudherbe's corpse, naturally, was no longer there; they'd taken him away yesterday. Some blood left on the floor might still be there. Alain Grau stuck his head in to confirm this. They would talk it over in detail later, at lunch, when they pulled a table out from Madame Colombe's stall, set it equidistantly from their doors, and sat around it to eat a spread of *saucisson* and *salade*, as was their habit every weekend. Her wooden horses and the two statues of jockeys stood guard holding a little sign reading DÉJEUNER.

Anne-Sophie's stand and the others along Allée Onze backed up to a long two-storey warehouse of cement block whose main floor was taken up in part by Boudherbe's depot, and whose up-stairs formed a kind of storage attic for the dealers of the various stands appended to it. Though individual spaces were loosely delin-eated, there was no formal partitioning, and all the dealers stuck their wares up there at random, under a prevailing honor system that prevented one dealer from mistaking his neighbor's dusty ar-moires, stacks of chairs, canvases awaiting restoration. All this stuff together constituted an ensemble of ghost objects like souls in an attic waiting to be born. "I think I may have something like that upstairs," Anne-Sophie could say to a client and, if it was heavy, could count on her colleagues to help her haul it down the narrow stairs. This afternoon it was she who was helping Monsieur Grau, who wanted to bring down a marble plinth.

In the storage area something seemed wrong, disturbed. She could not have said what emanation of disorder, or displacement of shrouded furniture, or mere derangement of the molecules of the attic space chilled her, communicated danger. Someone had been there, and it was easy to imagine it had been, say, the murderer. Grau felt it too, at least he looked around with extra attention. But nothing, no one was there. And people went in and out all day, moving things, taking down their stock, storing something or recovering it, things changed all the time. Grau shrugged. Anne-Sophie could not resist opening an armoire door wider to half peek inside, where there was no one, of course. They each took an end of the column and struggled with it down the stairs.

For a Sunday, it was rather a slow day, but with the weather growing colder, the heaviest season of tourism was behind them now. In slow times Anne-Sophie read a great deal. The usual lot of a shopkeeper included long hours when there was no one much around. She loved the active part of her métier—the finding of things to sell, trading with other dealers, country markets, the annual trip to Provence. She also liked the sociable part—her colleagues, their lunches, the slightly déclassé side of it she would not have encountered in the daily life of an *attaché de presse*, for example. But she didn't really like waiting on customers and she hated the sitting around, so she read.

She read with a love of reading seemingly incongruous in a girl who loved horses. She read English well. At the moment she was reading a book by Henry James, a man who had spent a lot of time in France. This was a book about a French girl whose mother is having an affair with a younger man, American. The girl is in danger of being married off to someone she doesn't love, basically so the embarrassing mother can carry on in an unsuitable way with the young lover, taking long weekends in country inns and such. Fortunately, an older American man comes and breaks up the affair on the grounds that the lover has to go home and tend to his duties at the family factory. But it is too late for the girl. Anne-Sophie suspected that the girl had a crush on her mother's lover.

After lunch and throughout the afternoon Anne-Sophie, half

unconsciously, found herself eyeing the passage leading to the upstairs depot, to see who came and went. No one unusual, no one unauthorized. At four, she went back upstairs to have another look.

This time, she noticed something she hadn't noticed before, a *porte-clefs*, a key chain, with two car keys and a little flashlight inscribed with the name of some American company: Nolinger-Webb Rent-a-Car, Portland, Oregon. It was the key ring presumably of the person hiding in the attic. This confirmed her impression that someone had been up there and he was American.

She was somewhat pleased to notice the surname Nolinger existing in some independent context. She had been sure Tim was the only Nolinger on earth and that she, therefore, was singularly cursed with this hard-to-say name, which Tim pronounced with a series of hard glottals or whatever they were, Anglo-Saxon sounds she herself was incapable of pronouncing, a disadvantage when it came to your own name, or what would be your name; she and Estelle pronounced it Tim Nolanjay which she privately thought a much prettier way of saying it. She had thought of calling herself by various softer combinations: Nolinger-d'Argel, or d'Argel-Nolinger, which was an easier elision. However, you could not hold an accidental matter like his surname against your betrothed, a man so exemplary in other ways, and she was unaware of the homonyms invoked by her and her mother's pronunciation of his first name. To his ears, his first name in their pronunciation sounded like "teem."

Anne-Sophie thought Tim superb, ideal apart from his income and sometimes a certain vague, detached quality more or less common to all men except—this she had gathered from the works of Estelle d'Argel—except jealous men, and even they, between bouts of their irrational affliction, were probably distractable and preoccupied, like Tim. In general, she believed, Anglo-Saxons were less prone than Frenchmen to jealousy, though eccentricity they had in abundance. She could have wished Tim were more interested in horses, but, unlike her mother, she was not at all disappointed that he wasn't French. She thought it a great adventure to have a husband who wasn't French, especially since the defects of French husbands were so plain to all. And Tim had a pretty game of tennis, and his articles seemed very clever—she could not be the best judge of this, their being in a foreign language where she was sure to miss a number of points, but people said they were clever. Eventually he would write an important book. But anyway love should not yield to rational analysis.

She took the key chain and flashlight and went back, resolved to watch intently for developments.

After hearing about Anne-Sophie's ordeal, Estelle d'Argel hurried via the metro Porte de Clignancourt to Anne-Sophie's stand to reassure herself that Anne-Sophie was intact and calm, and to provide motherly solace. Her novel-writing line of work had taught her to value experiences, but, like all mothers, she didn't want her children to have to have them. Like all daughters, Anne-Sophie was glad to see her mother and embarrassed when she turned up here at work. With this mother in particular, Anne-Sophie tended to feel washed out and clumsy. Estelle was small, expensively dressed in knits and scarves, was occasionally photographed or written up, went on TV, and hadn't a clue about Anne-Sophie's chosen calling. She also had an aversion to horses. She kissed Anne-Sophie and studied her.

"Ames telephoned me. It's blood we're smelling, isn't it?" Estelle said. "Even today, the smell of blood. Like *boudin noir*. Was that where it happened, over there?" The police had set a stepladder decorated with yellow tape in the doorway of Boudherbe's depot. "How can you bear it?"

"I think you're smelling Yvonne's *rillettes*," Anne-Sophie said, noticing her neighbor beginning to set out the lunch.

"Teem didn't come out here with you?"

"I didn't want him to, Mother. I wanted to just face it by myself."

"Still, shouldn't he have insisted? This terrible thing you've gone through!"

"I just want things to get back to normal."

"I'd take you to lunch, but I have a rendezvous I can't change," Estelle said. "This visit is just to reassure myself."

"Really, *Maman*, I'm fine, it's fine." Though it wasn't really. She kept remembering the strange blackness of blood, and a cry she had heard, perhaps? The death cry of Monsieur Boudherbe just now returning to her mind.

"Look at this little flashlight I've found, with the same name as

Tim's on it! Can you keep it for me?" she said, thinking it might be better for Estelle to carry it away, for fear it was a clue unfairly linking Tim to the crime scene—or something.

At five-thirty, just when things were winding down—shutters closing, the scrape of chairs and tables being dragged into the stalls, carts and wagons collecting in the alleys to take away the deliveries, last-minute negotiations, and she herself putting her horse figurines back in the vitrine and retiring the little table where they had stood to attract horse-minded strollers (English, often)—then she saw, she was pretty sure, the same American who had discovered Monsieur Boudherbe sidle along the passage and quickly, furtively, dart through the door that led to the stairway.

Her immediate feeling was joy or glee at this deepening of mystery, this complication, added to the events of yesterday, seeming to ensure prospects ahead of interesting drama, and questions beginning with: Why had the American gone up in her attic? Who was he? What had he to do with the murder of poor Monsieur Boudherbe? An American man of unusual beauty, about her age. Her eyes had caught his—he had large brown eyes, like a horse, long hair and a shadowed jaw, and muscular shoulders. She did not think he had anything to do with the murder, but he had undeniably been on the scene of it, and here he was still, and no one but her had seen him sneak upstairs.

Her first impulse was to call someone, Pécuchet or one of the many policemen still milling around in Monsieur Boudherbe's depot, unless they'd left for the day, as it appeared. Her second impulse was to wait a little while—she didn't have to be home quite yet—to see if he came down again, and if it really were he. The third was to go up there herself. Though she knew she oughtn't to do that, the situation had an allure, as if she, Anne-Sophie, were the center of these events swirling around. Very little had happened to her in life, she sometimes felt, at least since she stopped competing in the dressage, when she was nineteen, and went to university instead. People assumed that getting engaged was something happening to you, but it didn't exactly seem that way to her, not an end in life in itself, but only the inevitable march of predestined events. The prospect of catching a murderer—a fugitive at least—had an element of thrilling danger. She should act, she knew.

In the end, she did nothing, Monsieur Martin, the *gardien*, passed through locking the stair corridor, as he always did at the end of the day, so the American was stuck up there, if she wasn't mistaken, and couldn't get out unless he jumped from a window. Anne-Sophie rolled down her shutter and walked with Nathalie Serre to where she had parked her Mini. She turned once, in case she could catch him watching from the window of the loft; but there was no one.

Making love later that night with Tim, just for a moment over his shoulder she saw that empty window and expected to see the dark face.

9

Hôtel Le Mistral

Anne-Sophie had dropped Tim off at the Gare du Nord on her way to the *puces*. From there he walked round to the Hôtel Le Mistral to talk to the young Americans whose plight he had heard about from Clara Holly. He was thinking that this could be a story either for CNN (Dream Trip to Paris Turns into Nightmare) or for *Reliance* (American citizen, deprived of passport, held without charges on flimsy grounds). He hoped that the young woman would turn out to be pretty and photogenic. With no idea of her name, he had to rely on the good nature of the desk clerk, who at first resisted, as was typical, saying that there were dozens of Americans registered in the hotel, how should she know which one he wanted? Trouble, police, only been here two days? he persisted. Finally, with a kind of surly smirk, she allowed as how it must be 204. He then tackled the problem of convincing the occupant of 204 to come down and talk to him. Why should she? She did, though, plainly having no idea about her privacy rights in this situation, or was perhaps responding trustfully to his American voice.

"I heard about your situation from Clara Holly." He smiled as winningly as possible. "It sounded interesting, an interesting piece for my paper, but also I wondered if I could actually be of help?"

"You could, but I don't even know what's happening," she said. A small, worried-looking girl in her twenties, with hair the color of maple syrup, and transparent skin, and a kind of malnourished, ethereal quality, less robust than he imagined the usual Oregonian. She wore jeans and a T-shirt and wire granny glasses. She had a bad limp; her little pelvis was tilted like a roof, probably from a deformed hip. Something about this was shocking: He realized you didn't see Americans limping or deformed very often, orthopedists having intervened in their cradles.

In answer to his questions, she explained that she had surprised herself by not being panicked or desperate through all this, until now when she could feel panic coming on. It wasn't her personal safety that worried her. What could happen to a woman, middle-class and American, even in France? She was trying to maintain a certain center of confidence in her general human status, white, innocent of murder, possessor of a legal passport (though it was gone), with access to money and the phone number of a respected local woman who could speak French, and at the moment a roof over her head that the French police would prevent her from being kicked out from.

Yet indignation and fear swelled her throat when she really faced it. You heard of American tourists being put in Turkish prisons, drugs planted on them, executed in Singapore or wherever—though not in France. She had gone over in her mind all the worse things she'd seen, albeit only on television—stacks of Rwandan corpses, festering Bosnian graves, skulls unearthed from cornfields, blood-spattered shacks in Mexico, Algeria, Indonesia, Pakistan, Kurdistan, Turkey, Iraq, where the terrorists or police forces had stormed in, automatic weapons spraying the occupants.

"Clara Holly said she'd pay for the room," Delia said.

Tim asked, "How did you get along with Clara Holly, is she nice?"

"Fine," said Delia. "Better than I expected." He could see she hadn't actually liked Clara Holly that much. Why not?

"It might have been her fur coat," said Delia, as if divining the question. "Okay, I was surprised that an Oregon native of Clara Holly's age would wear the skins of dead, endangered animals. But of course I know that attitudes differ in Europe, and also that there is no logical moral difference between fur coats and shoes." She sighed.

Tim went over her story, not mentioning his connection to it via Anne-Sophie, but she had little to add to what he knew already. Other concerns came out, in an aggrieved rush: How can people sleep in Paris? Horns, sirens that warble in a way that vibrates the nasal passages, loud car alarms setting themselves off in series, like jungle messages being passed along. Enormous clashings of broken glass, as if tons of bottles were being crushed, cars, voices laughing under her windows, motorbikes starting up.

"I'm stuck here I guess till I can get a passport, but nobody tells me anything," she complained.

"What about your companion?"

"I don't know where he is," she blurted out after a pause thinking about it. "He's disappeared. I'm not worried for myself. . . ." A new set of fears tumbled out in the grammar of old films. Arrested maybe? Maybe in France they don't permit you a phone call? Torture, Amnesty International, films of ragged men in undershirts, cigarette butts clamped in their moist derisive lips, defying brutal guards. Tim could read her concerns: Would her so-called friend really leave her just sweating here, passportless, speechless, moneyless?

Never, she said. Gabriel would never do that. That she was sure of, after what had happened between them.

Even without experience it was easy to tell police when they came in, their movements slower than normal, eyes not synchronized with the movements of their shoulders but slanting off at odd angles around them. These police were unmistakable even though well dressed in European tailoring. Tim assumed they were French detectives, but it turned out they were Americans. Delia got up as soon as she saw them inquiring at the desk, turning their heads toward her. Tim followed her, intending to help with the language, but there was no need.

"You're Miss Sadler, I guess? I'm Frank Knowles and this is Frank Durkin. FBI. Both Franks. We'll be Frank with you." He smiled professionally. "European special section." He flashed a badge at her, exactly as on television. She peered dutifully. "Guess this isn't what you had in mind on your vacation."

"It wasn't a vacation, exactly," she began. "I'm . . . I have a brother Frank too."

"An era of Frankness." They all laughed and grimaced. "Not really our thing to look after tourists in trouble, but you're in a special fix."

"Did the French police call you?"

"Right."

"Then you know my personal fix is really that my passport was stolen! I went right to the consulate and filled out the papers and they were getting my records from the States, and I am to go back to get it Monday, but now . . ."

"We put a hold on it," said Durkin, "at their request. You can't get it Monday, not until they decide you aren't involved in their thing. We cooperate with these French requests and vice versa, most of the time."

"We'll get you to tell us the story," said Knowles, and went to sit with her on the lobby chairs. She repeated the story Tim had heard, the flea market, her friend Gabriel Biller, then the man with his throat cut.

"So where is Mr. Biller?" Knowles asked.

"I'm not sure," she said. "He'll be back."

"We should talk to him too. His dealings with the victim. When did he leave?"

Here Delia paused, either counting the hours or deciding to lie, or not knowing. For such a puny little person and inexperienced traveler, she seemed to have a certain moral stoutness, Tim thought.

"I haven't been paying attention. Too busy—telephoning the U.S. and trying to straighten things out. I hope you can help us."

"You didn't see him go?" Skepticism.

"We aren't 'together.' " Her voice bracketed the word. "We're just traveling together."

"Let's get a little background here," one of the Franks said in an equable voice. "What exactly are you doing here?"

They didn't seem to object to Tim listening, nor did Delia, as they drew out some of her history. Not drew out, exactly, for she seemed artlessly comfortable talking to them, the Americanness of the two visitors outweighing the fact that they were FBI men. She didn't mind telling her story yet again: business trip, to buy linen napkins, and wanted to go to the Louvre. At one point she had to excuse herself to take a phone call from Oregon—it was her partner Sara saying she'd sent emergency money, eight hundred dollars via American Express, all Delia'd have to do is go to American Express. Delia thought she had explained she wasn't supposed to stir. However, this seemed a surmountable problem. It was a relief to hear Sara's normal voice from America.

She was an antique dealer, she explained to the two agents named Frank, with a stand in a mall in Sweet Home, Oregon, a kind of big warehouse in a shopping center, where a number of dealers banded together. She and her partner, Sara Towne, dealt in old linen, green china, baskets, potpourri, flowers, that sort of thing, and hoped one day to have an entire shop in a fancier location—Lake Oswego or even downtown Portland.

"And your friend? The other dealer?"

"Sara?"

"The person you came here with."

"Gabriel Biller, rare books, prints, documents. He's not so happy with the location either, since the casual book buyer isn't after his level of things, but more and more the collectors find him, and with the Internet he can be anywhere."

"Does a lot of work on the Internet, does he?" asked one Frank. Something in his tone, Tim saw, now affected her and qualified her candor. Something worried her.

"I don't know," she said. "I don't really know the details of his business. Plus the Internet's a mystery to me."

"You said he did business on the Internet."

"I've heard him say the Internet has revolutionized the rare book business. Before, you had to mail catalogues all over."

"Would you happen to have a catalogue?"

"Why don't you look on his website?" said Delia, wiggling, not liking this now. "His name's Biller." She spelled it. "I'm really not privy to his affairs."

"He said he was going to change money, that was when, what time?"

"I don't know, I'm still kind of jet-lagged."

"This morning?"

"Last night, I think, or early this morning."

"You think? And he hasn't come back."

"I wouldn't know, maybe he has."

"Wouldn't you have expected to see him?"

"I was upset and went to bed."

"You didn't see him? Didn't eat dinner together?"

"We had an early dinner, that's when he said he'd need to change money."

"So you don't know if he slept here last night?"

Suddenly she didn't like his tone, or something scared her. Her teeth clamped her lower lip, her eyes sought Tim's.

"I was just wiped out and went to bed about ten," she said.

"I guess you know that your government can't protect you under these circumstances. Accused of a crime, the foreign government takes over," said Frank Knowles.

"I'm not accused of a crime?" Delia asked, suddenly bewildered. How could she be?

"Their rules apply. I hope you know that. But we do what we can."

Tim suddenly felt a wave of chivalry. "You could help get her passport for her," he said to the FBI men.

When he had said this, one of the Franks, Knowles, who seemed to be the point man, studied him with a look of special concentration, as if memorizing his face for a later lineup. "Who did you say you were with?"

Tim listed his credentials.

"Why are you interested in little miss here, Mr. Nolinger, what's the story here?" he said, suddenly unpleasant.

"Just as a person who could help," Tim said. "We have a mutual friend. I thought I could help, get her passport, speak French, whatever she needs. My girlfriend was there yesterday at the flea market."

"Speak French, do you?" as if it were seditious and unbecoming. "Ask the desk clerk to let us into his room. You could tell her we're friends, needing to get something from his room."

"I don't think she'll do that," Tim said. "You'd have to get an order." He noticed that Delia was looking at them in surprise.

"Ask her."

Tim went over to the desk. The clerk had been watching them the whole time, and probably had formed her own opinion about the meaning and tone of their conversation in the corner of the lobby. He smiled as persuasively as possible and repeated the request.

"Impossible," she said, as Tim had expected. He was just as glad.

"Fuck it, these Frogs just have a thing against cooperation," Frank Knowles snapped.

"When Mr. Biller comes back, give us a call, will you?" said Frank Durkin, handing Delia a folded paper. "Meantime we'll see what we can do vis-à-vis your passport. They'll let you charge your food here?"

"It's more of a snack bar," Delia said. "But, yes."

"Okay, we'll be talking to you," said the other Frank, and they left, leaving Delia sitting in the lobby.

Tim lingered kindly, concerned for her dinner and who she would talk to, but finally took his leave. He wrote out several phone numbers for her, approximately describing his whereabouts in the next couple of days, in case she needed help or thought of something he could do to help. Not much of a story here yet, he reluctantly decided, but the girl had caught his interest. So had the presence of the FBI.

Delia sat awhile longer watching the progress toward evening, lights going on, the desk clerk scouring the ashtrays in the tiny lobby. She couldn't help herself from watching the door for Gabriel, but he never came; after another hour he hadn't come.

How do you know when a man is sincere in what he's saying to you? A woman just knows, Delia thought. Of course you have to ask, sincere about what? It wasn't love or commitment she required, so why this certitude that Gabriel also had begun to feel love, if that wasn't too big a word for the way she felt, her passion building during their morning exchanges at the Antiques Barn in Sweet Home, Oregon, of hello or the few times he helped her unload a box of green dishes bought from someone's attic. Requited and fulfilled during the ardent hours last night, kisses more than expert: sincere, somehow.

Delia reflected that kisses, like toothache, were unrecoverable. What you remembered were the words you described them in. Fabulous, wondrous? It had been a night to influence the future, that had been implicit in his embrace. Her breast burned as if beneath his fingers. She had felt love before, though not often, but this was different and holy.

Which was how she knew something had gone wrong, some problem, he wouldn't just disappear like this leaving her stranded in this French hotel without explanation.

Her room was too horrible to go up to. It came to her she was uneasy in her room. There, it seemed, someone could force the cardboard door, and with no one in the corridors, no one to hear, could come in and do whatever. She could not see exactly what they would do. She couldn't really believe anyone was trying to hurt her.

And they wouldn't come and try to hurt her with these FBI men around. Frank and Frank, and the journalist. They all seemed like creeps but harmless. The journalist was handsome, at least.

She reviewed all the comforting telephone conversations she by now had had with Sara, her mother and father, her brother Boyd still at home. There had been an envious note in their commiserations—envious that she has having an adventure in far-off Paris. She agreed that this was an adventure, but there were these disquieting elements, mainly the disappearance of Gabriel. The money, the passport, being confined to a sleazy hotel—all those would be straightened out.

Yet the man in the flea market had been lying there dead all the same, and he had something to do with Gabriel, and Gabriel was gone. She kept trying to break through to a sense of peril, even of reality, but she could not. Some thick brain fog kept impeding thought. Murder, theft, FBI sleuths, even movie stars had failed to dislodge a heavy miasma of fatigue and lethargy. It came to her that this was probably jet lag, deferred the last two nights by the bracing distraction of Gabriel's company but now hitting her like sleep serum in her veins. Her eyes sagged as if beanbags were attached to her lids. She'd come on Friday, this was Sunday. It was four P.M., the devil daytime hour of jet lag. You heard, under no circumstances nap. Coffee, she thought, a walk around the block, they wouldn't put her in prison for that.

She limped outside and looked up and down the *rue*. It was always painful to walk but not a pain she noticed anymore, just the one hip, congenital. This was almost the first moment she had had a chance to study a Paris street. The past two days, including the stimulating blur of her adoration of Gabriel, murder, being stolen from, emotions of astonishment, then fear, people coming at her, new faces, talk—all this now receded a little. A bus going by, taxis rattling, more people on the street than in Sweet Home or even downtown Portland. She looked a long time in the window of an African couturier who displayed bright costumes in printed cotton, with wonderful headdresses and lavish skirts. She thought about these for export, decided they wouldn't do for Oregon, not even at its most folkloric. Who wore these in Paris? Paris, France, an alien place where she could speak to no one.

For reassurance she thought about the Americans she'd already met—the two FBI Franks, Clara Holly, Tim Nolinger—wondering briefly how it would be to sleep with him, then embarrassed at the thought. It seemed as if her libido, now liberated by Gabriel or by France, had begun raging around uncontrollably looking for objects of desire, like Frankenstein's monster. Of course, she was mad at Gabriel for not being here. It was him she was afraid for. Her heart speeded up. Where was he?

10

Goddess of the Hunt

Outside of Paris, with the autumn, with the shrivelling leaves and stiffening breezes, with the graying light came the unmistakable signs of the hunting season. Dead pheasants hung in the butchers' windows, brought in by the first shooters, tiny black wounds barely noticeable in their sumptuous plumage, leaden eyes staring open. A new pack of spotted dogs rushed to the fence at the neighboring farm to bay at Clara's car. People in vaguely Tyrolean costumes, with epaulets and brass buttons, drove up and down the lanes; everyone was wearing smart, shined riding boots.

Clara and Serge were agreed about stopping the wanton and cruel killing of deer and partridge on their ample hectares, a practice traditionally enjoyed with great fanfare by the local hunters during the season. Serge defiantly went out with his own shotgun to look over his allées and check the chains that secured their gates. It was the invasion of his sacred precincts as much as the slaughter of the animals that angered him, though he was no hunter either. Had been taken rabbit hunting by an uncle near Cicero, Illinois, and could still remember the gunpowder smell of the dead stiffening creatures lying on the oily cement of the garage. Then he had cried because what had been alive was now dead, and that they hadn't had to kill what they did not need, secret tears to avoid the derision of the uncle.

And Clara, though she had a fur coat, was sufficiently an Oregonian to have also objected to the hunting rituals in the neighborhood, especially where they affected their property, people with guns crashing through their gardens, horses occasionally, horns, baying dogs, the destruction of flowers. Once Clara was sure she had heard the crashing of a stag through the underbrush, the creature dismayed, hurtling, breaking its hooves against branches, and the hounds baying, in their own wood, this was last year. There had been horns, certainly. How was it possible that barbarous troops like figures from a tapestry, like the chorus of an opera, could blast their horns in her wood? And then she had seen the stag, or another stag, dead, being carried off in the village, quite a small animal, and someone had told her it was the hunter who killed it with a knife, the dogs did not rend it with their teeth as she had feared, and as you would think from the paintings in the Louvre; she had seen paintings in the Louvre of dogs tearing the flanks of the exhausted, anguished stag.

In a way she had been shocked to learn that the whole elaborate ritual of hunting—dogs, red coats, horses—was done in France, which seemed too, well, too small a country to let people loose with weapons in, and anyway she had always thought of it as an English barbarity, especially the red coats and the dogs baying like the hounds of hell. It was true that hunters killed animals in Oregon, but they dispatched their prey mercifully with rifles, and only wore red to keep from shooting each other.

In general she and Serge had decided, or rather she had taken the lead from Serge, to keep a low profile among the locals, down-play their own foreignness, blend in with France. More than this, they tried to be good citizens and neighbors, always contributing to local fund-raising events, even church ones, though neither was Catholic and Serge was Jewish. The amount of their contributions was carefully calculated in the hope of seeming neither miserly nor ostentatious, despite which they always had the feeling of getting it wrong. When it came to the hunting issue, though, principle was not to be sacrificed. Serge was definitely at one with her on this, or she with him—they both objected. Every year he had had his own lawyer write a letter to the master of the local hunt, notifying them they were not to hunt on his property, and every year the locals had resisted, with delegations and appeals, and had hunted as they pleased, claiming that until the matter was adjudicated, tradition would prevail. Men had ranged these woods for centuries, and that was the tradition.

"It is considered an act of great valor to give the *coup de grace*," the mayor had said, that first year that a delegation of men in sweaters and neckties had come to talk to Serge, and he had made Clara talk to them instead.

"You mean you can just come onto our property?" she had asked.

"In pursuit, if they have already wounded the animal, certainly," said the mayor. "By law. It would be inhumane, an unforgivable cruelty to let him die slowly, he receives the *arme blanche*. Madame," added the mayor, clearly irritated that it was she and not Serge hearing them. But she had afforded them a ceremonious hearing, in the salon, still a bit of a mess at that period from the studio carpenters who were continuing the repairs and repainting.

Every year for four years they had had one of these stiff encounters with the local mayor. In the meantime they had put heavy chains across the paths at the perimeter of the property, and built a strong gate across the road. They had been advised by their lawyers they perhaps had no right to do this. "If you had more hectares they would not have the right—it's the Loi Verdeille—to hunt on your place. You seem to have just below the minimum hectares required to keep them off. Then there's the status of certain rights-of-way across your land." Serge had discussed patrol dogs, but they hadn't yet got any because of the feelings of their house dogs, Taffy and Freddy, mild yellow Labs who were no use at all at keeping out strangers.

It was Clara who managed the affairs of the château without complaint, almost as a form of atonement for a certain restlessness she felt sometimes. She thought of herself as having made a mistake in life. She had no particular name for it, just a mistake. Maybe it was overreaching—setting out to be an actress, thus making a claim of superior beauty and worthiness of being seen, a claim on the attention of others. Or else her mistake had been not sticking to acting, letting herself be dissuaded in the name of wifedom and motherhood.

Or was it in marrying someone she didn't truly love? Of course she loved Serge, but not in that swept-away, sexual way she tended to doubt really existed. Had she married in bad faith, for conventional reasons like pregnancy, or because he was famous, which is easy to confuse with love? She had been young. The mistake, whatever it was, though, was a decade behind her and she was used to it, she was comfortable. Only, sometimes, when she read something slightly New Age, about getting clear or about atonement, she paid attention.

So, in atonement, this year as in other years, it was she who would receive the delegation, obey the summons to the *mairie* in response to the letters, writs, forfeits, contraventions, that were laid on them about their chains and gates. This year's ritual confrontation was today.

She went looking for Serge, hoping he would come with her to the meeting. The mayor, members of the local hunting association, and a magistrate were coming.

"Don't discuss anything. We have lawyers to talk to their lawyers. Just tell them our position is unchanged, tell them to ask the local stags to run somewhere else," Serge said, barely looking up from the television. In Georgia, a twelve-year-old had shot up the schoolyard, killing four other children, and the images of consternation now appearing on CNN absorbed Serge, who sat watching at the kitchen table. An ambulance, men with stretchers, a neighbor and one of the teachers sobbing to the reporter, cut to the principal making an announcement about grief counseling, cut to a crowd around a woman lying on the ground.

"The mother of the shooter," Serge said. "Fainted."

Clara thought of Lars, almost this age, and of how there had been an incident like this in England, Scotland maybe, anyhow the British Isles, where Lars was, though now they had tightened the gun laws there. Her throat constricted with fear for Lars.

"There's something wrong with the people, in the town, look at them," Serge said. "They look retarded."

"They're all fat," Clara said. "The fatness is what always strikes me when I go home."

"These people are fatter than other Americans," Serge said, sunk in thought about this. "They look mentally defective because they look as if they were all fed in the same mental institution. Even the children."

Clara said, stiffly, "I'm sure they're just as sad as if they were thin." Serge was not thin.

This year's meeting would be in the office of the regional manager of the commune of Lanval, above the Mairie/Bibliothèque Municipale, a small converted building in a patch of wood outside the village. One entered through the library, where Clara nodded at the usual women; she used to come here to check out library books, but by now had read the small stock in English, by Poe, William Styron, Melville, James Fenimore Cooper, and Erica Jong.

Men were waiting in the room at the top of the stair. It was plain she was meant to sit a little apart in the one vacant chair by the window. They rose as she came in, a collection of local men, ruddy, sturdy in corduroys and country jackets, one in jeans—the committee, she supposed—and here was a man she had once thought was the librarian but had eventually learned was the mayor of Etang-la-Reine, Monsieur Briac. They were dressed like peasants and farmers, but she knew they were all stockbrokers and engineers, registered to vote out here at their country houses. Most Frenchmen were engineers, it seemed to her. These were all hunters, in any case. She smiled. She was used to the power of her smile, especially on a group of men, but this time it did not have a palpable effect, the atmosphere was too strained, the subject of *la chasse* too solemn, Serge's hectares too critical to the orderly management of the sport in this region.

The points were the usual ones, beginning with the point about the effective management of the deer population, each year on the verge of crowding out human civilization if not culled. She smiled and observed that there were more humane methods of population control than running each deer to ground and stabbing it. Her acerbic tone deteriorated the atmosphere rather quickly. A stout man by the door barked in irritation. The protests rose, the arguments, the usual arguments, marshalled as usual.

There was the matter of the law, which permitted pursuit onto private property of game that was in the course of being hunted, a condition left undefined. They had discussed this with their lawyers. So had Serge, but it was here, she knew, they were most vulnerable, and had chosen the path of deterrence with the physical impediments of gates, chains, piles of brush across roads.

She had heard all this before, they had said it before. Her mind fastened on the tapestry on the wall behind the mayor: Three plump, shimmering female nudes slept in a forest, in abandoned, sprawled positions with parted legs, surrounded by the corpses of rabbits and squirrels. A pack of dogs, held in check by a cherub, waited for the goddesses to wake, and from the gloom of the overhanging branches, satyrs stared down at the voluptuous breasts, inviting clefts, and lavish buttocks of the beauties.

A man sitting near her, following her eye, said, "*Diane la chaste et ses nymphes, d'après la toile de Rubens.* Diana the goddess of hunting."

Clara felt a start of blood in her cheeks. Despite herself she glanced at the speaker, a tall, balding Frenchman in a khaki jacket, very handsome.

"The tradition of the hunt," Mayor Briac was saying, "the formal tradition as we know it, for, obviously, man has hunted from time immemorial—the formal tradition was codified under Louis XIV, who was also a great scholar and encouraged the great naturalists like Buffon. . . ."

Clara shifted restlessly. Invoking the centuries of tradition, the history of France, royal privilege, did not seem fair or germane either to the reality of cruelty, suffering, blood lust, the love of killing so easily transferred to one's fellow human beings. She had copied something down from a painting by Dürer, and found it in her purse, prepared to read it out:

Qui tue la bête par plaisir plus que par nécessité offense le Père.
He who kills animals for pleasure offends God.

But the scrap of paper stayed in her hand, hand limp with self-consciousness, she could not speak. Perhaps it was the leering satyrs of Rubens's imagination, or the naked sex of the sleeping Diana and her maidens, in their defenseless sleep so like the dead prey. How odd that this picture, pointedly associating hunting and sex, should depict the goddess of chastity. What did the word *vénerie* mean to the French? She was all at once uncomfortable, miserable, at being in this room with a dozen male hunters. Predators. In the bright autumn sun coming through the long windows, dust motes danced as the room heated up. Worse than discomfort, it was misery, welling up from she knew not where. She stared at the floor to avoid looking at any of the pictures; a row of sporting prints showed hunters, hunters, hunters, and their prey. They kill for pleasure.

Tuer par plaisir. The association with pleasure was suddenly clear to her. *Plaisir* with its sexual connotations. Male energy warmed the room, charged the dust motes like ions of some alien force, stifling her, frightening her. An unfamiliar and brutal sensation pulsed at the bridge of her nose, as if a hole, a shot, pierced right there. Her eyes filled, she remembered this sensation, it was tears. She was going to cry. Her throat swelled, the first tear spilled, the hand of some unnameable sorrow or exasperation pressed her breast. She quickly stood, feigning disarray, allergy, she knew not which, or why.

"Thank you," she said, "I'm afraid I'm late—I'll leave you— I'm not in agreement—my husband—"

She stumbled out, her adversaries too astonished to do more than half rise and watch her. The woman at the library desk wavered between a rhetorical farewell—"*Bonne fin d'après-midi, madame*"—and saying nothing. Clara bolted across the gravel forecourt and climbed into her car.

11

Will You Wear White?

On Mondays the flea market remained open but somehow folded in on itself with a quiet sigh of pleasure that the Sunday strollers had gone back to work, the knots of tourists were gone. Now dealers talked to each other, or to the few people who came back to look again at the vase, little table, terra cotta bust that had drawn them the day before. Serious transactions unfurled, cash in envelopes moved from breast pockets to desk drawers, *pâté* and *carottes rapées* perfumed the air with garlicky pungence. Anne-Sophie had lunch with a print dealer from Lyons in the Resto Pergolèse, but it was all she could do to tear herself away from the vantage point of her stand, with its full view of the corridor leading to the stairs, where she could see anyone who went up or came down from the *grenier*.

It had already been unlocked by the watchman when she got to work this morning, no way of knowing whether people had gone up or come down. Whether the American man had come down. The mystery unresolved deepened its charm, its vexing charm to distract her from the normal transactions of her Mondays. After lunch she went up there, alone, though with the precaution of telling Monsieur Pécuchet that she was going. No one was there. As before, she had the sense of an alien presence, though there was no real change or disarray. As before, this infected her with a dangerous excitement. It was almost with regret she rolled her shutter down at the end of the day and set out to do errands and have dinner with her mother, to discuss matters relating to the wedding. She had several errands.

It was now October, and Anne-Sophie and Tim were to be married December tenth. Most of the arrangements had already been made by the efficient Anne-Sophie herself, in consultation with Tim and the marriage consultant, Madame Louise Aix, at the Bon

Marché department store. Madame Aix was a bosomy black-clad woman with red hair and glasses on a string, and an air of seriousness that Anne-Sophie found reassuring after the slightly dismissive participation of her mother. But certain problems had arisen with the invitations. It was time, and even a bit late, to have ordered them, but the issues of format were by no means clear, given that one of the families was anglophone.

Though Estelle agreed with the idea of marriage, Anne-Sophie never knew which detail of the traditional ceremony her mother would find ridiculous or unnecessary. She had laughed derisively when Anne-Sophie had broached the idea of a morning coat for Tim. Her heroine Raymonde, in *Les Fruits*, had protested going to the *mairie* and the church! "What do I want with stupid legalities," etc., with her marvellous tempestuousness.

So Madame Aix for her part had quickly seen in the motherless young career woman a need for advice and mothering. Their relationship had grown to where Madame Aix ventured counsel on a wider range of subjects than mere formal details. Madame Aix found herself in such a relationship with a number of young women, and often their mothers too, women worried to distraction by the realm of possible error a wedding opened up.

"Will you wear white?" she had asked.

Anne-Sophie thought so. Madame Aix frowned slightly. "It is so—*jeune fille*."

Did Madame Aix think of her as old? Anne-Sophie feared so, she feared it herself, knew she was slightly old for a first-time bride.

"A very young girl in her teens might." Madame Aix appeared to struggle for the tact needed. "It's just that the significance of white, an ancient symbol of virginity, is so much part of our collective unconscious that a bride in white prompts speculation, if not amusement, and people draw their conclusions better not drawn. You see? Whereas, I would propose, *ivoire,* ivory satin, or even *rose-ivoire*. With your high color it will be very lovely and blushing, and, after all, nearly white."

To Anne-Sophie, and to Tim when asked, it was clear that the same customs prevailed in France as in America, of ignoring the symbolic significance of white when it came to choosing a wedding gown: Anne-Sophie's white satin gown was coming from Inès de la Fressange on the Avenue Montaigne, where a school friend of

Anne-Sophie's was the head of public relations. The religious ceremony would be at St. Blaise, in the village of Val-Saint-Rémy, where Anne-Sophie's grandmother, her father's mother, still lived, though now quite senile. The cocktail reception would be across the square from the church at a little restaurant, Père Norand, and the dinner at Anne-Sophie's grandmother's house in the same village. Cases of champagne had been ordered from Monsieur Braquer, who had been her father's vintner, but it remained to be decided who would do the hors d'oeuvres and where to honeymoon.

Estelle was not much use in all this, and had complained about the hypocrisy and trouble a fancy wedding was—she would have preferred the registry, or barefoot in some tiny Alpine church. But of course, Dorothy Minor pointed out, Estelle was the *soixante-huitarde* of the family, while the younger people were the more conventional. Tim pitied Anne-Sophie Estelle's detachment; he had the male belief that young women and their mothers collaborating on weddings should be very happy and close. He knew it had been so with his sister and his mother.

About his part in the wedding itself, Tim had only the normal male attitudes, cooperative, sentimental, and resigned. He had assented to the caliber of the champagne and the nature of the food, and had reservations about the religious side of it. Estelle derided his reservations, saying it was very American and literal of him to take religion seriously enough to have reservations. He did not in general see anything too different between American and French nuptials, either in their premises or their details—the bridal gown, the cake, the tent if it would have been summer, the striped awnings beneath which he had delivered several of his American friends after college into their new husbandly states. It was all something men went through, and he felt generally positive about the traditions as well as toward his choice of wife. Anne-Sophie had not visited America and Tim's side of the family, but his father, often in Paris, had met the Argels, and indicated to Tim that he thought Anne-Sophie a lovely girl, despite the eccentric mother. His mother and Anne-Sophie had not met, though they had politely corresponded.

*   *   *

Tim and Anne-Sophie came to Estelle's a bit early, before the other guests, to discuss something important with Estelle, the apartment they had found. To have found an apartment at last was a great relief to both of them, as each had devoted what seemed like numberless afternoons to the ongoing project of the search for one big enough and nice enough and affordable, to accommodate their new married life.

This had not been Tim's favorite pastime. It was his appointed task to do the preliminary looking on the days when Anne-Sophie could not; otherwise it was she who rushed out to get *Le Figaro*, scan the ads for three- or four-room apartments in the acceptable arrondissements (fifth, sixth, seventh) they had agreed on, with a glance at the first, second, eighth and ninth, and maybe the four-teenth but that would be getting too close to *maman*. From the few times they'd looked at things together it was clear that it was Tim who was temperamentally better suited to do it. The merest eccen-tricity in arrangements, the least ugly improvisation sent Anne-Sophie into paroxysms of discouragement and fear. "How can people live like that," she would moan, feeling herself and Tim to be on a similar precipice, easily to be tipped over into a chasm of squalor and expedience. Not at all what she had dreamed for their perfect union; an ugly apartment would symbolize the compro-mises of this world, the mockery of human hopes. Tim had found her emotion puzzling; he had always thought that newlyweds would be indifferent to their surroundings. He pointed out they were just going to make love all the time. But he accepted that Anne-Sophie must be sheltered from too much apartment-hunting. Also, it was he who had the flexible hours.

He had tried not to think too much of the practicalities of mar-ried life—he assumed he and Anne-Sophie would address them when necessary—but the process of looking for an apartment had brought practicality home to him in an uncomfortable way. Seeing the details of the lives of others, so forlorn and shabby, so rickety and extemporaneous, depressed him almost as much as it did her. French apartments were small. Laundry rooms were used as nurs-eries, kitchens were in closets. The *cuisine américaine* depressed him, it seemed too pointed a criticism of what the French appar-ently felt was the ruthless pragmatism of the American character: the kitchen in the living room where necessary. Never mind that in

America kitchens were never in the living room, he felt that this label, *cuisine américaine,* pointed to some capability for improvisation in himself which he hoped never to have to use, but which would involve moral failing if he used it. It also seem to allege bad taste.

In another way, the *cuisine américaine* spoke of the merry resourcefulness of the French to put the best face on having to have their kitchens in their living rooms, in the modern world where six apartments were carved out of some nice old private house once belonging to a haughty family. Trying to inhabit and personalize their cubbies, people had painted their walls navy blue, or lowered their ceilings with fiberglass panels. There had been an era of orange and pink. How many flights would one walk up without an elevator?

One particular day, Tim suddenly knew he had found their apartment, on the Passage de la Visitation—the name itself so charming, the arrondissement so correct. An apartment of four rooms, with a small kitchen. With an actual dining room, which he believed in having, as he had been brought up with dining rooms. And he'd come to learn the value the French put on certain things— windows, for one, which direction they faced, and whether there were any closets at all. The price was only a little too high for them, and he felt sure Anne-Sophie would like the herringbone floors, and the bedroom fireplace with its marble curlicues, the second WC, the large entry hall. His heart lifted with the optimistic sense of the future that only real estate can bring, and stepped up with the simultaneous anxiety that someone else would buy this place before Anne-Sophie could see it.

He called her at work and made an appointment with the agent for them both to come back that afternoon. She was dismayed before they were even inside by the discovery that the apartment he wanted her to see was on the *premier étage,* one floor up—the American second floor. Plenty high up and still not so high you had to get in an elevator, a great advantage in Tim's mind, completely unacceptable in hers.

"It will be dark," she said.

"No, it has good light," he said. "When I was here it was getting morning sun."

"I never imagined living on the *premier étage*," she said, a remark he found completely inscrutable.

"It's charming, you'll see," he said. "There's the guy." The agent solemnly shook their hands, more or less overtly sized Anne-Sophie up, and gave Tim an important, conspiratorial smile. They climbed the stairs.

"Monsieur was the first person to visit this apartment," the agent said to Anne-Sophie.

Inside, her manner gave no indication of her views. She looked with censorious thoroughness into the closets and inspected the floors with scientific attention to the width of the cracks between the boards and how many of them would have to be replaced.

When they were outside, they stepped apart from the agent, and she said "*Très bien*, by and large."

"You didn't like it?"

"Yes, I liked it. There are problems though. The street is *très bien*, but the *premier étage!*"

"I like being one floor up. Not right on the street but not in the elevator all the time."

"You don't understand the French attitude about the *premier étage*." This was said affectionately, as if he were an educable child.

"How can I understand? It's completely irrational," he said. After some rational discussion, centering on the prestige of the street, charm, and useful features especially a *bibliothèque*, a handsome set of built-in bookshelves, they decided to go back to the agent's office and make an offer. They knew they shouldn't hesitate, as really good apartments got snapped up on the spot.

Anne-Sophie's father, a doctor, had been dead for a decade, but Estelle had stayed in the family apartment, a large nineteenth-century apartment in Montparnasse in which all the rooms were oval and painted tasteful shades of gray. Estelle had a new book coming out, and a photographer there to take the jacket photo had stayed longer than expected, so that when Anne-Sophie and Tim arrived it was in time to hear Estelle saying to the photographer: "Of course, I have no sense about men, I've never understood them, my heart is constantly being broken." A startled instant of reflection showed on Anne-Sophie's face, though she had long since learned to separate her mother's fictional persona, the warm, worldly sensuous woman who narrated her works, from the comfortable family member who scolded her about her career choices and had been more or less happily married to her father.

From the hall where Elvira had let them in, they could see the expression of passionate chagrin on Estelle's face, presumably to do with her own inept conduct of love affairs, though so far as Anne-Sophie knew, her mother's only boyfriend was the elderly academician, Cyrille Deroux. The photographer was packing his gear. Tim and Anne-Sophie had no further clue as to the subject of their conversation, for Estelle then saw them and gave a cry of greeting. She was wearing jeans and a photogenic sort of ruffled shirt.

"*Ah! Ma fille, Anne-Sophie, et son fiancé Monsieur Nolinger!*" she explained. They smiled at the photographer, and dipped their heads in greeting. He struggled to collapse some sort of giant silver foil umbrella into a tiny packing case. Estelle embraced them.

"Anne-Sophie has undergone the most horrific trauma in the past days, the appalling murder in the *puces*, did you hear of it?" she asked her photographer friend. The event was recounted even as the silver umbrella, having a mind of its own, snapped back to its full size with an indignant report, and the poor man was obliged to wrestle with it anew. "That apparatus reminds me," Estelle said, "of the diaphragms of one's fertile days."

Tim and Anne-Sophie ignored the poor photographer, whose struggles they sensed must embarrass him. Estelle, herself embarrassed at being caught playing the novelist in front of Anne-Sophie— she always tried to downplay that side of her life *en famille*—briskly launched them into the aperitifs and listened to their account of the apartment, which she agreed sounded good. This was important because she would be advancing part of Anne-Sophie's share of the purchase price.

12

Tears at the Tennis Club Marne-Garches-la-Tour

When Tim came to dinner, Estelle tended to invite other Americans, usually Dorothy Sternholz and sometimes Ames Everett. This had the effect of making Tim feel more, rather than less, strange, emphasizing his non-Frenchness as if his odd nationality had to be considered. Soon, when the princess Sternholz and Ames Everett had sipped their port for a few minutes, she led everyone to the table.

"We are having something delicious, of my own invention, that is, you will tell me what you think." Estelle was not a great cook, but prided herself on straightforward ingredients of perfect quality, rather as did her creation the countess Morilly, in her books, which were apt to digress into rhapsodies on a *courgette* or *betterave*. "This is an *omelette aux truffes*, but what you might think is an extravagance is not, for these are Chinese truffles! Really, they smell identical and the vegetable man swears they have the same *parfum* in the dish. So we'll see!

"I hope Teem will eat eggs? I know how Americans are."

Anne-Sophie realized she had never seen Tim eat an egg, but had no idea whether this was by conviction or because she had never offered him one. The question was put to Tim, who absently declared himself ready to eat eggs, Ames and Dorothy too. In reality, his heart was a turmoil of anxiety about what he and Anne-Sophie had just done in pledging themselves to a hugely expensive real estate transaction.

Everyone gave the dish a suitable moment of reverence. Estelle had a Frenchwoman's way of presenting each favor, each dish, each idea, as if it were done especially for the lucky guest. Perhaps that was the essence of literary style too, Tim thought. "I want you to have this delicious *confiture aux groseilles*," Estelle would say, as she might say, "I want you to have this rare, perfect adjective," and she was right that the confiture, or the adjective, would seem an especially delicious one, even if Anne-Sophie remarked later with slightly unfilial cattiness that it came like other jam from the Monoprix.

"Anne-Sophie," said the princess Sternholz presently, "may we know about the wedding dress?"

"Yes of course! I am very happy with it. From Inès de la Fressange. Well, it has a bustier in *soie blanche*, covered with a sheer tulle caraco, long sleeves, round neck, and then the skirt is organza, with silk ribbons. Completely simple, but pretty, I think." Tim was surprised that she said she was happy with it, for Anne-Sophie had a Frenchwoman's way of saying "Oh, it's just a little nothing much" at a compliment, where an American would say "Thanks."

Her mother grinned at Tim. The two of them shared, or Estelle assumed they did, a patient but rather patronizing view of all this ceremonial fuss. Luckily Anne-Sophie did not notice. When she caught them in these conspiritorial glances, always initiated by Estelle, she was apt to pout childishly and complain to Tim later that she was being treated like a child, a *femme-enfant*.

"You have to get married in something," Tim now said loyally, ignoring Estelle's smirk, "and the guests expect a pretty dress."

"We are having a most traditional wedding," said Estelle, with asperity, to Ames and Dorothy. "I believe Anne-Sophie has not yet introduced Teem to the idea of what he is going to have to wear."

"Men like to dress up," Anne-Sophie asserted. "Only think of their uniforms and hunting outfits. Kilts. Headdresses. It's clear, men are never happier than when dressed in costumes."

When the argument over this had subsided, a lull in the conversation prompted Tim to fill it. It usually fell to him, who was more in the world than Anne-Sophie, restricted to her stand all day, or than Estelle working at her sedentary art, to provide anecdote or gossip. Tim often embroidered stories for Estelle, for her universe of desperados. He continued to hope for her absolute approval as the husband for Anne-Sophie. And Estelle liked his stories, and made him feel at such times that he was more perceptive than other men. She sometimes even seemed to fear he might in time be a bit bored by Anne-Sophie. In his view, she constantly underestimated Anne-Sophie.

So he told them about seeing Clara Holly and a strange man at the Tennis Club Marne-Garches-la-Tour, near Boulogne. In the habit of playing tennis Monday afternoons, Fridays too if he could make it, he had been at his rather inconvenient and distant tennis club with Adrian Wilcox, the British sculptor. Tim usually beat Wilcox, but today Wilcox completely obliterated Tim, and was so pleased about this he suggested going into the bar for a couple of beers; he would want to rehash the game, and Tim was too good-natured to refuse. Wilcox invested winning and losing too heavily with metaphorical implications of decay and impotence, or, as today, having won, rejuvenation, art, and immortal life to take his wishes lightly.

Agreeing, Tim said he just had to be in town in time for dinner with Anne-Sophie and her mother, the normal Monday night custom Adrian was well aware of. By way of hors d'oeuvres they shared an *assiette anglaise*—so typically French to assign to this slightly guilt-making snack of sausage and rillettes an English origin—and a couple of beers. Tim was facing the door, so that he instantly saw Clara Holly come in. She was preoccupied-looking, even distraught. She didn't see him.

"What should I have done?" he wondered now. "Greeted her immediately, I now see. But by the time I decided, it was too late. I'd seen too much.

"She was half in tears, and ordered what looked like a gin. That already put me at a disadvantage, that is, I thought she might not like to be seen crying and drinking straight gin alone in the bar."

"Zat is so American," Estelle commented. She spoke English with a theatrically French accent—Anne-Sophie's English was really much better than her mother's; she had been sent to London summer after summer to perfect it. "Why should she mind? Has a woman no right to an aperitif in America? Is it so deeply compromising?"

"Well, I wasn't being judgmental about the drink, but she seemed upset. You don't like to intrude on some grief or distress."

"You must be the first newspaperman in the history of journalism ever to feel that," Estelle remarked. She often made jibes at Tim's profession, which was after all rather like her own.

"She must be used to having a certain effect, she's very pretty. The very pretty lead their lives in goldfish bowls," Ames Everett said.

"It could have been vodka," Tim agreed.

"I think you are awful, all of you!" cried Anne-Sophie gaily. "Condemning the poor woman as if she were an *alcoolique*. So she was drinking alone in the tennis club! Perhaps she had asked for a glass of water! I expect you will say she came in to pick up men, too."

"I'm trying to explain that my moment of hesitation in not greeting her was fatal, as it turned out, because you've guessed it. In a minute, a man came in, and sat beside her. I guess she hadn't been expecting him, or didn't like him—at first she nodded rather icily— but they seemed to have seen each other before. A Frenchman, a member of the club, I've seen him. Balding, handsome in a way, but about fifty, maybe less."

"Antique," said Estelle, who was in her mid-fifties. "A man so ancient, how could it be anything but innocent?"

"Whatever he said, she smiled at last."

Adrian and Tim ordered another beer, and by the the time they had drunk them, she was laughing. They were relative strangers, Tim thought, barely knew each other, but there seemed to be a context for their conversation. He felt awkward to be sitting there watching them, because something was happening to them, it was clear on their blazing faces. It was their faces that compromised them. Some self-conscious emotion had transfixed them.

"Anyway, I finessed the moment I would have to acknowledge my presence, as it turned out, because I went to the men's room before we left, and when I came out they were both gone."

"Had they left together?" asked Estelle.

"I don't know, and Adrian had his back to them."

"He was probably her broker, or her dentist," Estelle said, defending this unknown Clara against the new suggestion, so Anglo-Saxon and prudish, that she had practically been discovered *in flagrante*.

"Probably. He looked like a banker, something like that."

"How useful to have a lover who is a banker," Anne-Sophie said. "One who makes real estate loans."

Tim didn't ever really feel comfortable at these domestic dinners with his future mother-in-law, unlike many Frenchmen who would enjoy them, gossip and food both, and now he felt mildly ashamed of himself for having told the story about Clara Holly to people who knew her. No doubt it had been an innocent meeting, now turned by him into gossip or low-key scandal. But he had been touched by it in some way. Seeing emotion in others always touched him; he knew it to be the worst propensity for a journalist. If someone had tears in her eyes, his eyes filled. When he saw desire, he felt it. Anyone would desire that beautiful woman, it wasn't so weird of him.

At about ten, Tim's portable rang. He discreetly stepped away from the table for a moment or two, then returned and settled uneasily into his *tarte aux pommes*. It was the American woman, Delia. "She's scared," he explained. "She says there's no one in the hotel, the manager's not there, and she's hearing noises. I told her to go sit in the cafe next door until the desk clerk comes back. The hotel's not very nice. I'll look in on her tomorrow morning."

13

Who Is Tim?

They drove home, Tim's long legs tucked up uncomfortably in the front seat of Anne-Sophie's Mini, its canvas top unrolled where she had earlier transported a screen. In the night air they could feel the chill of approaching winter.

"I wonder if we ought to go up to the hotel where the American girl is staying?" Anne-Sophie said.

"She'll be all right."

"*Maman* was nice about the apartment. I'll show it to her tomorrow if I can get the agent."

A certain apprehensiveness crawled in Tim's stomach; he'd forgotten the apartment.

"*Comme je suis contente.*" Anne-Sophie sighed. She was expansive in her feeling of happiness and love, generated by the new apartment, the approval of her mother, their American friends Dorothy and Ames, both Protestant but not too puritan, Tim's interesting profession that prompted dramatic phone calls during dinner, a promised future of harmony, against which the plight of the American girl saddened her.

"The poor thing. What is her name?" she asked.

"Who?" he cried guiltily, for his thoughts were a welter, on the rash venture of the apartment, and on Clara Holly—on her expression as she had looked at the handsome man and the self-conscious redness had risen to suffuse her neck and face.

"The American woman who called? Who found poor Monsieur Boudherbe dead?"

"Delia."

"What is she afraid of tonight, exactly?" Anne-Sophie asked.

"She didn't say. I don't know why she called me, except she thinks of me as a fellow American in a wasteland of Frogs, and I had given her my phone numbers."

"What could happen in a French hotel at ten at night? Nothing. *La pauvre*," Anne-Sophie said, wondering if she should mention having seen the other American, the man, in her depot attic, and somehow not wanting to. "Of course we must help. I remember how frightened and pale she looked, looking at the dead body."

"No doubt," Tim agreed.

"There were two," said Anne-Sophie, "a man and a woman."

"I didn't see the guy, he'd gone somewhere to change money."

Anne-Sophie paused. Eventually she asked, "Are you really going to interview Serge Cray?" Tim knew it impressed her that in his line of work he sometimes had access to famous artists and politicians.

"Tomorrow."

"I could see that you were falling into one of your hopeless quarrels with *Maman*," Anne-Sophie said after another moment. Tim and Estelle did sometimes argue about politics, each taking extreme positions, his usually to the left, notwithstanding his association with *Reliance* magazine. At first, he couldn't remember any incipient quarrel, though there had been a tentative discussion of the American character, which had been averted.

"We French are often criticized for being elliptical," Estelle had said, in a leading tone, moments before the arrival of Ames and Dorothy.

"Elliptical? You mean not straightforward? Devious?"

"Put it as you will. I am saying that, *au contraire*, we are much more straightforward than Americans, with their implaccable, unfathomable smiling. Their orthodontics. Their claiming to love each other, then murdering each other at the lift of a foot." But Tim hadn't been in the mood to be maneuvered into defending the American murder rate.

"Why are the French accused of being elliptical?" he had mildly answered, thinking, though, that this conversation was a good example of elliptical. "They can be very direct."

"Oh, you are thinking of Anne-Sophie," said Estelle, herself having always deplored Anne-Sophie's fatal lack of nuance. In Estelle's view, Anne-Sophie was directness itself, and with her bluntness came a complete failure to understand flirtation; it was perhaps this that had suited her to an American fiancé.

But this was the closest they had come to a subject of dispute, this particular night. It always slightly irritated Anne-Sophie that her mother would talk to Tim about subjects she didn't bring up with Anne-Sophie—general topics, adult talk, as if Anne-Sophie were still a child or hopelessly unintellectual, while Estelle and Tim were writers, and it was that, not their future legal bond, that seemed to bring them together.

Yet it wasn't that Estelle was a writer—it was what she wrote about that was sort of a problem for Anne-Sophie. It was often fascinating, but also appalling and intimidating. When she was younger, she had pored over certain passages, for instance the description in *Estragon* of Maude's young lover Pablo, with his "enchanting rosette of an anus, surrounded by the most tender and adorable ebony hairs, and when she, arching ecstatically beneath him, could just manage to reach and could just insert the tiniest bit of her little finger into it, this sent him into such amusing paroxysms of delight—not, luckily, the ultimate one until her own pleasure was vertiginously achieved, but . . ."

Without putting it to herself specifically, Anne-Sophie was left wondering if Tim would really like a finger up his asshole, but even if so, it was physically impossible, given their respective heights; she could not reach it. And there were several other problematic passages, and the unthinkable questions they raised.

To her actual daughter, Estelle had always given only the most mundane advice, for instance another piece of advice as universal as the maternal strictures on clean underwear: the one about how one should marry for love, but it was just as easy to fall in love with a rich man as a poor one. Easier by far, some would have said, but not Estelle, who despite her own comfortable bourgeois style of life had a romantic view of poverty as liberating, even noble. Whatever her reasons, until recently she hadn't asked Anne-Sophie too pointedly what Anne-Sophie might have gleaned of any distant Fitzgeraldesque midwestern lawns, columned porches, fireflies, safe deposit boxes full of long-term certificates of deposit and whatever else she had begun to hope for from Tim. For poverty, however noble, is not necessarily something you want in the family.

"As you know," she said to her friends Dorothy Minor and Ames Everett, when Anne-Sophie and Tim had left, "I have no intuition, absolutely no common sense, am absolutely the worst judge of human nature. . . ." This was one of her vanities, for though she was astute, she liked to pretend that she had meager powers of observation and filled her books from the wellsprings of the heart. She seemed to feel that there was something a little vulgar and prying about mere observation.

They had no idea who Tim was, really. Now her concern was animated because Anne-Sophie had shown her the little flashlight marked with the name Nolinger, and because an apartment would have to be paid for. And of course, being literary, Estelle was aware of the many archetypal tales—the student prince, Cinderella—wherein the foreign stranger, once he has arranged to marry your daughter, turns out to be a rich and noble person in his own land.

"I have no sense of these things, but I am so determined that Anne-Sophie be happy. If the wretched Teem makes her unhappy I will personally kill him."

"Why should he?" Ames asked. "He'll treat her wonderfully. It always seems to me the slightly rootless Tim must long for the stable peace of a French family and the effective ministrations of an organized French wife, or he ought to."

"Why are you having worries now?" Dorothy asked.

Estelle hesitated. She hated to be thought of as showing any interest in money at all. She was not avaricious—she scorned money, or at least people who tried too obviously to get it, and the characters who tried to get it in her books came in for a great deal of misfortune, for instance Monsieur Todeaux in *Plusieurs Fois*. Up until now, even with only eight weeks to go until the wedding, the *liste de mariage* formed and most of the arrangements, she had shared the curious constraint—perhaps very French—about making inquiries about Tim. There was also a little of the French belief that all Americans were rich. So she could hardly justify showing too much interest in Tim's "background" now, except as a kind of maternal curiosity, for what good mother does not wish her child supported by a safe income?

"Something a little delicate. We know Teem, and his father is a delightful man, so American, in the hotel business, there has never been any mystery about this. Paragon Hotels."

"I met the father one time," Ames agreed. He saw how Estelle and Anne-Sophie could have no idea of Tim's social background—neither had ever even been to America.

"Do we have any idea if this is a big hotel business? Do we know the scale of it?"

"Paragon Hotels, it's a chain—why?"

"Could it be connected to the name of Nolinger-Webb?"

"That's a hotel chain, car rentals and such. I very much doubt that Tim is the principal scion of Nolinger-Webb, if that's what you're hoping," Ames hastened to say, it occurring to him for the first time that maybe he was. Could Tim be a hapless younger son, a disowned rebel from the great airport services fortune? Still, any whiff of a major American fortune always drifted over to Paris, and none had wafted in to wreathe and perfume Tim.

"But you are not sure!" said Estelle in what sounded a very encouraged tone.

"Nolinger is not a common name. It could be the same family, but that still wouldn't tell us if Tim's father is distantly connected to it or intimately connected. One would have to ask him. Anyway, I don't get it. These are Tim's keys?"

"No, no, nothing to do with Teem, but it set me to wondering about the name. I could hardly ask Anne-Sophie—but I wonder if she has any idea if Teem is connected to a chain?"

"They must have discussed their families," said Ames. "She probably has a very clear idea, Anne-Sophie is eminently clear."

"It's very vulgar, isn't it, to be reassured by the idea of a big chain lurking in Teem's family tree? All the same . . ." Ames could hear that Estelle was indeed reassured. "What do you think? He has good manners, but then his mother is French-speaking. Also he went to school in Switzerland. He was brought up in Istanbul or some odd place like that. What does that tell us? Nothing."

"Those years his father spent in Istanbul say 'distant cousin' to me, at best—but why don't you ask him?" Ames suggested.

"Ask him! Impossible."

"It's a nice family, *Maman,* really," Anne-Sophie had said once. "I've seen pictures of where his parents lived, a very pleasant white house made of wood, in America, but most of the time they were in Europe on account of his papa's work, and you have met Monsieur Nolinger."

"His *portefeuille*—you call it the 'beelfold'? That used to be an infallible index of a man's affluence, but now it is often made of an ambiguous nylon. The same with shoes, by Reebok or Neeck. I can get no clue," she complained to the princess Dorothy and Ames.

Ames remarked to Dorothy, in the taxi going home, "It hadn't occurred to me, heir to a great fortune. But there is something slightly off and mysterious about Tim. Could that be it?"

"More likely a prison term," Dorothy disagreed.

She and Ames laughed with the slightly guilty pleasure of people who knew themselves to be breaking a sacred taboo—the taboo among Americans abroad against investigating each others' former lives back in America or questioning the version of himself that each expatriate has the right to put forward unquestioned.

"And then there's Clara Cray and the mysterious man," said Dorothy.

"Tell me more about this person who, as you said the other morning, seems so to have fascinated Teem," Estelle had asked as they parted. Few French people had seen the obscure Hollywood film, which fixed her identity in her hometown and for the odd film buff as Clara Holly; the French thought of Clara as Madame Cray, in the normal way. Estelle had already conceived an abstract dislike for this woman, in Anne-Sophie's behalf, and from some French-woman's reflexive mistrust of other women in general, except for certified friends, and no exceptions for friends where men were involved. "Blond?"

"No, no, short dark hair—curly. She has rather deep color and a very large bust, like an Italian actress."

"She does, doesn't she?" Ames Everett agreed.

14

Where Is Gabriel?

Tim and Anne-Sophie found Delia Sadler sitting at a little marble-topped table in a shadowy corner of the cafe next to the Hôtel Le Mistral, an empty coffee before her. She looked forlorn, agitated and scared. Her thin little shoulders in a ribbed shirt seemed to tremble slightly and she was scrubbing at the table with her napkin, trying to order and calm herself. When she saw them she smiled and waved, relieved. It was Anne-Sophie who barged briskly over to Delia, exclaiming, "I was there, you know, I saw you! At the *puces*. I saw the whole thing! What a terrible sight!"

Delia recognized her, the pretty blond young woman smoker, who was still smoking. Anne-Sophie always smoked, as if a cigarette were ballast to hold her upright. Tim saw Delia's eyes recognize Anne-Sophie, then take in the cigarette, then look behind Anne-Sophie at him. She was puzzled at the conjunction of Tim the helpful American reporter and the young Frenchwoman she had seen at the flea market.

"This is Anne-Sophie," Tim explained.

"I saw you that morning," Anne-Sophie reminded her, extending her hand.

Delia Sadler looked a little disoriented by all this, seeming to wonder what Anne-Sophie was sticking her hand out for, for an instant before shaking it. Did women shake hands in America? Tim couldn't remember. She looked happy to see them. "I'm sorry to have bothered you, I shouldn't have called, I just panicked. I think they've got Gabriel. My colleague," she explained.

Anne-Sophie sat down and waved for the waiter. "*Je prends un café.*"

"Have another coffee," Tim said to Delia. "*Une bière, s'il vous plaît.* So what happened?"

She began her tale.

Unsuspicious by nature, certain of her basic security and rights and status as an American citizen even without passport, and beloved of Gabriel Biller, Delia had nonetheless woken up this morning feeling even more embattled than yesterday. She had thought back on the FBI men and the newspaperman Tim—they had all seemed to want something from her she wasn't capable of giving in the way of information and theories, cooperation, keys. Though they had begun in the guise of friendliness, they had soured on her and abandoned her. The men named Frank had told her to hang on, they'd be back to see how she was coming along.

"But they didn't come back today, I spent the whole day here, this was my fourth day in France. I wanted at least to go to the Louvre, that was the whole point of coming," she complained. "I was going to go every day, for a week, I've only got four more days."

In the morning, she had dawdled over her coffee in the tiny breakfast room off the lobby of the hotel until the maid began to glare at her. Dealers and salesmen slurped their coffees, ate their bricklike chunks of jamless untoasted bread, there was no orange juice. She thought of her passport, and of how the FBI men had said to the guy Tim, "You probably shouldn't write about this case, not that you would want to, there's not really much here, but the French are touchy, and a news story could complicate things for Miss Sadler here."

Tim had doubted this, but seemed to accept, as a sort of compliment to the powers of journalism, the idea that it could affect legal procedures, bring international complications.

"I wondered about that too," he said now. "Why would I want to write about it, and why shouldn't I?"

"This morning I still had the five hundred francs Clara Holly had loaned me on Saturday, but by now I'd begun to get good and sick of the hotel restaurant, where I could put food on the bill, so I told myself some money would come soon from Oregon, so at lunchtime I decided to go somewhere else to eat, not far enough to count as leaving the scene." The shabby street was lined with small cafes, and there was a largish brasserie on the corner, Le Bon Tabac, another of those cross-cultural mysteries.

"In Oregon you would instantly go out of business if you called a restaurant The Good Tobacco," she said.

She had sat at a table outside, for it was sunny enough to cut the chill October air, and being visible outside would prove she hadn't meant to run away, in case the police came. Being vegetarian, she ordered a cheese sandwich, which turned out be enormous, a whole half a baguette, which was great because it would last an hour if she nibbled it slowly. Twenty-two francs. Once she was installed and served, her mind fastened on her plight, on the whereabouts of Gabriel, on the side of all this she'd be telling about once she got home.

When she got back to Oregon, she'd tell about the man dead in the flea market of course. She could also tell about the disgusting thing that happened in the rest room, in the basement of this brasserie when she went down to pee. As she recounted this episode to Anne-Sophie and Tim, she watched them closely, as if to see whether it shocked them.

"It was a unisex rest room, the kind with individual little cubicles with solid doors, but they were all taken, and they cost two francs. Two francs! So I hung around waiting for someone to come out, so I could go in. Eventually a man came out, but when I tried to catch the door and thereby save the two francs, he resisted. Well, imagine! So selfish! That would never happen in America. At home another woman would pass you the door without letting it latch, I don't know about men!"

This man shut his door firmly instead, and then when she tried to put a two-franc piece in the latch, she found it was still locked and resisting her money. The man languidly washed his hands at the basin and went upstairs.

Then, while she was waiting for the other toilet to be free, the first door opened again, and out came a woman. From the same stall where the man had been! It shocked her. Perhaps everyone knew this place, Le Bon Tabac, where the stalls were soundproof and people could rent them for two francs to screw or do drugs or whatever they were doing! She tried to imagine doing it standing on a toilet.

The woman, in her twenties, hadn't looked like a hooker. There was no aura of abandon or defeat; she looked rather smug, in fact, and patted her hair in the mirror, smiling a smile at her reflection that contained no clues to her mood.

Anne-Sophie and Tim laughed at this story, and their laughter seemed to shock Delia even more.

She had gone back upstairs and ordered a coffee, seven francs, and tried to string that out. Then she went across the street to a sidewalk cafe and had another coffee—"cafe"—six francs fifty centimes. There were things to learn! How strange that unless you were a murder victim (of course) there was an interest in the tiniest mystery of travel, there was a richness to things, like a rich brocade, but also a tarnish, like the antique table napkins she sold in bundles back in Oregon, monogrammed sometimes with the initials of a bride, but also bearing faded stains that wouldn't come out from tea parties long ago. All that she saw from her little table of black formica in the wall aperture of Café Le Destin, half indoors, half out, bore the faded stains of other centuries. The butcher shop had a blackboard in its window, with writing on it in chalk, the handwriting illegible even if you knew French.

Wandering on, she began to wonder if spending money on a magazine would be worth it, since she couldn't read it. She spent a long time at the newsstand, comparing the prices of magazines. Because she couldn't read any of them, she wanted to find the one with the most photographs for the money. Finally she bought *Marie Claire*, twenty-five francs, and went to sit in the hotel lobby to look at it. She kept thinking about the odd fate of being a whore who had to screw in toilets, and of a society that let that happen. Revolting, sinister things about France were beginning to pile up.

In fact, the horrors of France had begun to assume a kind of abstract fascination. She had a little notebook that she wrote them down in, beginning with having her wallet and passport stolen but that was just the beginning. Hotel: the mattress was thin, the room ugly, and the desk clerk had a snooty, hostile manner even though she could speak English. And though she could speak English she often pretended not to. And the employees at the American consulate were not American but French, probably owing to some French law. She had witnessed their browbeating scorn for a poor old man ahead of her in line, an old harmless man, not well dressed, his yellowish white hair stringy. He was trying to get a birth certificate or something about his late wife's social security. He wanted to marry again and needed some paper about his dead wife.

"Don't want to lose her pension?" the girl had sneered.

"Well . . ."

"We like to keep every bit we can get," the girl pressed, with dreadful contempt.

"As if it were her business," Delia objected, "as if the money were coming out of her pocket. 'You want to make sure you get all the pensions coming to you,' is what the desk girl said, in this mocking tone." The bureaucrats laughing at him, this was another instance of hated government interference, insensitivity. "What did she know about the poor man's life?"

By four in the afternoon she was sick with sleepiness again. How long could jet lag go on? She knew she oughtn't to sleep, but she couldn't stay up anymore. She had a cold sensation of mercury leaking out of her brain stem and rising to the top of her head obliterating thoughts, now soaking her eyeballs in nightshade or hemlock. She told herself that maybe one good afternoon nap would clear these impediments. She thought of sleep tortures.

Sleep. She yielded up to this powerful idea and crossed the lobby of the Hôtel Le Mistral. The irritable woman at the desk eyed her. Delia couldn't tell if she was well disposed toward her or not. It had been brave of the woman to refuse to let the FBI men into Gabriel's room, that had been the correct thing to do. On the other hand, she might not like Americans or tourists. She didn't seem as if she did. As Delia passed the desk, the woman said in a horrid voice, "You know, madame, even if monsieur does not use his room, he pays as long as he has not given it up."

Delia shrugged and kept on going.

"So far, I'm not impressed with the friendliness of people in France, frankly, including the people at the American consulate," she said to Anne-Sophie and Tim.

She had taken off her jeans and lain down on the bed in the rest of her clothes, as a pledge of her intention to get up in an hour or so maybe, then she fell into a stonelike sleep. Sometime later, no way of telling what time, she was awake, as awake as if it were morning, though a pattern of neon light coming through the shade from some sign outside flashed on the ceiling and told her it was night. "I had no idea what time it was, but my brain was clear and noonlike, and right away I became aware of sounds through the wall from Gabriel's room. Maybe it was these that had woken me. I could hear drawers sliding open and shut. Now I think it was the two FBI guys," she said. "They wanted to look in his room, and they found some way to get in."

Anne-Sophie and Tim advanced objections and questions. Why would the FBI want to go into Gabriel's room, he who had nothing to do with the French murder and had been with her that night? Why would Gabriel murder an unknown antique dealer? She began to feel the fragility of her certitude, and even of her safety, depending as it did on an absence of malice, on cooperation, on goodwill from all concerned. From the Franks, specifically.

"I know it sounds paranoid, but it crossed my mind that the killer saw me and Gabriel arrive at the flea market, and thought we had seen him. So he stalked and murdered Gabriel, and would be looking for me too. That was just my paranoid thought. But he wouldn't try to kill me in the lobby of the Hôtel Le Mistral. Or would he?" So she sat in the lobby, not going upstairs, her room too little and with ugly blond furniture, thin green bedcover, hard chair and ripply mirror that made her look as if her face swam, and she thought of calling Tim.

"I've been sitting here trying to figure it out. Something's happened, Gabriel's just gone, disappeared, and I think someone's got him, the police or the murderer of the man in the market, and they could hurt me too."

Tim still didn't know if he agreed. Why should it be any more than bad luck or bad timing, unless she was involved in whatever it was—drugs would be the likeliest thing, or possibly art theft, since this was a flea market crowd.

"Why couldn't it be he himself who went in his room?" Tim asked, but Delia seemed injured by the suggestion that Gabriel would sneak back without telling her.

It couldn't be him of course, or why wouldn't he have tapped on her door, and who would he be talking to? Maybe the two Franks.

"Maybe you shouldn't stay there," Anne-Sophie put in. "We could find you somewhere else to stay and let the police know your whereabouts. Move to another hotel meantime, where you'd feel safer?"

"Then Gabriel couldn't find me, if—if he comes back."

In my attic, thought Anne-Sophie, thinking of Gabriel. She felt a connoisseur's pleasure in knowing something the others didn't. In a sense Gabriel was hers, like any secret, like finding an under-valued object at a jumble sale. Was it disloyal of her not to tell Tim? She didn't know, she only knew that it was hers to think about, and in the meantime no doubt this American girl had nothing to fear, for after all this was France, unless these Americans were all drug runners, though the young woman didn't look like a criminal, and it would be too bad if such a good-looking man was.

"He hasn't checked out?" Tim asked. "Would the hotel let you into his room? He might have some money there. He might have left a clue. Could you tell if anything had been moved?"

"I don't think they would open his room—they didn't let the FBI guys in. We could ask, though. You could ask them like you did before, in French? Tell them it's an emergency, he's disappeared? I could keep his stuff in my room, at least we wouldn't have to pay for two rooms," she said.

"Well," said Tim, "they wouldn't do it tonight anyhow. We'll go back with you now and wait till the desk clerk comes back. Meantime don't worry. Nothing much could happen in a French hotel."

The hotel was certainly not very elegant, Anne-Sophie agreed, as they passed through the dimly lit lobby, but she reflected that she herself had stayed in worse places in the country, on buying trips. She understood that Delia was probably especially timid because *handicapée*. "Would you like to borrow my portable *téléphone*?" she asked. "Then you could call for help directly if there's no one at the desk." She gave Delia her cell phone and instructions about numbers for the police. Then they went with her to her room and looked in it—empty. Delia's sigh revealed her conflicted desire to leave and stay, and that she was afraid, but she gamely bid them good night.

15

The Clipping Box

The first thing in Clara's thoughts Tuesday morning was not her little boy, as it usually would be, but the French hunter she had talked to the day before, Monsieur de Persand. She had left the confrontation at the library already agitated, thrown into a state of emotion she couldn't account for, by her meeting with the mayor and the hunters. And then came her encounter in the tennis club with the balding Frenchman who had spoken to her at the meeting. Had he followed her? Was it coincidence he had come into the Tennis Club Marne-Garches-la-Tour? Fate or design? Did she care which? At any rate, he had been nice, trying to cheer her up and make her laugh, saying that his friends were terrible shots, for one thing.

"Where were you?" Serge had asked when she got home. "I thought you'd come home right after the thing." And she had felt a little stab of irritation, to be quizzed as if he had guessed at her state of mind, about a meeting he hadn't bothered to go to.

"It was upsetting," she said. "I don't know why—there was nothing new. For a while I didn't trust myself to drive."

And this morning her thoughts were still on the way she felt herself to have lost emotional equilibrium, at the meeting and then later, talking to the man. The few minutes of flirtation, the attraction, had caught her unaware. Perhaps the encounter had startled him too. He hadn't had the air of a man who usually prowled after women in tennis lounges.

He was married, wore a ring. She certainly was. Before putting the whole thing out of her mind, she allowed herself to dwell for just a self-indulgent instant or two this morning on his very long eyelashes, some men did have them, and the unexpressed power that went with baldness, the power that underlay, perhaps also, the myth (or reality?) of extra virility that supposedly went with it. If the man is handsome otherwise, she thought, baldness is strangely compelling. Large gray eyes, rather heavy-lidded, she imagined them staring down other men in boardrooms. She shook off the reverie. Why was she even thinking like this? A bourgeois of no interest, possibly the executive of an insurance company, maybe a banker.

She was still thinking about him when the phone rang, and it was Cristal, blighting any further moment of solitary reflection she might have wanted before Serge came down. It was unusual for Cristal to call first thing in the morning, and it meant she was up late in Oregon—insomnia or crisis. Clara felt the familiar tug of fear.

"I'm getting some help with my anger," Cristal said. "It won't always be like this. Sometimes I can't breathe."

"What are you angry about? Mother? I know she can be trying. Is she all right?"

"Your mother is an angel, she is sweetness itself. We have such good times together, she's—I think of her as my dearest friend."

"I don't understand, then." It seemed to Clara that Cristal was getting much more tiresome than before.

"I know I'm too emotional, I'm too emotional, out of damages that happened to me in the past. Plus the strain of my daily life, it's not your mother, but it's SuAnn, she's on some new medication, it's not helping, and . . ."

Cristal's daughter SuAnn was manic-depressive and was frequently hospitalized. She had a little girl. Clara understood how that would be a strain for Cristal. Because of Lars, she knew the constant knot in the breast of something unsolved, the concern for your child, the longing. But Cristal was very whiny all the same. Clara was always sending money.

"Cristal, let me know if I can help. You know I'll help. Should SuAnn see someone new? New doctor?"

"I can't see just throwing more money at it. Your money, ha ha. She's already seeing the best doctors, they're using her for a guinea pig, far's I can see. Let's just drop it." She went on to report on Mrs. Holly, who was asleep.

"All right," Clara said, thankful to drop it.

"The doctor gave her some new medication, she goes to sleep earlier, thank God. Your mom I mean."

"You're still up."

"Now I'm in the habit," Cristal said.

She was just putting the phone down when Serge came in with a fistful of clippings. "Here," he said, showing her the article he had just taken from the *Herald Tribune*. He kept these clippings carefully together in a fireproof storage box, and it was nearly full.

"Four men, break-in, a gun shop in Kansas. That's the farthest east so far," he said.

Clara read it and put it on top of the stack. The question was where to set his hypothetical movie. He must have been discussing this the other night with Woly and the men from the studio. He had been discussing it for some years, filling up the box with clippings, and supposedly working on a script, but with little to show for it.

"Kansas? Wheat fields, those farmhouses, it could be very pretty," she said by way of encouragement.

"If you put together in the last six months only what is reported, it's a considerable civil armory these people have accumulated," Serge said, "not even counting Waco or Oklahoma City."

He imagined America as a nation in right-wing revolt, made up of desperado school boards, subversive Boy Scout troops, renegade Chambers of Commerce, Lions Clubs and Elks secretly arming—a nation on the brink of revolution. Serge would never argue with her about this, considered her disqualified by her Americanness from seeing it, or by her sex. The box of clippings told of gun shop robberies, bombs in village halls and bandstands, the occasional fully covered media-blown outrage: Waco, Ruby Ridge. Yes, true, she conceded there were the odd nuts, the tragedies. He imagined a film of enormous sweep, catching all this prairie angst, and it would by extension reflect all the protest lying in the hearts of all patriots in all the world, and the depravity of all oppression.

For film, for all its limitations when it came to the flexible expression of ideas, had the advantage of movement, and of width. He thought of the frame, and the screen, as infinitely wide, as expansive as the mind, did you but find the right image to fill it with. There were images for the abstractions of freedom, nature, the potentiality pushing outward inside the human breast toward the infinite, could you but find and express it, also all the comedy and beauty and sweetness of life. He always saw "life" as a man sitting contentedly against a sunny wall, sombrero pulled down over eyes that watched, with a smile. Wrapped in a blue cloak, the eyes alert. Then the organization of the frames, like steps in a game. So beautiful compared to the crampedness, crabbedness of books, with their yellowish paper and spotted spines, though these he loved too. He loved them for their role as forerunners of film, clumsy, flat, redolent of human commitment, effort, passion.

"Don't forget the man is coming today, the journalist. His name is Tim Nolinger," Clara said.

16

Illuminating Manuscripts

Tim took Anne-Sophie's car for the various things he had to do today. He was no sooner behind the wheel than his portable phone rang. It was Delia, breathless and scared. "Someone tried to get in my room last night," she said. "I know it—someone's after me, someone's got Gabriel . . ." He calmed her down as best he could and told her to wait for him in the cafe next to the hotel, he couldn't get there before one o'clock.

His appointment with the Crays was this morning. He followed the directions to their place given him by the Paris business office of Monday Brothers Films. It was outside of Etang-la-Reine, nearer to Marne-Garches-la-Tour than he had realized, and not far either from Anne-Sophie's ancestral village of Val-Saint-Rémy, off a side road through a wood of spindly trees planted in rows and large rhododendron shrubs. A beautiful large house, or small château, whichever you would call it, probably eighteenth-century, needing exterior *ravalement*, set in this pleasantly neglected forest of many hectares, with some English-looking flower gardens nearer the house, some asters still in bloom. You either approached it by coming up a long drive between imposing gates, or by parking on the main road, which had been built since the eighteenth century, so that one side of the house abutted it, and had in fact attracted a few nondescript graffiti. He sensed that one was meant to come in by the gates and driveway.

It was Clara Holly herself, not a maid, who came to the door, though he could hear a vacuum cleaner and voices elsewhere in other rooms. In the morning, in jeans, she appeared even more beautiful than the other night, her beauty more emphatically an innate physical quality and not some trick of costume or makeup— the large dusky eyes, the mouth without lipstick as deeply red as if bitten, the shiny, luminous skin. He couldn't tell if she remembered he was coming.

Clara led him into a superbly proportioned salon simply painted plain white—it must in its day have had boiseries and gilt—and left him standing by the fireplace. The room had a sparse but inhabited quality, as if the vanished eighteenth-century furniture were still there in spirit. Objectively visible were some classic, even predictable modern pieces—Eames leather lounge chair, Mies coffee table, Noguchi lamp, the inevitable Warhol stood against the wall, and the bright blue of an Yves Klein *Venus*.

Seeing her brought back the events of the previous day. It was strange, he'd been shocked to see Clara Holly so unguarded, sitting at a bar like a tart in a film, even if it was the bar of a completely correct tennis club which she probably was a member of. His mind kept going back over the scene; it was of no importance, but it had been intruding on his thoughts more than he liked. When the Frenchman talked to her, she had been as flushed as a maiden. An old friend? No, he would swear a stranger, that had been clear from the tentative manner of their falling into conversation, and her smile had been reluctant at first. He thought of her drinking gin and laughing, and of how her expression, now so politely impassive, had been stirred and excited when talking to the man. She had rather childish dimples. It might have been a scene from a film; he could imagine someone saying "cut" and she would have reverted to the detached civility of her manner to him now.

He thought it was peculiar how the idea of a person's character can have been influenced by the movies one had seen—or was it the other way round, that film has taken from life the image of a woman sitting at a bar looking sad, and then perking up when some man talks to her, using it as shorthand to question her character? He should ask Cray about this archetype that film avails itself of, books too—all those Hammett and Chandler heroines. Ah, but it wasn't the heroines who sat at bars, those were the bad girls, the temptresses, even the murderesses. They were never good.

Women at bars never up to any good, that was the lore, and had flouted his earlier view of her as correct, calm, poised, rather chaste in her reserve. Was he at some level worrying about Anne-Sophie, wondering if she would ever—did ever—sit at bars, say in country inns when on buying trips? Certainly she must, why not? What was the matter with him? He thought of Emma Bovary. Would Anne-Sophie be unhappy after they were married? Was Clara Holly unhappy? When she looked at him and said she'd just go let Serge know he was here, he was painfully conscious of her allure and of how this was a sort of illicit reaction in himself, an engaged and committed man.

In a few minutes, Serge Cray pawed and puffed his way in, bearlike, pent up, tossing his head with huffs and chuffs. Tim hadn't expected this radiant animal energy—the man's film style was languid, even precious. In person Cray seemed to be bursting out of a cave. It was hard to imagine his association (not to put a clearer name to it) with the flowery, abstracted Clara. Hard to imagine their embraces, but it was always hard to imagine anyone's embraces.

Cray was a stout man of medium height, or shorter by a little, burly, with thinning salt-and-pepper hair, wearing a green alpaca sweater and cords and copper bracelets on both wrists. A glittering, wary expression in his eyes was extraordinary, but maybe only if you were looking for some evidence of his genius. Seriously, Tim asked himself, if this man were, say, selling ice cream or fixing the pipes, would you notice anything special about him? Yes, the eyes were strange. It was not an illusion.

"Oh, yes," said Cray in a sarcastic tone, following Tim's glance at his wife as she left the room. "Sometimes 'in a way that transcends nature, a single person is marvellously endowed by beauty, grace, and talent'—those were the words of Vasari about Leonardo." He left the impression he was talking about Clara and that he disliked the qualities of beauty, grace, and talent.

"Leonardo was superhuman, don't you agree? There is something megalomanic about collecting Leonardos. Leonardos are for megalomaniacs. Bill Gates buys Leonardos. Could you say about the queen of England 'megalomania'? Probably not, one of her ancestors began that collection. I met the man once who looked after the queen's Leonardos. . . .

"Come this way, upstairs. I never show people this stuff, but I will this time, at Clara's urging," Cray said, without other introduction. "Come this way. I believe she thinks I lack for fellow collectors and the chance to talk about my treasures. That must be why she asked you here."

Tim was distracted by the thickness of his glasses, which magnified his eyes into a mesmerizing glare. The staircase was wide and steep, with a corridor at the top leading to, it appeared, several bedrooms. Cray unlocked one of them. "Precaution. These locks. There is a certain amount of burglary in France.

"She thinks I lack for fellow aficionados," Cray continued. "Of course I'm not in the Bill Gates league moneywise, buying Leonardos and Gutenbergs. There's no challenge in that even if you could afford it."

"No," agreed Tim, seeing that no response was required.

"Which in particular did you want to see?"

"Just, I don't know, what you have, no one thing in particular," Tim said. "I don't know that much about manuscripts. If you have one that would resemble the one that was stolen in New York." He assumed the police had already contacted Cray about the theft, and the possibility he might be approached.

Cray had a cabinet with wide, shallow drawers with lids and dust covers. The first was labelled "Apocalypse."

"There were a number of these copies in the Middle Ages, of apocalyptic prophecies, variously illuminated. Some of which have come true, down through the ages, some of the details of which . . . For instance, the Holocaust, that was foretold. I find them especially fascinating, not to say alarming, as we draw closer to the millennium."

Tim dutifully inspected a large stiff vellum, brown-spotted, in unreadable Latin, and then some other foxed sheepskin pages encased in linen swaddling.

"Acid-free linings and the rest of it. All the most advanced conservation techniques. Naturally I am not the expert, someone at the British Museum advises me."

"Very important."

"I'll tell you something else interesting that Interpol told me. Four or five of these Apocalypse manuscripts have been stolen this year, mostly from Spanish monasteries, one from the Isle of Wight. Before the art theft registry thing, this would not have been apparent, but now the coincidence or coordination is apparent. No one knows if it's coincidence or by plan."

"As we draw closer to the millennium," Tim agreed carefully. "Interest grows."

"And you are interested in biblical prophecies? Are you a believer?" Cray asked.

"Not exactly," Tim admitted.

"Don't misunderstand," Cray said. "*Moi non plus.* I'm a skeptic, not a believer. All the same, we must behave as if we believe. I know if I were a believer, I would give time and money to what I believed in—religion, politics. So I do it anyway, with or without believing. Give money, anyhow. I've read a certain amount of theology and political theory, I've decided on a rather arbitrary set of convictions, then I stick to them. Not based on faith, on decision—which is not so subject to temperament, and not as shaky as faith. Would you characterize your own faith as unshakable?"

Tim was somewhat nonplussed at this abrupt excursion into schoolboy philosophy. He muttered that he too had thus far avoided subscribing to any one rigid moral system. Together at the same minor Swiss boarding school, he and Cees had had a chemistry teacher, the same one who said that mixed nationalities were like unstable compounds. He said, in another context, that whatever you think you know absolutely as a fact, is the thing you must most distrust. Tim had taken this to heart, so although he had not given up some absolute notions, such as that, say, it was absolutely wrong to kill, he otherwise had discarded any moral tenets that seemed too fanciful, like those concocted by religions, in favor of a rock-bottom instinctive decency—no lying or anything worse, no unkindness, obviously no murder or theft.

Beyond that, he was ruled by a kind of mild hedonism and a sense of responsibility only for things specifically entrusted to him, and not too much to spare for the great world, which did seem beyond the efforts of one hand-to-mouth writer, though he noticed a sometimes exercised tone creep into his writing on certain obvious subjects—African massacres or political corruption in France. If he had thought anyone actually read what he wrote, he would probably have indulged this polemical streak at greater length.

"What is the general gist of these manuscripts?" he asked.

"The end of the world, of course, in more or less specific detail, sometimes quite colorful, like the Spanish prophecies of fire dragons who will spread the fire by igniting forests with their scaly, incendiary tails. Here's a little picture of a fire dragon."

The morning went by almost before Tim realized it. Cray was a compelling companion, with a vast amount of lore.

At noon he took his leave and headed for the Hôtel Le Mistral. The clerk, as predicted, was scandalized at the idea of opening the room of the vanished monsieur, until she came to see the sense of it. Monsieur had been gone since Saturday afternoon, nearly four days, without indicating his intention to be absent. It did not strictly speaking violate any hotel law to open a room and take the things out when it appeared that the renter had disappeared and had no intention to pay. But she would not consent to Delia's taking Gabriel's luggage; it would be locked into the luggage room, that was correct hotel practice, and the clerk demanded that they come with her to supervise its removal so the hotel would not be liable nor suspect.

Delia went with the clerk, and Tim with them both, curious. Like Delia, he half expected to find the room had been tossed by the people Delia had heard the night before, but it was in only normal disorder, a jacket laid across the bed, fresh soap left by the maid, a suitcase open on the luggage rack, a paper sack and a small rucksack on the dresser, razor and comb on the shelf in the bathroom.

"Close the cases and we'll put them downstairs," the clerk said as Tim took his leave of the young Oregonian captive. "Monsieur has to pay, nonetheless, the four nights, plus the late occupancy charge for today, or someone does."

In a low voice, as if she feared being overheard by the hotel, Delia told him she was resolved not to stay here another night. "There is something so definitely not okay."

"It could be, that could be," Tim had to agree.

"I'd go to some other hotel, but my money still hasn't come, I know they're stopping it some way. And they don't always tell me if I get phone calls or else they're stopping them too."

Tim could think of nothing to suggest except that she spend the night with Anne-Sophie.

17

The Invitations

It wasn't that Estelle was heartless or indifferent, she was just not good at ceremonies, or that was her own explanation. She had sometimes talked to Tim about the wedding, so that he found himself in the role of go-between, between her and her daughter, explaining her misgivings to Anne-Sophie. She confided to him that she hated letting Anne-Sophie down by not being able to rise to a sense of occasion, let alone be really helpful, by knowing about the ceremonial details, or at least by having inspired, creative ideas about decor and the wedding dinner.

"It takes a sense of play, of fantasy, I know all that, it is just that a love of ceremony was left out of me. *Au contraire,* rituals drive me to tears of skepticism, at the misplaced hopes, the ultimate doom of all hopes. Yet I am as full of hopes as you are, Tim dear, for your lovely *mariage.* Why should it not be perfect?"

"It'll be perfect," Tim assured her. "Anyhow, Anne-Sophie loves doing the plans and she's a well-organized woman."

"Isn't she? I marvel, really, she is so *étonnante.* I almost cannot intrude on her perfection." He couldn't tell if she was being ironic.

Regarding the invitations, it had been necessary for Estelle to write to Madame Nolinger, even both Mesdames Nolinger, in Michigan, unless Tim could supply certain information as to how his parents would want their names expressed. He had never dwelt on their divorce, and wasn't sure either Anne-Sophie or Estelle had fully realized his parents were divorced, even though they had two different addresses in Michigan. Also there were questions of whether there were any titles, degrees, military decorations that should be mentioned. Had his father served in the war, for example? (As an enlisted sailor in the last year of it, he knew.) He was able to say that his father had served, and that though he believed his father had received a master's degree in theater arts at an early age, he doubted that he would want this mentioned on the invitation. As to his mother, he had never heard of any title or decoration of hers that could ornament the pages of the thick vellum leaflets being printed up.

Estelle thought it better to write to his parents directly, which she had planned to do anyway, regarding whether there were anything she could do about the hotels, and what relatives would be coming. She was not entirely confident of her written English, so wrote in French to Tim's mother. The reply had been disappointing, though, as Madame Nolinger had volunteered very few things of interest except that she had graduated from the Académie du Sacré Coeur in Bruxelles. Anne-Sophie was now taking the replies to the invitation consultant.

Madame Aix concluded that the invitation would begin:

Madame Louis d'Argel
(referring to Anne-Sophie's paternal grandmother, the
ancient lady living in Val-Saint-Rémy, where the wedding
would be)

Madame Philippe d'Argel
(they debated whether to put 'en littérature Estelle
d'Argel' and decided against it)

sont heureuses de vous faire part du mariage de

Mademoiselle Anne-Sophie d'Argel, leur petite-fille et fille,

avec Monsieur Thomas Ackroyd Nolinger

et vous prient d'assister ou de vous unir d'intention

à la cérémonie religieuse qui sera célébrée vendredi le

10 décembre, à 16 heures, en l'église de St. Blaise,

Val-Saint-Rémy. Le consentement des époux sera reçu par

Monsieur l'Abbé François des Villons, l'oncle de la mariée,

et le Right Reverend Edward Marks.

Then on the overleaf, to be folded in such a way as to be the front when sent to America, it would read, in English:

Mr. and Mrs. Gerald Franz Nolinger

Mrs. Cécile Barzun Nolinger

are happy to invite you to the wedding of their son and stepson

Thomas Ackroyd Nolinger to Miss Anne-Sophie d'Argel

and then the rest of the information. Anne-Sophie thought it looked correct, but worried that people might not recognize her mother in the unfamiliar "Madame Philippe d'Argel," nor Tim's mother in "Mrs. Barzun Nolinger." It had not actually crossed her mind that his mother might not use his father's name.

In any case, she needed to rush these proofs to Madame Aix, though today her mind was not completely on the wedding but rather on a new development with the American still camping in the flea market attic, still slipping out in the mornings. She had gone out to her stall even on the Tuesday and Wednesday, pottered, and read for a while, eye on the stairway. She was reading *Jane Eyre*, the story of a little French girl, Adèle, whose rich father, a surly Englishman, had locked his poor wife in the attic and had taken up with a puny, conniving governess. Early this morning, Thursday, when few people were around, saying ha-ha to danger in the French fashion, she decided to go up to the attic and confront the interloper.

"What danger means to the French I have never understood," Tim had written once. She had read this passage over several times. "They seem drawn to it in a way we are not. Perhaps it is to atone for the crucial national moment when by and large they avoided danger. Or perhaps, belonging to an old civilization gives a certain perspective that we, fragile in our optimism, and convinced that we have yet so much to teach, lack. We are prudent, they drive too fast, race cars across deserts, sail in little boats alone across the open sea, scale skyscrapers, tightrope-walk, assault their arteries with rillettes and patinate their lungs with Gauloises." Estelle had congratulated him, he thought without irony, on this passage, but Anne-Sophie had found it completely untrue and unfair.

Ignoring the possible danger of surprising a cornered felon, she found Monsieur Martin, the *gardien*, and instructed him not to unlock the door leading to the attic for the rest of the day. "If anyone wants to go up there, ask them to check with me," she directed. When someone did, Monsieur Henron at about noon, she took charge. She, Henron, and Martin would go up together. Anne-Sophie marched up the attic steps with a pack of Marlboros clutched in her little hand. There, as she had known he would be, was the American, sitting on a chair. He had been reading a newspaper, but rose when he heard their steps. After a second of dismay, his smile was debonair, his manner composed, almost as if he had been expecting them. He spoke in accented French. He smiled at her and looked intently into her eyes.

"*Excusez-moi,*" he said. "Someone must have locked me in. I was hoping someone would come before I had to spend another night here."

He smiled again, and with brisk aplomb he gathered his jacket and the newspaper and moved toward the stair. "*Merci* to have liberated me." He had a dark, Byronic beauty. Anne-Sophie had read the poetry of Lord Byron and other Englishmen. She admired his insouciance.

"Monsieur, please tell us what you are doing up here?" she began.

"Is everything here?" cried Henron.

The watchman broke in with further expostulations, threatening him. Monsieur Martin was feeling guilty, Anne-Sophie imagined, for having let a non-professional be up there all these nights. "Please explain, monsieur, what you were doing there!"

Without replying, the man went down the stairs, trying to conceal his haste under a calculated calmness.

Anne-Sophie lingered a second to look around the storeroom. Her heart fluttered just a little. Disappointment was already setting in. The mysterious guest was leaving. She would learn no more about the mystery of his presence. Here were the cardboard container from his *pommes frites*, some orange peels, a serviette. He could have been here for days—he had been peeing into a ceramic umbrella stand, with a plate for a lid to stifle the sharp ammonia stench that bit her when she hesitantly lifted it.

When she and Henron came downstairs, some *policiers* were already holding the American by his arms, and Monsieur Martin was gesturing and speaking, the American angrily responding in passable French.

"If I'd been running away, I wouldn't be here, would I?"—defending himself, exasperation in his voice and, she thought, fear. Anne-Sophie, seeing this, was flooded with remorse to have rousted him.

Then the police took him away somewhere, and none of the beholders could say why. These hadn't appeared to be the usual police charged with the security of the flea market but those attending the murder of Monsieur Boudherbe. The American glanced over his shoulder as they led him off, looking at her, a significant communication if she had known how to interpret it. Reproach? Pleading? There was poetry, anguish, intimacy in his backward glance.

Anne-Sophie had the usual French predisposition to champion victims of bureaucracy and indifference, or the suspected criminal, or those oppressed by police brutality. Such generous sympathies are a moral luxury all but gone now in America, Tim would have said. But how should he know? He was always in France.

So, having caused the American's discovery, her impulse was to do what she could to save him from the clutches of the police, first by protesting that she had had no objection to his being in their attic. She found phrases of slashing indignation racing through her mind, addressed to the officious policemen. But since the ones who had led the unfortunate man away could not be denounced, she was obliged to direct her denunciations at those remaining in the still-taped-off cavern of Monsieur Boudherbe's storeroom. They told her she was uninformed about the situation. They would not say where it was the man had been taken.

Anne-Sophie's indignation grew with her sense of having turned him in; she was a collaborationist! She tried to undo her work.

"As a witness and neighbor, *je vous assure*," she could swear that he had only just arrived at the murder scene and had nothing to do with it. Nor were she and her colleagues troubled by finding him in their attic. "*Non, non,* nothing was stolen from any of us."

The officers listened impassively to the agitated, pretty young woman with the short plaid skirt, pretty legs, and Hermès scarf bearing pictures of stirrups and buckles. The sergeant lit her cigarette, his hand lingering on hers, and assured her they had nothing to do with the man's arrest, it was another division entirely, which had been hunting him for a number of days.

"Mademoiselle should not reproach herself."

"*Quand même,*" she said, disconsolate.

18

The Houseguest

Leaving Madame Aix, stirred by unease, indeed guilt, at her recent role in the arrest of the poor American, Anne-Sophie nonetheless stopped at the butcher and exerted all her concentration on what to buy for dinner. At the butcher's she bought a demi-kilo of *tendron de veau* with a blanquette in mind. At the vegetable stand, little carrots, little turnips, a handful of pearl onions. *Blanquette de veau* was one of her most successful dishes, nearly foolproof and greatly liked by Tim. They would have boiled rice, and strawberries for dessert, with sugar but no cream—a good dinner, after which they would make love, two activities firmly associated both in life and in literature, as in the works of Estelle d'Argel, say where the worldly *Anglaise* Madame Foster cautions against serving cream or spices if sex is envisioned afterward.

Why should this be? This brought to Anne-Sophie's mind the rest of the passage in *Les Fruits*, a most humiliating one in which her mother launches into a particularly minute discussion of *crème féminine*, as she calls it, and, with her vaunted specificity, compares it not just to some delicate marine scent but to *haddock fumé*, which messed up Anne-Sophie's confidence regarding personal hygiene for years—she had been about eighteen when she first read *Les Fruits*. . . .

She knew she was only postponing the moment when she would have to tell the young woman at the Hôtel Le Mistral that her friend had been found and lost, and was probably in the hands of the police. She faced it that she had to go over to the Hôtel Le Mistral at once but she did not. She was considerably amazed to find Delia in her own living room.

"Someone was trying to get in my room!" Delia explained, in a voice now firm with conviction. "I know it sounds paranoid, but I saw the handle move on my door last night, and there was someone waiting in the street every time I looked, the same man. So Tim brought me here."

"Someone might well have tried your door," Anne-Sophie pointed out. "Hoping for the best. It happens to me all the time, when I'm in the South. I have a little thing to secure the door."

Delia sat in the living room while she fixed dinner. Tim came about seven-thirty and poured them glasses of port. He held his questions as Anne-Sophie told them both about the arrest of the American man, and about her part in it, and about how all week she had thought about the man hiding in her attic, wondering if he were still there, and thinking that he was probably Gabriel. She could not explain her failure to have mentioned him before now. Perhaps it was curiosity to see what would happen, or fear of looking foolish if she were only imagining he was there, or a desire that the man be safe and not arrested, or an unwillingness to give this American girl what she wanted, though she hoped this was not the reason she found she could not speak.

"Or perhaps he is a dangerous murderer and I will get a medal!" She laughed, so preposterous was this idea. Delia didn't seem to understand she was only joking; all at once tears stood in the girl's eyes and her voice trembled with rage.

"I knew he wouldn't just leave me stranded that way," she cried. "He doesn't speak French, he's got an unrefundable ticket, he—"

"He speaks French quite well!" objected Anne-Sophie. "Tim will find out where he is."

Anne-Sophie carefully skimmed the simmering bouillon in which the cubes of veal were emitting their furzy scum.

"Why didn't you tell him where I was?" Delia was asking.

"But he knew where you were."

"We have to get him a lawyer," Delia persisted. "How do I do that? Should I call the American consulate? Even if I had my passport, I couldn't just leave him. . . ."

She talked on in this fashion; her anguish was only natural. Anne-Sophie put the carrots and tiny vegetables into the broth and listened to Delia's story.

*   *   *

The night after the murder, her second night in France, was still
vivid now. Delia had lain awake far into the night thinking over
how Gabriel had come into her room and sat on the bed. There was
nothing else to sit on but the hard chair, and Delia had sat beside
him as he kept going over it and over it. He was more shaken than
she by the day, she knew from his preoccupied stare into the corner
of the room, his frown. "Oh, shit, why would they kill the guy?
Who would do that?" His dismay had seemed greater than the ug-
liness of the sight would explain. Delia had seen that it might be
more than human feeling that dictated his sighs. He sweated as if
in fear.

"Who? Gabe, tell me?"

"Who? I don't know. I don't know anything about it, but
Christ!"

"Does it have anything to do with you?"

"Me, no, how could it?" he said. "Still, there he was dead, and
I was supposed to go see him, he was the person I was supposed to
deal with."

There was no mistaking Gabriel's fear. He was foreign-born,
no doubt he had seen horrors, and all of them were brought back.
She had never seen horrors, so was less troubled. Sure it had been
gruesome—she had turned her eyes away, she would never forget
the sight—yet the curious unreality, the unlikeliness, kept her from
feeling much for the unknown clay at her feet.

She had comforted him. She did not tell Anne-Sophie and Tim
the rest. How suddenly they were kissing. In his kisses some intimation of wild regret, of fear and mystery. Her sense of danger arose
from the lack of playfulness, the strength of his grip on her
shoulder. His fervent murmurings made her feel she was his buoy,
his mooring on some sea washing around them. He was strong. His
eyebrows nearly met over his black eyes, like the eyes of the corsair
in a poem, her favorite childhood poem. Had she not always sensed
this wildness behind the disguise of a bookseller? And that there
had always been more between them than the cheerful collegiality
with which they had planned the trip? And then they were un-
dressed, and there was much more than cheerful collegiality. It was
the most wonderful night of Delia's life, to date.

Looking back now, she could see he had been scared to death, and in kisses there is something that combats fear. She raked and combed now through all their words for some clue to what might have happened to him, what it all might mean and what to do now.

"We could call Madame Cray," Anne-Sophie agreed, warming to the thrill and danger of harboring a fugitive against the explicit instructions of the flics, thus atoning in part for her role in turning in the man. "She is interested in helping you. Tim says her house is very large, it is outside of Paris, maybe you could stay there."

Delia sighed. Panic seemed to rise up in her again. A young law-abiding American female was something of a stranger to peril, except in parking lots and the like, when you watched yourself. Yet now she was a wanted person, in that she'd violated the French policemen's strictures to stay put, and the FBI too, in a country where she didn't speak the language and had no money. Here she was in this strange woman's apartment—should she have stayed at the hotel? However murky, however dusty the corners, however alien the creepy fingers on the door handle, there was something generically reassuring about a hotel, its hotelness, its rules whereby she wasn't allowed to walk off with Gabriel's stuff, the desk clerk, tireless toiling chambermaids, not that they seemed to toil all that much.

It now was borne in upon her that she was in a much worse situation than at the hotel, because now she was somewhere where no one, not even she herself, could find her, in some Paris apartment of which she didn't know the address or phone number.

The young couple, having installed Delia Sadler on their sofa, lay chastely down to sleep in the bedroom and slept badly. Anne-Sophie woke at one and lay awake. The sleeping Tim took up most of the bed. There was something alien about a large foreign presence occupying your territory, your personal bed. This would happen for the rest of their lives. She willed away any trace of disloyalty in this reflection. Tim was working on a story that sounded so interesting, about the simultaneous theft of several ancient manuscripts to do with the end of the world. With the end of the world in mind, it was reassuring to have a large man in bed with you.

Beds in America, she had heard, came in vast sizes, even round. She and Tim had discussed briefly whether they would have the normal French bed of 140 centimeters such as they were now lying in, or would they adopt the more modern 150? The latter, they agreed, or even 160, though it was harder to get sheets for 160, but easier in America. . . . Why does the mind awake idle over such subjects?

Following the story of the manuscript theft, he might have to go to Spain, to visit the monasteries where the thieves had gone, pretending to be monkish scholars, and made off with the treasured parchments. She would not be one of those silly, insecure wives who minded when their husbands went off on faraway missions. Never ask a man where he's been, said the countess Ribemont in *Against the Tide.*

By leading the party into the flea market attic, she felt like Pandora who had hesitated to open, then had opened, the box of furies or imps. There was the imp of remorse as she saw the police arrest the Byronic young American, her frustration as she tried to protest that she was not lodging a complaint against him but found no one to listen, and now the fact that she had taken in charge the young American woman, had given her dinner and a sofa to sleep on for the night, thus incurring an obligation and probably committing a crime. Such thoughts tormented her until two, when she fell asleep at last.

Tim woke up at four, trying to remember a dream. Having a beautiful woman in the afternoon . . . in a hotel room . . . As it took fleeting form in his imagination, he remembered there was a hot breeze blowing through an open window, and song would come in. Then he remembered that such musings were already illicit, he was a man about to be married. For the woman was Clara Holly, plum-toned and voluptuous, not the rosy, pert Anne-Sophie. Was he to confirm the dreadful Freudian problem about a wife never being an object of desire?

But the sleeping Anne-Sophie did excite, first his tenderness, then his desire. Unfortunately she was really out cold, and who knew what their visitor could hear, however furtively they might make love. What the hell were they going to do with Delia? And how was he to go about finding her friend, as Anne-Sophie so trustfully believed he could do? Fully awake to the forthcoming problems, it seemed to him he would never sleep again. Then Anne-Sophie made a promising stir and sighed as if she were waking. Tim stroked her temple, then her breasts, tentatively. She woke a little and reached out for him. She whispered to him. It could be done if they did it very quietly, without a sound to wake their visitor.

Delia didn't think she was a prude, but there was an awful lot of screwing in France, in the public toilets, or with people listening two feet away—for of course she was awake, four o'clock, the *heure blanche* of jet lag. They had told her it would take a day for every hour of time difference—nine—and it was true, she had been in France a week and still her eyes flew open at four, and could not stay open at four in the afternoon. And from the next room she could perfectly well hear the fall of bedclothes, the slapping sound of surreptitious slippery friction, a stifled giggle, gasps.

People having intercourse at her elbow, she uncomfortably installed on a sofa, using somebody else's bathroom, strangers, with their toothbrushes there, their mouthwash and stuff, no way at all to find out what happened to Gabriel except if they would help her. "Don't abandon me, remember," he had said lightly but seriously. He'd been scared and the man in the flea market had been dead. Something grim was afoot. But if female friendship and resolution could save Gabriel, she would summon that resolve.

19

At Madame du Barry's

They all slept, eventually, and awoke Friday morning to face the first question of what to do with their Oregon visitor. Anne-Sophie, always cross when she had slept badly, insisted that Delia must go to Clara Cray without delay. Not entirely without reasons of his own—fascination with Cray and with his beautiful wife—Tim thought Anne-Sophie's idea about calling the Crays a sensible one. To his surprise, it was Delia who resisted it.

"I can't sponge off her. I shouldn't have called her to begin with. It came to me that though I'd asked for help from Clara, I'd never even been to see her mother, even though Mrs. Holly is right down the road from my own mother, and I had known that Mrs. Holly was old and housebound, because she used to come to the library all the time, and would always be there when I went to the library. And then she wasn't there, so I asked the librarian who told me she doesn't come in anymore, Cristal Wilson comes and gets her books."

So Delia cursed herself about that, should have seen from that that Mrs. Holly was housebound and would appreciate visitors. She was so insensitive sometimes.

"But Gabriel had given me Clara's phone number, and I just panicked and called it."

"He had their phone number?"

"I don't know why he had it. It is sort of odd, when you think of it," she agreed. "He gave it to me, I see now he must have known he wasn't coming back."

Anne-Sophie gave the phone to Delia with a compelling scowl. Clara, sounding surprised, said that Delia was welcome to stay, and Tim could drive her out this morning. He had almost had the impression, speaking to Clara about the time, that she—something in her voice had intimated—that she would be glad to see him. Anne-

Sophie could see Tim was not reluctant at the prospect of another visit to this glamorous domain.

"I will come with you," she said. They were speaking in English for Delia's sake. "I die to see this place, and maybe Serge Cray himself?"

They finished their buttered toast, an American habit Anne-Sophie had adopted, and prepared for the trip to the Crays' château, a pretty drive through the forest via Saint-Cloud, Tim's familiar tennis route. Despite herself, Delia seemed to enjoy the bare trees, many with petals of gold still clinging to them, the russet carpet of fallen leaves, and the pleasant impression of the sumptuous and orderly *banlieue* beyond Paris. A smile replaced her scowl, and the slightly pinched air of mistrust they were used to her wearing.

The Crays' big house rose before them at the end of an allée of the soldierly trees outside the village of Etang-la-Reine. As before, Clara opened the door herself and greeted them warmly, though it seemed to Anne-Sophie not very warmly. She saw Clara look twice as Delia walked, perhaps had not noticed before her lameness? They declined coffee, so Clara said she would show Delia up to her room. Delia seemed dazed by the size and age of the place, but of course she had as yet seen almost nothing else of France.

"Would you like to see the rest of the house?" Clara asked them. Anne-Sophie eagerly agreed. Tim would have gone with them, but just then Cray came in, wearing slippers and a sweater.

"Let me have a word with you," he said to Tim, without any greeting. "Come upstairs." As the two men turned toward the stairs, they could hear Anne-Sophie happily commenting in the hall on the features of the château for Delia's benefit. "*Imaginez! La du Barry* herself! Which was her room? *La pauvre!* You know what happened to her? They cut off her head, though she was not at all a haughty traitor to her class, she was a nice woman. Even if she took up with a king, she remembered her roots!"

Clara's lower voice was describing what she and Serge had done to the place, a railing restored here, a room scraped down to its original color, a new bathroom, mouldings to replace those that had been taken away sometime in the past.

"This is my little boy's room," she could be heard to say as Tim

and Cray climbed the stairs behind them. "He's away at school."
This was the first Tim had thought of Clara as a mother. It was hard
to think of Anne-Sophie in that role either, though presumably he
would be the agent of that change in her life. From time to time
these implications of marriage would attack and slightly disconcert
him for a second. "*La du Barry,*" Anne-Sophie's happy voice was
saying. "Imagine her walking on these stairs!"

Then other voices and car doors slamming could be heard
below outside the house. From Cray's study window they could see
a party of men in two cars assembling in the courtyard.

Clara continued with Delia and Anne-Sophie up another flight
of stairs to the small third floor, to a pretty room with flowered
wallpaper and mirrored cupboards. Seeing it, Delia looked radiant
at this hopeful change in her fortunes. She began immediately to
unpack her few things, and though she continued to complain that
she ought to be doing something about her plight, she saw there
was nothing whatever to do.

It was apparent to the others that she was relieved that she now
found herself in a luxurious country home instead of a seedy
fleabag hotel. But she had yet to see the Eiffel Tower or the Champs
Elysées or the Louvre, especially the Louvre. She lamented that it
was entirely possible and maybe in the cards that she'd be back on
the airplane without having seen any cultural landmarks of Paris
whatever and without eating anything specifically French unless
you counted the toasted cheese sandwich with an egg on it in the
brasserie by the hotel, or the veal stew Anne-Sophie had made last
night, which she hadn't eaten on principle.

Anne-Sophie put the purse full of Delia's belongings on the
dressing table. "How pretty, *dix-huitième*," Anne-Sophie said,
peering with expert interest at the dressing table itself.

"Serge is the great flea market person," Clara Holly said. "He
goes all the time. No one recognizes him. He buys everything there.
All the chandeliers in the ballrooms and restaurants in *Queen Caroline* came from there. Did you see it?"

"Yes, *très bien, superbe,*" Anne-Sophie said.

"No," said Delia. She had, though. She didn't know why she
didn't want to admit it, or be obliged to say how wonderful everything was, or acknowledge Clara's high connection to the glamour

world of film and money, in case Clara would think that was why she had called her in the first place.

"After it was shot, we brought all that grand stage stuff to our house here," Clara said. "It all probably came from someplace like this in the first place, was sold off, and now it's just back where it belongs. We didn't try to restore the place, really. You can't be slavish about the past. . . ." She had an air of inattention, as if she merely repeated what she had heard somebody else, probably her husband, say.

Clara was listening to cars in the drive outside, and looked out the window. "It's the hunters!" she said.

Anne-Sophie did not at first understand the note of disapproval. She knew people in the local hunt, including the president, Monsieur Crépin. Leaving Delia to arrange her things, she followed Clara downstairs again and outside, and cheerfully advanced on the party to greet them. She had not realized that Antoine de Persand hunted; she knew the Persand family in Paris, yet there he was with the others, a party of men in green felt hats. Persand, apparently, had just come from town, and was wearing a business suit and Burberry raincoat, with the requisite scarf.

Hearing the voices in the courtyard, Cray frowned and rose, signalling Tim to follow him. When they came downstairs, Clara was just coming in the front door, and Anne-Sophie was chatting with the party of men that now stood, in yellow green-collared jackets and boots, looking restlessly at the woods. One of the many things Tim admired about Anne-Sophie was her sociability, her perfect recall of names from the *Bottin mondain* without ulterior motive, her perfect ease in greeting people and introducing herself if they didn't remember her.

"It's a delegation from the *mairie*," Clara said to Cray, rather grimly. Tim didn't then know the history of their standoff with the mayor. "The shooting of small game opens tomorrow and they want to talk to you."

Cray gave an irritated snort. "I thought you had dealt with this." He pushed past her and crunched across the gravel toward the group gathered there looking into his woods. Tim saw at once that among the visitors was the man he had seen Clara talk to so warmly at the tennis club, tall and balding, dressed unlike the others in city clothes. She seemed acutely aware of him—her beautiful face was pinkish and self-conscious, in contrast to the languid detachment he had first seen, though it could have been because her husband had spoken so brusquely to her in front of others.

"A hunter, monsieur!" Anne-Sophie smiled archly at this very man, whom she evidently knew.

"Not a dedicated killer of animals, I have to say," replied the man, kissing Anne-Sophie in a fatherly manner, with a glance at Clara. "It's the same to me if we fail to see a deer. I enjoy the day in the field. How is your mother?"

"I could let you ride across my land provided nothing was killed, if riding is the thing," conceded Cray.

"Antoine de Persand," said the man, extending his hand to Cray. "I am your neighbor to the rear. You've not met monsieur the mayor? Monsieur Briac." Briac and Cray shook hands, but they had met, were old enemies.

"I've always wanted to see your house, it is said to have belonged for a moment to Madame du Barry, did you know that?" said Persand.

"Thank you for agreeing to receive us, monsieur," said Mayor Briac. "If we could, as you once suggested, look at your avenues?"

"Can we come too?" cried Anne-Sophie. "I long to see your beautiful *forêt*."

Tim and Anne-Sophie strolled diffidently behind the men of the mayor's party, curious to see what was going on, but knowing it had nothing to do with them.

"*Vous savez,* monsieur, that the master of the hunt and the others now believe some of your fences are illegally encroaching on public thoroughfares and traditional rights-of-way in such a manner as to forbid the rights of hunters and passers-through," the mayor explained. He had a xerox of a statute, which he sternly passed to Cray.

Cray glanced at it, handed it disdainfully back, and strode off into his wood toward the fences in question, his accusers at his back. "You can look at my fences anytime," Cray said. "They are utterly legal. I've gone into all this with my lawyers." While his English was perfectly unaccented and American-sounding, he spoke French with a heavy Polish accent.

Tim followed along with Cray and the other men, striding at a faster pace than the women. He noticed Persand's backward glance at Clara, as if seeking just the smallest verification of her presence behind them, walking with Anne-Sophie. Tim had an intimation, a reporter's sense, perhaps, of impending developments. But nothing yet had happened, really, had it? There were but little quickening currents trickling around stones, which would converge into a more insistent torrent, sweeping things along—things floating and then sucked under, the little matchsticks and dandelion spores. It would have been twice as entertaining to speculate in advance which, who, would go under. But things were never apparent except in hindsight, when it was too late to write about them.

Delia had followed the others downstairs, her heart lighter to find herself safely under the roof of an older female Oregonian; her thoughts could now turn more fiercely to her poor friend Gabriel, with the particular intensity born of guilt for having forgotten him for moments at a time. Was he in a cell somewhere or a police gallery, brutalized with rubber truncheons, or being shipped to the Foreign Legion? Her intention now was to make herself useful to Clara Holly, and also to try to enlist these people in his rescue, for she knew she herself was powerless. The man Tim, she was thinking, was the key to finding out where Gabriel was, he was a reporter who presumably had contacts. The consulate would be another route, where they spoke English and would have been notified, maybe, of the arrest of one of their citizens, or he would have called if they allowed him a phone call. Was Gabriel a citizen? Yes, he'd had an American passport.

This was underlined when she followed the voices through the entrance hall outside where Clara, Anne-Sophie, and Tim stood talking in the chilly morning air to the group of strange men who were not policemen or the American FBI. She hung back but was near enough to hear that, as they were all talking French, even Clara, she would have no way of being a part of this. Abruptly the group turned toward a path that led to a wood of spindly trees behind the house. They were led by a fattish man with a thunderous scowl whose expression made it plain this was not a pleasure party but a problem. Should she go along or stay? It seemed the part of a cooperative houseguest to go along.

In the woods—this was the nicest part of France, you could be in Oregon, nature's beauty bestowed neutrally on France as on Oregon by the beneficent creator—Delia could feel an inner knot of worry loosen, its tendrils unfurl. She knew she wouldn't catch up with the others, so she didn't try, but limped at her pace, enjoying the turning leaves and odor of winter damp. In sunshine the wood at this season would be aflame with golden aspen, but now in the gray light of impending weather it was sullen, with gloomy caverns of shrub.

Then, as the others stood at the first of the heavy yellow-painted chains Cray had slung across his paths, the French sky with its painterly property of mirroring human emotion turned hostile, and clouds chased before a sudden cold autumn wind. Leaves chattered and fell under the weight of thick raindrops and lay sodden on the ground. Like the impulse of a black heart, the rain struck right down the collars of the party and rolled down their chilly sleeves. Was it hunters on whom heaven scowled, or those who would interfere with a hunter's rightful pursuit of balance in nature?

Rain! So productive of instant camaraderie. The French of course had umbrellas, which they stiffly proffered to include the improvident anglophones, and the party turned back for a dash toward Cray's house. Tim took Anne-Sophie's umbrella and held it higher to include Anne-Sophie and Clara Holly. He was aware that the Frenchman—somebody Anne-Sophie seemed to know—had stepped forward with his own umbrella for Clara, but she had dashed off with Anne-Sophie, laughing with the gaiety that getting wet seems to bring out in people. Alone, Delia limped along behind them but, like any Oregonian, was untroubled by the downpour.

20

Hospitality

As they had gone fifteen minutes into the woods, they had as far to go back, and it seemed much farther. The trees bent and swayed, the better to let the rain through. Umbrellaed or not, the party arrived soaked, jackets sticking to their backs. "You'd better come in," Cray said, expressionless, motioning them inside his house. The hunters came into the foyer stamping and shaking their heads like drenched hounds. Clara could see Serge did not like having these their enemies in his house but liked being able to render them beholden for a moment of warmth and dryness.

Monsieur de Persand, however, did not come in. He murmured some excuse to the mayor, shaking his hand, and then bowed over Clara Holly's hand. *"Madame . . . malheureusement, je suis pressé . . ."* He nodded to the others and dashed to his car.

Antoine de Persand had hunted his whole life, a pastime shared with his father and brothers, a part of the local tradition in the countryside around their weekend house, an invigorating outdoor pursuit welcome in the life of an indoor man, a banker and father and the *responsable* of an extended family. In fact he had no particular liking for killing animals, and didn't actually like *gibier* to eat, except for certain rabbit terrines, but that was just a matter of taste. He did like to tromp the fields with his gun. Technically, he didn't hunt, he shot, but his social stature and his upright, somewhat inflexible rectitude and moral authority had earned him a place on the committee of the local hunt (as well as on various philanthropic and civic boards). And when shooting, he usually did not even fire his gun. This had had the paradoxical effect of making the others think he was the most important man among them, the only one so busy his mind wasn't on his aim. Once, in pity, his companions

awarded him a *demi-biche*, the hindquarters, which he was obliged
to carry to the butcher on the hood of his car.

He was married to *une Strasbourgeoise* of German background, Trudi, and had two children. A recent tragedy, the murder
of his younger brother by the husband of his mistress, had devastated his mother and placed Antoine nominally at the head of the
family interests—investments and such—in the place of his older
brother Frédéric, who lived a raffish life in Nice. Antoine was forty-
seven and in a high position at Maller et Cie, the bank, for whom
he was also one of the leading counsels.

His decision not to go inside the film director's house with the
rest of the hunt committee was a considered one. The tragedy in his
family, arising, basically, from adultery, had been a lesson to him,
and he knew he couldn't bear, or afford, even the smallest self-
indulgence of talking to that beautiful woman again. He placed a
lot of faith in the virtue of self-control.

It occurred to Tim, watching Persand's departure, that perhaps
he'd exaggerated to himself the idea that there was some special
thing between this guy and Clara Holly. On the other hand, the
man looked especially uncomfortable, and reluctant about something. Tim's thoughts kept returning inexplicably to the sight of
that chance exchange in the tennis club—and with it a suggestion
he did not bring to consciousness, that if anyone could have her, he,
Tim, also could have her. He was aware of Anne-Sophie's little
hand in his raincoat pocket, looking for a handkerchief she'd put
there.

"I know this house, monsieur," said the mayor to Cray. "It
used to belong to the municipality. It was sold first in the seventies.
The decision to sell was not mine, a predecessor's."

"I bought it from an ad in *Maisons et Châteaux*," said Cray
sharply. "Never met the owner."

The mayor sniffed, perhaps at the memory of the previous
owner, the one who presumably had stripped the building of its
eighteenth-century grandeur.

Clara had gone for towels. She came in with a stack of them.
The hunters refused them, *"Non, non, ça va."* Tim and Delia also
refused, but Anne-Sophie and Cray dried their faces.

"Sherry," cried Clara. "I insist that you drink some sherry and eat a sandwich while you dry, it's dangerous to be so wet." She did not quite know why she said this or was moved to be hospitable to these unfriendly forces. But she and Serge seldom had visitors, and it had something to do with a liking to have people in, and put her in mind of her first French social mistake, not asking people inside. The large Fourth of July outdoor barbecue to which they once invited the village, soon after they had moved here, had seemed instead to irritate the locals, who had been hoping to be asked to see the interior, confusing Clara, who had noted that many French celebrations were held outdoors, often in the same sort of tent she'd taken pains to organize.

Now she was a little surprised when the mayor agreed they would drink a sherry, and not refuse a sandwich. She led them down a corridor to the large family room she had installed, a south-facing, sunny room open to the kitchen. Anne-Sophie followed, chattily giving them a little lecture incorporating notions she had gleaned from Tim: "It is the existence of the 'family room' that causes French people, failing to realize that there is a living room elsewhere in an American house, to believe that American kitchens are in American living rooms, hence the *cuisine américaine* with which they deface their own interiors." Or so she was saying, in a tone of gentle affection for French ideas.

Here they would dry off by a fire in the giant stone fireplace (not original to the room). Senhora Alvares would make sandwiches. Delia went to help her while the drowned hunters stood in a group in the middle of the room. Tim engaged one or two in a discussion of rain in October. It was often rainy at the outset of the season for *petit gibier*, pigeons and partridge, they said.

Cray had disappeared. Tim had seen his frown when Clara had offered sherry, and took note of his significant glare at her. It had not deterred her hospitable impulse. She liked the sense of having people in her pretty house, here with the Aga stove brought from England for its radiant welcoming warmth, her little pantry where napkins were folded and stacked by the dozens, the image of order, and the pile of little cocktail plates people could hold on their knees.

They found various ingredients appropriate for the construction of sandwiches, and Delia helped Senhora Alvares by spreading peanut butter and cutting off crusts. Clara too pitched in with the emergency sandwiches, spreading butter on the bread, slicing cucumbers—she was a lot like her mother, she supposed, remembering how Mother enjoyed fixing food for a big group, all the football parents or all the King's Daughters or her bridge club or for after the library sale or when they closed the polls on election night.

As she spread the butter she found herself thinking of the man, Antoine de Persand—just as well he didn't come in, how could she have thought he would have any special reason to do so? What did it matter? She felt a little silly to have imagined that he would come in, that he would want to see her. Not that she would ever get mixed up in something like that. Like what? How embarrassing to have made this silly, unwarranted mental leap.

Clara brought sherry, and Senhora Alvares passed the little glasses and the cocktail-sized plates and half-sized napkins with little roosters on them. Delia looked at these with professional interest, correctly identifying them as American, 1930s.

"Lake Oswego," Clara said.

Eventually, warmed and dried, the mayor shook Clara's hand, then Tim's, Anne-Sophie's, and even Delia's, and then each of his men performed this ritual, a protracted few minutes of handshaking and au revoirs. They went out to their cars. At the end, the Frenchmen had seemed convivial and made pleasant conversation about the weather, the village *bibliothèque*, the little collapsed bridge at the crossroad and the plans at last to repair it. Hunting had not been mentioned. Clara noted this scrupulous reluctance to abuse their hospitality.

She set about restoring order, aided by Anne-Sophie and Delia. They gathered the glasses and plates, the crumpled *serviettes*, the ashtrays. Women, thought Tim, seemed to find something enjoyable about cleaning up after guests. Clara in particular wore a satisfied air. On the platter a half dozen sandwiches remained—most of the peanut butter sandwiches they had made.

"I noticed no one asked whether this was a smoking household," Delia said, frowning at an ashtray.

They became aware that Serge Cray had come down and was surveying with a directorial eye the dismantled scene of plates, glasses, and crumpled napkins as the females picked them up. He

noticed what Tim had noticed too—that the peanut butter sandwiches had all been left. One, on a plate, had a bite out of it. Cray
smiled and said sarcastically to his wife, "Only you would serve
peanut butter to a bunch of Frenchmen."

She smiled a little, turned away, it might have been without
noticing, but the unpleasant tone of this phrase shocked Tim with
its unintended revelations about Clara Holly and her husband, and
maybe about marriage itself? He had never devoted much thought
to the everyday side of marriage, with its inevitable small rancors
and collective joys or disappointments. The rude things you might
hear yourself saying to your wife? So far he had never said anything
rude to Anne-Sophie—hadn't felt the impulse to. At the doors
of consciousness, however, were several of her irritating traits.
Smoking, for one. And sometimes, failing to recognize a simple but
Anglo-Saxon cultural reference. "Satchmo?" These had now (only
you!) revealed their landmine potentiality.

The revelation that the husband was cruel and curt raised in
him a stab of chivalrous feeling for Clara. He wanted to reassure
this poor beautiful lady that all men would not disparage and condemn her and that peanut butter sandwiches were well within the
purview of human hospitality. He had the impulse to take her in his
arms and soothe her—anyone would.

Anne-Sophie too recognized something alarming and disappointing in Cray's mean phrase. Only you would do *une telle bê-
tise*. With two words a man could humiliate you, and so unfairly,
since it had been the girl Delia who had made these sandwiches
which, though repulsive and looking like *caca*, were surely harmless and well meant? Madame Cray had almost appeared not to notice, as if her husband's habit of making rude criticisms no longer
had the power to wound, so much had she suffered.

So! This was marriage! It was the hint of female subjection that
alarmed Anne-Sophie. She, Anne-Sophie, would have cracked a
dish over his head. Instead Clara Holly had affected not to notice—
perhaps really did not notice—that her husband had made a rude, a
withering remark to the effect that she was the stupidest woman in
the whole world. Only you! And then too he had made this observation in front of other people—Tim, the Oregonian girl, and some

new man who had been introduced as a garden designer and was still there. Anne-Sophie's breast burned with sisterly commiseration.

Her eye caught Tim's. She saw there, she hoped, an implicit commitment to love her and never speak to her that way. Their accord would be perfect. She was thinking how handsome her loved one was, how she loved him, how lucky they had met. If only she were as pretty as he deserved! If only she were always good-natured and calm, as Madame Cray evidently was. These notes were the chord of her love for her intended husband. Only you!

"Peanut butter is too American for them or what?" asked Delia, thinking, who cared what the mayor thought anyhow? What assholes. How horrible to be married to someone fat, even if famous, who pitched a fit over a peanut butter sandwich and spoke to you like that in front of others, or even in private.

"It's one of those cultural gulfs," Clara said.

21

The Driad Apocalypse

Cray motioned to Tim to come back upstairs. When they had shut themselves in Cray's study, he said, his strange eyes glaring excitedly behind his thick glasses, "Yesterday someone called me about a manuscript, I assume the one taken from the library in New York. Exactly as predicted."

Tim nodded, gratified. It was indeed happening as Cees had said it would.

"The price is high, five hundred thousand dollars. The conditions are the usual ones—I don't tell the police and so on."

"Have you?"

"I've accepted the conditions. It seemed to me the responsible thing would be to buy the thing, take it out of the hands of the thieves at least. I'm not worried about the money—the library's insurance will cover it, I'm sure, or there'll be a reward. I'll restore it to its owners, of course. I temporized. The man was to have called again this morning for my answer and with instructions—he hasn't, as yet. Someone will have to deliver the money and pick up the document, something I don't want to do myself."

"You want me to do it?" Tim said, thinking without hesitation, why not? There was nothing illegal, or dangerous either, probably. And there was a story in it. They would alert Cees, of course.

"Yes."

"Okay," he said. "Just let me know when, and how I'll know if it's the authentic document."

"You can study what I have. Interpol sent a Xerox of the stolen manuscript along with the original alert."

Tim examined the Xerox, and the information sent along from the American authorities. A spotted handwritten document in Latin, apparently Xeroxed from a microfilm, the words light, the background black.

"There are clever forgeries, of course. They might try to sell a fake."

"Maybe I should look again at some original manuscripts from the period." Neither the original nor the clever forgery would look anything like this.

Cray shrugged and turned to his cabinets.

Tim thought about what to do. Given the events of the past week, it seemed reasonable to wonder if the theft, the murder in the flea market, and the disappeared American had some connection to each other, though it was hard to imagine what, since the American had been with Delia at the time of the murder, as innocent as she, and was now presumably in the hands of the French police and hence could not be the person calling Cray.

Cristal took the four-thousand-dollar check written by Serge Cray for Lady's vet to the Ben Franklin Bank and put it in her account, saving a thousand out in cash. Looked at the five stacks of twenties on the counter as the teller counted them out, thinking it was more money than she had ever had at once. She folded the deposit slip carefully and put it in her purse. The cash she put in the bottom of her grocery bag in case someone should snatch her purse. Her daughter SuAnn always kept all her money in cash and paid her bills, even the doctor, in cash, it was one of the convictions of the group she was a member of, and you couldn't object, it was a good principle, or would be in a perfect world. In a perfect world no one stole from you or was bipolar either. SuAnn was involved in a struggle for a perfect world.

Cristal was jittery driving back to Mrs. Holly's with a thousand dollars in a bag like that, but nothing happened. Mrs. Holly was watching television in the den, so she took the stacks of bills and put them in Mrs. Holly's bedroom closet under the bedpan and foam bedpad they'd had to use that time, repellent gear no one would look under or want to touch.

If Clara should ask what about Lady, she could say she died after the surgery, after the bill was paid. Yes, that's what she'd say.

So that when next they talked, and Clara fell into a mood of self-reproach about not coming home, as she often did, Cristal deflected any talk of Clara coming home.

"I'll come over," Clara said, choking with remorse about who knew what.

"No, that's okay, you should come in December for her birthday, that'd make her so happy."

"Yes, December, that'll give me time to get my husband used to the idea," Clara agreed.

"Yes, only a month."

22

The Arrest of Monsieur Savard

The next morning, Saturday, a flea market day, Anne-Sophie, having only a portfolio of prints to carry, took the bus to Clignancourt and walked through the still-dark streets to the Marché Paul Bert. An air of excitement reigned there. Many of the dealers were already open, people unloading nested chairs tied with clothesline, and a gilt mirror of unprecedented size that looked like it would crush the gallant little Arabs in blue work clothes bent under its weight, and Huguette Marsac waving them along. But the buzz mainly emanated from a congregation of fellow *antiquaires* in their yellow *imperméables*, corduroy collars turned up against the chill, rubbing their cold fingers and talking animatedly.

It was Huguette who interrupted herself to give Anne-Sophie the news. "Monsieur Savard, stall ninety in Allée Four, has been arrested for the murder of poor Monsieur Boudherbe! Are you stunned?"

She was stunned. Only yesterday the American was being carted off—she had assumed for questioning about the murder. Now Monsieur Savard, a mild, distant, but exemplary dealer in small bronzes, had been definitively accused.

"It appears they went to his apartment last night and arrested him!"

Rumors swirled and fell like tides throughout the day, and with the waning sun of the afternoon. Monsieur Boudherbe and Monsieur Savard had been partners in a crooked scheme gone wrong, a criminal enterprise like drugs, arms for the Irish or Algerians, Russian prostitutes, the theft of art treasures from emerging Eastern European nations. Or, they were lovers and it was a jealous quarrel—though nobody had ever thought of the stout, tobacco-stained Monsieur Boudherbe in the role of sexual animal, Monsieur Savard even less. By the end of the day, it was known definitely that Savard had been found to have three million francs in his drawer at home, probably stolen from Boudherbe.

Anne-Sophie was thoroughly staggered. *"Ce n'est pas possible,"* she said again and again. She had constructed for the romantic-looking American a desperate role as intruder, victim of police injustice, stranded prisoner, even as guilty fugitive from a ruder, more dangerous land. She was sure he was a murderer too.

But the regret she felt that he was not also a murderer was made up for by the excitement of having misjudged Monsieur Savard. This misprision introduced a whole new shaken appreciation of the limits of human intuition. Her respect for the police went up; they were seen to be keen in their impartial search for truth, impartial even to the extent of arresting a Frenchman instead of the tempting American *étranger*. Had they let the American go? Anne-Sophie acknowledged to herself that she'd better alert Delia about these new developments. She realized, though, that she didn't have the Crays' phone number and would have to wait for Tim to come home.

23

Confidences

Over the next week, life fell into a new but fairly regular pattern. Out at the Crays', Delia had come down early the first morning, a little relieved to find no one up, and yet dismayed to be alone lest she be thought to be snooping in their kitchen. She was thinking about her new hosts Clara and Serge Cray. Mr. Cray was clearly a pig where his wife was concerned. She began to see there were upsides and downsides to having a famous but temperamental husband. The maid or cleaning woman who had been there yesterday, small and wide, came in at eight and nodded from across a gulf of language.

"*Bonjour,*" said Delia, conscious that this was the very first word she'd spoken in French apart from *merci*.

"*Bom dia,*" said the woman in a language Delia didn't recognize. The woman made coffee and gave Delia a plate of croissants.

She had lain awake in the night ordering in her mind the things she had to do today. Now, safely away from the hotel, she must call the consulate, notify her parents she'd moved and give them the new phone number, tell Tim her money hadn't come, and call the airline, for it was tomorrow she was to have gone home on her one-week nonrefundable ticket. It seemed a kind of catch-22 situation, no passport, no hope—unless she could get some sort of attestation that would let her reschedule her ticket, which you practically had to die to get, but probably a police order would count as much as death.

When Clara came down, a reassuring figure in her bathrobe though rather blowzy in Delia's opinion, the dowdy effect of a big bust when you weren't wearing a bra, Delia explained all her problems to her.

"And Gabriel too, his ticket was nonrefundable."

"We'll make some calls," said Clara vaguely, thinking that though she had feared the intrusion of Delia, it was sort of nice finding someone in the kitchen to chat with in the morning.

"I can't just go home without knowing where he is and what's happened to him."

"Do you love him?" Clara asked. "Is he your boyfriend?"

"He's not my boyfriend, exactly," Delia said. "He lives with someone else, she's slightly crazy, I think it's mostly that he feels sorry for her, and worries about sending her right over the brink."

"I think we can have confidence in Tim Nolinger," said Clara. "He strikes me as competent, a responsible person, he's supposedly trying to find out where Gabriel is and so on."

"Competent and responsible aren't the same thing, though," Delia pointed out.

The naturally beautiful seem to fall into two camps, those who think nothing of their looks and those who think of nothing else. Clara was one of the former, yet when she waked this same morning after the visit of the hunters, she had looked a long time at herself in the mirror. She was still wondering why the nice Frenchman who had been so kind after the meeting (he was called Antoine de Persand) hadn't come inside with the others. She had expected he would come in, they would have exchanged a few harmless words, he would have seen her pretty house and eaten a sandwich.

Had she let herself go? If she'd continued in films she would have had to monitor the tiny changes, the incursions of a decade; but the isolation of her situation, her preoccupation with little Lars and his problem, had put them out of her mind until now. She was alarmed to find that a power she had had, she perhaps had no longer, and vowed to renew her plan to garner the beauty and sexual secrets of Frenchwomen, and put them in a little book. Struck by how much they seemed to know, she had mischievously started compiling such a book a few years before, thinking she needed a project; but now she would also apply these secrets, if she found out any. It occurred to her that Anne-Sophie d'Argel would be a good source, so lively, fresh, and pretty, obviously the repository of centuries of French female wisdom. She wondered where she had put the notebook where she'd begun noting things down. She wondered if Madame Antoine de Persand was very beautiful.

Tim and Anne-Sophie found their new connection to the Crays and their charge Delia not entirely welcome. When he had first heard about the thefts, Tim had planned to go to Spain to visit the two monasteries and a library in Seville from which Apocalypse manuscripts had been stolen by a man with German credentials costumed as a monk. In all three thefts, leaves from the writings of St. John about the end of the world were the object. Tim had assembled information about all this from newspaper reports, the Internet, and Cees. But now he had agreed to act as Cray's agent in acquiring the latest stolen manuscript delaying his Spanish trip.

He asked himself why, and answered to his own satisfaction that his line of work required him to let things lead where they would, up to a point, and the possible stories and articles to come out of it were well worth the expenditure of a couple of weeks.

The association with Cray had another upside too. There was the proposal that Cray would pay him for his time—would in fact put him on the Monday Brothers Films payroll for the period involved as an assistant on the film Cray was planning. Cray assured Tim that this was normal practice, in case Tim had scruples, before Tim could analyze whether he did or not. It was easy—he'd welcome the pay; he was a man about to be married.

He drove out to the Crays' each day at noon, when the commuter traffic was over, and hung around for an hour or two. Tim was surprised at how easily he slid into this arrangement, and it made him think generally about questions of vocation. He knew he wouldn't want to spend his life as anyone's assistant, but did he in fact have anything better to do? Shouldn't he have a long project? Write a novel? About what? Or a book about European politics? All he really knew much about was being in France—its history, wines, social conditions. Maybe he should learn something systematic about medieval manuscripts. But then he'd have to learn Latin. . . .

In any case, his travel plans had evidently now to be put on hold, waiting for the thieves to contact Cray again, and he needed to resolve the whereabouts of the missing Oregonian, presumably in police custody and therefore not the German monk thief or manuscript seller. Though he had agreed to do both of these things—deal with the thief and find Gabriel—he unfortunately had no particular contacts in the French police. But he had a friend with the *New York Times* who did, and she had reported back this morning that while several Americans were in custody in Paris—shoplifting, a visa problem, and assault—none of them was Gabriel Biller. Meantime, Cees in Amsterdam confirmed that none of the other people on the list of collectors had been contacted. As nothing else was happening, Tim wrote a restaurant review for the *Wine Observer* and spent some time in the library, where he was always happy, reading about the Apocalypse.

Clara Holly had become less distant, was at least polite, would drink a cup of coffee with him before Cray came down and ask questions about his life, or the wedding, like a hostess.

"Serge has given me some of your articles to read," she said. "They're very interesting!"

Tim was complimented and surprised that Cray had read his stuff, but it went with the man's reputation for excessive thoroughness. "In *Concern*?"

"In a magazine called *Reliance*. It struck me that you and Serge have similar politics," Clara said.

"I don't know that I have any politics," Tim said. "I try to be objective, even for *Reliance*."

"I don't think being a journalist excuses you from having politics," she objected.

Another time, she brought up the wedding.

"Your wedding is nearby, in Val-Saint-Rémy," she said.

"In six weeks," he agreed.

"Anne-Sophie is so delightful. So French! Americans are just clods next to them. The French seem to know everything about—well, everything important. Gastronomy. Eros." Her mention of Eros quickened Tim's pulse just a little.

"I've always thought this house would be nice for a wedding reception," she added presently. "It's too bad we didn't know you back when you were making the plans. I'd love it if you were having it at our house."

"Thanks," he said. "I guess it's long since been decided."

"Do you feel your life's beginning or ending?" She asked this with a lightness of tone that was meant to mitigate the solemnity of this painful question. He'd asked it himself, and answered it.

"Beginning, mainly."

"I read somewhere that for most men in the world, their wedding is the most important thing that will ever happen to them, and almost the only time they'll get new clothes and be the center of attention."

"What an appalling idea. But, isn't it true for women too?" he asked.

"Oh, women have childbirth," she said.

Tim was in fact slightly worried about a detail of his life with Anne-Sophie. Anne-Sophie, until now a merry and ardent mistress, had seemed suddenly to become insecure about the sexual side of their life, despite his being thoughtful and aware of this, he hoped, and always reassuring her about her beauty and sexiness. So far they had not had any of the problems you heard plagued some people— frigidity, premature ejaculation, lack of desire, and probably there were other things. At first, sensing her concern, he'd feared some deficiency of his own, but he also wondered whether it might be because of the lurid sensuality of Estelle's writing that Anne-Sophie had begun to find things a bit flat. Though Estelle's language was ladylike, her literary personae descended from Huysmans or Pater, and were given to disquisitions on the difference between *parfum vert* and *parfum fruité*, or the range of sensations peculiar to the inner thigh. Her protagonists hinted at languorous but insistent sexual appetites in a sophisticated *monde* where the orgasm was discussed at luxurious hashish parties. ("Ah! the greedy pulse of *le bouton*, the tiny tympanum at the centre of the universe! curling the toes in that delicious rictus . . .") All this could well have put Anne-Sophie off somehow.

Then Tuesday morning when they were making love Anne-Sophie had said, in English (he remembered that detail especially, for they always spoke French together when talking of love), "I want you to fuck me as if you had never had me before." He had been startled, even while trying to oblige, at this completely out-of-character declaration, and in his brain there lodged an echo. Was this maybe an English translation of one of Estelle's lines? Or was Anne-Sophie getting tired of their usual range of positions (basically, him on top or her on top) and in need of something more? *En levrette?* What did this predict for long years together? He had no answer, but noted the development.

She had also become exigent about her car, claiming to need it, often on days he'd asked to borrow it, so he couldn't go out to the Crays' as often as he had been doing. He understood that this was a symptom of something, he just didn't know what, perhaps only the strain of impending marriage.

"I think it is a little bit normal, I fear, before the wedding, for men to get restless and wistfully to eye other women," Madame Aix assured Anne-Sophie, who was telling the older woman about certain concerns she had about Tim, especially that he was spending all this time at the Crays' and often mentioned Mrs. Cray. "I hear this all the time."

"I don't think there is anything to it, but . . ."

"I hear horror stories. Men go off with their former girl-friends, they take up with dancers and prostitutes—it's a kind of panic reaction."

"Prostitutes! *Quelle horreur.* Certainly not, not Tim."

"No, certainly, but I wanted you to know there is a wide range of behavior. It's not so strange to find him looking wistfully at other women."

It had got her to thinking about the whole problem of keeping a man sexually interested for a lifetime. Wild, uninhibited behavior was always advised. Maybe more *soixante-neuf?* They occasionally did this, but she sensed that Tim preferred the *soixante* to performing the *neuf*, a universal male characteristic according to the countess Ribemont, one that should not be endlessly indulged.

"Did you realize that Tim Nolinger is the Nolinger-Webb heir?" said Dorothy Sternholz to Vivian Gibbs at the hairdresser (Nigel Coiffure, the Englishman). "You'd never have known that, he's a modest, a sweet boy."

"I didn't know, but it doesn't surprise me," Vivian said. "Though would I say modest and sweet? I think he has a somewhat princely air, if only because he seems so at home in the world, and, like a prince, he seldom has money in his pocket."

24

The Arrest

Clara and Delia fell into the habit of talking in the mornings over coffee. Clara would talk about her little boy, Lars, or she would reminisce about Lake Oswego to refresh her memory of certain landmarks, however banal, like the Safeway or the so-called City Hall or the Ben Franklin Bank, none of which Delia found that remarkable, though she was willing to correct or update Clara's memory of them. These conversations appeared to increase Clara's pleasure at being in France, which gave Delia the feeling she was abetting the crime of nonpatriotism.

It took them no time at all to establish that the vanished Gabriel's live-in girlfriend was none other than Cristal's crazy daughter SuAnn—unstable, medicated, given to strange causes and beliefs, and, to boot and especially, a Y2K person. This connection to Cristal gave them another, unforeseen, bond.

Clara began to be aware that Delia's emotions had somehow transferred to her, reposing in Clara her need for a friend, her confidences, her fears about the things that were happening. It seemed natural. Clara could see the young woman was a little frail, far from home and family, and had the generally dependent nature of a youngest child, and also her handicap, whatever that meant to her. Delia virtually followed her around, and Clara often slowed her pace to accommodate the girl's slower walking.

Clara took her to the American consulate to discuss the passport, there being no reason now not to issue it, since someone had been arrested in the flea market affair. At the consulate, the clerks had not heard from the French police, but said they might now reissue the passport. Clara and Delia had the feeling that the clerks in the consulate liked to defy the French authorities when they were on sure ground doing so.

"But I really want to go to the Louvre, that's why I came over really," Delia kept saying, and Clara promised to take her soon.

For her part, Delia learned quite a bit about Clara, not from anything Clara confided—Clara was almost strangely self-composed —but by inference. Delia figured out that her life was not just a glamorous piece of cake, though it wasn't hard either. Apart from the giant house, it was rather normal, or even tinged with sadness, on account of the curt, remote husband and the little boy sent away to school and not even allowed to have e-mail, only a letter once a week. Yet she was a good, hardworking wife, with an almost puritanical view of marriage. She would never be unfaithful to her husband, she said, and once when they were talking about a particular Lake Oswego scandal, she had said, "Why would she throw everything away like that for a moment of pleasure? It doesn't make sense. What would be the point? You'd only end by making yourself unhappy, never mind your husband. Sex is sex, after all, with one person or another."

Once when Delia talked about her business, antique linen and green plates, and making her way in the world, Clara said, "I don't know, I was married when I was twenty, I've never really been on my own. I probably wouldn't know what to do."

Delia wondered if it was time to mention God to Clara Holly.

Delia, even now not sleeping beyond five o'clock in the morning, usually waited till seven before coming down. The sky was still black, the moon bright when she heard a car drive up, heard the rasp of the hand brake. It seemed too early for anyone to call, and even creepier that someone should ring at the front door, but she went to answer it.

Outside stood two men who carried radios or phones, and a woman police officer. In her nightie and robe (one of Clara's), Delia shivered in fear. She had known they would come for her.

But the first man said, *"Madame Clara Cray, vous êtes en état d'arrestation."*

Delia stared and said, "Uh—I guess you want Clara."

"Je regrette, il faut que je vous prenne en garde à vue," the man went on saying.

Delia backed away from the door, and they came in. Miraculously, Clara was up too, and stood behind her, looking sleepy.

Though she could not understand what they were saying, Delia could tell from Clara's expression that it was Clara they'd come for.

Clara was just standing there with a look of amazement and indecision on her face. She indicated her robe, the need to get dressed. All that was plain enough. The visitors said something, and she turned to Delia. Her voice was shocked.

"Could you wake up Serge and tell him to come down? I don't know if I have to go with them?" Then she spoke in French again to the men, and started up the kitchen stairs, followed by the policewoman. Baffled, Delia went as fast as she could up the main staircase, and knocked on Serge Cray's bedroom door. Behind her the men stayed in the hall, watching the women up the stairs.

Cray gave a groan, she heard the thrash of bedclothes. The door opened and Cray peered out. He was wearing pajama bottoms and a T-shirt that was pulled up over his fat belly, and exuded the smell of sleep.

"Some police have come and it looks like they're arresting Clara," Delia whispered. "I mean I guess they're police. They look like police." Cray came further out of his door and peered at her, blinking like a mole through his thick glasses.

"You better come down. I guess it might have something to do with me being here?" Delia added. "She sort of made herself responsible at the hotel? And the consulate? They're in the hall. Clara's getting her clothes on."

"It's the fucking hunting." Cray snorted and started down the stairs to the kitchen, his heavy body suddenly agile as a pony. He thought of the chains in his woods, possibly illegal considering the law—some fucking *loi* or other—about enclosure. His American lawyers hadn't been sure about the chains.

Then there was the other *loi*, the Loi Verdeille. This law, the one that most exasperated Clara and him, maintained that hunters and strangers had the right to come and hunt on your private property under circumstances defined, as far as he could tell, as broadly as possible, resulting in practically total freedom to shoot near your living-room windows, rattle the china in your cupboards, assault your sensibilities with the corpses of once lordly animals dragged through your bloodstained shrubbery. There were these private-property issues involved which outweighed with him even the objections to hunting, and he would not shrink from getting his lawyers further involved if that's what the locals wanted. His temper began to rise.

He hadn't seen these two men before, and they weren't in police clothes. Clara wasn't there. "*Messieurs?* What's all this?" he asked them. "What do you want with my wife? I've made my position plain to monsieur the mayor, and in any case my position has nothing to do with my wife." His dark skin darkened further with an angry flush, like a furious, fat gypsy.

"It is Madame Cray who is cited," said the first man politely. They were looking anxiously up the stairs, as if fearing her escape.

"Please sit down," said Cray, leading them into the salon. "I'll telephone my people." It was only seven-thirty; who knew what time the lawyers got in, in no way before ten. "Delia, you could give them some coffee." The men did not sit down. Given to abrupt exits, Cray now left without another word. Delia waited for the men to indicate if they wanted coffee. But maybe they hadn't understood. They stood with wooden faces.

"Cafe?" she asked. They shook their heads no and tried to wear amiable expressions, as if to smooth and pacify the rearing awkwardness. They smiled at Delia, to underline their commendable Gallic tact.

Clara came down, in a suit and stockings and heels, sort of churchgoing clothes. What did you wear to be taken away by police in?

"Did you tell Serge?"

"He was here," Delia said. "He went back upstairs to call the lawyer or something. 'His people,' he said."

Sometimes "calling his people" took the form, Clara knew, of Serge calling lawyers in Los Angeles, who would then call the office in Paris, which would then enact Cray's wishes, except at the moment it was not a possible time in Los Angeles, he'd have to get Woly out of bed.

"I don't know what this is about. Do you know, messieurs?" Clara asked the men. Perhaps they were just process servers, *huissiers.*

"It appears to be about theft and desecration of French property, madame. The destruction of a listed building—there are a number of counts."

Delia could see Clara had no idea what they were talking about.

"Can we wait for my husband to come back?"

"A few minutes, no more. I am afraid you must wear these. It is the same, I know, in your country."

Cray came back just as Clara was being led out. She seemed calm enough, but she was in handcuffs. She looked pleadingly at him, trying at the same time to give a reassuring, if ironic, smile. He was stymied for a few seconds, then hurried to his car, scowling and cursing violently. He didn't suggest that Delia come along.

25

Prison

Clara sat in the back of the little Renault in handcuffs; the *mag-istrats du parquet* in front kept craning around to look at her, as if they expected her to try to leap from the car. She wondered why she didn't feel more frightened, no doubt it was her conviction of innocence, her sense of being a pawn in the hardening hunting standoff, her assurance that Serge (famous, influential) would know what to do, or Woly's lawyers would, and finally that none of this could be true. One minute in her robe in her kitchen, the next en route to the jail in Versailles in handcuffs.

It seemed useless to ask these men anything, they wouldn't tell her or they didn't know, though they seemed to bear her no malice and the one gave an encouraging smile. She wondered why it was she who had been arrested, not Serge, or why not the both of them?

She sat back and thought of her little son Lars, as she did innumerable times a day, this time thinking it was just as well he didn't know about what was happening to her, it would scare him. Or maybe he'd think it was funny and exciting, like a television drama. It was, in a way, funny and exciting.

They arrived at the jail, a place she passed three times a week on her way to the open market without ever glancing up at its barred and grimy windows behind which prisoners sat, some perhaps as pure of heart as she. She didn't know the name of this prison. The wooden doors, heavy as granite, opened to allow them to drive into the forecourt, and, more ominously, closed behind them. Clara had not thought before that wood, blackened, ancient oak, patined by the centuries of misery they had seen, could be more final and grim than metal. They conjured centuries of royal power and indifference, brutality, boiling oil. It made her heart begin to quail a little to feel the doors closing like jaws behind them. She was in a foreign land, and did not know her position, her rights, or her chances. She held her head high. She had a position, and rights, nonetheless.

Now the officers, who had almost been nice, apologizing for the handcuffs, became rough and brusque, pulling her from the car as if she had been resisting them and pushing her with heavy hands on her shoulders toward the building. She imagined eyes watching them, approving the force of their magistrates against the evildoers that threatened France. She shook off the hands, which were immediately withdrawn, and gazed up at the impersonal windows with her own eyes blazing.

"You will see a representative of the *procureur*, she will tell you what it is you are charged with and *tout cela*," said the smiling man, returning his hand lightly to her elbow. Now she saw that his eyes were indifferent, the smile a mere grimace. They delivered her to a big woman who waited in the hall and took her into a vestibule with a brown linoleum floor. The woman inside began to put her hands all over Clara, searching her. Now Clara began to be really shocked. She had nothing concealed in her underclothes. She surrendered her purse.

Down another hallway, in an area that looked like an infirmary, another matron waited, carrying a towel. "This way." The woman led Clara into a bare room. *"Prenez une douche, madame."* For an instant Clara heard this in the English sense: douche, the word in English so intimate and intrusive, a kind of rape. But they were talking about a shower. Take a shower?

"But," Clara began, indignant. She'd just had a shower at home. She'd just got up. Did she smell? Did they think she might have lice? What had been irritation verged on panic. With the arrival of the deepening flush of panic came the simultaneous realization that panic was useless. She tried to stifle the pounding of her throat, and the impulse, as they pulled her forward into the shower room, to scream and struggle. The woman nodded again toward the shower in a cement-floored room beyond and thrust the thin towel at her.

The shower room was cold. The floor was cold and vaguely slimy, or maybe that was imagination, the corollary of her revulsion. The walls were peeled and scabbed with blistering paint and scratches like primitive first writings. Someone had had time to scratch "Jacq-" in the paint. Clara took off her jacket and unbuttoned her blouse, and when the matron went out, she turned on the tepid water. Could anyone see her? She ran the water but didn't stand under it.

You had to hold the water on. Her arm was getting wet as she held herself away from the stream of water. All the horrible associations of showers came to her mind—death camps, *Psycho*. When would the woman come back? When she thought the length of her shower was convincing, she let go the button, dried her arm, and waited. In seconds the woman came back, smirking as if she knew well that Clara had not subjected her body to the prison water.

A few steps farther, to a cell. A cell! A tiny room, a bunk, a rough table, a toilet in full view. Cigarette butts on the floor, and the stink of cold tobacco. She sat in shock through the long morning, unable to think straight about what to do about anything. It was hard to bring the mind to bear, it tended in the boredom of waiting to drift into strange, contentless lethargy, from which she would sternly recall herself, only to drift again. An hour passed, hours and hours it seemed. They had not taken her watch.

She had been put in here at nine. At one-thirty they led her down an interminable corridor, her footsteps ringing as in a Kafka film, reverberations hollow and portentous. She realized she could not just turn and say enough of this and leave. Each time this reality penetrated a little deeper into her numbed comprehension, it became more difficult to keep her self-possession. In an office, a slender, even chic woman with a dossier sat at a table, as if this were a job interview, and motioned Clara to sit down facing her on a folding chair. Clara felt herself hoping to make a good impression, as if her life depended on her eager expression of complicity.

"You know why you are here?"

"Not at all," Clara said, smiling tentatively.

"You are charged with theft," the woman said. "For stealing the property of France, and of the Commune of Val-Lanval. There is a list—nine fireplaces, nine mirrors, the boiseries of the salon, and parquets. There are some other charges, to do with the desecration of a national monument. When you removed the fireplaces and the rest."

For an instant Clara had no idea what the woman could be talking of, but of course it was the house. "But there were no fireplaces when we bought it," she protested. "No mirrors or anything."

"These are very serious charges, punishable with prison. But I believe the charges could be reduced for restitution, the *état* would discuss you restoring the original pieces to the château."

"But I don't have them! I—there wasn't anything there!" cried Clara.

The official did not seem surprised at this. She rattled the papers briskly and glanced at the officer who stood by the door. "*Détention provisoire*. You will be incarcerated pending the hearing. Would you like to speak to a lawyer now? He will advise you of your rights and how to proceed. Please sign these papers at the bottom there."

Clara sat staring. "Do I have the right to call my husband? Can I get my own lawyer?"

"No doubt, in time. These are the procedures after arrest, and you must follow them like everyone else." Her voice was stern but not unkind, as if she were instructing a mutinous pupil. Clara stared at the papers. Seeing no alternative, she signed them. The woman waited, seeming irritated at Clara's slowness in rising to her feet, in backing toward the door, looking around for someone to show her what to do. Then the big woman was back and took her arm.

26

Have You Heard What Happened to Clara?

Delia watched the car depart with Clara, then went back inside. She stood in the kitchen, more bemused than alarmed by this new turn of events, events not unexpected in an unreliable country lacking in due process, a country of which she herself had been a victim: Clara Holly dragged off by French authorities. Obviously this was a country with no civil rights whatever, and she felt bad about it more for Gabriel's sake than for Clara's. She believed Clara's arrest must have something to do with the events surrounding Gabriel, or maybe her own hotel bill, or the FBI men both named Frank, from whom she'd heard nothing since the day they came to the hotel. She felt the sense of duty she had in Gabriel's case; it was now more incumbent upon her than ever not to get caught, but to remain detached somehow, to testify and bear witness, to rescue the others, honest Americans under the paw of France.

"I saw it all," she assured Cray. "They treated her roughly."

"I want you to remember everything you saw," he said.

In the afternoon, Mayor Briac came to Cray, who had spent the morning on the phone. Briac was dressed in a business suit, and was accompanied by a secretary, a young man with a notebook. Cray took him into the little book-lined room off the salon. It had a globe, leather chairs, the fittings of official consultation.

"It is most unfortunate about Madame Cray," the mayor had the effrontery to say. He would not sit down.

"Hypocrites," snarled Cray. "What do you want?"

"The law is indifferent in the operation of its just provisions. They must be enforced, that is all. You have defied the Loi Verdeille in excluding hunters from your hectares, for example, but the commune has strictly enforced its provisions about *monuments historiques, c'est tout.* There is not one law for Americans and another for everyone else, monsieur, despite what you appear to believe."

"Are you telling me there's a connection between the so-called law and this thing with Clara?"

"Indeed."

The mayor assured Cray that the commune would be prepared to reconsider the charges against Clara if Cray would reconsider his attitude to hunting. Cray's enraged roaring could be heard throughout the house. In the kitchen, Delia and Senhora Alvares looked at each other.

"There will be no hunting on my land, monsieur," Cray shouted. "Cowards who would persecute a woman!" and much more in that vein.

A dark woman brought a meager dinner, announced as *purée de pommes de terre avec cornichons*, the taste watery, inedible, and a few lumps of mucilaginous meat. She was made to eat in solitude, but later she was led to a corridor, with a few other women there talking among themselves. Was it exercise time, a privilege? They were all white women, without notable marks of life's hardships. They were combed, and dressed in pants or shapeless dresses. They stared at Clara, one or two smiled and Clara smiled back but stood to herself. Even in jails, the French were so French, she thought, reserved and polite. These didn't look like wild hookers or con women—she couldn't tell what they were.

"Tu es Américaine, toi," one remarked, smiling with satisfaction. Even foreigners do not lie outside the purview of our mighty institutions. Then the women ignored her and went on talking among themselves.

She had imagined from prison movies that inmates were always flaunting their guilt, using it as a way of intimidating the other menacing people with whom they had been thrown. In a prison movie, each man strove to look more hardened and bitter than the others. But here the women were all innocent, as they loudly protested to the directrice and each other. A haggard woman of a certain age turned to Clara to tell a story the others had apparently heard too often, of the indignity of being so rudely treated by store personnel when they suggested she was trying to leave without paying for some items "which were not, after all, valuable, I told them, madame, just personal, feminine necessaries."

"And how could they think I was a *pute, moi?*" another, fat and hennaed, said, laughing. "No prostitute has my sort of shape."

Clara didn't know how to explain her presence without revealing that she lived in a splendid château, which didn't seem sisterly. "They think I stole the woodwork from an historic monument," she said. "But I am innocent." This was not an interesting crime, she didn't interest them. At eight-thirty a matron led her back to her cell.

In the night, lying trying to think of subjects to think about, she thought of Edmond Dantès and the Château d'If, and *The Prisoner of Zenda, Soul on Ice, The Man in the Iron Mask.* She thought of Serge, wondering what he was doing to get her out of here; and she thought of Monsieur de Persand, imagining him to be a kind of lawyer or powerful judge who would come and rescue her. Her thoughts dwelt longest on this theme. Serge's activity she took for granted. She tried not to reflect on how Serge had made her owner of the house for tax reasons, or else it would be him in jail. Eventually her thoughts melted into incoherent fatigue and she slept, but only for an hour or so, and then waked, disbelieving, remembering that she was in prison.

Tim Nolinger learned of the arrest of Clara Holly from Ames Everett, whom he happened to talk to at the American Library. He hadn't planned to go out to the Crays' today, had work to do in town, and she said again she didn't like him borrowing the car all the time. A few times when she had asked for it, and he had argued his superior need of it, she had seemed seriously irritated. It was her car, after all, and he'd been using it every day. She had always given in. He had not really heard her underlying complaint, the amount of time he was spending out in Etang-la-Reine with the Crays.

Among Serge's phone calls was one to the American ambassador, Charlie Nolan. The news of Clara's arrest thus spread through the embassy staff and then to others. Dorothy Sternholz heard it from Ames Everett and immediately called her friend Vivian Gibbs.

"You've heard about Clara Holly?"

"No, what?"

"Arrested! Supposedly for defacing a French national monument. That is, their château. It's apparently a move to try to get them to relax their opposition to hunting."

"I didn't know they were opposed to hunting."

"Violently opposed. My dear, she's in jail!"

Everyone agreed the idea of Clara despoiling a national monument was ridiculous on the face of it. The American community drew together, via the political clubs, Democrats in Paris and Republicans Abroad, united in excited indignation. Everyone knew the place had been sitting in rack and ruin, and that Serge Cray had saved it, and that Clara Holly had showered it with virtuous and tasteful attention, restoring the gardens and so forth. But for the Crays, the place would have been torn down, for all the attention the Ministry of National Monuments had paid it. Committees were formed in emergency sessions on the principle of the thing where the rights of foreign residents were concerned.

Of course, there were some reservations.

"However, I always did think they were a little high-handed with their *travaux*, not even going to the Monuments people," Dorothy Sternholz confided to Ames.

"I never thought it was wise just to slap a coat of white paint on it," Ames said. "All wrong for the period."

"Clara tends to think that everything she does is perfect. . . ."

Other Americans rallied. Though Serge Cray was not someone you could take casseroles to, both Alena Coe, in her capacity as program chairman of Democrats in Paris, and Maydie Bailey of the Union Interallié called the business office of Monday Brothers Films to ask that messages of solidarity be relayed. What was particularly interesting and disquieting to everybody was that if such a thing could happen to the Crays, which of them might not be the next to be dragged off in the night for having put a nail in some wall that Chateaubriand had peed against?

All the bellowing of Cray, however much it might shake the earth in California, had no power to speed up the processes of

French justice. All agreed he had made a mistake in having gone through Biggs, Rigby, Denby, Fox, the California legal team relied on by the Monday Brothers studio, who, even though they had a French branch, lost hours every day because of the time difference. Only by the heroic maneuver of beginning the workday at 8 A.M. in Los Angeles (meaning overtime pay for an attorney willing to come in that early) could the lawyers achieve a maximum of two hours of overlap with the French office, assuming these latter stayed until seven at night. Also, it didn't help that the Paris branch of the venerable old law firm had taken on a French sense of time, stately and historical, and the French certainty that events will unfold in their preordained way.

27

The Prisoner

Three days passed and, to Clara's astonishment and mounting fury, no one came to rescue her. Her initial disbelief had been replaced with the anger that set in the next day. She paced, she grimaced, she shook at the bars of her cell like prisoners in films. She shouted, which brought people running, who then threatened her. She must not shout, she would be put in a tiny *cellule isolée, un misérable cachot*. She stopped shouting.

The hours stopped being interminable, became merely thick and dull, she stopped feeling them. She was in here forever and might as well stop feeling it. She knew she had succumbed already to the diabolical forces that were using her, she was inferior stuff. When you thought of Edmond Dantès learning Latin and other languages, of prisoners who learn whole grammars of unknown languages, and recite the periodic tables stored somewhere in their minds! She had nothing in her mind, no store at all of rote memories.

But she didn't believe it possible that no one was trying to get her out; it must be that her case was insoluble, that there was some proof existing against her of some crime, in violation of some inexorable French law no one could do anything about. When she asked to telephone Serge, she was told that responsibles of the jail would convey messages from her. But her messages lacked conviction; she had nothing to say. Knowing he would naturally be trying to rescue her, she fell back on reassuring him, that she was okay, that she was being fed. She asked him not to notify Lars, who was timid and would have been frightened for her. It went without saying she wanted to get out.

How in just three days could you begin to feel all vitality ebb, and passivity and despair crush in on you?

She slept badly. After the second night, she asked for sleeping medicine and finally was allowed to get a prescription sent over from her doctor. She didn't sleep all the same, lay awake going over things, even things unrelated to her predicament, the nightly roll taken of concerns, intentions, failures. Her mother, Lars, her mother, Lars, the garden, the poor deer and rabbits, Lady the dog, the Frenchman, her mother, Lars. The handsome Frenchman, Antoine de Persand. Serge.

Her innocence of theft got her to thinking obsessively through the long nights about all the things she probably *was* guilty of— neglecting her mother, not going home, and Lars, she'd been too docile about Serge sending him away, and before that, that rash during her pregnancy, was it measles? No, nothing could have been done, they always assured her of that, but was it true? And his whole life now a vast silence.

Serge believed, now that Lars could lipread as well as sign, the child could lead a normal life, more or less, and must learn to get along with normal people, as if it hadn't happened, and not to think of himself as apart. And he believed that English schoolboys would not be cruel to a deaf boy, which she didn't believe for a minute. Not that she had anything against the English, but. They wouldn't be cruel to a boy who had his mother's good nature and looks (said Serge). Clara wasn't so sure. She worried all the time about Lars at a subconscious level where worries are put that are not likely to go away. These would never go away, and Lars would never hear them.

He would be so big before her mother saw him again, they must go this summer, must positively go; no one must tell her mother about this, she would blame Serge, she didn't like Serge as it was.

And had Monsieur de Persand had something to do with her arrest, was that why he didn't come in for sandwiches? But of course it was probably the mayor or one of the others who had thought up this vengeful action. She reviewed their malicious faces in her mind, studying them for signs of treachery. How odd that her usually indifferent memory now became as sharp as a pain in the heart, almost photographic when it came to the expressions of the men, the choler in the mayor's eyes, or in those of the sandy-haired master of the hunt, always in boots, with creases in his earlobes they say will kill you. No doubt they thought it was only she who hated hunting, they hadn't reckoned with Serge. Only you. How lucky she had discovered that Persand had no particular feeling for her, didn't come in with the others.

She thought of men's bodies. Their grace and strength stirred her. She was glad that even though faithfully married she retained this abstract erotic admiration of how men looked, the potentiality of their bodies. The way she had noticed certain things about Persand, really inconsequential things, that to judge from his open shirt collar he had a hairy chest, something she didn't really like, but why had she noticed it? She kept seeing his open collar, the strong neck, his rather high color, the tuft of hair. . . .

She thought of women touching men. She never touched Serge, he was not a person who accepted caresses. She wanted to touch the hard shoulder of a man and stroke his back, caress his hard sex.

Tim Nolinger went out to the Crays' the second day after he heard about the arrest—the soonest he could tactfully take the car—hoping to be able to help in some way, and wondering if the thief had called and so on. He seemed able to contrive reasons ad lib to go out there, though he knew she would not be there. He parked on the main road and walked to the house. The house was emitting a sort of heat of wariness, something hostile and electronic and charged. As he stood at the door, he realized that with a strange silent step, not even crunching on the gravel of the courtyard, a massive Rottweiler had come out of the shrubbery and stood, ears up, watching him. The Crays had house dogs, the yellow Labs named Freddy and Taffy, but he hadn't seen this dog before. Then there was a second Rottweiler, two silent creatures watching him, both wearing heavy leather muzzles. He had a feeling that if he'd stepped off the path they would have approached, maybe attacked him. These were dogs with orders, baleful and conscientious. No question that dogs are intimidating beyond the extent to which they could actually hurt you. Unmuzzled these would kill you.

Senhora Alvares let him in. *"O senhor está em cima."* Tim knew from her distracted manner Clara was still in jail. She took him to the table in the breakfast room and brought coffee, and presently Cray came down.

"Did you have trouble with the dogs? They have orders not to bother people coming to the front door. They patrol the woods, but

I suppose their main instinct is to protect the house. There's a *maître-chien* who sees to them."

"No, they stood and watched me. They're muzzled."

"I'm told they are nearly as deadly with the muzzle on, they strike the intruder with the heavy leather tip. I should have got them here before this."

"Intruders, that is to say hunters?"

"Exactly."

This was an escalation, undoubtedly. Tim wondered if the local hunters would now make a point of stomping through Cray's land to defy the dogs, and so on.

"Is there anything I can do for your wife? For you?"

"I think they'll let her out on bail tomorrow. Then we'll see," he said grimly. "As to the other matter, there's no news at all, only silence."

He meant the Driad manuscript. Tim was just as glad nothing had been heard on that. Later that day he was to face another legal matter, the signing for the apartment he and Anne-Sophie had bought, which was enough entanglement in the murky mire of legal matters and debt.

He hung around the Crays' a few minutes, then went to meet Adrian Wilcox at the tennis club. The next players were late, and they got to keep their court an extra three-quarters of an hour, so he was obliged to take the *périphérique* at an illegal speed to get to the *notaire*, in the Sixteenth Arrondissement, in time for the signing of the *promesse de vente*.

He saw at once it was a mistake to come to this ceremony wearing his tennis clothes, but he was late as it was, with no time to change, and, innocent of real estate transactions in either society, had opted for the American take on such procedures, to wit, that the signing of one's name to a document obliging one to pay hundreds of thousands of francs and take a mortgage forever should be greeted with the same insouciance we admire in the march of great rogues to the gallows.

Anne-Sophie was in her most serious suit, high heels, flushed with excitement; Estelle was there, and the sellers, a Monsieur and Madame Flieu, whose birth dates, marital history, progeny, and addresses were all listed on the document read out and then placed before Tim for initialing on forty-seven pages, turned one by one. All were as dressed up as Anne-Sophie, as was the *notaire* behind his desk. Tim assumed, at least, a grave demeanor, and indeed felt gravely uneasy, beset by the specters of mistake, overreaching, no turning back.

The Flieus pressed their hands, wished them marital happiness, and remarked that they should all meet now or later to decide the cost of such things as the light fixtures and the bookcases, or perhaps they would not be wanting these items?

"*On pensait,* we were thinking, thirty thousand francs for the total," said Monsieur Flieu. "Is that good?"

Anne-Sophie sighed. "We'll have to think."

Tim had no idea what they were talking about, though there were some built-in bookcases in the dining room, and one serious chandelier he thought a bit overdone anyway.

They shook hands again. "We'll be in touch very soon," Anne-Sophie said.

Outside Anne-Sophie explained to him that the seller was now suggesting they pay an extra thirty thousand francs for the built-in bookcases. They had discussed it before, she reminded him.

"I can leave these bookcases for you, if you like," Madame Flieu had said amiably when they had gone back for a better look at certain features and at the *cave*.

"I love your bookcases," he had said, with some happy image of himself surrounded by his books, which were at the moment in haphazard squalor under his bed and on kitchen counters.

A little note had come a day or two later, listing several things Madame Flieu was prepared to leave—bookcases, medicine cabinet, heated towel rack. But she had said nothing about thirty thousand francs, nearly five thousand dollars! Tim was stunned. Anne-Sophie was less stunned, though she pursed her rosy good-business-woman's lips and thought about the sum.

"We have to bring them down a bit," she said as they left the notary's office. "I think that is high."

"Thirty thousand francs! What are they talking about? We can go to the BHV and buy some fucking bookcases."

Anne-Sophie pursued her dealer's train of thought: "They want us to buy the bookcases, which of course you must have, but I don't know about the *lustre*. It is eighteenth century. Of the *trente mille*, the *lustre* must be worth the half. We can tell him to keep his *lustre*, and thus pay only fifteen for the bookcases. I can do better on a *lustre* at the *puces*."

"Wait a minute, these things were part of the apartment! Bookcases are built in, attached!"

"Sometimes people take over their new apartment and all the door handles, even the plumbing, is gone," Anne-Sophie said. "But these people seem very nice, I am not in the least worried. Anyway the agent will check before we sign the final sale."

Thus did he learn that all is not what it seems, and that if they weren't careful, the Flieus might carry off the toilets and sinks on the grounds that in France you buy only the walls. He was shocked that he was now being held up for an extra five thousand dollars for the very items that had prompted their offer in the first place, and he found it infuriating in the extreme not to have been told all this beforehand. Would it have influenced his enthusiasm for the place? He didn't know. Luckily, Anne-Sophie did not seem to find anything out of the ordinary, so he let the matter drop, or rather tried to refocus on finding the extra money. For her part, Anne-Sophie seemed newly at peace with the apartment, her reservations having given way before the exciting reality of this significant step.

They kissed at the entrance to the metro; Anne-Sophie was rushing off to look at an estate sale.

"Well, *c'est fait*," she said, smiling.

"*Madame la propriétaire.*"

But they didn't go off to drink champagne as Tim had vaguely thought they would. They had lost an opportunity to celebrate a solemn, happy moment, the committment they had made as a couple for a place to live together, the sort of thing you ought to clink champagne glasses over. He went away with a wistful feeling of loss instead of accomplishment.

"Tim Nolinger has bought not too far from you," said Vivian Gibbs to Kathy Dolan, whose husband worked as a U.S. cultural attaché. "Passage de la Visitation. Did you know that behind those gates at the end of the street, there is a Rothschild?"

"Just your little newlywed starter nest?" Kathy wondered. The rumor of Tim's heritage had by now reached the embassy, probably explaining the fact the Tim and Anne-Sophie were invited to several functions there, one a dinner for lawyers and journalists, another to honor the conductor of an American symphony orchestra. Tim surprised himself by feeling rather pleased, though unsure why and how America had found him; Belgium had never invited him anywhere.

28

Stir-Crazy

By the fourth day Clara was sunk even deeper in a trance of misery and incomprehension, punctuated by moments of indignation at being persecuted for a moral cause, when her reverie was broken by a guard. She was abruptly led from her cell to the visitors' area and motioned to sit in a chair on one side of a pane of glass. She peered, heart beating with apprehension, at the empty chair on the other side, waiting for Serge to come in. Then the door beyond opened, and a man walked in with a guard behind him. At first glance she mistook him for a lawyer sent by Serge. A man in a beautifully tailored dark suit, scarf, carrying his camel overcoat. It was Antoine de Persand.

In her astonishment she had nothing to say as he sat down and leaned toward the little grille opening in the glass. It crossed her mind absurdly that she had no makeup on, and wrinkled clothes. She must look so haggard and depressed.

"Madame Cray."

"I am amazed to see you."

"I had to come. I don't know why I am, have come, I have nothing to suggest, I just—it seemed . . ." Here he stopped, it appeared baffled.

"It is very strange, this whole thing, I agree," she said.

"I disliked that you could think I might have had something to do with this, madame. I am a friend, be assured, and I part company with the hunt committee on this persecution. Your hectares aren't so important to the hunt, it is the ego of the mayor by now. I have a fear that monsieur the mayor has a long memory, and though he has no personal animus against you, his *amour propre* is now involved."

"Was it difficult, getting in to see me?"

"No, in my case easy. Perhaps it is difficult in general."

"My husband has not been able to come."

"Ah," he said.

"What do I need to do so they will let me out?"

"I have no idea. I'm not an emissary from the mayor. I came because—out of friendship. I have no idea why I am here," he added in a suprised tone.

"Thank you, all the same. I'm sure I'll be out soon."

"Are you—is it all right?"

"French jails are not comfortable."

"I'll go to see your husband. I'm sure he has taken measures. Technically I am a lawyer, I have certain connections, if I can help in anything—"

"Thank you, monsieur. I know he is doing all he can."

More—much more—was spoken by their intense exchange of gazes. Was he too feeling the mute, visceral experience of desire? For it was desire that welled up in her. She felt the inappropriateness of this. Perhaps it was akin to what hostages felt for their captors, some bizarre form of imprinting. You fall in love with the first man who comes to rescue you. The glass barrier seemed intolerable to Clara, and because it prevented so much as a handshake, it prompted fiery and rather abandoned speeches, which she swallowed as well as she could. She wanted to say, If I could just spend a night with you, an afternoon—

Then, against her will and against common sense, she heard herself say it. From a prison cell she, Clara Holly, was propositioning a strange Frenchman.

Monsieur de Persand stiffened. He seemed to pale, while her face flamed.

"I just need some strength," she apologized. "I didn't mean—anything. I seem to say and think wild thoughts, it's this place. . . ."

"I must tell you sometime what happened in my family this past year, and you will understand why I . . . do not permit myself wild thoughts. The death of my brother, the misery of my mother, the *orphelins*, the chaos of the heritage, the problems of an aunt and uncle—all because. . . ." He sighed.

"I agree, I agree, I am talking nonsense," Clara said. "You get rather unsettled in here. Excuse me." But he must have known exactly what she had meant. Probably female prisoners offered themselves to the lawyers all the time, in their desperate hope for liberty. . . .

At this moment, the stirring of the guards indicated that all were to rise and visitors to leave without further ado. Clara and Antoine de Persand stared desperately at each other, shocked, through the glass partition. Persand hurried out, clutching his coat.

Back in her cell, Clara's sufferings increased. Hot tears for the first time rolled on her cheeks. How had she dared say such a thing to Antoine de Persand? Why did she even have such a longing to be in his arms? It was a sign her brain had been turned by prison. She saw herself as a person crawling across a desert toward a watery mirage of love and wild sensuality. And why did this image of aridity apply to her life? Because her life was dry, devoid of voluptuous pleasure, with routine love, infrequent, lacking in true intimacy. It seemed to her that prison was just a metaphor for her whole life. Self-pity and misery overcame her. Four days of confinement had reduced her to a depressed and delusional state.

29

Word from Gabriel

Now Tim made his way out to the Crays' in Anne-Sophie's car or by train every day to monitor news of the manuscript thief and the progress of legal matters surrounding Clara's arrest. He had by now, even in this relatively short time, *faute de mieux*, achieved the status of family friend, sponsor of Delia, and general factotum. He realized that Cray had relied on Clara as his liaison with the outside world; that person in her absence became him. Why did he oblige? He didn't know, curiosity or charity, and the article or story that would come out of it. It was more than the paycheck, though he had got his first three thousand dollars from Monday Brothers Films and felt embarrassingly overpaid. It would help with the bookcases, that was for sure.

And there was the curious power of power and glamour to compel his attendance. He despised this in himself. Of his other reason for hanging around—being of help to Clara—only he had an intimation; but also, he did want to see the thing out, to stay to the end of the play.

He wasn't sure how well he liked Cray. The man was brusque, and had a short attention span that seemed to preclude conversation. He spilled things down the front of his clothes. But just when these characteristics would get irritating, Cray would return his attention to what they were saying, astonish with some insight, turn out to have been paying attention all along. When he talked about film he was impressive. Perhaps he was a genius. Tim could not tell.

He had begun in earnest to work on his film. The clipping box stood on his writing desk. He wore a preoccupied air, and made many, many phone calls to England and California.

Getting to know Cray, he found himself in a unique position to report on the doings of this reclusive and intriguing figure, but prevented by their growing friendship from violating the privileges of the intimacy. Meantime Cees was also urging him to stand by to handle any transactions with the thief, and this gave him a sense of double dealing, which was kind of irrational in that Cray and Cees both wanted in the end to catch the thief and save the Driad manuscript. Cees was right in imagining that intimacy with Cray would be enough inducement for Tim to hang around—that it was interesting to be in a position of privilege *vis-à-vis* this almost legendary figure. Cray must have assumed the same thing, that his very self made Tim's serving him worthwhile to Tim. He was used to being served. He also gave Tim a new assignment.

"Could we find out what happened to the fucking *boiseries*? Could you do that?"

Tim said he'd try.

"Do you have anything else to do?"

This startled and somewhat wounded Tim. Did he? Sure. What? Well . . . There were a lot of things he should be doing.

"I read some of your stuff," Cray said. "I had them get it for me. Where do you stand—with *Reliance* or with *Concern*? Aren't there some natural contradictions there?"

"I can usually see both sides," Tim said. "It's a kind of a curse."

When several days had passed, they still had heard no more from the thief/caller. Once when the phone rang, it was Clara's mother. Serge shook his head at Delia, signalling he didn't want to talk to her, Delia should. "Why hello Mrs. Holly, it's Delia Sadler? From down the road? I'm here visiting um Clara, she isn't here now." Delia looked at Serge for instruction.

They speculated that the millennium manuscripts, and specifically the Morgan Library document the thief wanted to sell Cray, the Driad Apocalypse, were somehow connected to Delia's absent friend Gabriel. Was that too large a leap? Not really, they thought. The man's elusive surfacings, lying low even when he'd been cleared of the flea market murder, and now his possible association with millennium cults via his girlfriend in Oregon, seemed to suggest it more strongly than before. Tim thought he might talk to Delia about this possibility, but he had no need to bring it up, for the thing clarified itself.

On Friday, the day Cray hoped to have Clara's release, Cray

and Delia and Tim were assembled in the family room. It had become like a war room, with three telephones. When one of them rang, Cray nodded to Delia, who was closest to it, to answer. (Often he had Senhora Alvares answer, or a workman primed to maintain that the caller had a wrong number.)

A look of joy and recognition spread over her face before she had said a word. Tim and Cray tuned in. How could someone be calling Delia? But of course she had given out the number to hundreds of her various relatives and friends, with whom she stayed in practically minute-to-minute contact.

"Gabe, it's me!" she cried. "This is so weird! How did you know I was here?" Tim heard her say this and drew nearer. One could imagine bafflement, even expletives on the other end of the line. Cray, who was reading in the corner, heard also and lifted his head. Gabriel, the mysterious young man whom Anne-Sophie had seen dragged off by the flics. The depth of Delia's enthusiasm for this young man as yet unknown to them was abundantly clear.

Then she was volubly telling the caller all that had happened to her, and she spent long moments listening, presumably to what had happened to him in the two weeks or so since they had parted. Gabriel the missing.

"Are you all right? Where are you? I had to leave the hotel, it wasn't safe," they heard her explain. On her face a reassured expression that life would now go on as she had known it, her friend was extant, the telephone was working, all was normality and hope.

She looked up at Cray. "Can my friend stay here? Just until we can get his passport and stuff out of the hotel and some plane tickets?"

Cray looked at Tim. Perhaps he had the same intimation that Gabriel was also the manuscript thief, for how, indeed, had this Gabriel known that Delia was here? And how had he got the phone number, which was *liste rouge* but known to the manuscript thief?

"Certainly," said Cray. "He would be most welcome. Tell him to come here." She told him, and nodded, beaming, at Cray. Gabriel was apparently accepting the invitation.

"Can you give him the directions?" she asked, handing Cray the phone. "Hello," Cray said, a note of joviality in his voice Tim had not heard before. "We are more than glad to have you here!"

He described the buses from Versailles, the walk from the village, precautions about the dogs. Cray was pleased by the dogs. He was always sending some luckless delivery man off the path to find himself surrounded by snarling Rottweilers, and made to submit to an inquisition by the *maître-chien*, a Belgian, booted like an SS officer.

"A relief for you, Delia," he said, putting down the phone. "Your friend is safe, the two of you can leave France as soon as you make arrangements, and meantime a safe haven here."

"This is so nice of you," said Delia fervently. "Oh God, what a relief."

But even Delia's rapture over Gabriel's surfacing did not seem to rupture her new bond with Cray, for shortly thereafter he took her into the other room, pointedly excluding Tim.

30

Out on Bail

It took a week to return the shaken and furious Clara to her home on bail. A *juge d'instruction* was assembling evidence for her eventual trial, promised for just before Christmas. Cray came for her with one of the lawyers, in the Land Rover—as he might have come to pick her up from the station after a shopping trip, she remarked bitterly when she walked out, shaking her hair and blinking in the bright autumn day, humbled, dirty, enraged. The forces of French justice arrayed themselves stiffly in the prison courtyard to watch her go. Cray sensed her anger.

"You wanted a limousine, you wanted some ceremony." Cray laughed. "I should have realized."

"No, no." But she was inwardly angry with her husband that it had taken so long, and he with her because he had not been able to be more effective, though he had done everything he could. It was rumored that the American ambassador had complained on her behalf at the Quai d'Orsay.

"Jean Beaumarché told me so himself," said Christophe Oliver, the French lawyer with Biggs, Rigby, Denby, Fox.

In the days following Clara's release, Tim became aware that the air at the château had continued to change and sour. Was it the drooling Rottweilers and the jackbooted keeper, introducing a note of danger to the comings and goings? Was it the note of energized involvement on the part of Cray, who now restlessly strode from room to room in the manner of a fevered sick person, or stepped outside to test the vigilance of the dogs, like one of those gothic lords of manors in the Victorian novels Anne-Sophie read? Was it the sense of irritation, even rage, emanating from the composed and ladylike Clara?

Thinking of herself as a calm person, Clara didn't recognize rage when she felt it, not at first. When Serge, with the lawyer Chris Oliver, came to fetch her at the prison, part of her was glad to see them, reassuringly reanimated with indignation at her plight, setting things in motion, pulling strings. It was irrational, she knew, to blame Serge for this, though blame welled up in her, with barnacles of other faults and disappointments stuck to it. Lars. Other things.

Yes, part of her knew it wasn't Serge's fault. She even more than he opposed hunting, and she was glad to be a martyr—up to a point—in such a virtuous cause. But when she thought of how Serge had not gone to prison, of how he had not rescued her until days and days had gone by, of how with devious foresight he had made her the owner of the house, of how he had sent Lars away, of how all her views were trampled and subsumed by his bulk, his money, his inactivity, the lethargy of artistic despair that enveloped her life too like a poisonous miasma, then a kind of despairing fury rose, the more powerful because she knew she had no recourse and would just have to endure it.

The first time Tim saw her after her release, she was standing in the courtyard when he drove in. She smiled in her heartbreakingly sunny way and took his hand when he got out of the car, as if to protect him from the dogs. She did look thinner to his eye, "drawn," whatever that meant, with a tinge of a shadow under her eyes—all this serving only to increase her beauty by lending it a doomed and fugitive quality.

"Welcome, Tim. You've been so great with Serge," she said, as though Cray were a demanding invalid she regretted having had to be absent from. They went inside. Another lawyer, Bradley Dunne, also from Biggs, Rigby, Denby, Fox, was there, following her around, maybe trying to assess the injury she had suffered, for some eventual claim.

How did you throw off the horror of all those days and nights in prison? Tim asked her this. Of course he wanted to hear about the prison, everybody did, and she had told her story, it seemed, numberless times in the twenty-four hours since her release. Her account already had acquired a certain practiced quality, all about the watery cross-sections of bony fish, the lack of coffee, and how chicory water was all she had had for seven days.

"Did you know about the coffee withdrawal headache?" she asked. "The most horrible headache, nothing works to help it. It sets in on the second day. After that you're content to lie on your bunk, the pain is so awful. I suppose it lightens eventually, but the first thing I did when I got out was have a cup of coffee."

"I can't believe they can do this to an innocent person," Tim heard himself say, though of course he could believe it.

"And surely the innocent must suffer more keenly than the guilty. For the guilty there must be a measure of compensation—you get a chance at atonement," she agreed, smiling.

But it was not only Clara's days in prison, it seemed, that lent the air of strangeness and irritation he was picking up on. She had got out to find that, in the week she was gone, Cray had become fascinated with Delia. Among his calls to California had been one to Woly, asking Monday Brothers to fund the sojourn of Delia in France for a few more weeks, to help with deep background for his movie. Since without a passport she had had little option but to stay, and since she clearly intended to wait for her friend to surface, it was not clear to Tim why he needed to pay her besides.

"Her little bones—delicious. Little twisted hip, don't you find it . . . ?" Cray chuckled. Tim didn't quite know what he meant. That he found Delia sexy? Or something weirder, that he had a sadistic wish to crush her damaged little bones? Or was it that to admire the imperfect was a sort of criticism of Clara's perfection? Or was it just that in Clara's absence he had focused on the other docile female to hand?

"She is a member of a cult, did you know that?" he said. "Or rather, a consortium of cults. It's very Oregonian, she tells me. The consorted cults of Oregon run the antique mall where she and her friend have a shop. She knows people who are into the millennium thing, Mormon polygamists, superpatriots, the black-helicopter people, nothing surprises her. I feel like she has been sent to me."

"It's the Far West," Tim agreed. Though he had never been to the Far West, this was well known to be where the Y2K people and such were concentrated. But he had thought more Idaho, Montana, and could not imagine the sane little middle-class Delia in an attitude of fervent worship or cult membership. "What kind of cult, anyway?"

"She says she's not religious but that she agrees with many of the ideas of many of the people she knows. Ask her about them."

When Delia came in, Cray would draw her away to the dining

room to eat their sandwiches, excluding both his wife and Tim. Since this left him alone with Clara, Tim didn't mind. His infatuation with Clara—he did not put a more serious name to it—welcomed any conversation, any accidental brush of hands, any confidence from her that might seem to privilege his friendship. Of course he knew that Anne-Sophie was becoming aware of this distraction that had begun to eat at his heart—he found himself adopting the fulsome language that seemed the only language for this sort of thing: his heart was being eaten—but he couldn't very well reassure Anne-Sophie, couldn't say, "My crush on Clara isn't serious, you know," without dignifying Anne-Sophie's suspicions and making them worse.

In the days that followed, the mysterious Gabriel still didn't appear. Delia could be seen staring out windows and jumping when the phone rang—as did both Cray and Clara, for their own reasons, to do, Tim imagined, with the legal problems hanging over Clara. Sometimes Cray amused himself by teasing Delia.

"This is foie gras, Delia. Do you know how they make it? How they put this big cone down the duck's throat and then pour grain in, all the creature can hold, force-feeding it endlessly so that its liver swells up huge—and that's this, what you're eating!"

"Ugh," predictably. Then, "You think I'm a total hick, but in fact I know about foie gras. I suppose you're just saying all this so you can eat mine."

Though he knew he should have better things to do, like researching the sale of the boiseries, or organizing his books, or writing about something, Tim was getting to be a regular of the Cray household to the point that he now felt comfortable sitting in the kitchen, where Cray tended to sit and read, or in the little breakfast room adjoining the family room, a small space painted yellow and decorated with silhouettes in narrow black frames, where the newspapers stacked up and a radio was sometimes on. In the kitchen, the warm Aga cooker was increasingly attractive in the chilly mornings—the château was not easy to heat. From the kitchen, tall windows opened out onto a garden landscape of cement urns and plants silvered by the several frosts so far. A defunct fountain collected brown leaves in its basin. Senhora Alvares now thought of Tim as a factotum of Cray's (rather than as, say, the admirer of madame), and greeted him with that mixture of deference and familiarity reserved by underservants for upper servants. On the payroll, Tim supposed he was Cray's man at this point. He hung around because the alternatives were worse—moving his books to the new bookshelves, for example. But they had heard nothing further from the manuscript thief.

Tim had been in touch about all matters concerning Gabriel with Cees in Amsterdam, beginning when they moved Delia to the Crays'. He knew Cees was interested in the Gabriel affair, but Cees had not said whether he thought it was connected to the Driad Apocalypse. Tim had discussed with Cees the possibility that Gabriel and the manuscript might be connected, and Cees had now told him that two other potential buyers on the list had also been contacted by telephone, by someone promising them the manuscript. Was it by Gabriel or someone else altogether? The other buyers, like Cray, had been told to cooperate with the thief and signal their willingness to buy his merchandise, but so far the thief had not made a second pass at any of the potential buyers he had lined up.

Tim wasn't the only person hanging around. He, after all, had a reason, the manuscript mystery. Antoine de Persand found very slim excuses to appear twice when Tim happened to be there. He and Delia watched the dynamic—the beautiful woman, the handsome man, their compulsive glances. Surely Cray must have noticed too the impression the pair gave of being in the grip of some invisible spell. But it appeared he did not.

Tim heard Clara in the hall one morning just after he had got there and was putting his coat in the closet by the breakfast room. He went on into the kitchen, where Cray sat reading and Senhora Alvares was making coffee.

"Will you have . . . ? We were just about to . . ." Clara was stammering.

"No. Thank you—*merci,* yes, *s'il vous plaît.*" Antoine de Persand advanced a few steps into the kitchen. Then Clara, apparently deciding on a fancier environment, led him to the breakfast room that adjoined the kitchen. For a second the others hesitated, but Senhora Alvares took the whole tray of cups in there, so they followed: Tim, Cray, Delia. Clara had positioned herself at the foot of the breakfast-room table like the lady of the château and was bent over the cups. Persand was just sitting down, nearest her.

Looking up from pouring, she saw Cray appear. "You have met my husband," she said to Persand. Persand stood and shook Cray's hand, then Tim's, then Delia's.

"So what is the respected mayor planning next?" Cray asked.

Persand hesitated. "I thought I should come and tell you. Are you sure of your *surface* here? I think he intends to challenge the legal status of some of your hectares, and perhaps make a right-of-way issue."

Serge said, "Sit down, monsieur. Could you explain?"

There was the passing of cups, the ritual of sugar, conducted by Clara, who had retreated into an appearance of maidenly shyness, eyes trained on the coffee pot. In her mind was the humiliating moment when despite her principles she had made a pass—face it, it was a pass—at this man and been refused. Not something she could ever have imagined in her life. Hubris, hubris. But neither could she have imagined being in prison. Her heart pounded, her hand—it was ridiculous—shook when she glanced up to see Monsieur de Persand sitting at her table.

"You are familiar with the Loi Verdeille?" Persand went on.

"Of course. A law of astonishing fascism—"

Cray had explained to Delia that this law provided that the owner of a property of fewer than twenty hectares could not prevent hunters from hunting on his private property. Cray could not comprehend such a violation of private property rights in a free, democratic nation. When he had vowed to take it to the European court in Strasbourg, he had been told that others, similarly indignant, already had. But the court had not yet pronounced, and meantime it was a law of France that the small proprietor could not keep hunters out, though a large landowner could.

"Right," Delia chimed fiercely. "Astonishing."

"That is another question," said Persand stiffly. "The mayor thinks that perhaps the legal status of some of the roads on the perimeter of your property, if reexamined, could further diminish your *surface*. You may have counted easements, et cetera. He's looking for another means of harrassing you."

Cray grunted. "Did my dogs annoy you?"

"I saw them, monsieur. They saw me, also."

"There are eight dogs loose on the property, and their master is instructed to set them on intruders and on the intruders' dogs. I am interested that they seem to be able to discern the difference between intruders and invited guests and friends such as yourself. Maybe it's that welcome visitors come properly up the path. Or maybe the *maître-chien* somehow knows and signals."

"The mayor also has the power to condemn certain parts of your *surface* for the public easement, which might have the effect of lowering the measure of your hectares even further," said Persand.

This did affect Cray, who at last saw the point. He scowled, his eyes glittered, his jaw darkened as if his beard had suddenly surged. "So that's their game," he said.

Persand turned to Clara. "And you, madame? You have survived the terrible ordeal of the prison?"

"It is something everyone should go through," Clara said, smiling in a sprightly, almost Frenchwoman's way. "You discover things about yourself, and you say and do things that are not like yourself at all. Things you would never do or say in the real world."

"I can imagine that. I suppose we all have an imaginative life we dare not let out."

"But in prison, it is free," said Clara. "You can think of doing any forbidden thing."

The wedding plans continued smoothly, but the apartment problem worsened.

"Tell Madame Flieu to take her planks with her," the agent coolly advised Tim and Anne-Sophie, when Tim remonstrated about the extra charges. But it wasn't so simple—they wanted the bookcases. It was a matter of coming up with the extra sum. Tim had a little money in an American account, and called his mother, who had a power of attorney to withdraw it.

"These are attached!" Tim continued to complain to all and sundry. "The sellers can't take things that are attached!" But it appeared they could, it was the French way, and all he and Anne-Sophie had bought, after all, were the walls. Any embellishment was a function of the goodwill of the seller, Madame Flieu. Tim could not master the irritation he began to feel about those bookcases, another instance of the sullying of their eventual nest by forces they could not control, as if heavy, ugly birds had thrust themselves in and squatted on the delicate eggs of marital content- ment about to hatch. He and Anne-Sophie found refuge in espe- cially passionate and frequent lovemaking, during which, once, Anne-Sophie said, "Oh, God, I'm horny." This non-French expres- sion, so unexpected in Anne-Sophie's prim, London-tuned, slang- free English vocabulary, caught Tim unaware and struck him as funny, as it had been funny when had she said the thing about "fuck me."

It was days later, when he was there in the middle of the day, that he saw a copy of *Sexus* in her apartment. She'd been reading Henry Miller, the evident source of her rather hapless attempts to speak sexy English when they made love. He wondered again if something was wrong for her, or if she thought something was wrong for him. Had his interest in Clara followed them to bed? He wouldn't have thought so, but it was hard to discuss sex without in- troducing something clinical and off-putting into an activity that had seemed spontaneous and happy. Just what he needed—another source of anxiety.

For her part, Estelle was interested to learn about Tim's trust fund, from which he was going to get the bookcase money. She had heard of this fiscal arrangement by which millionaire Americans supported their indigent sons or marriageable daughters.

31

Clara and Delia

Whereas Clara had at first been sympathetic to Delia, she now began to find her irritating. Tim thought maybe she was annoyed by Cray's fascination with the girl—they were always talking—or it could be that Clara rivalrously felt that her own problems far exceeded Delia's, which only consisted, after all, of an enforced stay in France in a luxurious château and a slight inquietude for her friend Gabriel, while Clara faced the probability of a further stay in prison, or so the French magistrate had made clear.

At first Clara had made allowances for Delia, thinking that although handicapped people often were sardonic and skeptical, overlaid with a slightly hypocritical patience—natural enough—this Delia seemed genuinely sweet, even rather passive, a person on hold. Maybe she was waiting for the operation that would allow her life to begin. As Clara's own growing up had been one of unencumbered running and jumping, and needing no one's forbearance, she would not judge Delia.

But it struck her that Delia seemed to have an amazing capacity to do nothing. They all noticed it. She could sit in a chair motionless for hours. They wondered if it was because her hip hurt her that she had cultivated this quality of inertia. Yet when she moved, she merely limped and did not seem to be in undue pain. She didn't like French television, didn't read, would watch CNN for brief bouts, inevitably ending with snorts of indignation and sighs of national shame at the intellectual level of CNN.

"CNN is not as stupid as this in the U.S.," she would say. "It's as if they think if you aren't in America you must be dumb."

She did help around the house, answering the telephone or carrying cups to the kitchen. And she would talk for long periods with Cray. Who knew what they were doing? Tim assumed they were just talking, but he had found out in life that the last people on earth you would have thought were fucking, were fucking after all. Still, he didn't think they were. The lumbering, fat Cray and the bird-boned young woman—it was almost as unimaginable as to think of Cray and Clara.

Delia seemed to think of herself as a victim, and of legendary proportions. She had enthusiastic conversations on this theme with the people back home, which he and the Crays were at liberty to overhear. Tim noticed she had given up putting her calls on her credit card; instead of faithfully reciting the endless digits for each call, she now dialed direct at any hour with a calm show of entitlement. Perhaps Serge had told her to. She also was in contact with countless people in Paris, whose phone numbers had been forthcoming by the dozens from people in Oregon, each of whom seemed to have an American friend living here. By this means Delia's plight also became widely known in the American community, and became thought of, even, as being as dire as Clara's. The girl who can't get her passport because of the mysterious misapplication of French bureaucracy was somehow connected to Clara Holly facing prison for the theft of historic panelling.

The U.S. consulate had assured Delia that the delay of her passport was probably nothing more serious than an administrative glitch whereby the French police had forgotten about her and therefore had forgotten to lift their request to the Americans to hold it back, or to notify the French immigration authorities that they had no more need of her. The French immigration authorities in turn, therefore, had not rescinded their request to the American authorities.

Tim suspected that someone still wanted to hold on to Delia until her friend Gabriel surfaced. And one day he did.

"Did you hear that *Mademoiselle Décor* is going to cover Tim Nolinger's wedding? His fiancée is a French socialite, but you've heard about him too? Are you invited?" Vivian Gibbs was asking Maydie Bailey at a co-meeting of Democrats and Republicans, to celebrate Thanksgiving and to review the rights of foreigners in France in the wake of Clara Holly's problems.

"Are the invitations out?" Maydie asked warily.

"I love a French wedding. I went to one which went on for six days. . . ."

"I'm afraid I don't know Tim that well," confessed Maydie.

"Why are the French so backward about the Internet?" Delia sighed, having no luck with the Minitel, the primitive French version.

"Well, they were so far ahead with the Minitel, everyone in France was online locally, so they just didn't notice the Internet until now. Then there's their thing about keeping out American culture—that made them skeptical of the Internet."

"So why do they have McDonald's then? Why did they choose McDonald's instead of the Internet?"

"There is no explanation," said Cray.

Anne-Sophie, finding Henry Miller hard going, was giving him up. She had been looking for anatomical slang words in English, to upgrade her erotic vocabulary, as suggested by the countess Ribemont in *Against the Tide*: "There is no secret to making a man happy: it's as simple as an aphrodisiac tone of voice, and a *vocabulaire dur, alors*. Use the words he has always dreamed of hearing you say." Finding what these were, however, was far from easy, and trying one or two of Miller's phrases had not had much of an effect on Tim, she had concluded. In fact she found the English vocabulary very deficient in general, when it came to a woman's anatomy too, so lovingly describable in French—*praline, petit pain, l'as de trèfle, lucarne enchantée*—while the words used in English seemed rather unpleasant.

"Yes, I see it all, the missing pieces are all here now, I can begin, we can get under way," Cray joyfully told Woly on the telephone. "You can start over there by organizing the second unit for the helicopter shots. I've begun work on a rough script."

32

Cave Canem

Gabriel suddenly turned up on the day Anne-Sophie was unexpectedly injured. Tim and Anne-Sophie had been invited out to Etang-la-Reine to lunch with the Crays and Delia, and had been asked to bring Anne-Sophie's famous mother Estelle, of whom Cray was an admirer, or so he said. Tim would also have expected Anne-Sophie and Delia to have much in common, both involved in the antiques business, but he had never once heard them talk shop. Perhaps it didn't occur to them that they had this bond.

Anne-Sophie was excited—thrilled—at the prospect of lunching with the famous Cray, despite his behavior the first time they had met. Tim considered French people very overly film-struck. In the French mind, Cray was a great *auteur* of legendary significance. And as Anne-Sophie was in some ways a compendium of received French ideas, she had never got over being amazed that Tim was seeing Cray so often, in a position of trust and intimacy. On the other hand, the Crays were impressed that Anne-Sophie was the daughter of Estelle d'Argel.

It was a Sunday, Anne-Sophie's busiest day, but she had arranged for Monsieur Lavalle to mind the stall, and they arrived about one o'clock. Senhora Alvares was there, though she didn't usually work on Sundays, and a waft of lunchtime cooking encouraged them as they walked warily up the steps, no dogs in evidence. Estelle declared herself ravished by the late flowers and general woodsy ambiance, and the encouraging smells of food.

Meeting Cray, Anne-Sophie was at her most Watteau-esque, rosy and dimpling; Cray, alas, was more taciturn than usual, impervious to pretty women. Tim wondered if that might not be a chacteristic of all directors, who are inundated with them. Still, he was civil to Tim, and even warm and welcoming to Estelle, whom he addressed formally as "madame," as if he were French, *"Asseyez-vous, je vous en prie, madame,"* and so on.

They were sitting on the terrace outside the kitchen in a drizzly burst of late November sun; they had all had the same impulse to catch as much of it as they could and store it against the oncoming winter. At first, Clara was nowhere to be seen. When she did drift in, she was civil but distant, especially to Cray. It was clear she had not recovered from her jail ordeal, and perhaps that was to be expected, and was perhaps irritated at having people to lunch. They sat rather stiffly at first.

"Ah, the waning of nature in autumn, such a pointed commentary on human life, it simply makes you burst with defiant libido," Estelle began, but it was a line the others did not pick up. Tim made the mistake of telling about the bookcase imbroglio, shocking himself with how his resentment came out about the five thousand dollars, and the hated sellers, the people named Flieu.

"Provençaux by their name," said Estelle, as if that explained everything. "Niçois, perhaps." Tim had often noticed how she and other French people spoke of "les Niçois" or even "the French" as if describing another group of people altogether. He used to believe this was a sign of alienation, but eventually figured out that it was a craftily inverted symbol of social solidarity—as well as a literal translation, as one must use the article in French.

"I know it was just my misunderstanding of the real estate customs, but that doesn't make it easier," he said.

"You have to be very specific with the French," said Cray. "They'll find a loophole if there is one."

"It's the principle," Tim added lamely.

Estelle laughed. "With Americans, it is always principle," she said. "It is their most disagreeable characteristic."

"If you could back out of it now, would you?" Clara asked. Her tone was pensive, as if she were thinking of something else.

"I think I would. I'd like to find another place, and start by building my own bookcases." As he spoke he realized it was true, he hated their apartment.

Anne-Sophie stared at him amazed. "*Alors*, Tim," she said, "it was you who loved it all along! I never wanted to be on the first floor!"

With an unusual display of tact, if it was not insensitivity to the potential unpleasantness of this discussion, Cray himself became talkative. He had sudden bursts of gaiety, like a man who usually lived on a desert isle, and this mood came upon him now. He liked to talk about things most people give up talking about after college—moral issues, the meaning of life, art, psychology. He had a scorn of psychoanalysis, though conceded it might be all right for others. "So you find out you hated your father, or that you're gay"—odd example, Tim thought—"what does it matter? You have the power to act as you will." Well, maybe.

But Tim liked it that he would talk unselfconsciously about art. Film was the art of images. Words had no place, almost no place, in it; the most important image in the modern world was the explosion, the way in the Renaissance the image was the triangle (why, Tim never understood), or the garotte. As the world had been created by the cohesion of matter, so it would disappear when the process reversed. He asked, did he think this was imminent, in the manner of the apocalyptic prophecies of St. John? He couldn't say.

When Cray began to talk like this, about art and apocalypse, Clara excused herself and went to see about something in the kitchen, and Anne-Sophie, who was still upset at hearing Tim's real view of their apartment, got up and wandered into the garden, around the house where vegetables were planted out of sight of the more formal area in front. She took her book.

Today she had been reading a story that had begun promisingly enough with a poor French girl just after the war who had barely enough to eat, and luckily met an American man who took her for a big meal at a restaurant where he knew all the other people, and just when she was wondering if she'd have to sleep with him, or with which of them, the book disappointingly veered off to become the story of the man character, Jake, who was not at all like Tim, and a sleazy Englishwoman, Lady Brett. Anne-Sophie had somewhat lost interest in these people but read lazily along, trying not to think of what Tim had said. It said on the jacket this stupid book was required reading for every college freshman in America, imagine!

They heard her scream.

They leapt up and dashed around the corner of the house, Tim in the lead. Anne-Sophie was sitting, stunned, on an iron garden chair, a strange man bending over her bleeding arm. The husky Tim grabbed him and threw him a few feet across the gravel, to the man's great surprise. Tim then saw from the innocent shock of his expression and Anne-Sophie's second scream that this hadn't been appropriate. The arm was laid open, and blood saturated her white blouse and jeans in pulses with the beating of her heart. Tim hesitated, would have taken her in his arms, but feared to jar her and increase her pain. All began to shout at once and stare, horrified, not knowing whether or how to stanch the wounds. They all continued to shout shouts of more or less simultaneous dismay:

"What happened?"

"Tim!"

"She's bitten, he bit her!" the stranger said, getting up. "The dog bit her!"

"*Oh, mon Dieu*" (Estelle).

Cray came lumbering around the corner with Delia limping at his side. Now Anne-Sophie was sobbing. The strange guy had a handkerchief (weird detail!) and handed it to her for a bandage.

"Gabriel!" cried Delia, seeing the man Tim had shoved. Gabriel Biller was here at last.

Tim swore. Her arm was raked with tooth marks, though perhaps superficial. "Those fucking dogs," he fumed helplessly at Cray, his eyes unable to move from the ribbons of blood soaking into Anne-Sophie's sleeve. But it was not one of the contract Rottweilers, it was a Cray house dog, a yellow Labrador, the mild-mannered Freddy, warily standing by the hedge, teeth bared.

"Freddy! Sit," said Cray, peering at Anne-Sophie's arm. The pretense of being in command when it is too late. "He's had his rabies."

Anne-Sophie still sobbed but, they now saw, more in shock than pain. How especially unsettling for her to be attacked by a dog—a woman who considered she had perfect rapport with animals.

"Sorry," Tim said to the stranger, who was brushing the gravel from his palms, Delia joyfully clinging to his arm.

"Stitches," Tim said, helping Anne-Sophie to her feet. She was already resuming her look of insouciance, the gallant sportiveness of someone who has fallen off a horse. She had a charming, brave smile for Gabriel. "The monsieur in my attic!" she said. "We know each other. I did not expect to meet again like this!"

They made her come into the house. Cray at second thought refused to believe it could have been Freddy who had done this savage thing. Anne-Sophie, assuring him it was so, was disposed to forgive the creature, who slunk behind them, abjectly cringing for forgiveness for the rest of the afternoon.

"I think he was trying to express his manhood—his doghood—he is jealous of all these fierce professional dogs," said Anne-Sophie, striving to smile gaily. The worse the things that happen to them—French people—the more admirably resolute their smiles, thought Tim.

Senhora Alvares had come with a clean towel for the arm. Clara hovered in distress, saying over and over, "He's never done anything like this before!" The man Gabriel had come to the kitchen with the rest of them, but stood diffidently in the doorway. Anne-Sophie included him in her smiles, and it emerged that they recognized each other from the flea market. Gabriel smiled too, in seeming appreciation of the amazing surprises the world contained. "The same little bitch who busted me!" he said, shaking his head as the pieces of further coincidence fell into place. The blonde with the cigarettes who had handed him over to the flics.

He stepped inside the Crays' kitchen. Delia had picked up his knapsack (did it contain the Driad Apocalypse?) and clutched it as if it were her firstborn, her eyes never leaving his handsome, unshaven, rather wild-eyed face. So they had Gabriel at last.

Some sentiment was for calling paramedics, but Cray insisted on driving Anne-Sophie to the emergency room. The nearest was in Marne-Garches-la-Tour, fifteen minutes away. Anne-Sophie was put in the rear seat of Cray's Land Rover, with Tim beside her, and Estelle rode in front next to Cray, chattering conspiratorially to him, as if they were both parents of the wounded one. At the hospital, the wound was cleaned and bandaged, the *médecin* accepted Cray's assurances about Freddy's rabies shots, gave a tetanus shot to be sure, and the party was dismissed.

Anne-Sophie insisted on returning to Etang-la-Reine. Even though this was a group of mostly Americans, because they were in France they continued with the lunch plans, knowing that meals are never skipped, even in the face of dogbite or the arrival of criminal fugitives. But Anne-Sophie was shaken and ate little. Tears occasionally sprang to her wide blue eyes, they assumed from pain, yet did not dare to touch her to comfort her, for fear of making the arm hurt more.

A place had been made at the table for Gabriel. A good-looking man about thirty, with a slight eastern European accent, but only slight, and plenty of American mannerisms, so that if you didn't know he hadn't been born in the U.S. you might not spot the faintly thickened *th*, the hardened *s*.

Over a rather haphazard entree of sardines and the fibrous, pallid tomatoes of autumn, doubtless an attempt by Senhora Alvares at some Iberian specialty, Gabriel recounted his adventures. He'd been afraid of being caught up in the murder investigation, and he had had clients to see, things to do, so he couldn't afford being detained. It was that possibility that had prompted him to skip the hotel. "I was scared at first," he said. "The guy's throat was cut. I was more shook up about that than Delia, because she'd never seen anything like that in Lake Oswego, Oregon. For her it was just sort of television. But I grew up in Rangoon."

"Rangoon?"

"It's a long story," he said, but he didn't tell it.

"It wasn't television, it was horrible," Delia protested.

"Horrible," Anne-Sophie agreed. "I nearly stepped in his blood."

Now he was relaxed and voluble, and seemed to regard the others as sympathetic compatriots, the way the runaway slaves, sure of a sympathetic audience, must have talked at way stations of the underground railroad.

There had followed two weeks of being on the lam in France. Evicted from the haven of the flea market attic, he had taken to sleeping rough or depending on the kindness of strangers—some sexual adventures were hinted at, but he did not elaborate—or in cheap hotels, with a dwindling supply of francs. There were the couple of hours of being in police custody after he was rousted by Anne-Sophie in the flea market. That had been about his passport, he said, and they had let him go when he had convinced them the passport was at his hotel, and that he had not fled, and was observing their instructions to stay around. It was the police who had told him his female companion had left the Hôtel Le Mistral, so he had imagined Delia had got her passport and gone back to Oregon.

"How I get my stuff from the hotel is something else," he said. "I guess I just go get it."

Tim told him where they had locked it up, behind the desk, and what the bill came to. It came to Tim that the Driad Apocalypse could be at the Hôtel Le Mistral too, a document worth half a million dollars languishing in the firetrap luggage room.

Gabriel didn't explain how he happened to phone the Crays' private number and find Delia. Nor did he explain how he had the Crays' phone number in the first place—perhaps he got it from Delia? The number of Clara Holly, formerly of Lake Oswego, call her if ever you get to Paris. He was animated, convincing; Delia never took her eyes off him. Nor did Clara and Anne-Sophie, Tim could not help but notice. No doubt he was a mesmerizing character, with deep-set gypsylike eyes, the longish hair, the poetic darkness.

When Delia told Gabriel about what had happened to her, she included the visit from the FBI, the two Franks like a comedy team. Hearing about them seemed to affect Gabriel. A skin of worry filmed his eyes for a second.

"I knew I had to stay away," he said.

"But why?"

"Well shit, the FBI is who I'm trying to avoid," he said.

"But why? You must have a reason."

He hesitated. "Well, I think they think I'm someone else. I don't want to be involved, whatever they think. I saw what happened to the guy in the flea market."

"That was done by Monsieur Savard," said Anne-Sophie. "He is in prison awaiting trial. A terrible thing. No one knows why he did it."

"Yeah, sure," said Gabriel glumly.

Tim would discuss all this with Cees when he could, to find out what he made of it. One detail especially:

"Well, we can put you up till you get all this straightened out," Clara said, "there's plenty of room here."

"Delia is staying here for a week or two, for work on a script," said Cray, studying Gabriel.

"Delia?" said Gabriel, as if surprised to hear about an unexpected literary side to Delia. "Great." And then, with a sudden afterthought, "Does the FBI know where to find Delia now?"

"No," Clara said. "Unless Tim told the hotel."

"I concealed your address from the hotel," Tim said. "But I gave them my phone number."

"The dress has fitted sleeves, my arm *comme ça*, how horrible," Anne-Sophie suddenly said, looking at the enormous bandage now doubling the diameter of her slender arm. As so often when she came up with references to the wedding, there was on Tim's part a second of incomprehension, of having no idea what she was talking about. Oh, her wedding dress.

Concerned that Anne-Sophie not overdo, Tim insisted they go home shortly after lunch. Gabriel was saying he'd like to take a shower, and it appeared he was going to make himself at home. Tim caught Cray giving him a significant look as they parted. Did it mean, Call me? Talk to you later? The thickness of his glasses in the slanting late afternoon sun obscured his expression. It was probable Cray would call Interpol and/or the FBI himself. Tim would call Cees, of course.

When they were alone in the car, Anne-Sophie said, "Why are we even buying the apartment if you hate it so much? It will be a curse."

33

The Shadow of the Altar

The Crays were already in defiance of the laws of France, both regarding hunting and for defacing national monuments, and now they were harboring an American fugitive, or so they assumed, though it wasn't clear which law enforcement officials were after Gabriel, if any, or for what. The French police had let him go after taking him in charge briefly in the flea market—they had let him go twice, in fact, since they had not arrested him after the murder of Monsieur Boudherbe, either. Nor did Cees think there was much reason to imagine that Gabriel was connected to the manuscript. Gabriel himself did not now emanate the acrid unwashed panicked smell of the hunted but the aftershave sweetness of the newly showered and inwardly serene. He apparently had used Cray's cologne.

Things settled into a strange impasse. There was still no way of knowing if the Gabriel they had was the caller with the stolen manuscript to sell. That was their assumption, for how else had he, like the manuscript seller, known the *liste rouge* phone number taken out in Clara's name? Cray didn't show Gabriel his manuscript collection. And Gabriel did not mention having a manuscript to sell. He stuck to some story about having been going to look at a consignment of books in cases from the poor man who was found dead. Cray got him to tell the story several times, but it was always the same.

Meantime Tim was deep in the task of finding out what had happened to the ancient boiseries and other features of the château. As it happened, this was a simple matter of examining the records of the salesrooms at Drouot. The boiseries of the salon and dining room had been sold anonymously just before the Crays moved in, and it should be easy enough to prove that they had not been involved. There were some strings that had to be pulled to learn the identity of the anonymous seller, but Tim was sure he could do that. So he now spent a large part of every day at Drouot or cultivating dealers and *commissaires-priseurs* who might remember the transaction, hoping to find the agent who had taken the panels on consignment. Cray demanded new developments every day.

Tim wasn't sure if it was marriage that was beginning to weigh on Anne-Sophie or the wedding, two things differing as a lifelong commitment to the theater would differ from stage fright. Or it could be her painful arm. She was becoming ever more testy. She snapped at little things and picked fights.

"You are absolutely uninterested in the wedding, you don't lift a finger!"

Or: "Of course it falls to me to write the thank-you letters, I don't know where that custom started, that it's always the woman."

Tim would protest, "Most of the things are for you, dishes and such."

"And why are those *my* dishes? *Merde.* I suppose you do not eat off dishes?" And she would eventually bring his nationality into it: "No American man could let himself show an interest in dishes, isn't it sad?"

"I think you are almost a feminist," he would say, teasing her, having heard that for Frenchwomen, for some reason, this was the utmost insult. She would protest noisily.

"Of course I am not a feminist! Now you are telling me I am no good at making love? You don't really want to get married, you are getting regrets. Well, maybe I am too!" She would scare herself talking like that, then kiss him with her most adorable, angelic smile.

But from these exchanges he would occasionally glimpse an inner complexity of her nature that she usually strove to conceal. In his limited experience of American women, she was the opposite of them in that respect; they were always wanting to tell you about their natures, their dark anxieties, their troubled pasts. Did a wish to talk about these things also lurk in Anne-Sophie? Was she hiding dark anxieties and a troubled past?

Anne-Sophie had been reading *Mariée* magazine, a magazine for brides which, when he leafed through it, he found was full of articles beginning "The most beautiful day of your life" or "Let us dream again of the fairy-tale day we will never forget." When she saw him reading it, she smiled, he assumed a little embarrassed at her enthusiasm, for Estelle's cynicism had tempered any uncomplicated joy she might have been feeling about the wedding with the knowledge that it might be silly, the day would pass, the bills remain, starving children could be fed with the cost of the ceremony and reception, et cetera. A wedding was just a party, made no promises, did not imply a future of felicity—that would happen or not. It was a social concession to the demands of the community that one be wed and briefly feted, then take one's place among the simple-minded breeders and wage slaves of the world.

"I was wondering if we shouldn't have *garçons d'honneur*, little pages and flower girls to carry the offering," she said. "Probably not. No. But they are sweet."

Many of her married friends by now had produced tots of four or five. "Little kids are cute in a wedding, if it isn't too late to organize," Tim said supportively.

"I'll think about it. I'll ask Madame Aix. It's probably too late." She sighed.

That the wedding weighed more heavily on her than on him was evident, for Tim would forget it for days at a time. He did think things would be easier for her if Estelle were more helpful. Many of the increasing pressures came because of Estelle. He was sure it was her popularity as an author that made *Mademoiselle Décor* ask to photograph the flowers and table decorations, and the charming young couple coming out of the church and people boozing their brains out at the reception and the like. (*"Une bouteille de champagne pour deux personnes—c'est pas possible!"* Anne-Sophie had objected, reading the recommended amounts.) Tim saw that Anne-Sophie and Estelle were both pleased at being featured in a national magazine, whether because of Estelle's eminence or their social standing, though both denied it. Both believed it would be good for their respective careers. The marriage advisor, Madame Aix, was thrilled. Her private inquiries later elicited from an American friend the probability that Tim Nolinger was the scion of an American fortune in hotels, which meant this wedding would interest a wide readership.

34

The Hunting World

Tim understood Clara Holly's attitude to hunting. Hers was a standard female American attitude—Green, tender-hearted, urban. But, though not a hunter himself, he had had no quarrel with it in the past. It just wasn't an issue he had taken much interest in. Now, when he came to consider it, he leaned toward the position of the Crays in opposing hunting, the more so since the mayor had begun playing hardball, with surveys and legal persecutions. And Tim agreed positively with Cray about the private property issues. It shocked him that the hobbies of hunters could prevail over something as basic as your right to keep people off your own land if you didn't want them there, even conceding the principles of easements and public walkways and beaches and the like. He had begun an article for *Reliance* on this subject, carefully avoiding any comment on gun issues, for *Reliance* would be convinced that Frenchmen almost as much as Americans had the right to be armed, though it might not say so in their constitution. *Reliance* believed that guns were an issue God himself had taken a side on.

"How come you write for a magazine like *Reliance*, it's for nuts," Delia said. "And then *Concern* too."

"None of your concern, ha ha," said Tim. "I can write for them both because I can see both sides."

"Both sides about gun control? Abortion?"

"Sure."

"That's disgusting," Delia said.

On hunting, Anne-Sophie was more of a *Reliance* person. Though she had stopped wearing ivory bracelets, she still saw nothing wrong with the age-old practice of shooting pheasants, which were hardly endangered. She had nothing personal against deer and rabbits, it was just that for her hunting and shooting were all about the horses and guns, the being in the woods, the camaraderie and hunt breakfasts. It was a social and even a business thing. Luckily for her business, every hunter had to have somewhere a set of hunting prints, and a decorative rack to hold his guns. This difference in their views was not something Anne-Sophie and Tim discussed, but it was there. He hoped he was not one of those men who believed their wives must agree with them in every detail.

The couple was somewhat frayed by exasperations developing out of their *travaux*, the work they were having done on their apartment. For separate reasons, they were both anxious to rid it of any traces of the previous owners, the Flieus, Tim because of the bookcases and Anne-Sophie because to obliterate the past, apparently, was the French way. So they were repainting, and redoing a bathroom. Anne-Sophie was dedicating her midweeks to supervising the work, neglecting her stand, as she recognized.

Clara was aware of her own growing detachment from the other household members, now numbering three: Serge, Delia, and Gabriel, not counting Senhora Alvares or the *maître-chien*, Patrick, or Serge's assistants Fred Connolly and Marc Duvall, who came and went, or a number of new people appended to film, who came and went at the direction of the mysteriously energized Serge. All these people seemed strangers, even her husband, and insensitive strangers, with cares of their own that rendered them incapable of seeing the great tumult she was going through. Part of her anger at Serge arose from his seeming to have forgotten her jeopardy. Even now, the Judge of Instruction was assembling a dossier about the things missing from their house, and about the sale at Drouot Tim had found, where the boiseries were sold some months before they moved in. The judges were trying to establish Clara's whereabouts at that time.

Unfortunately, no one knew who it was who had sold the boiseries. Tim had reached several dead ends. Whoever had sold them had done it anonymously, through an agent who himself did not know, or professed not to know, the identity of the seller. The trail had stopped with the Drouot records. Whether the French legal system would wring out more information remained to be seen, but Tim had done as much as he could do. Presumably it would emerge that the Crays could not have been involved, but it was possible that by some mysterious assignment of blame in French law, the Crays, in buying an already despoiled monument, made themselves legally responsible for its lack of fireplaces and denuded walls. The Cray lawyers were researching this fine point.

But the danger of Clara going to prison would vanish if they would permit hunters on their land. They were under no illusions about the quid pro quo. And her heart had hardened further about that. She had seen horrors in the village—the broken carcasses of deer, boar hanging in the butcher's shop window, their little bristly faces still wearing the expressions of fear and agony with which they had turned in their final moments to face the dogs or the guns—she could not tell if they had been shot or harried to death. It seemed especially ugly to her that a hunter would sell his catch to a butcher, giving the lie to their claim to kill for tradition's sake or even to feed their families. It was merely commerce and the love of blood.

Antoine de Persand came over a second time, this time to invite the Crays to his house for lunch the following Sunday. He had something to propose to them, and wished also to make a gesture of neighborly support in view of their increasing isolation in a sea of hostile press and legal jeopardy.

Delia's indolence continued to irk Clara, and so did the time she spent with Serge, or in endless telephone discussion with the antique dealers of Sweet Home, Oregon. Gabriel she found charming. He would talk with equal passion of books or politics—but he also talked of organizing his passage and leaving France. Serge had advised him to be on the safe side by taking a train to somewhere like Brussels or Amsterdam and leaving from there in case his name was down on some French list of people to be stopped at the airport.

Gabriel had the more immediate problem of claiming his belongings, including his passport, at the Hôtel Le Mistral. This he planned to do today; Serge had given him money and Clara had offered to drive him into Paris when she took Delia to the Louvre.

Delia had wanted to go every day to the Louvre. A few days before, when she tried it on her own, by bus and train, she had come back so tired that Clara had volunteered to drive her the next day and each day on the weekend. Today they would all go into Paris—

Gabriel to pay his hotel bill, Delia to go to the Louvre, Clara to look in on poor Anne-Sophie, whose bitten arm was keeping her home though she would usually be in the flea market on a Monday.

This would be the fourth or fifth time Delia had gone to the Louvre, staying only an hour or so each time, which had struck Clara as an intelligent, rather disciplined way to approach the vast riches of this monumental place. But she was a little surprised that Delia found so much to occupy her there. She did not think of Delia as someone profoundly interested in art, beyond the obligatory views of the Venus de Milo, the Victory of Samothrace, the Mona Lisa, and the strange painting of the two French duchesses or whatever they were, the one pinching the nipple of the other, always ogled by tourists, on which Delia remarked with disapproval.

Before the arrival of Gabriel, it had crossed Clara's mind that perhaps Delia and he had secret rendezvous there, she mentioned so often her wish to go there. The Louvre would be a perfect place to meet someone discreetly—her mind worked like this now. She imagined herself walking through the Flemish rooms with Antoine de Persand, hearing his thoughts on Van Eyck. Lunch at the Grand Vefour, then long afternoons of sex at the Hôtel du Louvre or maybe the Opéra Concorde, or maybe in an apartment he would rent, you heard Frenchmen had garçonnières where their wives never went. When she thought like this, her underthings would get damp. Antoine de Persand was on her mind almost as much as the imminence of jail.

Today she let Delia out on the rue de Rivoli near the entrance to the Louvre—"I'll meet you right here"—and drove to see Anne-Sophie, miraculously finding a parking place right in front of the building. She found Anne-Sophie apparently in the course of writing thank-you notes or dealing with responses to the wedding invitations. A stack of nesting envelopes and little cards of various sizes were piled on the coffee table. Anne-Sophie proferred one.

"Does this look right to you? Madame Aix says it is, but she's looking at it from the French point of view. Tim's parents are divorced, that's why Monsieur Gerald Nolinger and Madame Barzun Nolinger on a different line. You see we put their page in English? I have a friend who is marrying a man from Louvain and they put the page of invitation from his family in Flemish."

"Do you expect many people from America?"

"Many more than I thought," said Anne-Sophie. "I think a lot of his relatives had been thinking they were due for a nice French vacation anyway. We have already booked the hotels. Tim has *a belle poignée* of relatives. Also some of his friends from college."

"We're looking forward to our part—the rehearsal dinner. Serge is very involved, you know. Plans are progressing."

"Oh, we are very pleased," Anne-Sophie said. "It is *si gentil*. And for the reception after the wedding, what do you think about a cake? Madame Aix says that a 'wedding cake' with several tiers would be more chic than a croquembouche, especially as one is marrying an American. White icing, with amusing little figures on top, and decorated with flowers and sugar bells. There are a number of patisseries in Paris that would know how to construct such a cake."

"You should have both," Clara decided. "Croquembouche for the Americans, they've never seen one."

At five she went to pick up Delia at the appointed spot on the rue de Rivoli. Gabriel was with her, and without luggage.

"They're watching the hotel," he said. "A guy in the cafe across the street, it was completely obvious. I didn't go in."

"But they had you once, they let you go. Why would they be watching the hotel?"

"Not the French, the FBI," he said.

"Surely it can't be so complicated," cried Clara, suddenly exasperated with the cloaks and daggers, feeling, not for the first time, that Delia and Gabriel were carrying their strange game, whatever it was, too far. "Just write me an *attestation* and I'll go get your suitcase myself."

35

Take It Off, Take It Off

The arrival of the guard dogs at the Crays' meant that the local postman, who in any case would have sympathized with the mayor, refused to deliver mail to the house and instead left it in a big box by the front gate. It was necessary to go into town in person to pick up a registered letter, and when one arrived on Thursday, Cray suggested Tim go with Clara. Tim knew he was deteriorating into an errand boy, but he didn't care, he was interested in the whole situation, knew there'd be a story eventually, and felt quite reckless in his fascination with Clara.

But he was beginning really to suffer from the contradictions in his own life, marching steadfastly toward the altar with Anne-Sophie while hoping on some level to seduce Clara Holly, and knowing all the same there wasn't the least chance of that. He knew that to her he was just an eager man of her own age who danced attendance on her husband. There was also her curious (to him) attachment to the idea of marital fidelity. While he had no intention of being an unfaithful husband, once married—all this imagined torrid sex with the beautiful Clara having occurred like backstory before the present of married life would unfold—it was becoming troubling the way it kept popping unbidden into his reveries.

When Tim's five thousand dollars arrived, sent by his mother from his account, something in him rebelled—a huge sum to plunk down for some French bookcases he was already mortgaged for and morally entitled to. He thought he was probably being petty, and knew he was being unreasonable given that this was the French custom, but he brooded. There were a zillion better things to do with this money. A big diamond for Anne-Sophie, some crazy trip for the two of them.

"Ha ha, you look like a man who's getting married soon," Cray had said one day. "Who was it said that with marriage women change their names and men their natures? Relax. Marriage is an excellent condition. That is, for an uxorious type like me. The House of Uxor. I wonder if that was a pun in Poe's mind? I must check the etymology. . . ."

Was it true that men changed their natures? Apparently not, in Tim's case; he knew he was going to go along being the same old person no matter how much he would like to have the fresh heart and ardor of a newlywed.

Clara drove them in her car to the post office. She wore the vague, dreamily preoccupied expression she had worn since her week in jail.

"What do you think of Serge's plans? Do you think the film will work? What does he tell you?"

"Wouldn't know. It's Delia he talks to. All they seem to talk about is doomsday and black helicopters."

"I don't go to America often enough. I should know more about all that."

"You've read his box of clippings."

"If you believe what you read, the world is coming to an end next year. Serge believes there are millions of paranoids with guns, vast arsenals of white supremacist weapons, lone enforcers, vengeance-obsessed pipe bombers who'll be out there."

"The reality isn't in question. I kind of worry about what he's going to make of it," Tim said. "I'm not sure I understand his politics."

Clara sighed. "Nor I."

Clara double-parked outside the post office and went in. Tim got out of the car to watch the village doings, and could therefore see that three or four men in hunting clothes getting out of a van in front of the boulangerie had seen her and now were hurrying toward the post office shouting, *"C'est elle,"* and *"Voilà la dame."* The woman who stole the boiseries from the château. She who impedes hunting.

In the few minutes it took for Clara to collect her letter, a knot of about twenty people had assembled outside the post office. Concerned, Tim moved nearer the door of the building to wait for her. She stopped in the doorway when she saw the crowd, wondering what was going on. He moved toward her, but not before others began a demonstration of angry shouting, random accusations of troublemaking and variations on Yankee-go-home. They did not look like rough farmers so much as city people dressed in their weekend clothes, but they made a mutter that sounded rough and rural. "That's her." "Yeah." "Oh, so that's her."

Then one of them shouted, *"On voudrait te voir déplumée."* *"A poil!"* Strip, like you've stripped us. Somebody else added, *"Oui, à poil,* let's see her naked." This caused laughter and more shouting. Tim remembered that a woman government minister had recently been similarly harassed. The implications of depluming soon took on a rather lewd urgency, for Clara's beauty did not escape this bunch of Frenchmen. Take it off, they shouted. They advanced closer to her. Now Tim was seriously worried and began to push his way through them to her side.

"A poil, let's see her bare." It seemed that they might tear at her clothes. Someone shouted a solution à la Lady Godiva to the hunting ban.

Clara saw Tim and reached out for him from where she stood on the steps with the men pressing in on her. Tim threw his shoulder into the scrum, knocking one man who pushed him back. Tim might have hit him, felt inclined to start a fight. But he restrained himself. That wouldn't help Clara. Tim again threw his shoulders into the throng, moved a few more people, who stared at him as if his violence was excessive; he sheltered her in his arms. The crowd parted, and they hurried the few steps to her car.

She shook and was slightly damp with fear. He clumsily cradled her in his arms, and planted his lips to her brow where it was moist at the hairline, and pushed her into the driver's seat. That was the extent of an embrace he had often imagined in further detail. He got in on the passenger side. In the instant he had held her, he had felt her heart pounding. A phrase came to him from Anne-Sophie's wedding magazine—*coeur en chamade.* That he could feel her inner turmoil suggested that she was a woman of almost unnatural self-possession, protection against some violence or passion within her, that might someday break out. He was lost. He loved her hopelessly and against his will.

The hunters, half laughing, half angry, crowded the car but made no effort to impede them as they started up. Then Clara shifted into the wrong gear, first instead of reverse. As it lurched forward into the crowd of men, she slammed on the brakes and killed the motor. The men pulled back from this dangerous display of inept driving, except for one who screamed, *"Mon pied, mon pied! Madame!"* She had stopped on his foot.

"Oh no, oh shit," she cried. "How could I do that?"

Tim leapt out to stare at the man's foot pinned under the front wheel. The victim stood stone still for fear of further injury, or because he could not move. Tim growled something to the effect that he had better move his ass.

He couldn't, of course. Clara had to back off his foot. Staring at the gearshift as if fearing to make a mistake and run over him altogether, she carefully started the car, put it in reverse, and released his foot. She drove a few feet off, planning to get out herself to inspect the damage. But the injured man limped away, his face a scowl of imminent lawsuit. Tim watched him, got in, and Clara pulled into the road.

"I don't know if it breaks your foot to have it driven on, maybe not?" she said.

"It probably doesn't, those little flexible bones in the foot. He was walking perfectly."

"I didn't feel anything, I should have felt his foot," she kept saying, and "Are you sure you saw him walking away?" At least her mind was off the nasty little episode on the post office steps.

But she was shaken in several ways, and after that didn't want to go anywhere alone.

The registered letter, no surprise, turned out to be from the *mairie*, announcing a survey of local roads and the terrain adjoining them, which would require the presence of surveyors on the property of Monsieur et Madame Cray.

This incident more than rattled Clara. Emotions had got out of hand in a moment, but the larger implication was that she and Serge, despite the fact that people nodded to them in the shops or at the little concerts sometimes held in the Bibliothèque Municipale, were hated and had been insulted. The insinuating, lewd jeers, and someone actually pulling as if to rip her sleeve, had been as degrading as the jail, and in some way more frightening. The unpopular game she and Serge were playing had revealed its dangers. She thought of the oiled gun cases, the hand-carved decoys she saw in shops for thousands of francs, the boots and knickers—male privilege, old-world custom, a strange country and they had run afoul of some deep stream in it, some buried barbarism and passion. She thought of the American South, of the Klan—could the burnt crosses happen, or the charred corpses happen, in peaceful, semi-rural France?

She called her mother after this, not to talk about what had happened but to ask if her mother let hunters across the field behind the paddock in the pheasant season.

"Oh, honey." Mrs. Holly laughed. "That's years. Since they put those subdivisions in behind the Thrifty, they don't hunt around here, it'd be someone's backyard. Your father would go out for pheasant, but they had to go as far as Medford by the end," she said.

It was after the incident at the post office that he let himself realize that, more than wanting to sleep with her, he'd fallen in love with Clara too, by itself a fact he tried not to pay too much attention to, given the existence of Anne-Sophie and Cray, his ignorance of her state of mind about anything, and his general sense of unworthiness (though, to tell the truth, he considered himself less unworthy than the fat Cray or a balding Frenchman like Persand). He could just put up with the hot promptings of desire, the adolescent panic, the yearning, but he deplored his regression from the sincere, joyful, and easy love he felt for Anne-Sophie. He didn't like having to be aware of his emotions at all. He brooded. He felt love, but would settle for sex. If he could entice her to sleep with him once, it would ease his misery. He would settle for one time. That would get sex out of the way, relegating it to the status of mere memory, a dream of the ideal. Then he'd be ready for marriage.

36

Tim and Antoine Talk

Another thing that had shaken Clara was the realization that it was not entirely by accident she had driven onto the man's foot. For an instant, in a fury, in a panic, she could have driven straight into the throng of men without remorse, even with glee. The men who had said *"à poil"* and might have put their hands on her. Wanted to put their hands on her, in anger, and under their anger the thing they could do to a woman. She had liked it when Tim Nolinger had roughed up the one. She felt her life was descending into primitive regions of fear and lust, and that at some level she was finding these better than lassitude.

In her heart an elaborate set of rationalizations was evolving: life is so short, one must seize on happiness, even happiness as thinly defined as one moment of passion, a fleeting instant of being loved, of loving in a feverish paroxysm of sensation and emotion not destined to be repeated, after which you give yourself up to good works. She would promise to give herself up to good works and the devoted attention Serge needed for his genius to flourish, and to Lars if only he would be returned to her, in exchange for some happy uncomplicated sex soon, some kind of funny joy with a relative stranger, all the better, no complications or future. That the stranger was resolved against all this was a separate problem.

And she didn't even know the woman who was thinking, feeling this way. She was a stranger too.

Clara brought up marital fidelity as a subject so often that it must have been weighing on her. Or rather, Tim could see, infidelity was on her mind whether she knew it or not. Was it possible she was worrying about Delia and Cray spending so much time together? Delia was often up in Cray's study for an hour or two at a time. But Clara denied feeling concerned.

"Serge and Delia?" Clara would say. "Why would I care? It

could be a sign that his creative energy is coming back. Wouldn't that be more important than so-called fidelity? Fidelity and infidelity are nonissues for me—it's so unimportant which person you sleep with, finally. I can't see why people throw their lives away. Anyway, Serge?" Still it was clear she was irritated by Delia.

Cray for his part seemed irritated by Gabriel. "I'm throwing the bastard out on Saturday, forty-eight hours from now, regardless if he's made himself clear or not. This isn't a flophouse. Besides, I'm not taking a chance on pissing off the French, in view of Clara's problem. They accept you if you fudge the letter of the law, but flagrant defiance is not well received. If they're looking for him, I'm not harboring him."

"So far as I can find out, no one's looking for him, unless he's got the manuscript," Tim said. He noticed that Cray said "Clara's problem" and not "our problem." "Maybe we should just ask him, has he got the fucking manuscript?"

"Saturday he goes, manuscript or not."

Soon after this, at the Tennis Club Marne-Garches-la-Tour, Tim was surprised to be greeted in a friendly way by Antoine de Persand, who was changing into tennis clothes in the locker room. He was naked, putting on his jockstrap. Unwillingly, Tim looked at him—a strong guy, about his own height, with the pale torso and brown limbs of a tennis player, muscled, with a heavy penis, though he turned modestly aside when Tim came in. Persand made him promise to join him for a beer after their respective matches. After his hour with Adrian, Tim wandered into the lounge area. Persand, now in street clothes, was standing at the bar, broodily drinking a beer. He greeted Tim and ordered more beer. Tim thought of various things Persand could be wanting to say to him. It would be about the Crays. They moved to a table.

"I heard about the episode in the village. Deeply shameful. Lucky thing that you were there. My wife was in the post office and saw it."

"It might have turned ugly, but it didn't," Tim agreed. He strangely found himself unwilling to indulge Persand's plain wish to hear all about the incident at the post office, but he did, describing it in more detail. What, after all, did he have against Persand?

"Feeling is strong against the Crays, even among people who don't hunt. I don't include myself. I have nothing against them. I understand Americans. I have an American sister-in-law, for one thing," Antoine said. He didn't have to explain what the strong feelings were about. Meddlesome foreigners go home.

"I think the Crays are pretty stunned—her arrest, the attack, and so on. Of course they had nothing to do with removing the boiseries and fireplaces from their house."

"We've invited them to lunch on Sunday. I hope you and Anne-Sophie can come too. I haven't congratulated you on your *fiançailles*. We've known Anne-Sophie since she was a little girl, you know. Her father was my father's doctor."

"You heard she was bitten by one of Crays' dogs?"

He hadn't heard. Persand looked at him, as if trying to guess how this would have affected Tim's relations with Cray. They chatted a bit more. Against his inclination, Tim began to like Persand. He seemed gentlemanly and depressed. Tim waited for what he expected, some mention of Clara. This followed.

"Very hard for Madame Cray, I imagine," Persand said presently. "It seems unjust that she take the brunt of the man's intransigence."

"I believe she agrees with him. They're both opposed to hunting."

Persand said nothing to this. He mentioned other things—a proposed change in the dues at the club, Chirac, the longevity of the late René Lacoste, in his day the greatest tennis player of France, as an argument for tennis playing. Persand was charming, but Tim felt wary, and too aware of the unspoken subject, Clara. He accepted the invitation to lunch.

37

Public Opinion

In the villages of Etang-la-Reine and in nearby Val-Saint-Rémy, in all the commune of Val-Lanval, and as far as Paris, local sentiment was engaged on the issues of the boiseries and the hunting both. In a matter of days, in the minds of the hunters of the commune of Val-Lanval, Clara Holly had become the symbol of America eroding the rightful heritage of France. The word *déplumer*, to defeather, was seized on in the press for its apt allusion to fowl and fowl play. Critical articles about the Crays appeared in the local *Le Quotidien*; also a sentimental piece on Madame du Barry's legacy to the neighborhood, and the crime of obliterating it by remodelling her house.

Almost immediately after Clara's release pending the preparation of the dossier, French politicians and the French press also got involved in *l'affaire Cray*. The Green press seized on one fact that came to light: that the hunters of the commune of Val-Lanval were shooting—ducks, mainly, but also some species more endangered than ducks—ahead of the date approved by the European Community and longer. This splendid opportunity to attack the right-wing French president for caving in to chauvinist special-interest hunting groups did not go unused, as *Le Monde* put it. CHIRAC DEFIES STRASBOURG FOR RIGHT TO SHOOT.

On the other hand, the right-wing press attacked the socialist minister of the environment in the name of law and order, for not cracking down on these illegal game practices humiliating to the good name and honor of *la France*. Thus newspaper opinion from the perspectives of both left and right tended to be against the hunters.

But popular French opinion was quite understandably also against the Crays for monument desecration. There were some factions that believed the Crays were being treated lightly because of his fame, and others who thought the system was socking it to them for the same reason, inspired by the film protectionists.

The court date was set for Clara's tribunal to report on December 7. The American ambassador, Charlie Nolan, protested to the French minister of justice that American citizens with their papers in order were being unfairly prosecuted for things they could not possibly be guilty of. "Egad, Jean-Louis, the poor devils had not even bought the place yet!" The socialist minister of the environment protested to the press that Americans who had desecrated French national monuments were being specially protected by the president's opposing party—Americans who did not scruple to occupy and deface national monuments, and impede the hunting traditions of France, and must be punished. And so on.

Brussels announced that it would consider a complaint about the French violation of EC rules in the matter of the shooting dates, as a sort of amicus in the action brought in Strasbourg, so in a sense the issue was joined all over Europe.

L'affaire Cray, said Clovis Mornay, a leading French intellectual, on a panel on French television's Canal Plus on *l'antiaméricanisme,* was a perfect example of how the innate American desire for hegemony, expressed by private citizens as much as in actions by the state, was attempting to interfere with the centuries-old traditions of France. It also was an example of Hollywood arrogance, and Hollywood was itself an informal arm of the American state, perhaps even, covertly, an actual arm.

"Their ultimate goal is the simplification of the French mind, to prepare it for reprogramming by American moralizers. First you must obliterate history—in this case a tradition of hunting in this country probably going back to the Bronze Age."

"Yes, there's something to what he says," said Estelle to her longtime friend Cyrille Doroux, the academician. "The American lack of subtlety. Their minds are simpler."

"Decidedly."

"Even Tim, though very nice, has something of that tendency to oversimplification."

"They never think politically," agreed Monsieur Doroux. "Only moralistically, Mornay is quite right."

38

Lunch at the Persands

Anne-Sophie was not pleased that Tim had agreed to a country lunch at the Persands on Sunday. She had to work, she complained; she had a business, Sunday was her most important day. Was this a foretaste of his expectations when they were married, that she would drop everything on any Sunday for a trivial social engagement, or to oblige Serge Cray? But when the day was fine, she relented, provided Tim would drive her to the flea market at six A.M. in the pitch darkness, and return at noon to pick her up after his errand at the Hôtel Le Mistral.

This was the morning he had promised to try to redeem Gabriel Biller's bags. Cray had postponed his confrontation with the man pending the success of this venture, and Biller had figured that if Tim went on Sunday morning, at the change of clerk, there was a chance that the new desk person would be someone who had seen neither Tim nor Gabriel. To be certain, though, Tim carried Gabriel's credit card and driver's license, and though he and Gabriel looked nothing alike in person, the thuggish photo could be either of them or anyone else of a nice-looking, thirtyish, male sort, the coloring ambiguous.

There was no problem at all. The man behind the desk had never seen Tim or Biller. He calculated the charges, opened the luggage room, and brought out the jacket and rucksack and small suitcase, which Tim remembered was not locked. In the car he glanced inside it. There were a few papers, and nothing looking like a valuable medieval manuscript. He put it all in the trunk and went to pick up Anne-Sophie.

Monsieur Lavalle had not come in as he had promised, Anne-Sophie said, so she had to roll down her shutter for the rest of the day, doubtless losing enormous revenue. She had the slightly self-satisfied air of someone who is behaving handsomely. Tim kissed her, careful not to press her injured arm, which had been re-dressed in an even bigger roll of batting and tape, and they headed toward the Porte de Saint-Cloud.

Until the lunch invitation, Clara had not realized the Persand place adjoined theirs in one spot where there was no fence. Through the woods one could just see a pleasant stone manor house, eighteenth century, mansarded, on a sizeable number of hectares, although probably fewer than once had belonged to it. She and Tim had walked along the property line one day earlier in the week, looking for the explanation of Persand's saying that he was their neighbor. Waking the day after that, she put her opera glasses in the pocket of her Eddie Bauer jacket and walked in the woods alone before Delia and Serge got up. But of course it had been Wednesday, and no one lived in the Persands' place during the week.

When she realized it was his house, she had felt a sense of embarrassment almost as strong as when she had spoken so boldly to him in the prison visiting room, those impulsive words that, since then, she had gone over and over in her mind, hoping to find room for ambiguity in them, so that he, in reviewing their meeting, might think she had not at all meant what she had meant. He would see he had been mistaken to think she meant anything, let alone a bold sexual overture. Alas, her words had not been ambiguous at all.

Today Cray, stout and no great walker, announced that he and Delia would drive to the Persands'. "I'm not really invited," Delia protested, "I don't think they meant me." But Cray insisted she was coming. He seemed not to mind when Clara said she would rather walk through the woods. The day was crisp and sunny, a day for tramping over the fallen leaves, for enjoying the fugitive dappled motes of light through the thickets. The woods were silent, with no sounds of hunter or hunted. She set out in advance of the others, and would meet them there.

Thinking of this now, when she came to the Persand land, she could see the back of the stone house, a tennis court, tricycles. Surely he didn't have young children? Her heart raced in consternation. That would mean a young wife. Perhaps a second wife?

Grandchildren were not impossible. Her spirits were in a considerable turmoil generally, on the one hand hoping she would notice something disappointing that would diminish her fascination with him and on the other hoping there would be a significant moment, perhaps a moment alone with him—she thought of scenes in film in which the lord of the manor shows the heroine the billiard room or wine cellar. . . . She feared equally that Madame de Persand would be beautiful and that she would be ugly, which would remind her that Monsieur de Persand was after all only a middle-aged banker from next door. She derided herself for these really infantile emotions. Nothing in the least like this had ever happened to her.

As she walked around to the front, she could see that Tim and Anne-Sophie were there already, and Serge's Land Rover was just pulling into the drive. The door was opened at once, by Monsieur de Persand, in khaki pants and an open shirt like an American. She had a quick impression she herself was overdressed in a smart pantsuit and cashmere sweater. She looked beyond him to see what Anne-Sophie, the perfect Française, was wearing and was relieved to see she was wearing the same.

Clara smiled at Antoine with distant friendliness; he might have been the *boulanger*. She put her jacket on the pile of jackets on a little *canapé* in the hall and looked around. A comfortable country house with a certain air of disorder—innumerable mud boots of all sizes, umbrellas, and a nice but chipped porcelain vase on the table. Beyond, in the next room, she saw books, and curtains a century old of faded puce velour beside the long windows. But she was not able to sustain the smile of perfect indifferent friendliness she had hoped for, for inwardly her heart had lurched at the sight of the boots—those must be his, calf-high, for riding or hunting, boots bringing thoughts of his strong calves, of a man's strong thighs, of men riding, of white breeches, of— She felt herself flush. Was she in such a state of heat and vulnerability as to be provoked by even mud boots into this painful state of desire? His handshake was friendly, without pressure. He did not kiss her on both cheeks as he might have, perfectly customary between neighbors. She felt that desire was just another humiliation in store for her; probably there were others too; she was doomed to live in torment like someone in Dante. She smiled radiantly.

There were antlers at one end of this hall, she noticed, over a wide door leading to the salon, where Persand led them now, with affable, welcoming, rather general words for Serge and Delia who had entered too.

"Madame my mother is here this weekend, my daughter, also one or two of my nephews, as usual," he explained. "We use the house all winter when the weather is good like this."

Anne-Sophie, in the salon, was already greeting an older blond woman, small and handsome, wearing a skirt and high-heeled city shoes. For a second Clara wondered, could this be Monsieur de Persand's wife? But of course it was his mother. "My wife, Trudi," he went on now, of another woman who came in, in her mid-forties, hair brown with blond streaks like half the women in France, smiling in a friendly way.

"I'm Trudi, welcome," she said, clearly less comfortable than her husband with English.

The older Madame de Persand spoke it with great precision. "We've been rather negligent neighbors, I am sorry to say. We have been reclusive but now we are resolved to reform. We heard about the appalling way you were treated at the post office, madame."

"Thank you, it was a harmless thing really," Clara said.

"It *was* appalling," Tim Nolinger agreed. "I thought we had a possibly ugly incident on our hands."

"Tim was very gallant." Clara laughed. She looked more closely at Trudi, who was taller than she; an attractive woman, but there was nothing special about her.

Antoine turned to Serge and Delia, still lingering by the salon door.

"What will you drink?" He suggested that they usually drank kir vermouth at this hour, on this day of the week. An orderly Sunday lunch—Clara began to relax a little.

"I know it is usual for people of my age to rail against the manners of the modern age," the older Madame de Persand went on, "but really! And do not think I imagine that those were simple farmers, no, those were our bourgeois neighbors in their weekend clothes. Or some of them were. Of course they were imitating the recent episode with the cabinet minister, amusing themselves. They would not behave like that in town. *Déplorable.*"

"It was awful, the how do you say? the bad manners—I saw it

all," Trudi agreed. "I was inside the *poste*. I was going to call the police—I had my portable. Then monsieur broke it up." She smiled at Tim. "Of course, I don't think they really meant Madame Cray any harm."

"I was sure they would not hurt me," said Clara loftily, though she had not been sure.

"We might almost play tennis today," Antoine remarked. "Did you bring your things?" Tim was the only one who had tennis stuff in the car, so they had to play singles.

In the garden room, a glassed-in addition looking into the garden, the others had their kirs. It seemed to Clara the talk was entirely of misfortune. Besides the incident at the post office, there was Anne-Sophie's arm, a blight in a small champagne vineyard still owned by the Persand family, the general deterioration of things in the Balkans. Tim and Antoine played a set of singles, the players visible from here, Tim perhaps prevailing, though not soundly enough to irritate his host. The women could tell the game was amicable and well matched.

How beautiful men were at play, Clara thought. She thought of Greek vases, of the naked men with javelins or wrestling.

The long oval dining table could extend, she inferred from the leaves that stood unceremoniously against the wall, to huge proportions. Today they were merely eleven: Serge and Clara, Delia, Anne-Sophie and Tim, Trudi and Antoine, two nephews, a demure fourteen-year-old daughter named Garance, and Madame de Persand. Clara was put on Antoine's right, with Anne-Sophie on his left. Madame de Persand had Cray and Tim; the others ranged up and down the sides, with Trudi amid them, closest to the kitchen and in a position to keep order among the teenagers.

Clara watched with interest and the triflingest pang as Antoine shelled the bandaged Anne-Sophie's *moules* for her, which caused him to turn more often to Anne-Sophie than to her. Did Anne-Sophie find him attractive? Was she as aware as Clara of his manly allure? Or was it her reflex flirtatiousness that made her dimple up at Antoine and laugh, it seemed to Clara, a bit too much? Yes, there was definitely some extra sparkle to Anne-Sophie's smile, some consciousness of her own femininity. Antoine turned to Clara with hostlike regularity, interrupting Anne-Sophie's chatter to pass Clara a dish or make some polite inquiry.

She asked about his American sister-in-law, whom she knew slightly, and was told she was well. She tried to think who else they might know in common. She complimented his backhand. She mentioned a trade dispute that threatened to deprive Americans of Vuitton handbags.

"What are you working on, Monsieur Cray?" asked Madame de Persand. "Can we expect another film? I expect you detest being asked about that."

"Not at all, madame," said Cray, who was being heavily genial and neighborly. "I am making a film about American right-wing protest. Of course it's more complicated than that. About little people in barns and covens, planning to hide from the black helicopters. People storing up food for the millennium when the world comes apart. Vast tracts of land in Montana and Idaho where the guns are cached. The Rapture—trying to get all of this in. A film about America. Modest-sounding?"

He laughed, and his strange, smart eyes watched the listeners, gauging his effect. His effect was to silence the rest of them for a moment. Clara could hear the practiced paragraphs of a pitch, as though they were a group of studio heads. Not that Serge was obliged to pitch to studio heads. They let him do what he wanted, if he would only do it.

"Who do you hope for the stars?" Trudi de Persand asked eventually.

Cray frowned.

"'Whom', *chérie*," said Suzanne de Persand. "In English one says 'whom' at the beginning of a sentence. For some reason."

"Whom," repeated Trudi in the resigned tone of someone who knows she will never really speak this foreign language.

"Are you in sympathy with all these people, or against them?" Antoine asked Cray.

"I suppose my ambivalence will show. There's much to admire in them, and much to fear. Much that is creepy, scary, and much that is noble. Fanaticism has its noble side." His voice took on an interviewed intonation.

"Difficult to agree with that, monsieur," mused Persand. "Fanaticism seems always bad."

"Delia has taught me a lot. She's in the thick of it." Cray smiled at her. "Especially the Y2K thing. She thinks the world is going to end at the end of 1999."

"Well, not really. I don't know what to think," Delia said. "There's plenty of evidence, people who look into it. I just don't have that much of a tendency to think about it. Some people are more religious and spiritual than others. If the world ended tomorrow, I'd just think, shit, I never got my hip fixed. But I respect their concerns."

"Whom would like some more *moules*? Will you have some?" asked Trudi, getting up and moving toward the kitchen.

"Fanaticism is always ugly—and, finally, futile, does not history show?" Antoine went on, with the merest undecipherable glance at his wife.

"Not at all. History shows that eventually it works," Serge said.

"Of course America does not feel an interest in history, I realize that," said Persand.

"We have history," objected Delia.

"It's not fair to speak of 'America,' " objected Clara at the same time. "It's so big and various."

"That's right," agreed Tim. "Europeans tend to think of it as one place."

"Where is the real America located, then?" asked Madame de Persand with polite interest. "Washington, I suppose. Or New York?"

"Oh no!" cried Delia and Clara and Serge separately.

"No one agrees," Tim explained. "There are so many Americas. Europeans don't realize this. It's something I've tried to write about."

"Perhaps that's why no one seems to take responsibility for America's more mischievous doings," mused Madame de Persand. "If you ask Americans about what their country has done in Bosnia or Vietnam, they just stare at you, as if to say, what could it possibly have to do with them?"

"I always used to think the reason I didn't feel guilty for American problems was because of being brought up in Europe,"

Tim said. "But in college I realized that no one feels guilty for the behavior of America because it's so big. Everyone is so far away from the policymakers. America is too vast to generate much solidarity."

"He means we each feel the problem is all the other assholes— the Southerners, or New Yorkers. But Europeans think we are all the same—all assholes." Cray laughed.

"You are not familiar with *moules* perhaps, mademoiselle? I urge you to try one," said Suzanne to Delia, noticing her plate still heaped with mussels in their shells. Perhaps she wanted to avert a serious discussion.

"I have this shellfish allergy," Delia said. "We *have* mussels in Oregon. They *grow* in Oregon."

"Really?" said Madame de Persand.

"Give them to me," said Serge and pulled her plate nearer himself. Clara could not look at him lifting the shells and popping the gruesome little gobbets of flesh into his mouth.

"I was wrong to say history. Perhaps it is memory that America does not seem to have," began Antoine. "She seems to live in the now."

"We are having pheasant. They were just brought in, but perhaps they should have been hung," said Suzanne, persisting in changing the subject. "We shall see."

Clara in her mind's eye saw the hanging of pheasants in the butcher's window, their shimmering breasts dulled, their crests limp and eyes unseeing. Could it be Antoine who shot these pheasants? Her throat suddenly felt very dry, so that the food was hard to swallow. Was this some sort of joke or criticism of their attitudes to hunting? Or had they simply not reflected? She did not eat. Her mind drifted into a reverie of being somewhere else, alone with him.

When she returned her attention to the table, Antoine was saying to Serge, "My idea is to sell you some hectares at my back, which will expand your holdings into safe territory. I can spare two or three without myself coming under the twenty-hectares limit, and it would just suffice for you."

"That's a damned generous thing," Serge said, startled.

"I don't mean to make you a gift of it, to be sure." Antoine smiled. "Land in this region is expensive. It would set you back some."

Suzanne and Trudi were staring at him in disbelief.

"*Mais, c'est vrai,* this is not the moment—we can discuss—
another time." He seemed suddenly embarrassed to have made
public this handsome offer, as if asking for his good nature to be
noticed. Or perhaps he was unnerved by the disapproving astonishment of his wife and his mother.

"It's a good idea," Serge said. "That could checkmate the
mayor nicely."

39

A Walk in the Woods

As all French Sunday lunches must, so this one ended in going for a walk, the obligatory brisk, restorative, health-preserving tramp, whether along country lanes or adjacent green spaces, around a park, or even in the street if one is stuck in the city. Even Cray was bound by this imperative. The party set out together into the public *forêt* between the Persands' and the village of Etang-la-Reine. Now, by common consent, conviviality was no longer required. Civilization understands the limits of its dominion. Digestion, intimate confidences, personal reflections, and the need to sober up have their places too. In the perfect freedom of after lunch, they fell into knots of two or three according to their pace and interests, trailed, separated, wandered off one by one. Suzanne de Persand had changed her shoes for a pair of mud boots from the hall, and botanized at a leisurely pace along the paths with Garance and Delia, telling Delia the French names of things.

She had not recovered, apparently, from the shock of Antoine's offer to sell a hectare or so of land to Cray. It was clear he hadn't mentioned it beforehand. She was pensive, markedly less animated. Her experience had taught her to associate Americans with trouble, and here were more Americans.

Trudi de Persand walked briskly with Tim and Anne-Sophie, then fell back to let her mother-in-law catch up. Cray walked for a time with Persand, perhaps discussing the land sale, then, Tim saw, struck off to find his car.

"Let's go back to Etang-la-Reine to the stables and rent some horses, just for an hour or two," Anne-Sophie proposed to Tim. "It would be so nice to ride, and we could go all the way to the *grands rochers*," the site of great boulders deposited by some ancient glacier in the center of the forest. Though Tim was not especially fond of riding, he had no objection beyond the danger to Anne-Sophie of riding one-armed. She was scornful of his concern: "Riding stable horses? Nonsense, *pas de problème.*"

They debated the direction of Etang-la-Reine. Anne-Sophie's sense of direction was not good, but her feeling about which direction they ought to go was strong, and completely at odds with Tim's. He pointed out that as it was well past three in the afternoon, the sun would soon be lowering in the west, in the direction of the village, i.e., the other direction from the one she wanted to go. Tim as usual prevailed, but now it could be said, somewhat to his relief, it was too late to go riding. The nights were coming early, it was nearly December after all.

They were startled by a low growl and a snap of twigs in front of them in the underbrush. Tim, who was ahead on the path, stopped, putting up his hand to signal Anne-Sophie to stay back. At first he couldn't see the source of the menacing noise, but then, through the heavy bushes, he did make out people, a man and woman frozen in alarm, and one of Cray's Rottweilers, in his heavy leather muzzle, crouching nearly at Tim's feet, eyeing them. It turned its eyes to Tim and again to its prey, back and forth, uncertain about its course of action.

Tim understood that he had happened to make the gesture that controlled the beast. When he lowered his arm, the dog crouched lower and prepared anew to rush the luckless pair in the brambles; when he held his hand immobile in this way, up, the creature froze on its haunches, its eyes never leaving Tim's hand. The animal must have associated Tim with Cray, with the *maître-chien*, with the other white hats of the place, and was prepared to take orders from him.

"Stay still," he said to Anne-Sophie, who had crept near enough to see what he had seen. For a second Tim was filled with dread that they would see him there and think he was a spy. She made a *moue* and mimed a giggle. The figures in the shrubbery slipped hastily away.

Only seconds had elapsed. The *maître-chien* came up the path behind them, whistling for the dog.

"*Ça va?*"

"*Ça va, gentil chien.*"

"Could you see who it was?" Tim asked Anne-Sophie. Anne-Sophie had had an impression of khaki *pantalons* and white shirt on the one figure, dove gray top and black pants on the other;

the two people were to anyone with clothes memory perfectly recognizable.

"*Pas vraiment,*" she said. It amused her at first—she remembered Tim's story of seeing the two at the Tennis Club Marne-Garches-la-Tour. But then she thought of plays by Feydeau, where the naughty and guilty married people are always popping out of closets and crawling under beds, and this was called French farce. *Alors*, why French?

A feeling of deep uneasiness came over her. French people in and out of closets, whereas in an American play the wife was always in tears, with no friend but a dog or cat, and she was always a drug addict or an alcoholic. So, would you rather be the wife in a French play or an American one? Should an American man and a French wife settle beforehand which kind of play they were in? What kind of play were the American Madame Cray and the French Antoine de Persand about to open in? And she, Anne-Sophie, didn't want to be in a play at all, but in the life that was soon to begin, of real *mariage*.

What was it that made you desire one woman above another, Tim asked himself guiltily, and what made her desire another man above you? Something more than beauty, something infinitely chemical and resonant of past encounters, dreams, early imprints—it was out of your control. What made you act in a way you clearly did not intend to act? Were the people in the woods about to act in a way they didn't intend?

Cray had taken his car and gone, so Tim and Anne-Sophie drove Delia back to the Crays' house. Delia was ebullient; she had evidently enjoyed the afternoon, the neighboring house with its orderly grandeur, and the salad. She had also enjoyed the walk.

"I must have walked two miles. Did you notice that? I couldn't have done that two weeks ago. It's definitely working."

"Working?"

"Going to the Louvre. I've been doing it for a week now. If I could do it another week, I know the improvement would definitely be permanent."

The idea of the improving powers of art made Tim laugh, and he found himself wanting to tell Clara about it; the funniness wasn't something Anne-Sophie would see.

When they got to the Crays', Tim was surprised to see his friend

Cees—there was his official-looking small Renault parked by the front door, and Cees himself standing leaning against it, and another car, in which Gabriel sat in the backseat. Delia rushed over to him. The driver did not seem alarmed at the approach of a screaming young woman.

"I waited in hopes you were coming here," Cees said.

"You didn't say you'd be in Paris. What's up?"

"I rang your apartment. Also here, but someone said you were out."

"Paris weekend? Is Marta with you?"

"No, no, business. We came to pick up your captive, on suspicion of stealing the manuscript. If he won't tell you, he may be induced to talk to us. It appears there's enough hanging over his head to keep him on a few other charges for at least a few days. I began to feel he wasn't going to make any move toward Cray."

"Where are you taking him?"

"The warrant was issued in Amsterdam, we'll keep him there. We have the permission of the French."

"But . . ." Tim was stunned, he hadn't realized Cees would or could do this.

"God damn you," screamed Delia at Tim.

Tim was appalled. He, Tim, had in effect set the guy up. He hadn't meant to do that. It had the taste of treason, of tattletale, of teacher's pet, of collaboration—all the tainted and despised stances a man avoids. Not that he condoned lawbreaking, but informer was just not a role he saw himself in. Yet he realized that all along he had been informing, by keeping Cees informed. How had he not thought Cees would be acting professionally? He was aghast.

"I think he's just the seller," Cees said. "Not the thief."

"He hasn't sold it, though," Tim said. "What has he done really?"

"No, we're saving him from himself." Cees laughed. "If he helps us recover it, we'll have little to charge him with, and things may go a bit easier on the American weapons charges. That's the something in the past, apparently."

Anne-Sophie was also shocked. She came up to remonstrate with Tim and Cees. "But he is a nice young man, he spent days in the *grenier* at Clignancourt. I knew he was there, and I did not turn him in. Not exactly. I kept watch. But obviously he was not the murderer. He did not interfere or harm in any way. It's awful to turn someone in"—here she remembered that she had in effect apprehended him in her attic—"the people who did that in the war, for example."

"I didn't turn him in. I don't know that he's done anything," said Tim miserably. "What would I turn him in for?"

"What a jerk!" Delia limped toward him, denouncing him in high wailing tones. "You never said you were working with the police." She began to cry.

"But I'm not," Tim protested. "I just—Cees is my old friend, we talk all the time."

"It may be nothing, young lady," said Cees, "but if you would be candid about what you know of his business, it could help him. Ah—is this Anne-Sophie?"

"No, this is Delia, a friend of Gabriel's from America. *This* is Anne-Sophie. This is Cees, my friend from Amsterdam."

"*Bonjour, monsieur,*" said Anne-Sophie in an unfriendly tone.

"This is horrible, he was so happy, he was safe, he'd been hounded—" Delia went on.

"He had not been hounded," Cees said. "Whatever impelled him to hide out all this time, it was not the police—he was twice interviewed and released."

"I suppose we should look in the suitcase," Tim said. "It's in the trunk." Determined to be forthright, and hoping to find the rare manuscript before their eyes, he brought it into the kitchen and opened it, with Cees, Delia, and Anne-Sophie crowding round. Razor, change of underwear, toothbrush, several book catalogues. Nothing at all incriminating.

"What did I tell you?" Delia said.

40

The American State of Mind

O ver the next days Delia's rage continued to erupt, an immod-
erate fury, frantic and shrill, but not really directed at Tim; she
had accepted his apology, she apologized, saying she knew he
hadn't been trying to betray Gabriel. She was on the telephone constantly, or closeted with Cray, who began to turn into a Gabriel
partisan. In the course of the many phone calls—it appeared they
were to her colleagues the antiquarians of Sweet Home, Oregon—
it was decided that now she would have to stay longer in France to
help Gabriel. What good luck that she had a free room. The antiquarians would send money, Sara Towne would shoulder the burdens of the boutique without Delia, everyone in Oregon appeared
to agree it was for a good cause. Forby Anderson who had connections in the legal profession was getting the names of some international lawyers in Paris. No one was quite sure about the fee of such
a person; the solidarity eroded a little there. But probably Gabriel
himself could raise the money, or had the money to pay it back,
or—what was never said—he would after he sold whatever it was
he had been going to sell Monsieur Boudherbe.

Of her private devotion to Gabriel, Delia said little. Tim and Cray
were allowed to speak to him once, from the jail in Amsterdam,
and to his Dutch lawyer, who spoke to them guardedly. The lawyer
was also a friend of Cees, so there was a clubby, almost gentlemanly thing about everything surrounding Gabriel's incarceration.

"What worries him is extradition," said this Dutch lawyer.
"Though the Americans have not yet asked for it. Why would he be
worried about extradition, if he's innocent? He seems especially
afraid of the FBI."

"He knows why the FBI wanted that poor woman dead," Delia
explained.

"What woman?"

"Mrs. Weaver. At Ruby Ridge. And some of the other things they did, too."

Tim was exasperated with Delia's know-nothing air about Gabriel and the manuscript, and he suspected her. One day shortly after this, he waited till she wandered toward the bathroom and, alone with her in the corridor, he took her arm, twisted it painfully behind her back, pushed her head up against the wall, and hissed at her.

"Now you're going to tell me everything you know about Gabriel, and the fucking manuscript, and the murder."

She struggled and tried to hit him with her other hand, so he pinned that too, holding both her little wrists behind her back in one of his big hands.

"Let go, I have, I told Serge."

"What. Tell me." He dragged her into a bedroom, noticing peripherally that this must be Clara's room. Large bed, somehow solitary-looking, covered in an American quilt, with embroidered white pillows tossed on top, and some silver-framed photographs of what must be her little boy. Delia evidently believed that he would hurt her. So he would, he thought, he would twist her arms to match her hip. She looked scared but didn't scream.

"Did Gabriel have the manuscript?"

"I don't know what he had. He had a valuable thing to sell to the man in the flea market."

"Which he stole?"

"No! He sold things. He's a book dealer, a broker, like he said."

"Not too particular about the provenance of his wares?"

"I don't know. Let go."

"Commission?"

"Sure, of course."

"What's the commission on five hundred thousand dollars?"

"How do I know?"

"Say half. He's taking some risk. What does he do with the money?"

"It's for SuAnn, I suppose, for her group, how should I know? Anyway he didn't get it, did he? The murderer must have got it, mustn't he? He killed the man to get the money." She lunged backward into him and kicked at his shins. He unwound her arms and blocked the door.

"Come on, Delia. SuAnn. That's the crazy daughter of Cristal the crazy caregiver?"

"They aren't crazy. Well, SuAnn is, technically, I guess. They belong to a group, they aren't violent or anything, they're buying land in eastern Oregon for the millennium, or for when the marshalls bust them, or it's an ashram—I don't follow SuAnn's group."

"So what is going on? You're mixed up with a sophisticated theft here, some kind of international fencing operation, murder, and a bunch of Oregon hippies—what's the connection among these things?"

"I don't know, Tim, so open the door."

"Gabriel's relation to SuAnn?"

Delia was vulnerable here. She hated the relation of Gabriel and SuAnn. "I think he feels sorry for her," she said.

"Okay, Gabriel in Amsterdam. Why is he afraid to be extradited?"

"I told you, he's afraid of the FBI. He knows he'd never make it back there, they'd kill him and say he was trying to escape. They do that all the time."

"Why would they want to do that?"

"I told you. He knows why they killed Mrs. Weaver, and some other things. The FBI is funding some of these groups and they don't want it known."

"So you do know something about it." He wasn't sure whether Delia was as delusional as the people she described or whether she was right. Who the hell was Mrs. Weaver?

"I read the papers, like anyone else. Like Serge. Ask Serge, it was Serge who figured out about why Gabriel would be afraid of the FBI."

"You didn't hear that from Gabriel, or SuAnn or—who? Your friend Sara?"

"No! Sara and I have a business, we rent space from—I think the owners are Moonies."

"Oh Jesus," said Tim, despairing of making sense of all this.

"I don't keep track," Delia said. "They might be Church of the Remnant. I think they are. It doesn't matter, they're all more or less the same, they make the same points. They want to remedy problems in our society. They none of them like the government, or the police. The idea of Russians never bothered them, though. But they hate Planned Parenthood and you name it else. The Triple A. But it's one thing to be wacko and another thing to be wrong. They could be right, you know."

Church of the Remnant. Tim was beguiled by this name. What could its beliefs be? What was the matter with Delia, that she took all this stuff for granted, and seemed without the faculty of judgment? Nothing seemed strange to her. Was this the normal Oregon state of mind? Normal American state of mind?

41

Cécile

Anne-Sophie had been dedicating her midweeks to the painting being done in their new apartment, neglecting her flea-market inventory. Luckily she had a certain backlog of figurines and hunting prints in her attic, but she needed to buy. On Monday she tended her stall; on Tuesday she and Tim went to Arles to an antiques fair, where she hoped to find some fine old tack, and Tim started a travel piece. It was nice to get away alone together, more normal, things as they had been, with no reference to Oregonians, the Crays, or the wedding. Anne-Sophie had finally conceded that Tim had not informed on the poor young man, not really, and he could put all the Cray matters out of his mind for the moment.

Certain problems loomed that meant they should not be away too long, however. First, there were the *ennuis* with the apartment. As far as Tim could see, Anne-Sophie considered it to have been completely defiled by earlier habitation, and she was determined to rid it of all traces of its history—and she an *antiquaire*! So they were repainting and the rest, but they were far behind schedule with the bathroom, with the moving-in planned for the week before the wedding.

Then, too, Tim's mother was to arrive this Thursday, ahead of any of the other guests from America. She intended to go to Brussels to see some of her relatives, cousins too distant to have been invited to the ceremony; and she planned to bask in French-speaking, and to shop, and of course to help Tim and Anne-Sophie, and Anne-Sophie's mother whom she was looking forward to meeting and had read one or two of the books of, trying not to form any judgment on poor Anne-Sophie, who was doubtless quite different.

Despite his affection for his mother, Tim had a sense of strain at the prospect of her arrival. His mother was yet another person he was in some way responsible for. He included in this throng Anne-

Sophie, and now Cray, Delia, Clara, and even Gabriel Biller, the latter deeply on his conscience. He knew that in the great scheme of things his was a minor set of burdens, but he felt them. He hoped that his mother would have a good time, that she and Anne-Sophie would like each other, that she and Estelle would like each other, that there would be no unpleasantness between his mother and his father, or his mother and stepmother, that somehow he would be absolved of setting up Gabriel, that he would be cured of the crawl of desire in the pit of his stomach when he saw or thought of Clara Holly, that *Reliance* would take his piece on the growing anti-Americanism of French foreign policy, that *Travelling Light* would be interested in his observations on Arles, that he would find some time to visit the Spanish monasteries—when, for God's sake?—and that he would find his father well: emphysema had threatened. In no particular order, these concerns, like balls of bobbing styrofoam from a disintegrating wreck, would break the surface of his ordinary thoughts and float into view, disturbing his sleep at night and his concentration by day.

Estelle had invited them to dinner the first night of his mother's visit, to dine early on account of Cécile's probable jet lag, and Tim and Anne-Sophie had accepted, recognizing that the meeting of their mothers was a hurdle that must be got over, and agreeing that the two mothers would probably hate each other, even if they were both French-speaking—the one so scornful of America with its moralism and obesity, the other so conventional, golf-playing, and someone who had in Estelle's eyes had the unforgiveable bad sense not to come back to Europe once released from matrimony. What could account for that? Estelle had never quite said out loud, the woman must be an idiot, but the tenor of her questions had implied it: "Will your mother be unhappy if we can't find a member of a golf course near Paris? In Normandy of course I know people—Jacky Borde would know. . . ."

Another strike against Cécile Barzun Nolinger was that after the divorce, she had chosen to remain in Bay City, Michigan, while Tim's father and stepmother Terry lived in Grosse Pointe, a suburb of Detroit. Both Anne-Sophie and Estelle had found it natural that a person would prefer to live in a city distinguished by a French name, and so had obscurely concluded that Tim's father, even if not

French-speaking, was likely to be the more intelligent of the two unknown parents. Grosse Pointe and Detroit they pronounced in the French way, Daytwah, and Grosse Pwahn, which Tim found irritating.

He had not seen his mother for two years, and was surprised at how glad he was to see her. Living in Michigan, she had kept the lineaments of Frenchness—was slender, with short-cropped, blonded hair. Though she no longer smoked, she retained a smoker's voice, and her strong French accent, though she never spoke French now.

"Do you know, four years since I was here!" She kept exclaiming in the taxi. She was excited and kept patting Tim's hand. "At last I will meet darling Anne-Sophie!"

The Nolinger family had reacted without surprise to his choice of a French wife. With a Belgian mother, and since he had stayed in Europe, it followed, in that you tend to marry a person you've met. But it was not until the wedding plans were announced that they had really focused on the individuality of this Frenchwoman, Anne-Sophie. Cécile planned to love Anne-Sophie. Tim's choosing of a francophone bride she had taken as a compliment to herself, and even as a reproach to his father, and also as natural. "I hope I can go to the *marché aux puces* with her—she must know so much about it."

It was true that she was obsessed with golf—her game, her handicap—but assured Tim she would have no time to play on this busy trip. Tim took her straight to her hotel, with the suggestion that she have a nap before going to Anne-Sophie's and on to Estelle's, so as to be able to stay up until at least ten that first night.

"Whatever you think, sweetheart, I am in your hands," she said, and Tim realized again that she was, indeed, for two weeks.

Anne-Sophie waited at home while Tim picked up his mother at six in Anne-Sophie's car. Cécile embraced her directly and looked at her, and raved enthusiastically. She was *ravie*, Anne-Sophie was *ravissante*. They spoke in French.

"Just as beautiful and charming as I expected!" Though it was against the nature of a French mother-in-law, Cécile said, to take instantly to her son's choice of a wife, so she had. It was true. Cécile and Anne-Sophie looked at each other, trim, blond, and sportive, and each saw herself. The resemblance of Anne-Sophie to his mother gave Tim pause—were things so heavily determined after all?

"The apartment is adorable. Let me see the dress!" cried Cécile. "Let me see everything!"

Instant rapport did not describe the meeting between Estelle and Cécile. Far from being bonded by their mutual *francophonie*, their common tongue seemed to render more irritating their differences. The small Estelle, smartly dressed in black pants and turtleneck, with silver slippers, appraised the tweedy Cécile, who may have sewn the violet velvet blazer she was wearing. This in itself was alarming, because it perhaps indicated the meanness of Anglo-Saxon men, even colossally rich ones like Monsieur Nolinger, when it came to their ex-wives, something that boded rather ill for Anne-Sophie if the son took after the father, and if things did not go as harmoniously as one hoped and as the novelist in Estelle assumed they would not.

"So brave of you to carry on in America, are you not ever tempted to come back to France, that is, Belgium?"

"Oh, I've lived in the U.S. a long time now, my friends are there," said Cécile mildly.

"I have always wanted to visit America. Some day I shall. New York, at least," said Estelle.

"Few French people come to Michigan, it seems," Cécile agreed wistfully. "Do you play bridge?"

"Bridge? No!" said Estelle. "Regrettably," she added in an insincere voice.

Cécile abandoned that subject. "I want you to call on me for any help with anything—with the wedding in two weeks, you must be frantic. You must be sure to call on me."

Tim and Anne-Sophie exchanged glances of dawning discomfort. Estelle was far from frantic, had not even concerned herself with the details.

"I shall certainly ask much of you as the day comes near," Anne-Sophie assured Cécile. "I want you to see the *liste de mariage*, and the gifts that have come so far."

"Tom's father's family has some beautiful china, Limoges, which I hope they'll give you," said Cécile. "I didn't keep anything,

I gave it all back. The silver too, but I always said Tom's wife should have it."

"Dad's coming to the wedding, you know. Dad and Terry," Tim said, suddenly fearing she might not know. He could not tell from the fleeting change of expression whether she did know.

"I would hope so!" she cried gaily.

42

Principles

Clara was in effect waiting by the telephone and thinking over and over about the moment in the clearing on Sunday with Antoine de Persand. Had they gone a few steps farther, deeper into the woods, had they had another moment, they might have kissed. She had moved toward him, he toward her, was just reaching for her, both caught by some involuntary, powerful need that precluded discussion and was now directing their bodies. Then the low growl of the animal, a snapping twig, the quick sense of other people near, and of the lawless nature of their impulses, and that it could be Serge or Trudi behind them. They had darted around the rock as guiltily as if they had been caught *en flagrant délit*.

"I'll telephone. May I telephone?" he had said miserably.

"Yes," she had whispered. "Yes," and they hurried in opposite directions through the shrubs.

But when the phone did ring, on Monday, it was a reporter from *Le Monde* calling to ask Madame Cray when the Lady Godiva solution was actually to be put in place. Clara gasped; how could they have heard about that ugly scene?

"You have not seen *Paris-Match* madame?"

Clara flew to look at it. There was her picture (rather good) on the steps of the Etang-la-Reine post office being menaced by a throng of what appeared to be Tyrolean peasants. In color.

Cray was enraged, far more enraged after seeing it in a major weekly magazine than after Clara's account of it. The American community saw it and was newly enraged: it appeared that Americans were no longer safe even at the post office. Segments of the French community were enraged as well on Clara's behalf. The Crays hadn't realized there would be people on their side, but with the publicity over the incident, the press had ignited in some quarters the high feeling against hunting, as well as for it, and the Crays were duly visited by the Saint Hubert Society and the Saint Eustache Society, by the Ligue des Opposants à la Chasse and the Association pour la Protection des Animaux Sauvages, people opposed to the shooting of birds "prenuptially," people defending the rights of private property, people petitioning the European Parliament, people advocating no hunting on Wednesdays when schoolchildren were out or on Sunday afternoons or when drunk. Touched, Clara and Serge invited all their partisans in and gave them tea, and Clara took all the brochures, to send donations. The LOC left big signs for them to post:

REFUGE, CHASSE INTERDITE
Nul n'a le droit de chasser sur la propriété d'autrui sans le consentement du propriétaire ou de ses ayants droit.
ICI COMMENCENT LE RESPECT DE LA VIE ET
L'AMOUR DE LA NATURE

The mayor of Etang-la-Reine quickly moved against these anti-hunters too—and some of them were proprietors of large domains—by interdicting the gathering of mushrooms on community-owned lands consecrated to hunting. "And in the spring, we will see about flower cutting," he announced in a menacing tone.

Time magazine, European edition, published an account of the affair, and found some old studio photographs of Clara. When she saw how she had changed from then to now, she was dizzy with dismay at how fast her life was fleeting by. She could not expect that Monsieur de Persand would be attracted to her, how could he be? She knew it was crazy to be sick with love when you ought to be worrying about prison, or your child in England, or the destiny of innocent forest creatures.

At the same time, it was not unpleasant to be the heroine and poster child of a just cause. At Dorothy Sternholz's instigation, Americans were organizing a fund-raiser for the American Freedoms Defense Fund.

"Arthur Pearlberg has explained that there are issues here, more's at stake than this one case," said Dorothy Sternholz *née* Minor to Ames Everett. "If Americans can be persecuted so unjustly, then they will be. It's the reflex of the unofficial French foreign policy. Arthur says it's important that the French remember from time to time that we do put a lot into the French economy here, to say nothing of buying their exports."

"I know there will be plenty of French people who feel as we do," Martha Jacobs, the librarian at the American Library agreed.

"Not that Serge Cray can't afford her defense, but nobody can afford a really irrational persecution by an entire nation. Everyone knows the Crays moved into a shell, a hulk, a ruin."

"Isn't it true that the boiseries issue is trumped up, to pressure them about their stand on hunting?"

"Probably. Yet the boiseries were removed by somebody and sold. The commune and French history are the poorer, and somebody must pay. You can't entirely blame them."

"I'm wondering if we can put Tim Nolinger down tentatively for ten thousand—he sees a lot of the Crays."

"Ask him now. He's bound to be more generous before he gets married than afterward." Ames laughed. "As the saying goes, if you want a bookkeeper, marry a French wife."

Arthur Pearlberg arrived before the others, and they stood talking affably. It was always surprising when the great lawyer, so small and gray behind his horn-rims, swelled to such immensities of eloquence as they had heard him do, and as he now did, about how the developing pattern of anti-Americanism in Europe, paralleled, paradoxically, the rise of antigovernment ferment at home in America.

"And now if Americans aren't to be safe at the post office." Dorothy shuddered.

"They aren't safe in the post office in America, remember—you've heard of going postal," someone reminded her.

Tim and Anne-Sophie attended the fund-raising event and the musical part of the evening, comprised of art songs by Samuel Barber. Anne-Sophie, no more than ordinarily musical, was restless during these and remarked peevishly to Tim as they left, "American music is really rather ugly, admit it. Except for jazz and popular music. Once we heard Ferde Grofé and I thought I would die."

"Do you really think Samuel Barber is worse than Gabriel Fauré? Ravel? Do you willingly listen to *l'Enfant et les sortilèges?*" snapped Tim. Luckily for his peace of mind, he had misread his suggested pledge and kicked in ten dollars with a great feeling of rectitude.

A new aura of activity enveloped Cray, to do with cinema. He called several people who had worked on earlier projects with him, among them Les Chadbourne, the art director for *Queen Caroline*, and Gus Gustafson, a cameraman who had headed the second unit, to whom he talked about finding locations, if not in France then in Spain, that could serve as the American West. There were his long consultations with Delia, some discussions about the time to bring in a screenwriter. He seemed to move lightly in his heavy body now, he no longer drooped at the kitchen table reading. Clara couldn't altogether tell whether all this had to do with his film or with their hunting issues, or whether in some way the two were intertwined, the one invigorating the other. Once or twice, he wanted to make love, a relatively infrequent event.

"SuAnn isn't crazy. Yes, she's high-strung and gets excited, she might be disturbed when she's not on her meds, but she's not wrong about what's going down around here. There are plenty of signs of what the Feds are planning when the problems start. See, that will be the excuse, the riots and the food shortages, then the Feds will move in. I don't believe it's no foreign government, of course not, it's our own government. Though there are people who believe it's foreigners, and now they've arrested SuAnn's boyfriend over where you are, that makes you wonder if the French nation is in on it too."

"Delia is trying to find out about it," said Clara vaguely.

"Delia Sadler?"

"Yes."

"The girl from here? She's stuck on SuAnn's boyfriend, she's kind of a problem," Cristal said.

"Poor little thing, her hip . . ."

"You want to talk to your mom?"

"Just a word or two."

"People have seen tanks not far from Hood River. It's much, much worse here than you think, you don't know."

"Please let me talk to Mother, Cristal," Clara said.

43

Self-Denial

When Antoine de Persand did call, in a few days, he sounded neighborly but brusque. She thanked him for the lunch on Sunday. He asked, did she ever come into Paris during the week?

"Lately, yes. We have a houseguest who is spending a lot of time at the Louvre. Well, you met her. I take her there most every day."

"*Déjeuner* one day? Maybe Thursday?"

Her hesitation was real. She knew this was a bad idea. "All right." A deeply satisfying passivity directed her responses.

"*Bien.* One o'clock at—say, Pierre Traiteur? It is on the rue de Richelieu across from the Palais Royal. It is near the Louvre, so that should be convenient."

"All right. Yes," she said. "One, then. Goodbye," and hung up. She hoped he would think her lack of conversation was something to do with a lurking husband, not basic dullness. Her excitement at this conversation was such that she half expected Serge to have been listening, wiretapping.

Waiting for Thursday, Clara fell into a kind of bemused trance of expectation. She expected that the text of this lunch would be him telling her "we mustn't" and "this is madness." She could hear his arguments and had no counterarguments. On the other hand, there had been something in his resigned smile, in the woodland clearing, that suggested his misgivings were behind him. She didn't care which way things came out; they would be together at least for lunch, the one person in the world she most wanted just to talk to and to feel was her friend.

Life can light up in unexpected ways. There was a sparkle on things that could rout at least temporarily the dark specters of prison, Lars, Serge, and Mother, and it didn't need to have anything to do with sex. What was her attitude really, now that she was faced with a clandestine lunch?

On Wednesday, she awoke sweating with panic. It had come to her in the night that she had stolen the boiseries after all. "Boiseries" had always suggested fancifully carved panels of pale wood, or perhaps they were painted and gilded, with insets of Chinese wallpaper or murals by Watteau. But now her mind's eye in dreamlike sequence saw workmen dismantling what looked like battered pea-green plywood wallboards, maybe having some rectangular indentations such as a door might have. Were those the boiseries? Chilled, she thought of going in to Serge to ask him. He might remember. And what had happened to those green wallboards? She had supposed the dump, or firewood. Wallboards such as you saw when any old house was demolished, shreds of wallpaper sticking to them, covered with water stains and plaster dust, and the repellent detritus of past lives.

She would call Tim Nolinger, tell him all this. Tell him she may have stolen the boiseries, though even if she had, that did not solve the question of who sold them at auction at Drouot. But if he could find the person who had bought them, maybe they could buy them back, and things would go easier.

On Thursday morning, she woke with a lighter heart because of coming to the absolute resolve in the night not to have an affair with Antoine de Persand if the question should come up. It made no sense to begin a new relationship, even if it were practical and moral. She might go to prison or be deported, she needed to focus on saving her life; it was a question of priorities as well as of virtue. There were some things she believed deeply in, and one was honoring your commitments in life, for instance marriage vows. She would apologize again for her thoughtless confession of love made from jail. A jailhouse confession. She rose, mentally purged and pure, rid of the prurient, inexplicable hopes of even the tiniest caress. She was Diana again, chaste, an antihuntress.

Despite her fears for Gabriel and her constant consultations with America over his fate, Delia continued to want to spend a couple of hours a day at the Louvre. To Clara's relief, this included the day of her lunch with Antoine, and so she needed no further excuse. Delia agreed to start out at noon.

In spite of her pure intentions, Clara bathed and dressed carefully. She had her views of what a Frenchwoman would wear in this circumstance, a lunch date with an attractive man you weren't going to have an affair with. What to wear had been an epiphany dating back some years, from her early life in France when once she'd seen, in a boutique, a rather plump and normal-looking middle-aged woman, neck beginning to fold, put out her head from the dressing room to ask for something, and one could see she was dressed in a black bustier trimmed with pink ribbons, black lace panties, and matching lace garter belt and stockings. Under her ordinary dress, this French housewife was dressed like the madam in a western, like a dance-hall girl!

This had impressed Clara. The woman's lingerie suggested realms of eros and of self-indulgence, and probably self-respect, an Oregonian had no notion of. Perhaps the woman had put on that sexy gear to impress shopgirls, but it didn't seem to be that. She wore it for metaphysical reasons. Clara wore normal American underwear, Olga or Warner's, plain white.

Now she rummaged in her drawer for panties and a bra that at least matched, to be hoped with a smattering of untattered lace. Of course she didn't own a garter belt. She shivered a little; her room was cold, the château of Madame du Barry had been cold. This dressing up was stupid because there would be no lovemaking—never!—but inwardly she would be fortified by these pink satin matching components.

She dropped Delia at the usual spot across from the museum and went to park in the underground parking and walk the little distance across the Tuileries, through the Place du Palais Royal, and up the rue de Richelieu, a region of Paris where gallantry and sexual encounters had flourished since the seventeenth century or before.

Estelle had on the whole been disappointed in Cécile. Upon inspection, the clothes had been normal not expensive clothes, even allowing for American dowdiness, and there was the Belgian accent, and the rather tame aspirations. On the good side, she had appeared to admire Anne-Sophie, and be prepared to love her, and would not be a troublesome mother-in-law.

"The father only comes the day before the wedding, I suppose very American male, always the fiction of busy," she laughed to Cyrille Doroux. "Undoubtedly he mistreated poor Cécile—that's *maman*—and the new wife will be showy. Tim has said nothing about his views of his stepmother. A mystery, and I hope not a disaster."

44

Lunch Date

Monsieur de Persand had just got to the restaurant and was talking to the maître d'hôtel, who evidently knew him (ate there often? with mistresses?). He wore a dark business suit and striped silk tie, and handed his briefcase to the girl in the *vestiaire* with the air of an habitué.

"Ah," he said, seeing Clara, "*bonjour.*"

She smiled at him, and at the maître d'hôtel, who demonstrated by the merest discreet but not impertinent millisecond of eye contact with Antoine that he was impressed with her beauty and Monsieur de Persand's excellent judgment and good luck. Antoine bent over her hand. They followed the headwaiter to the table. A small restaurant, everybody visible to everybody else; people noticed the lovely woman in the smart suit and soignée pearls who dropped her purse. Face aflame, Clara sat down.

Antoine de Persand appeared calm, experienced in the matter of settling into a good French lunch. "Aperitif? A porto?" They were speaking French, which increased her unease. Though she spoke French, by now almost perfectly, it could desert her at any stressful moment, and usually did.

"A *kir champagne,*" he suggested. Her apprehensiveness grew. It was the aperitif of seduction and celebration.

"How lovely you are, Clara. Clara, if I may."

"Antoine," she agreed to this escalation, resolution a bit shaken by his own beauty, his cleft chin, his remoteness, his air of being a lofty beam in its sweep happening to fasten on her. Should she just say what she had to say immediately? Get it off her chest at once, apologize, explain that she had been vulnerable, who wouldn't be, in prison, had not been herself? Yet how explain the magnetic moment in the forest when she would have fallen into his arms?

He ordered the drinks. They were given their menus, but he left his lying closed. "What do you hear about your case?"

She told him what she knew of the progress of the *juge d'instruction*, her decision coming up, the search for the truth of who had sold the boiseries.

Antoine laughed. "You Americans have a bizarre idea of truth. In France, the judges don't care about truth. What is truth, after all? Everyone's truth is different anyhow. A French judge tries to arrive at a situation where people can get along. The lawyers too, they try for an arrangement where the people can *vivre ensemble*. Social equilibrium, social stability. That's the whole point. Real truth doesn't matter. Napoleon saw that." He opened his menu.

"It is because we are Americans, isn't it, that they are persecuting us?"

"There's a pattern developing of hating Americans, yes. It seems to happen in cycles. At the moment, it's in the form of trade disputes, and new objections to NATO. The French are always nationalistic, their right wing frankly so, and the left—well, it arrives at the same conclusions by a different route. It says let everyone be himself, thus let us be French, therefore down with *Jurassic Park* and other evidences of American cultural takeover."

She sighed. "All the same, I don't understand how they can say we sold something we didn't have." She didn't tell him about her dream, just two nights ago, that it was so. The panels of green plywood were as vivid today as that night. "What do you think we should do?"

"You and I?" He smiled.

"Well, I meant Serge and I, about all these difficulties?"

"Ah. Here they make *oeufs meurette* especially well. The kidneys in mustard also."

"I'll have a salad, then the *steack de thon*," she said, barely looking.

"Do you like a light red with the *thon*? Would you rather have a Pouilly Fumé?"

"Red, by all means." This appeared to exhaust the possibilities for discussion of the menu.

"I'm pleased with my idea of selling you two hectares in back of me. Though my mother may make trouble about it, I'm afraid.

Nonetheless, that will settle the hunting issue. There are plenty of French people on your side, by the way, plenty who oppose hunting. We are not an entire nation of killers."

"Why are you doing this, exactly?" Clara asked.

"You have the normal American directness." He laughed. "Probably basically because I am in love with you. I hate to think of you languishing in prison." This was said flirtatiously, not, it appeared, altogether seriously. "I want to oblige you. Of course I don't especially want to oblige your husband. *Au contraire.*" This too was said in such a light tone it took her breath away. A tone that said it was not to be taken seriously, or only a little.

"We should talk about—what we have to talk about and just get it over so we can enjoy our lunch," said Clara, unable, with American directness, to bear the slow evolution of such an important conversation, especially now that it had been taken to heights of candor, however lightly said, and must not be allowed to continue its visceral hold, its potential for disturbing and unleashing hot promptings. "I'm sorry I spoke to you that way that day, I was just . . . mistaken."

"I'm sorry to hear that," nodding to the waiter to pour the wine.

"I mean, I meant it," she said, "but it isn't anything we can do anything about, so it would have been less unruly not to have said it." Less unruly, *moins indiscipliné.* Why did everything have to be said negatively and backward in French?

"Why had I even come to the prison? Because I had to see you. Because I was already in the grip of 'wild thoughts.' I agree a rather inconvenient passion." He smiled to indicate that there were *guillemets*, quotation marks, around "passion." He seemed as regretful as she, only he appeared to have come to the opposite conclusion now, and seemed to be saying that perhaps they should act on their attraction. She shook her head firmly to indicate that it was not to be, and introduced some bland inquiry. Beside hunting, did he ski, or sail?

They launched into a getting-acquainted conversation. He didn't know where she was from or that she had a deaf child; she didn't know what he did for a living, exactly, or that he was in charge of Roxy de Persand's affairs—an American Clara knew slightly. He asked her how long she had been married to Cray, and about Lars. Did she cook? Was it she who saw to the lovely gardens? They didn't talk further about their feelings. Beyond or above that kind of confessional conversation, so mined with traps for exaggeration and insincerity, they didn't know each other well enough.

They did not talk about their spouses or whether they were unhappy or happy. Clara strove for the gaiety she so admired in Frenchwomen, and truly felt elated at the evolution of a new friend, the luck of them being neighbors, both dog lovers and admirers of the work of La Tour. Clara did not know many Frenchmen, she realized. They saw visitors from California, admirers of Cray, other Americans, like Tim Nolinger or the Paces, Episcopalians, for sometimes Clara had the impulse to hear music at the American Cathedral, and journalists—but not French men except Mayor Briac or the *commerçants* of the village. She knew French women somewhat better.

Persand knew American women, all right—his late brother's family—and found them often exasperating, with their insincere, expensively aligned smiles. Clara too smiled in this American way when something amused her; otherwise he thought she had a beautifully pensive demeanor.

That showed her depth of feeling, someone over whom real shadows hung, of which he gained fugitive glimpses through her merriment. He liked it that she loved to eat, appreciated each thing and ate it up. In New York, where he went occasionally, people ate only half of what was on their plate, wastefully and rudely; he always noticed this, a carryover from childhood training by parents who had been through the war. People who went through the war never left things on their plates. She ate everything, and was so beautiful, and had such an unfulfilled, yearning center—or so it seemed, not that one could know—in need of awakening.

Eventually they were having a lovers' conversation—two people who had never even kissed, dissecting the circumstances of their meeting, each syllable of things they had said to each other, and what they had meant. It must stop, of course. Yet she had a racing sensation of freedom, as if on a sailboat in a high wind, hurtling toward a shoal. They desired each other so much, they could say, but now in lieu of becoming lovers, they would become friends.

That in itself would be a precious and neighborly manifestation of good fortune. She thought he might conceivably be relieved by this outcome.

A stiff, even prim man across the table in his beautiful suit, almost blue-black with the faintest stripe, perfect white collared shirt, grayish tie, smelling faintly of shaving soap. He seemed to her the most desirable man she had ever met. In his dark, remarkably fringed eyes she sensed a sort of pain or longing at some sincere level beneath the cynical very French social manner, pleasantries and gallantries and careful choice of wine. Civilization is painful, she thought, holding us in our chairs. She wanted to know—she asked—how he got the scar on the back of his hand (excuse to touch it). She asked about the talents of his children.

The coffee came. Persand called for the bill. They looked at each other with infinite regret and a certain consoling feeling of rectitude, kissed cheeks in the correct French manner, but three kisses, rather lingering, implanted on her perfumed cheek not in air, and Antoine was given his briefcase.

"Well, Madame Cray," he said. They had not really argued about how it was not meant to be, him taking one side, her the other, then switching sides, going over all the reasons, moral and familial and the rest, though they could have, they knew them by heart. She shrugged and smiled, and thanked him again for lunch.

Anyway, where could it end? It's better not to begin, she thought again, quashing the tentative arguments, the same ones she had run through herself, on the brevity of life, the fugitive nature of happiness, the imperatives of desire once love has been spied out— Eros, that god who reveals his face only to the luckiest mortals, of whom there are so few.

Once outside, Clara looked at her watch. How possible that it was nearly four? Delia would have long since exhausted her short attention span for Art. Clara hurried toward the Louvre. She found she had a headache of terrible intensity, she who never had headaches. This one had begun in a knot at the back of her neck— was that the brain stem, among some primitive functions there like breathing?—and proceeded like an earthquake fault between the two halves of her skull up over the top of her head to a point between her eyes. On either side of the splitting pain, a dull expanding ache she had never felt before. It was so sudden—could be some sort of weird aneurism, you heard those could strike young women. She felt she must get home or throw up, she must lie down. She bypassed the long line of restive tourists waiting to get in, explained to the guard her missed rendezvous, and looked around the pyramidal space for Delia.

45

Chestnuts from Suzanne de Persand

Tim had called Cees for news of Gabriel, wishing to be reassured that the luckless American incarcerated in Amsterdam hadn't been rubber-hosed or extradited.

"A strange detail," Cees told Tim. "Did you have any idea Cray has been funding an Oregon terrorist group?"

Tim thought this could not be, though Delia might have hit him up for a donation to one of the causes she had told him she was involved in.

"Yes, yes. A check for—not much, but four thousand dollars, has turned up in the account of someone linked to a group suspected of bombing a church in Lake Grove, Oregon, several years ago."

"You people are marvellous," Tim said, unable to fit this together at all.

"There were eight hundred churches bombed last year in America, what does this mean, do you think, Tim?"

"No idea," Tim said cheerfully. "The spread of anticlericalism?" He hadn't noticed in Cray any special animus against religion. No, it wasn't possible that Cray was supporting Oregon church bombers.

In Etang-la-Reine, Cray, having lunched with Chadbourne, the British art director, was just going up to his workroom when Madame de Persand was announced. His first impulse was to have Clara deal with her, but there was something in particular Delia had told him that caused him to change his mind, and anyway Clara was at the Louvre. But the visitor was the mother, not the wife, of the affable neighbor Antoine de Persand. She was dressed in a gray tweed tailored suit, with decorations in the buttonhole which must denote some service to France.

"Monsieur Cray, so nice to see you again. I hope you'll forgive my popping in like this. I have brought Madame Cray some chestnuts, I left them in the hall."

"Uh—sit down, madame. I take it you have some business to discuss," Cray said, ignoring this neighborly proffer of chat about chestnuts. "We seem to be the object of some neighborhood enmity here. Did the dogs bother you?"

"Your man prevented them."

"Good."

"I'll speak frankly," said Madame de Persand, sitting down. "I was most surprised when my son announced his idea of selling you two hectares of our land."

"You don't think it's a good idea." This was a statement, not a question.

"He is so good-hearted, he would naturally want to help a neighbor. The whole thing has gotten out of hand, the hunting *contretemps* and the matter of defacing the château both. Very vexing for you, I know. However, I am quite sure I have some influence with *monsieur le maire*, Mayor Briac, and I think I can be of help."

"We need all the help we can get."

"For one thing, I am prepared to tell him that we, on our side, having more than twenty hectares, will also no longer permit hunting on our property, deviating from our practice in previous years, if he does not cease his determined effort to hunt over here. Since our two properties adjoin in such a way as to make it impractical for people to hunt your woods without access to ours, that should ensure that they let you alone. You see the point of my threat? He can't but agree. There is no need for you to buy, nor for us to sell. If I say so, they will not hunt on your land."

"That would be very handsome, Madame de Persand. But what do you have against the sale?"

"Just the usual things. We have a large family, there are a number of grandchildren, it just would not be responsible to sell land at this stage."

Cray laughed. "I understand that. And is your son always such a nice neighborly guy?" Cray was remembering that Delia had remarked, after the lunch at the Persands' house, "Obviously Mr. de Persand is very turned on by Clara, did you notice that?"

Suzanne de Persand said nothing. Something in her manner

suggested that her son was in no way a nice guy, and his inexplicable behavior now filled her with concern.

"In the matter of the mayor's persecution of my wife, madame, I'm sure you know we did not deface this house."

"Yes, that is a more difficult issue. I have been *inquietée* about poor Madame Cray," said Madame de Persand. "Nothing has occurred to me yet, because the forces of justice, once invoked, are hard to restrain. We must think."

46

Pyramid Power

Clara found Delia sitting almost in the center of the vast ground-floor space of the massive glass pyramid covering the subterranean entrance to the Louvre. She was sitting with her coat and big purse and notebook all in a mound, so that people had to walk around her. It was surprising the guards let her camp there like this, but there was a camplike air about the vast space, bright even in the gray late-autumn light, people milling around, coming up off the long escalator or stepping onto the down one to descend deeper into the ancient palace, people standing waiting, eating, or reading their guidebooks, assembling their tour groups in the luminous structure that came to a point above them.

"Hello, Delia, are you ready?" Clara asked, fighting tears, wondering if pain showed on her face.

"Could I stay ten more minutes? I didn't get started on time because first I went inside and saw the Venus de Milo," Delia said. "I thought I should at least see some of the art."

What was she talking about? "Isn't that what you're here for?"

"Well, more for the treatment," Delia said. "An hour a day is recommended, or, you know, as long as you can sit. The Louvre?"—seeing Clara's incomprehension—"The powers of pyramids? Concentrating the universal energy? I've been doing it more than a week. If I could do it another week, I can definitely feel I could be well."

"Oh God, Delia," Clara said, touched all the same. Tears came again to her eyes, and she wanted to laugh despite the horrible pain in her head. Pyramid power! "I've noticed you're walking better." She hadn't really, but whatever placebos might be worth, she thought, why not? Then the tears almost overbalanced the laughter. She had to get a Kleenex from her purse. How her head hurt.

When they were back in Etang-la-Reine, she could not master her tears, and hurried to her room.

In only a few minutes, Serge knocked at her bedroom door. "Clara—something unpleasant has happened in Oregon. Come out." But he came in. Sitting on her bed, she waited to hear the news without surprise. Something had happened to her mother, brought on, she understood, in the great karmic way of things, by her flirtation.

"My mother?" It was inevitable that she would have to pay for her infractions of duty and loyalty, and for acknowledging the desires of her heart. Had this been something her mother had obscurely suggested to her all her life, that one way or another we must pay?

"In a way," said Serge. "She seems to have been kidnapped."

"Oh God!"

"Delia's mother called. I talked to her. Nothing to do with the police, it may be nothing. Come down, Delia can tell you."

Clara hurried down the stairs to hear Delia's account.

"My mother called to say that she'd stopped by your mom's house because there was some activity in the driveway, people carrying things in—at first she thought out, a burglary. Anyhow, my mom wondered, and she thought maybe someone new was moving in, and she just hadn't heard that your mom had, you know, maybe moved. So she just put her head out of the car window and asked where Cristal was, and some guy said Cristal was gone, and they were just putting some stuff in the basement. And then she said— my mom said—where's Mrs. Holly, and he said, with Cristal. After that he just said he didn't know anything more, so my mother called here to find out from you."

"Did she call the police?"

"I don't think so, I think she thought you might know the explanation."

"Something is obviously wrong! We have to call the police. I'll have to go there!" Clara cried, feeling at the pit of her stomach the wrongness and danger, and remembering all the weird things Cristal had been saying lately.

The last thing she had said was, "Something will happen pretty soon. I want you to know we'll be safe here. There are people who have promised to protect your mom and me." These words came to her as clearly as when Cristal had spoken them.

"Probably you should definitely go," Delia agreed. "My mother is not an alarmist."

"I'll go, of course," Clara said, organizing her thoughts: airplanes, schedules, probably a night flight tonight. "There must be someone I can call meantime."

"Aren't you forgetting?" Serge pointed out. "You're under indictment in France. You can't leave France."

It was true, of course. It would be jumping bail. She would become an international felon. Distress mingled with an obscure relief. "You go, then," she pleaded. "Somebody must go right now."

To her surprise, Cray said, "I think that would be best. I'll go. Delia and I will go."

"It's not surprising," Delia said. "I think Gabriel's arrest has meant big changes in plans. People will be scared of what he's going to say. They'll move sooner than they'd planned." But she could not or would not explain, and Cray would not press her. He seemed to delight in her most enigmatic pronouncements, and to feel that like delphic utterances they should not be too carefully examined lest their fundamental meaninglessness be revealed, and their force lost.

47

Take Me to the Shining Shore

"You are spending every minute with the Crays," Anne-Sophie had snapped last night as they waited for a taxi in the midnight street, after a dinner party of mostly French friends of hers. As the wedding approached, her friends had come to accept the new reality of Tim as a permanent addition to their set, and had begun to invite them relentlessly.

"We are moving in a few days, your mother is coming back, there are so many things to be done, you can't imagine, now the flowers, I have to spell out every little detail for you—what is so fascinating about the Crays, oh, ha, don't answer that."

"Mostly it's Gabriel," said Tim, untruthfully. "I feel like it's our fault the poor guy is in jail—my fault. I feel like I have to do what I can to help, I have to live with myself."

"You have to move your books, only you can do that and put them on the shelves the way you want them."

"Yes, in the famous bookcases," Tim snapped.

Now Tim was putting books in the bookcases, his resentment subsiding in the fascination of the task, books he had forgotten, books he hadn't got around to reading. Anne-Sophie was in the newly painted kitchen when Tim's cell phone rang. It was Cray. Cray put forward a case for Tim accompanying him on a trip, three days maximum, to Oregon, Cray to look into a problem with Clara's mother, Les Chadbourne the art director to look at some locations, Delia to show them some of her alternate thinkers and New Age paranoids in the Sweet Home Antiques Barn and incidently to return home. Cray would continue to pay Tim, of course, on the same basis he was paying for the detective work on the boiseries. There'd be a story in it too. Tim thought of all the reasons this was a big drag, and said okay despite them, dreading Anne-Sophie's reaction. They would be going in the morning, probably, or as soon as Monday Brothers could send the plane.

"Three days!" cried Anne-Sophie. "Perfect. I can buy some Americana at that place of Delia's, she will know where, and, my dearest, I can see with my own eyes your native land, though not Michigan. Is Oregon very different from Michigan?" For Tim was always going on about American regional differences.

"Not so different," he agreed. "Both northerly, with pine trees and bears." He could see no reason to object to Anne-Sophie going along, though he didn't know the size of the Monday Brothers plane. He called Cray back.

Estelle was astonished and quite encouraged by Anne-Sophie's madcap plan to take a three-day trip to Oregon in America a week before her wedding. This spontaneous, unexpected, and impulsive idea indicated, Estelle hoped, a new freedom, a spontaneity, an adventurousness in Anne-Sophie rather as she had always hoped. Perhaps Tim would be good for Anne-Sophie after all. She was not free from maternal concern about the small private plane, however.

"I wonder if the Americans will be, well, like Tim, *alors*—their jackets won't match their pants, they'll wear tennis shoes in town, that sort of thing," said Anne-Sophie happily.

"Oh, yeah, I'm happy to be going home, except I worry about leaving Gabriel," Delia said. "In a way it's so disgusting here, I mean it's beautiful, but if you think about it, it's disgusting too. Take you, two people living in a giant mansion big enough for twenty, everyone around here is rich, the food is death food of fat and cream, people have servants, they make the black people sweep the streets, or the Algerians—and America might as well not exist. No one here knows anything about America, and the Americans who live here are the worst, they forget what it's like at home where people are hungry and angry, and the whole country is shifting like a big mountain with some sort of geologic activity pushing up from inside it, it's just going to split open like a big baked potato. At least Serge wants to wake people up. He can imagine it, no other American I've met here can imagine it, and no French person can imagine it, *no way*." She had a cheerful, expectant, almost radiant expression as she recited these conclusions.

"Prairie angst in Kansas among the creationists, polygamist

anger in Utah, killer cops and soldiers of fortune hiding out in Montana, those poor loonies in Texas that got fried," Serge suggested, like a hovering parent prompting a bright child.

"And the Feds were using inflammable gas, they lied about that. They intended to burn those people up!" cried Delia excitedly.

"And the French have problems of their own. The National Front, the skinheads," said Serge.

"Yeah, but I'm not talking about people like that. Not racists or white supremacists," Delia said. "None of the people I know are into that. Those people are out there, but we don't have anything to do with them. Not that that makes any difference to the government. Talk about hate groups—the government hates everybody. They don't mind who they kill, you could be racist or you could be religious. . . ."

They continued in a rather festive frenzy of denunciation. Listening to them, Clara felt apologetic that she had been thinking only about the killing of deer. The modesty of her indignation struck her. Still, you have to object to the evils you find to hand. She'd never even seen violence against a person. The episode at the post office, against herself, had been the closest she'd come.

"I would say *you're* disgusting if it wasn't rude to say it—disgusting in the sense of rolling in luxury and giving nothing back," Delia said, turning to Clara.

No doubt she was. Clara thought of something she had seen in the metro. On the curved vault of the wall, a giant poster for the African charity Alliance Faim. Two images of a smiling African girl of about seventeen. In the first, she was haggard, her teeth in her shrivelled gums were huge, and there was something diseased about her watery eyes. The same girl with "100 francs of your donation" was beautifully plumper, her gums no longer showed, she glowed with health. But what struck Clara was that the girl smiled in both pictures. Even when starving, she was a human being hoping that her life would turn around. Maybe she was thinking that having your picture taken could turn your life around, and of course in her case it did, since they would have had to give her food and medicine so she could be well for the second picture.

Clara did not like photographers, especially the ones who would pause to snap the dying child, the quivering antelope about to be pounced on, but would not save him, nor take the child to shelter, saying there were too many. Clara knew it was not the photographer who gave the girl the hundred francs.

She knew too that going to jail to keep hunters from killing the fawn on your lawn did not keep them from killing the fawn, was sentimental, was only a small blow against a cruelty so pervasive, so entrenched, and so minor compared to the suffering of people— she knew all that. Her headache had not really abated, and now it threatened a renewed intensity.

"Oh, I know, you're perfectly right," she said.

48

Lust

"Goodbye, goodbye," Clara said, embracing them all, when the taxis arrived to take them to the airport of Le Bourget. "Call me all the time, I won't budge, I'll be waiting by the phone." Tears stood in her eyes at what they might find, and at her own failure as a daughter not to be there to help her mother.

When they had gone, she wrote Lars, morosely read yesterday's *Le Monde*, and drank her morning coffee. She let Senhora Alvares answer the door. Her heart leapt with amazement when Antoine de Persand came in, looking exceedingly grim, though he kissed her politely on each cheek.

"Come in, won't you sit down?"

He followed her a few steps into the salon. "I'd like to see your husband, madame—Clara—if I may? It appears my mother has been here to see him, with a monstrous proposal."

"Monstrous? Good heavens, surely not!"

"Unacceptable, in any case. Idiotic."

"Doesn't that seem the simplest way?" Clara asked, unable to see anything humiliating about Madame de Persand's proposal.

He shook his head, his dark face darkened further. "I've been a member of the hunt, even the secretary, for probably twenty years. To suddenly tell my longtime companions—the entire village—that they can no longer hunt on my land? Impossible, it's impossible. There has to be a sale, and quietly, if it's done at all. And there's the matter of handling my mother. She can't in fact impede the sale, but . . . I can't tell you how infuriating and embarrassing this is. . . ."

"My husband is away for a few days," Clara said.

A silence. The silent moment extended. As soon as she said these words, she heard them with full orchestration, with all the clashing cymbals, the drumrolls of significance, the beautiful climactic chords, and he too appeared to have heard, or felt, these drums in the visceral way one hears drums.

With the possibilities so clear, the objections melted away, the defenses equally. "Immortal words, 'my husband is away,' " said Persand. "Boccaccio and so forth. Many plays begin that way." He paused uncertainly.

"There begins many a tale," she agreed.

"For how long?"

"Three days, possibly longer."

They looked at each other. It seemed fruitless to delay; they were going to act now and face the consequences later, so be it.

"Then . . ."

"Yes," Clara agreed, appearing composed, the wild elation continuing to grow.

"I . . ."

"Oh . . ."

Antoine glanced toward the kitchen.

"Senhora Alvares," Clara called, "could you pick up the papers, and the things I ordered at the butcher?"

Senhora Alvares put her head into the room. She did not miss much. She had no expression.

"Right now?"

"Yes, I said I'd be in about ten, and the bread too."

When they heard the front door close, Clara put her hand on his arm. They began to climb the stairs. "Just this once, to get over this terrible feeling," Clara said.

"Yes, once."

After a few steps, he put his hand lightly on her elbow. At the top of the stairs, they kissed hungrily and began to tear at their clothes, which fell in a trail to Clara's room, and with sighs they sank onto her bed, at last, God, how altogether starved they'd been. He gasped with admiration at Clara's luxuriant bosom, she at his imposing and ready penis; she opened her legs directly.

They did not even hear Senhora Alvares when she came back, in a couple of hours, having taken her time in the village. She heard the moans and thumps, the ecstatic screams, from madame's room. She gathered up madame's blouse and monsieur's tie, and hung them on madame's doorknob.

It was nearly three when they came down to lunch, eyes never leaving each other, wearing smeary, satisfied smiles, hands drawn to touch when Senhora Alvares was not serving at table. I'll talk to her later, Clara thought. They were both a bit stunned, she and Antoine, by their sexual appetites, and what this very vigorous interlude must say about what they'd been missing, or were feeling for each other. When they looked at each other, they tended to laugh for no reason, or for all the secret reasons they didn't need to discuss.

After lunch, they went back upstairs for a time. Antoine left about five. As he left, he fixed her with an intense, rather anguished look, and said, "I had always thought, more or less, that a man has to deny himself joy."

49

Oregon

Anne-Sophie was comfortable aboard the Monday Brothers' Hawker-Siddley 800 six-passenger executive jet, and did not experience a moment's anxiety. The pilot exuded both competence and deference, and spoke in the drawling American way all pilots speak. The seats were leather, and wide. The copilot brought tables that they might dine, the smell was of new car, or luxury boutique. There was a tiny galley, and a bar. Beneath them, through the window, the brilliant Old World lay; a France of castles and fields and the nuclear reactors in Picardy lay like a board game. They would fly west, west, to the New World.

She was thrilled. She knew it was not Tim's plane, nor his standing that had put them here, yet here they were, so it *was* in some sense him, the people he knew. Becoming quite close to Serge Cray, it seemed to her, had brought them closer to the world of private planes, a rarefied world not really theirs but amusing to try on.

Eventually she peeked into the cockpit and was received with a welcoming grin. The pilot was beguiled by her French accent.

"Ooh, is that *Eeng*-land?"

"Yup."

Cray was a restless flier, unbuckling his seat belt to stand up in the aisle, or playing solitaire. Tim tried to work on his piece for *Concern* on the plight of African immigrants in France. They had wine with lunch, and salmon pate, and trim little sandwiches ordered earlier from Fauchon, after which he slept. Chadbourne and Cray had desultory conversations about what visuals to look at in Portland. Delia's eyes were riveted the whole time on the little digital airspeed indicator winking at them in the cabin, urging them through the sunlit sky, taking her home.

They had left Paris at seven that morning, their trajectory intersecting with the receding clock in its bewildering way, through seasons and away from night, earlier and earlier according to the clock, so that when they stepped into the rainy, morose Oregon day they were puzzled but full of vigor, and it was still only ten in the morning.

Anne-Sophie was thrilled at last to see the reality of America. Despite what you heard and read, the country that had in part formed her darling Tim must have vast ranks of intelligent and benign citizens, and calm communities and scenic beauty, for Tim was *intélligent, gentil, beau*. From the first, her impression was favorable—the *sympa*, unpretentious little hangar, the affable official who glanced at their passports, the clean-enough ladies' room where she straightened up. Delia's mother and father came to meet them. They were like Americans in a movie—the *papa* wore a buffalo-check shirt, the *maman* a print dress, they both wore anoraks. Their car, a large jeeplike vehicle, was called an Explorer.

They embraced Delia with relieved elation, as if she had just been released from unjust imprisonment in a foreign jail.

"Delia, honey, you're walking so well!" said Dad.

"Great pleasure to meet you," said Mrs. Sadler to Cray. "I just loved *Queen Caroline*." Rather self-consciously they said *bonjour* to Anne-Sophie, and to Tim, evidently thinking he was French too.

The Sadlers said there was no more news about Mrs. Holly and Cristal Wilson. They had talked to the police and to some of Delia's friends at the Sweet Home Antiques Barn. The police were not too concerned. Their inquiries had revealed that the people moving things into Mrs. Holly's house had been SuAnn Wilson and a couple of other dealers, and SuAnn had said that Cristal and Mrs. Holly had gone to Hood River on a little trip.

"I'm not so sure, though, and I know Clara must be frantic," said Mrs. Sadler sympathetically. "Neither SuAnn or Cristal are one hundred percent, in my opinion."

The Sadlers of course wanted to hear all about France, and the perils Delia had endured there. They could not seem really to believe that she had spent a whole month in a luxurious château, though here was the famous Cray, they had seen the private jet—it was all amazing and delightful. Delia herself now seemed disposed to view her return as a narrow escape, and her sojourn in the grand French château no more than a usual condition of life. In France, danger was everywhere. Her friend Gabriel had been obliged to hide from hostile French police, she herself had been menaced in a hotel, authorities had refused to renew her passport when it had seemed to be missing—

Although it was cold and rainy, there were flowers blooming everywhere. Anne-Sophie exclaimed on the beauty of the planting they saw along the edges of the freeway and in the divider strip as they drove, and the abundance of green everywhere. All was verdant, piney, even the grass was fresh and new; it was as if Oregon was in an eternal spring held in good condition by the chill temperature, like flowers in a florist's fridge. Anne-Sophie thought everything beautiful, as in *Sylvie et Bruno*. "Yes, the rhododendrons will be early this year," Mrs. Sadler agreed.

Cray too seemed to feast on every detail of the drive in from the airport—the freeway, the four-wheel-drive vehicles passing them. He kept nudging Chadbourne and pointing things out. "I haven't been in the U.S. for twenty years almost," he said several times. "It's twenty years since I've been here."

"*Teem, chéri,* I want to go to the *supermarché*, for sure," whispered Anne-Sophie to Tim. "The Mall, all the *typique* things."

"The cars are so beeg," she said aloud.

"That's what strikes me too. By God, it's really important to have a look for yourself. The eye forgets," cried Cray. "Look there, Chadbourne, look at that!"

"*Quelle belle rivière,*" remarked Anne-Sophie, as they crossed the river. "What is it called? The Willamette? *Un nom français!*

"The Americans are wonderful drivers!" she exclaimed. "See how they stop for pedestrians. And how they wait for people turning left—really, it's very well organized. The French should learn from this!"

They would stay, except Delia, in a new bed-and-breakfast Mrs. Sadler knew of in downtown Lake Oswego, five minutes from Mrs. Holly's, overlooking the pretty lake itself. Cray in his own setting had never seemed that odd to Tim, but in Oregon the man's secretiveness and eccentricity stood out. He registered at the Tualat-Inn under the name Stan Carson, he wanted an inner room instead of looking out on the pretty if wintry lake, he made the others make all the phone calls.

Mrs. Sadler left them to get settled, hoping they would be comfortable there, and promised to drive them around once they got unpacked. "There are nice hotels in downtown Portland, but not so convenient, you'll be wanting to go over to the Holly house right away," she said.

The TualatInn was a refurbished Victorian house, furnished with brass beds, oak washstands with decorated china washbasins, Laura Ashley fabrics, and an infinite number of crocheted covers and hooked rugs done by the proprietor, Mrs. Barrater.

"Adorable," Anne-Sophie exclaimed. "I love the houses made of wood! Charming!"

Now they saw in what the skills of a great director consisted. In the little parlor of the TualatInn, Cray assembled, assigned, and organized a three-day program designed to find Mrs. Holly, scope out locations for a film, and also enter the bastions of the black-helicopter people and survivalists and religious fundamentalists, as many as Delia could come up with. Anne-Sophie and Delia would begin looking for these this afternoon. He summoned a sergeant from the Lake Oswego police, a locksmith to open the locked kitchen door of Mrs. Holly's house, and a couple of people Delia knew who knew the country roads. The finding of Mrs. Holly, it seemed to Tim, was distinctly second on Cray's agenda behind looking at the details of American premillennial protest. But they would begin at Mrs. Holly's. And despite the fact that sleepiness and jet lag were already overtaking them, they would begin now, not stopping to unpack.

"This can't take more than three days, because I figure I have about three days before the press gets hold of it that I'm here, and then the IRS and the rest of it," Cray said.

Mrs. Holly's house sat on a little knoll off a country road lined with blackberry bramble and rimed winter grass, and substantial houses discreetly separated from each other by a zoning requirement of two acres of land. Her house had a deserted air—

shades pulled and garage shut, a few flyers and newspapers lying on the steps up a long drive. Cray and Tim, driven by Mrs. Sadler, followed the police car up the driveway, which turned behind the house, where one was meant to enter, but it too was shut, and the low gate to the patio was locked. The policeman reached over the fence and did something to the lock, and the gate swung open.

It was clear to Tim as they arrived at the house that Cray had never been here before, had never visited Clara's mother, and wasn't particularly curious about her disappearance. Tim was curious—hoped to see Clara's room, some sign of how she had been in high school, maybe baby pictures. He had that form of romantic curiosity about Clara that Anne-Sophie seemed to have about him. She was extrapolating from Oregon a view of the way things must have looked in Michigan, where her imagination now had Tim growing up, though in fact he had spent very little time there.

The police had no objection to Cray, the son-in-law, going inside Mrs. Holly's house, though they hadn't done so themselves when Mrs. Sadler had finally called them yesterday. Then, at dusk, they had shone flashlights around the shrubbery and seen nothing amiss.

Mrs. Sadler came in along with the rest of them. As soon as the locksmith had opened the door and they went into the kitchen, they all could feel that something was different or wrong. Mrs. Sadler, who had been there before, confirmed it. Junk had been stored in Mrs. Holly's dining room—a welter of Exercycles, wet bars, televisions, stuffed toys—objects that by no possibility could have belonged there. Mrs. Sadler and Delia both uttered protests in Mrs. Holly's behalf. People had moved Mrs. Holly's furniture, it was an outrage, what did it mean? It seemed to mean something both sad and sinister. The tattered antler chandeliers and candlesticks, plaster lamp bases and cheap furniture covered with sheets were things that could only be valued by someone who had not much else to value. There was something desperate about saving this junk, let alone putting it in the dining room of some old lady, a sort of house invasion, you heard of those.

They were somewhat reassured to find that Mrs. Holly's bedroom was neat and her toilet articles gone, as if she had packed in an unhurried manner for a trip. But it was a little thing to cling to.

In the kitchen, wedged between the fridge and the corner, covered with a chenille bedspread, they found three assault rifles and two shotguns.

"All right, you folks, you're right," said the officer with satisfaction, "I guess this is a police matter, we'll take it over. I guess the first thing is find Mrs. Holly." He began to fiddle with his radio.

Cray stepped into the living room to call Clara on his cell phone.

"The damned thing doesn't work," he complained.

"American cell phones don't work anywhere else in the world, and European ones don't work here," Tim reminded him. "Like the televisions. It was never foreseen that an American might be abroad wanting to phone."

"I'll need to use the phone before it gets too late in France," Cray said to the police officer. Then he remembered. "I guess I pay the woman's damn phone bill, at that," he said, and picked up Mrs. Holly's phone.

Clara had apparently been sitting by the phone, for she answered immediately. Tim heard Cray tell her that they had arrived in Oregon, and that her mother was not found, but also that people were not too worried, no one feared foul play or danger; the locals felt that Cristal Wilson was not dangerous. Judging from Cray's replies, Clara received the news about her mother with distress but anxious hope.

With the evidence of real criminal intent, it now became plain that the police did not want the Cray party around, and so Mrs. Sadler drove Cray and Tim back to the TualatInn to wait for Chadbourne and Anne-Sophie, whom Delia had taken to the Sweet Home Antiques Barn. Tim went out to rent a car.

The Antiques Barn was a scene of some disorder, which did not strike Anne-Sophie as being too odd for a location consecrated to antique dealing, with its attendant pickup trucks, moving vans, items of furniture draped in padding being carried and stowed. These places were always confusion. Yet many people seemed to be moving out of the Sweet Home Antiques Barn. Stalls stood empty, with sawhorses or abandoned chairs blocking the entrances. Delia would not explain it.

Her business partner, Sara Towne, a plump girl in a granny dress, rushed to embrace Delia, and Anne-Sophie too, though they had never met. It was a sisterly welcome, to do with their shared métier. "I always knew it would be a good thing for Delia to do this trip, see how much better she is, I know it's owing to you, it was fabulous, it sounded fabulous. . . ." she went on. Anne-Sophie did not understand all the references, but she rejoiced in the Antiques Barn, which was full of delicious Americana including many things pertaining to horses. She bought tin trays with pictures of horses or horseshoes, lamps with horse bases, a lamp made out of a stirrup, mugs with famous champions painted on, objects formed from horseshoes. Things equestrian seemed to be a preoccupation of the whole culture. Anne-Sophie had not realized this, had always thought Americans were more interested in cars, though now when she thought of it, she saw those were named after horses, like Mustang and Bronco and Pinto.

Chadbourne too bought items of decor, seemingly unrelated in their theme: pennants from American high schools, tin wastebaskets, a doll carriage. Some of the things seemed strange to Anne-Sophie, but Chadbourne said they were for Monsieur Cray, for the film.

"Is there a recession?" Anne-Sophie asked, looking at the vacant stalls.

"I think they've heard about Gabriel," Delia said.

"Everybody looks just like in the films of Clint Eastwood," exclaimed Anne-Sophie, only half joking. She was surfing the television in their room the first night as they got ready for dinner. In her excitement she failed to notice that Tim was worried about poor Mrs. Holly and the things he had seen that afternoon. Her home invaded, her toothbrush gone, a woman in her seventies, with the police alerted, and messages going out on their radio.

"*Ravissants*. In their parkas and boots. The men here so handsome, just like Bruce Willis. Just like Teem! Now I find you are a regular American man, nothing special—you are all *très beaux*.

"What lovely sense of humors Americans have—the programs are so various and so silly, it's delightful."

After the Antiques Barn, while Tim and Cray dealt with the problem of Mrs. Holly, Anne-Sophie had spent the rest of the day looking at other things with Chadbourne and Delia. She had seen a supermarket and a Tower Records store choked with CDs and tapes of an unimaginable cheapness. Now Tim became irritated with her enthusiasms, implying, it seemed to him, some rather patronizing assumptions, for instance that the abundance of packaged food was magnificent for a nation of ladies well known not to cook. Such large, capacious vehicles—considering that Americans have to flounder in the rutted roads of their picturesque frontier and cover such inconvenient huge distances and have no trains.

"They have an enormous *camion* in the parking of the supermarket, called the Recycling, and people bring not only their bottles, as we do, but also their paper bags and tin cans! It is so virtuous! The French could learn from that."

Tim had never had a strong feeling of nationality. Though his passport declared him unequivocally American, he had never felt the need for deciding whether he was American at heart or really European, and he thought that the whole subject of nationality was arbitrary and divisive. But as Anne-Sophie praised just the things about Oregon that he himself found disgusting, paradoxically this reinforced his sense of Americanness. Instead of feeling alienated, he found himself feeling angry and involved at the wrongheadedness of strip malls and the vast cement shopping centers and freeways. Far from being politically correct food, it was a riot of junk food here, and Anne-Sophie claimed to love it, or maybe did love it. Or she was managing him, playing the wife of the typically obtuse and incompetent television dad who would believe anything his woman told him.

By dinnertime in Oregon it was too late to call Clara again, five in the morning in France, and they were bleary and ready for bed themselves. Insisting they stay up until ten, Cray took them to dinner. He invited the Sadlers and Delia as well, and they went to what was reputed to be the best restaurant in Lake Oswego, there to eat Pacific salmon, boiled potatoes, and cole slaw ("... filet of Pacific salmon, we leave the skin on and it's cooked on one side only, with a reduction of balsamic vinegar, lightly seasoned with chervil and shallot, served with small Washington Duke red potatoes, salt-roasted with a little olive oil, and a puree of red pepper, on a bed of cabbage . . .") As for the wine, "The Lorne Cellars is more oakey than the Knickerbocker Farm. Do you like the big buttery, or the flinty?" asked the waitress of the Chardonnay.

Tim watched Anne-Sophie pityingly as she struggled to peel the tiny potatoes in the French fashion. She had not noticed that the rest of them did not peel theirs. Certain transactions challenged her English: her brows knitted when the waitress asked, "Do you want me to touch up your water?" But her admiration was enormous. "*Saumon à l'unilatéral,* the cooking here is very advanced!" She did not in the least mind having to go to the foyer to smoke, she expected this. Chadbourne came with her.

As they drooped sleepily over their decaf, they discussed the day to follow, when Tim, Cray, and the police would continue to try to find Mrs. Holly and meet various followers of the various ideologies known to Delia. Anne-Sophie and Chadbourne would continue their sightseeing.

While they ate, the temperature outside dropped suddenly and the wind rose, turning a desultory rain into a blizzard that, this early in the season, shocked the people in the restaurant and rather excited the visitors from Paris. The local people hesitated in the doorway before dashing for their cars. Cray and his party walked quickly the short distance to the TualatInn with their coats over their heads.

Once back in their room, Tim and Anne-Sophie huddled in bed and watched television until they dropped off to sleep. The weather forecast was announced in the reverent tones always used for predicting disaster, but it seemed cozy in the TualatInn.

"Tomorrow I want to go to Taco Bell," Anne-Sophie sighed as she kissed Tim good night. "It is as if we are having our honeymoon before the wedding. If only we could go to Las Vegas . . ."

They woke at four, the *heure blanche* of jet lag. They could hear the wind whistling across the lake and, from somewhere, the sharp report, like gunfire, of an awning or a sail flapping. On her way to the bathroom, Anne-Sophie pulled aside the shade to look out. The world outside was white, and glittered in the moonlight; snow mounted on the sills and railings of the deck, and obscured the windowpane. How was it possible that nature had arranged such violent change in only a few hours? Tim got up to look, then they crawled back into the bed, wakeful and disoriented in faraway Oregon, listening to a storm that seemed to grow in ferocity as they lay there. It seemed like too much trouble to make love.

50

Guinevere Worries

Waking in the morning, Clara fell into a panic, knowing that her mother was going to die because of what she, Clara, had done with Antoine de Persand. She conquered this irrational but horribly present fear, and lay in bed trying to think about Lars, and her mother, but for the hundredth time she thought about making love with Antoine. She thought of all the legendary instances of husbands away from home: King Mark, was that in Tristan and Isolde? King Arthur too had been away, off looking for, was it the Grail? Or the sword in the stone? Both of these seemed not bad metaphors for Serge's trip to America, and for what had happened to her, too. She wondered what Antoine thought had happened to him. Was he up yet? Was he thinking about her at all?

She thought about sex in general, how mysterious it was. Her experience of it was not vast. There had been a couple of boys in high school, then there was Serge and marriage, and it had been okay, but for yesterday afternoon she had no adjectives. It had opened her eyes, had explained finally those rapturous passages in books, had elucidated sin and its eternal attractions, and why people went to hell for it. Decided on purpose to go to hell for the sake of sexual passion. Of course she didn't really believe in hell! Her whole notions of pleasure had to be reorganized; you had to have an attitude to pleasure, and to see how it was good and made you a better person. She thought of passages from the works of D. H. Lawrence that she may have once derided and that now made sense. Even those silly flower garlands . . . How to bear the wild vacillation between happiness and her conviction that she had killed her mother?

She got up; she would have to speak to Senhora Alvares, and she hadn't decided whether to make up an innocent explanation, or bribe her.

51

Snowbound

At six in Oregon, when Clara was well into her day, Tim and Anne-Sophie got up and turned on the television. The screen was already filled with images of stuck vehicles, officers in yellow slickers, highway machines, people standing around stamping their feet.

"It is so well organized, they give you the news immediately. In France you would go out and get stuck," Anne-Sophie said. Tim did not point out that in Paris you wouldn't have to drive out in a snowstorm.

They found coffee in the lobby at seven. As Tim was wondering if it was too early to wake up Cray, Cray appeared, looking apprehensive.

"Mr. Cray, I am such an admirer of your films," said Mr. Barrater, coming in with logs in a canvas sling. Since Cray had registered under the name of Carson, he glared at the man and made no answer.

"Assuming the roads are okay, Anne-Sophie and I can go to the antiques place and try to find if anyone knows where Cristal's daughter is," Tim suggested. They had discussed this last night.

Cray snorted. "She's not going to be there. They will have heard the police are looking for Clara's mother."

"I am looking forward to an American *petit déjeuner*," Anne-Sophie said.

"Hope you aren't planning to go far today," Mrs. Barrater said. "It's an ice storm. That's our local specialty." As if to illustrate the significance of this, the lights went out and the computer behind her desk, which had already been up and humming, and the television went black. "The lines go down," she said. "It happens every year and it always catches them by surprise."

By nine it had grown light and Mrs. Barrater had produced an elaborate Englishy breakfast of scones and clotted cream and Oregon Olalaberry jam ("Ooh la la," said Anne-Sophie). The lights had not gone back on. Mrs. Barrater called the power company but could not get through. "At least we got the phone and the gas stove," she said. "Storm mode." The TualatInn began to be chilly, then cold, and Mr. Barrater came in with more wood to build fires in the rooms.

"Is one safe in a structure of wood?" Anne-Sophie wondered.

The telephone rang. It was the police, saying they would pick up Cray and Nolinger; they were not to drive themselves with the roads in this condition. And they said that guns were not the only thing they had found at Mrs. Holly's residence; there was also twenty ounces of Semtex. The Bureau of Alcohol, Tobacco, and Firearms had been called in.

Though Anne-Sophie had been told that downtown Lake Oswego was within walking distance, there seemed to be nowhere to go, no obvious destination; there was a gas station, a cleaners, a pair of shops—both closed—and no warm haven of commerce in view. Anne-Sophie had never seen streets like this, sheeted with solid ice in which were imprisoned all the pebbles and litter as if preserved for all time like mammoths in permafrost. In Paris the streets were usually warm, radiant from the underground metro. No one could walk on this ice, yet the big Explorers and Tahoes and Broncos came creeping along, their wheels spinning with effort. Ice hung from the power lines, which sagged low over the street, and it built up on the roofs and railings, and broke branches and bushes, evenly glazing everything. Trees leaned against houses, limbs lay on roofs. She and Chadbourne stepped and slid. She grabbed Chadbourne, who grabbed the doorknob of a storefront dentist's office.

"Jesus Christ, what a place," he said.

Anne-Sophie in her little Parisian *manteau* looked tiny and cold in contrast to the few adventurous Americans in their puffy down jackets, stumping cautiously along, chipping at car windows with improvised implements, slapping their hands against the bitter cold.

"The bloody Jeeps are the only thing that get around," Chadbourne said. "Shall we carry on?"

"*Mais oui.*" They crept toward the stop lights. A police car passed them and parked at the TualatInn, perhaps to fetch Tim and Cray. From the chimneys of the houses they passed, sometimes, whiffs of smoke drifted, indicating the more resourceful householders. No lights or neon signs, nothing electrical worked. They worried, looking in at the window of the pet shop, that the owner hadn't been able to get there to feed a litter of young puppies, probably Labradors, who yipped beseechingly at the faces at the window.

"What if there is not heat in there?" Anne-Sophie wondered. "What shall we do?"

"Those dogs are Labradors, get it?" Chadbourne said.

They turned up the main street. Here was a Safeway, open and warm enough, though dark. They wandered the aisles, Anne-Sophie marvelling at the abundance, though admitting there was something to Chadbourne's "You wouldn't want to bloody eat any of it." She also thought privately that an Englishman had no cause to talk about terrible food, though you heard that English food had picked up tremendously now, since French chefs had begun going to London. They discussed such matters, and bought sandwich fixings—the local *pain de mie* and cheese oddly sliced and wrapped in little packets, and a quite okay-looking *pâté* from a reassuringly French-sounding maker. Cheerful Americans told them details of the ice storm: power was out from here to Gresham, and would likely not come on for days, a seven-car crash on the Hood highway, rescue operations for rounding up the sick and elderly and taking them to warm places. Four teenagers found frozen to death in a hut on Mount Hood. Poor Clara Holly, thought Anne-Sophie, she must be hearing this and worrying even more about her mother. She herself worried about the puppies.

"In five days I'm getting married!" she said several times, scarcely able to believe it.

At nine-thirty Tim and Cray went with two officers in a four-wheel-drive police vehicle that seemed no better than the other cars against the amazing ice that now coated the exterior world. They were to check several addresses contributed by people at the Sweet Home Antiques Barn: SuAnn's house, a summer cabin on the Beaverton Highway, a place out toward Mount Hood. Cristal and Mrs. Holly were in the third of these. As they had stopped for burgers at noon, it was already late afternoon, as dark as night, when they pulled into the driveway of a single-walled little frame house with a porch, set back from the road, with some dishrags and aprons frozen stiff on the clothesline. Tim noticed that the officers had their hands on their guns as they knocked and called out for Cristal Wilson.

"Police," they said.

"Coming," said a voice. A woman warily opened the door.

"Cristal Wilson? Is Cynthia Holly here?"

"Yeah. Why? Has something happened?"

"We've been looking for her. Someone reported her missing."

Cristal opened the door wider. A stringy woman in her forties, in jeans and a parka. "She's here. Why shouldn't she be?"

The house was cold. She led them into the kitchen. The stove burners were on, and inverted clay flowerpots were placed over the burners, radiating a little heat. Near the stove a thin little woman, presumably Mrs. Holly, sat on a chair under a pile of blankets, and next to her a child, similarly bundled, sat on another chair, knees curled up, staring blankly at the little visible heat waves emitted by the flowerpots.

"We aren't doing nothing wrong, we came up here, we didn't expect the storm, obviously," Cristal said.

"We went to Mrs. Holly's house," the senior police officer said.

"Yeah?"

"Found the guns."

Cristal had an air of innocent unconcern. "That's nothing of mine, or of Cynthia Holly's. Don't ask me what they put in there. They just pushed us out. They made us leave. They promised not to take anything of Mrs. Holly's. SuAnn's guru." She sneered, not convincingly, a scared woman.

"Mrs. Holly, are you all right?" the officer said.

She was looking at Serge. "That's Clara's husband, isn't it? Where is she? Is something wrong?" Her voice was querulous, and she was not too clean-looking.

"Yes, it's Serge, Clara is fine," Cray said, the tenderness of his tone surprising Tim.

"We should have called, I told you," Mrs. Holly said to Cristal.

"Okay, Thelma and Louise," the officer said. "You can't stay up here, it's looking like another few days of this freeze."

"We're happy to leave, believe me," Cristal said.

"Who are they, that came in to your house, Mrs. Holly?" the officer asked.

"I don't know which ones." Mrs. Holly began to cry, little meek tears that appeared to annoy Cristal.

"She's on medication, you know, and sometimes I can't convince her of things," Cristal said.

"Who's the child?"

"This is my granddaughter Tammi, SuAnn's. Something set those people off about a week ago, and that's when they wanted to put their stuff in our house," Cristal said. "Nothing to do with us. They just come in and made us leave. They're always reading signs and omens, I can't keep up with it."

"Well, come on, get your stuff together, you can't stay up here," the officer said.

"Look at the rocking chair and the old Arvin radio," Cray said to Tim. "I'd like to get a picture of that stove arrangement, and the stuff on the clothesline."

"We'll get Mrs. Holly to the hospital," said the officer. This, he explained to Cray, was not so much because she was ill, though she seemed frail, as because the hospital had emergency generators and was warm. A number of elderly people had been taken there, and the Red Cross was bringing in some cots. Meantime the police would impound the stuff in Mrs. Holly's house, and Cray could arrange to have the place cleaned up for her return. Cray wasn't sure she ought to go back to her own house—he'd discuss it with his wife when he got back to the TualatInn and could call her.

Cristal and the little girl got their clothes, stuffed them in paper sacks, and walked out to Cristal's old Civic. They seemed dazed, but perhaps were only so cold they were slowed down.

"Where will you go?" Tim asked, carrying a box for Cristal. It seemed to have mason jars and shoes in it.

"I guess SuAnn's," Cristal said. He found chilling her indifference to the kindness he meant to convey in his tone. It was the flatness of someone who expected no kindness.

They looked like they needed money. "Do you have money?" He didn't have much money in dollars himself, but he gave it to her, thirty-five dollars, he wasn't sure why.

"Just stick around, Cristal, until we look around," the officer said.

"I'd like to send one of my people up here tomorrow," said Cray to the officer, "to take some documentary photos. The decor is perfect, the yard, those things stiff on the clothesline."

Chadbourne and Anne-Sophie went back to the inn to make their sandwiches. It was colder than before. Mr. Barrater was falling behind in keeping the fireplaces burning, and they were inefficient anyway. Anne-Sophie stood for a long time with her back to hers, but it waned. She thought she might just get into bed and read or something. It was beginning to get dark.

"I think we should get into bed, Les," said Anne-Sophie, looking at the pudgy Chadbourne, his round body radiant with oxidizing calories. Chadbourne agreed. They took off their shoes and got into Anne-Sophie's bed, the door scrupulously left open so Mr. Barrater could come in with logs. They put the comforter from Chadbourne's bed on top of hers. Then, because it was four, the afternoon nadir for their deranged biorhythms, they fell asleep.

Tim was briefly disconcerted, when he and Cray got back about seven, to find Anne-Sophie and Chadbourne huddled in bed. But then, that was a good thing about French people, Tim thought, no false prudery in an emergency.

The sleepers stirred and sat up.

"Oh, *zut*, I slept, now I'll be awake all night," Anne-Sophie complained.

"Jesus, it does seem colder in here than outside," Tim said.

"Maybe we could get dinner in bed," Chadbourne suggested.

Serge waited until ten—seven in the morning in France— before phoning Clara to tell her her mother was safe, though in the hospital. Clara sat up in bed, tears overbrimming her eyes and running down her cheeks. She dabbed at them with the sheet. She had miraculously escaped retribution this time, her mother was safe.

"You're going to have to do something about Cristal, though," Serge said. "The woman is obviously batty."

He didn't tell her about the guns and Semtex.

Waking at four, Anne-Sophie had to fight back a wave of desolation. She was six thousand miles from France, in the freezing dark of a strange country. She stared at the moonlit wall, where she could read the cross-stitched sampler that said "Kissin' don't last, cookin' do." The exact opposite of what the countess Ribemont in *Against the Tide* would say. The countess said, "All men really require is extravagant admiration of their genitals." Anne-Sophie was in a world turned inside out and backward.

The sleeping Tim seemed to her to have strangely metamorphosed into an American cowboy. From his suitcase had come a puffy anorak from L. L. Bean, in which he lost any vestige of European cosmopolitanism. He spoke English all the time, even to her—she realized she had rarely heard him speak English except at the Crays'. Here he said "yeah" and also, once, "okey-dokey." He bought a bottle of bourbon whiskey to drink in the room. His handsome features seemed oddly to have melted or lost definition, so that he resembled the men on Oregon billboards, fair, bland, and beefy, with their small noses and strong chins.

In a few days he would be her husband. They would live in an apartment on the first floor even if on a chic street, on uncertain incomes, just thank God not in Oregon.

Yet Oregon was so lovely, if cold. She knew she was just rattled by the lack of electricity, a sense of nature's ferocity that fortunately did not apply in Paris, the sense of being on the edge of a distant continent from which some did not return. She told herself again that Oregon is really very beautiful, with lovely wide streets and convenient gas stations . . . No doubt in summer many golf courses, a great plus, and the food really good. How she wished she would fall back asleep and maybe tomorrow a thaw, and the chance to view American *objets* and *antiquités*.

For his part, Tim told himself it was only the discomfort of their situation that contributed to his poor impression of Oregon.

He had expected it to be more—ecological. It prided itself on ecology, did it not? Unlike the blighted, deserted towns of Michigan, the robust, cheerful little towns of Oregon had the reputation of being close to nature, citizen-friendly; their only social enemies were Californians, and the strange plague of gypsies that had somehow found its way here. It was a land of individuals, of freedom. With, alas, all that that implied of bad organization and inconvenience, ugly shopping centers, uncontrolled suburbs, fast food plazas, between which the lovely large trees struggled and an occasional natural weed asserted itself. Why could these people not see what they were doing to the place?

It irritated him that Anne-Sophie seemed to admire it. Was she being diplomatic or sincere? He wanted to shake her and say, "Come on, level with me, you can be honest."

"Oh, Teem, I have been to Circuit City." She sighed. "It is heaven, what is left for me in life?" When she heard herself utter this outrageous hyperbole, she had the grace to laugh.

Cray did not want to leave before he could meet some of the characters of his movie, correct the exaggerations of his imagination, fine-tune the details of their rhetoric, observe their normality. "Caricature is the enemy of the painful realism I intend for the style of the piece," he said. They would visit SuAnn, if Delia was right about where she was living.

It was a kind of compound, formerly a little cabin court of small cottages in a semicircle off a street in Westmoreland. A variety of old vans and autos were pulled up to the various cabins or on the grass in the side yard. At random, they knocked on a door and asked for SuAnn. The plump, rather normal-looking woman had not seen her, thought she might be with her mother. "Come in, though, it's cold out, maybe I can call someone who knows. She might be in the hospital again." They stepped into the little house. Four children sat on tiny chairs in the living room.

"We're having school," she said. "We're home-schooling them."

"Good, very good, excellent," said Serge Cray, all but rubbing his hands.

"You realize there are human beings on this earth, formed by alien sadistic child-rearing methods, who do not resemble us in any way, you hope they are of another species. Like the people in Rwanda, for instance, who hack each other up. No, we school our own," said the woman matter-of-factly. "Would you have some coffee?"

"Tell me a little about the curriculum," said Cray happily.

52

Meanwhile Back in Paris

Clara saw that Antoine was a nice man. That would not have been a prerequisite—he was a handsome man—but it ensnared her love absolutely. He was her male equivalent, a modest, correct person until now leading a correct life—"quiet desperation" being too ridiculously dire a phrase for two privileged people to claim. A correct life, a pleasant life, and then suddenly a life infused with drama and self-indulgence, born of desires heretofore unexamined. Only for three days, they promised themselves, and then a future of glimpsing each other in the village, smiles, the pledge of a certain permanent place in the heart. That would have to be it. But their hearts raged against this cold projection, or at least hers did.

God knew what Antoine was saying to his wife, or at his *bureau*, to explain his odd absences, his sudden departures without explanation, so unexpected in a dignified, self-controlled man. At his *bureau*, the *secrétaires* exchanged sly smiles.

He came for breakfast, they made love, they had lunch and made love, they went to an early dinner, they walked in the woods. They laughed and talked, their hands on each other—they had a lot to catch up on. They had a sense of Plato watching from Beyond with a gratified smile that these two people, some kind of test case, had proved his theory. Antoine could not spend the night, of course. Clara tossed with longing in the night, and stayed up till two to talk to Oregon again, with Serge's reassuring news that her mother was safe.

Antoine came out from Paris in the morning and took Clara over to his house. They walked there through the woods, the Rottweilers incurious, now used to them.

"I just want to see you there. I want to see you in my house. We'll be alone. They don't come out here in the middle of the week." Like Clara, he was enjoying the sense of kicking over the traces. He had been the designated good boy of his family, the Boy Scout and peacemaker, had almost never been unfaithful to Trudi, and had certainly never been a source of anxiety to her, or to his mother, or to any female, till now. . . .

She would not look at the antlers in the hall, their symbolic power over her life too potent to examine. He brought a Gevrey-Chambertin 1985 from the cellar, she sautéd the wild mushrooms gathered by villagers, he made toast to put them on. They ate in the kitchen, talking, and eventually made love on the living room sofa. Perhaps he thought the sight of the connubial bed would be too distressing to her, or he could not be quite that sacrilegious, she didn't know, but was just as glad not to see the two pillows, the two nightstands, the toothbrushes in the bathroom.

Actually by now, the end of the third day, with Serge coming home tomorrow, the idea of the end was getting harder to bear. Why was it that the prospect of a future without pleasure, a hypothetical deprivation, could threaten the pleasure at hand?

"That might be a sort of Protestant problem," Antoine said, "but it is a problem for me too."

"It isn't as if we were in love, this is just—is just . . ." The sense of being wildly gone in love was not one they had either of them expected ever to have. There were other words than love—addiction, desire—they used instead. Yet despite the circumspection of their vocabulary, Clara knew she and Antoine were out of control, were in a state of anguished rapture. It was as if they'd been told they had only three days to live—the duration of Cray's trip. Since the world was coming to an end in three days, who cared what you did? Was it a time for caution and self-control?

And was the impulsive affair the sweeter for its foregone conclusion? At any rate, the precious moments brought meaning to so many things they hadn't understood. They talked about these things. Clara knew she would be a better mother now, and a better wife in future, even if it was hard to describe how. Even if it was only sex and pleasure he had taught her about, those were mighty things she now understood the value of. Antoine seemed so gleeful about his own metamorphosis from staid *banquier* to romantic lover, he swore he didn't plan to revert, was now a permanent outlaw, in his heart. People crossed over. Had she crossed over?

Late on the third afternoon, Clara heard from Serge, who had

just got up, that he and the others would be leaving later that day
from Oregon, in order to arrive in Paris tomorrow before noon.
This would be her last night with Antoine. They must have a festive
dinner—she would take him to the great restaurant Taillevent. He
would have to make an excuse to his wife, then they could make
love somewhere, his office or a hotel, for farewell. You would think
they'd have got tired of all this fucking, but they hadn't.

Clara in a plain black dress was nonetheless almost too con-
spicuously beautiful for Antoine to feel quite comfortable even in a
restaurant where he was not well known. She stood out like Venus;
no one looking at her wouldn't think of venery; he prayed for a discreet table but was pleased too, and a little dazed, to be the possessor of this creature. Neither was hungry, they realized, had
somehow to get through three courses, what a mistake to be ad-
dressing *haute cuisine* with divided attention; great restaurants
were for the settled and bored.

Clara knew if they started talking about their parting, she'd cry,
so embarrassing in a restaurant, so she smiled and spun general
topics. Antoine was good at general topics. Literature?

"Adultery is the great subject of nineteenth-century literature,"
he observed. "Even of medieval literature, when the context is
secular."

"I love adultery," said Clara. "A hymn to adultery."

"An acquired taste, certainly."

"Madame Bovary, Anna Karenina—it always ends badly!" she
suddenly remembered. Every other topic too had a way of leading
straight to the questions of the longing of their bodies, and the perfect congruence of their interests, against the certainty that they
would never meet again like this; this was the last of their secret life.

53

Farewell to the New World

Highway crews with shovels and salt had worked through the night, so that by this morning most roads were passable, though electricity was still out in many sectors. The visitors decided to use what they had of their last day in Oregon to top up their experience with the things they most wanted to see or do. Cray wanted to see more of Delia's believers, millennialists, and Moonies, and perhaps more of Delia herself. Anne-Sophie wanted Native American artifacts and any item patterned in buffalo check. Chadbourne wanted to photograph exteriors in some of the little towns nearby, and since this could be done in the course of Anne-Sophie's antiques search, she and he would go together. The pleasant Mrs. Sadler would drive them.

Tim was the only one who continued to worry about Clara's mother, and Cristal and the poor little granddaughter. He started by going to the Adventist Hospital to see Mrs. Holly. Emergency generators were keeping at least this one area of the place warm, and patients in various stages of illness, attached to standing racks and tubes, had been grouped together in a sort of dayroom. Nurses moved among them, relatives in overcoats were allowed to survey from doorways but were not encouraged to throng in, as if they would soak up too much of the heat.

Tim saw Mrs. Holly slumped vacantly in her chair, near enough to where he stood that he could talk to her. He reminded her who he was, Clara's friend from France, had seen her yesterday. She seemed to brighten at the idea that someone knew her.

"Where's Cristal?" she wanted to know. Tim didn't know.

"This has happened before. Cold snaps," she said. "Cristal knows what to do when we are home, but they put us out, did you hear about that?"

"Who were they?"

"Some men. They said they wanted to put some things in the kitchen." She had an incurious, accepting tone, the absolute pragmatism of the old.

"They didn't say why?"

"They might have said, I didn't hear," she said.

How strange, thought Tim, to be so untroubled by powerlessness. Is that age? Or is it some American equanimity, some lack of imagination about bad things that can happen?

Tim tried to find out from the nurse what would become of Mrs. Holly when the electricity went back on, but of course she didn't know. It was easy to foresee that Mrs. Holly would be put in some nursing home, or left here, and she seemed to see this too, it showed in the bend of her contracted old spine, the forward, disconsolate droop of her head. She must once have looked like Clara. What would Clara think seeing her mother here, blanket over her bony little knees, breathing the vaguely uriniferous air? Mrs. Holly had not much notion of who Tim was, but accepted his ministrations as he tucked the blanket more snugly around her legs.

"Thank you, that's better. Do they say the weather's better?"

"Not much, Mrs. Holly. Looks like you'll be better off here for a few days."

"You come back and see us. Is Clara warm?"

"Yes, I'm sure she's warm," Tim said, preparing to leave. "Is there something to read? Would you like anything?"

"There's nine hours' difference between here and Paris," Mrs. Holly wistfully said.

He left, oppressed with thoughts of futility and age, and though he knew Clara had had no choice but to stay in France, he thought the worse of her anyway, for leaving this poor old lady to chance and neglect. He wondered if the warm smiles the nurses were beaming him were because he was almost the only man in here; the others attending to their elderly relatives were all female.

Before leaving the TualatInn, they had various phone calls to make and receive. Tim called his father's house in Grosse Pointe, to be told that Jerry and Terry Nolinger had already left for the wedding in France.

Cray arrived, fresh from visiting Delia's friends. He was high with joy and energy, infused by the weird energy of the fanatics.

"You'd think these people would be furtive, secretive. Not at all, no, no! Open! They have convictions. 'No works are good works other than those which God Himself has so designated.' Nor do the works of the creature—that's us—count toward a crown in heaven. Why the guns, then, I asked."

"Why the Semtex?" Tim asked.

"The answer," said Cray, "is you don't know which of your inner promptings are from God Himself, so you have to act with a broad scatter, like a shotgun. They seem to believe, also, that God favors the militant."

"It's about religion then, not patriotism?"

"No, it's the same thing," said Cray. "America is God's country. And why now? Because of the Apocalypse. The Mark of the Beast, the Whore of Babylon—these people are as literal-minded as they were at the first millennium. Great stuff!"

Delia had come with Cray to say goodbye to the others, which she managed to do without any suggestion that she had liked them. But now she had a smile for each of them, even Tim, whom she had avoided being alone with since he had twisted her arm. She hugged Serge. There was no clue as to whether those two bodies had been entwined in more heated conjunctions. She hugged Anne-Sophie, hesitated and hugged Tim, and even Chadbourne, as if not wanting to rudely leave him out. Good luck, they said.

"Could you kind of let me know if Gabriel gets safely back to America?" Tim asked.

54

Real Life

Madame Aix, very excited by the *Mademoiselle Décor* coverage, had involved herself, in Anne-Sophie's absence, with many of the wedding details Anne-Sophie would ordinarily have seen to. She was frantic at Anne-Sophie's unexpected and unorthodox absence this close to the day of the ceremony, and exasperated at Estelle d'Argel's indolence, though Estelle did agree to help take the flowers and several boxes of champagne glasses hired for the occasion, these things light enough to be carried on the train, and she had all along planned to host a cocktail-buffet two nights before the wedding. (For this, she did not involve Madame Aix.) Madame Aix found herself wishing she could expose this fraudulent excuse for a novelist, this unnatural *mère*, reveal to the world her detachment and lack of effort. She would never, ever, buy her books again. Eventually, she took the afternoon and went herself by train to Val-Saint-Rémy to look at the church and estimate the difficulties for the caterers and photographers, things Estelle should have done. Since, to a certain extent, the honor of her bureau was at stake, Madame Aix didn't want to leave anything to chance.

When she saw the tiny, dusty, undeniably charming church, she had an immutable premonition of what would happen: the stream that ran fifteen meters behind it would rise and overflow its banks on the day of the wedding. That this had happened often enough was clear from the stains on the walls of the transept.

The lawyer from Biggs, Rigby, Denby, Fox left a message for Clara. She should call him at once. The French magistrate had handed down her view that Clara was guilty, technically if not actually, and though her actual guilt could not be fully proven, she would have to serve some kind of sentence, *prison ferme*, he was afraid, though there was a small window for an appeal. Sentencing would be tomorrow. He, Chris Oliver, was on his way over. She was not to despair, they had many strings in their bow. . . .

At first, to the anguished Clara, this was only a minor and not unexpected grief. Parting from Antoine was so much worse. But the reality of prison soon asserted its due claim on her state of total misery. Nothing that the lawyer had to say, when he got there, was encouraging, but he spent a lot of time with the beautiful Mrs. Cray all the same, trying to calm her down.

On the plane, Tim had a couple of stiff bourbons, thinking it would be possible to shift his allegiance to bourbon; after the botanical mysteries of scotch, there was something fresh and uncomplicated about it, like mouthwash.

"Why is it called bourbon, though?" he said aloud. "Bourbon" suddenly sounded too French. It added to a certain reluctance he was aware of feeling to be returning to France. He remembered a fragment of a poem—he who had no head for poetry—it was by a Beat poet working in the bars and woods in Oregon:

> That short-haired joy and roughness—
> America—your stupidity.
> I could almost love you again.

Maybe he was more of an American than he thought. Or maybe it was just that what was in store for him in France, and the natural apprehensions all men are said to feel when getting married, was getting him down. The reality of the ceremony, and its imminence, and the rigors of the next few days had to be got through.

But, more than that, he was conscious of having enjoyed Oregon in a way, and he was still preoccupied with some of the problems they were leaving behind, even though, strictly speaking, they weren't his problems—poor Mrs. Holly, the poor little child Tammi or whatever her name was, poor Cristal for that matter, and the other desperate people, and the cold and poverty, and the purity of their craziness. Tim could respect Cray's preoccupation with all that, and the wish to tell about it and make it visible.

He also thought of Clara, of her glowing beauty and inscrutability, and of how he had felt her shiver when the hunters set upon her. Outwardly so composed, fear within, her emotions so smoothly packaged behind her lovely smile, like the smile of the Last Duchess. Maybe she maddened Cray, as the duke was maddened, with the indiscriminate way she bestowed her smiles. He ought not to be thinking of Clara at all. He glanced at Anne-Sophie; with her Dutch-girl fair coloring and Boucher cheeks, she suddenly looked like a marionette, though a charming marionette, slightly inanimate.

Ought one to marry when feeling reservations? But he had no reservations really, he didn't think. He loved Anne-Sophie. All this was nerves and culture shock.

Anne-Sophie sat with American *Vogue, House and Garden,* and *Bride* magazine in the rearmost seat of the little cabin. They strapped in, and the plane began to taxi. The thing felt small, all at once, like a balsa-wood model, frail to have to go over a pole, over an ocean. She continued to be gnawed by the certainty she would never get back to France. The wind would blow them off course, they would crash, a Branch Davidian had put a bomb aboard to head off Monsieur Cray's exposure of them in a film. Though it sounded as if he wanted to glorify them, so glowingly did he embroider on what he had seen with Delia at the fish camp, whatever a fish camp was.

"Delia'll be coming over, I've arranged it with her mother. The best hips are done in England now with a kind of reconstituted natural bone. They grind it up and form it, like particle board," Cray was saying of Delia. (Was there a liaison, Anne-Sophie wondered.)

But they would never even get back to France. She would never be married. The tragic loss of bride and groom on the eve, practically the eve of their wedding, the people actually gathered in the church of Val-Saint-Rémy, the priest giving a eulogy instead of the marriage, Estelle's exasperation at this ultimate mistiming . . . Though she knew it was silly, Anne-Sophie could not control this sense of rising panic to be far from France in an unreliably small plane with strangers. Even Tim, someone she slept with and knew intimately, now seemed a cold, insensitive stranger. She found one of the monogrammed mohair lap robes, pulled it around her, and tried to listen to music.

*   *   *

Cray told them more about his drive with Delia up the Columbia River gorge to a fish camp where SuAnn Wilson was, with others. It had once been a sort of forties resort, with a tottering dock.

"I think even Delia was scared," he said. He was pleased, they could see. "These people have guns. Ten or eleven families, they plan to go on to eastern Oregon, they're hoping to buy land out there. The famous SuAnn? It doesn't seem to matter if she's crazy, she fit right in. They seemed like poor people, is all, just poor people with poor taste in TV programs and a liking for junk food. And they have guns, lots of them, big ones, all loaded, and they have the idea that something, if only the forces of history, are after them, in the form of their neighbors, and the police, and the federal government. They have their exemplary tales—the Branch Davidians, the Weavers—even the names are perfect. Remember the sixties group The Weavers? 'Joshua, Row Your Boat Ashore.' Tim, you're too young, but Chadbourne?"

"Yes, sure, American group. Wasn't it Michael, though?" he said vaguely.

" 'Michael, Row Your Boat Ashore,' " said Cray.

Chadbourne, numbering and labelling rolls of film and stowing them in a green cloth bag, went on talking to Cray of the things they had seen at the millennialists' compound.

"We need a character like Delia," Cray said. "Perfectly sophisticated and yet disbelieving nothing. Waiting to see. This character functions as narrator in effect, whom nothing surprises. . . ."

"I need the gun store in downtown Lake Grove," said Chadbourne. "All the flags everywhere. And then I'd like some helicopter views of the Columbia River Gorge. . . ."

She thought all at once of Monsieur Boudherbe, and of the arbitrary nature of life. Someone could come and steal your money, murder you in your stall in the flea market. Your airplane would crash. You were going to marry this man instead of some other man. The orgasm was the orgasm, with one man or another. One spermatozoon and not another would do its work on your egg: France wanted Frenchmen. It was worse than depressing, it seemed so sad, so predetermined, what use was it all? Did one have options, or did you have to play the game?

* * *

At least she had stopped her senseless ravings of praise about the convenience and vigor of the American highway system and the remarkable cheapness of its goods, Tim thought. He was finding Cray's exuberance irritating too, he wished they would both shut up. Talk of these crazies in their abandoned motel conjured too many sad images of poor folks that well-meaning people ought not to abandon, i.e., he himself ought not to fly complacently off without seeing them safely into better situations. He could not shake off his concern with the whole state of things in Oregon. Poor little Mrs. Holly and the other old people at the Adventist Hospital, the freezing icy towns and the valiant strugglers chipping ice and fumbling with chains, and a sort of doughty courage going on in the face of nature. And the little girl and Cristal, like characters out of Steinbeck, and he would have liked to see the bipolar SuAnn. It was the edge of the world in Oregon, a whole society dedicated to struggle—tire struggle, ice struggle, carburetor struggle, safety struggle, struggle against (or with) bombs, and assault rifles behind the fridge. Maybe struggle was the spirit of the millennium, but the desperation and the disproportionate overreactions got him down: flight, arms, police patrols, all that development and asphalt in a state that was supposed to be Green . . . No, it didn't seem right to head off in a private jet to a big Eurotrash party—his own wedding—without adding his voice in protest somewhere in Oregon. France didn't need him the way Oregon did.

"Of course it isn't Delia's story, I don't know whose yet, probably the daughter's, SuAnn. Or Cristal? Shit, I forgot to ask about Lady. The dog. Clara will be sure to ask," Cray was saying. "Shit, Tim, call somebody, will you, and find out about the dog? Just say Lady, the dog, they'll remember."

We didn't make love once in America, Anne-Sophie thought. Making love puts a seal on a place. But we'll be going back often.

"It was smoothly done." Cray laughed, walking up to the cockpit. "This trip. In, out, mom rescued, plans in place for the second unit, and the IRS none the wiser that I was there at all."

"Can you really prefer Georges Gershwin to Delibes?" asked Anne-Sophie, who was listening to the earphones, of Tim, querulously.

55

Countdown to the Altar

It was well before noon when they landed, which meant they had almost a full day ahead, luckily, for there was much to do about the wedding, now three days away. Tim went to their apartment, but Anne-Sophie had the taxi take her straight to Estelle's; she would meet Tim before dinner and the events of the evening, and meantime Tim would try to reach his father and stepmother, who presumably had arrived.

The phone was ringing when he let himself in—Cees calling from Amsterdam to say that Gabriel was on a hunger strike because extradition papers had been filed by the U.S. Attorney demanding his return to the state of New York. Gabriel was claiming that the U.S. would try to bring him back and then charge him with a capital crime.

"If he can prove that, Dutch law would forbid extradition," Cees explained. Tim said he would tell all this to Serge Cray, but actually, since Delia's departure, Gabriel had ceased to interest any of them, though Tim was still burdened with a mild sense of guilt for his own complicity in jailing him. If the guy was guilty of some capital offense, however, did that put a different, more permissible face on his own collaboration?

There were messages from Tim's mother, who was back in town at the Lutétia. Tim's father and stepmother were at the Duc de Saint-Simon, which was very reassuring to Estelle's theories about his wealth and eminence, and also suggested a certain *connaissance*, though in fact this hotel had been arranged by Tim because it was around the corner from the Passage de la Visitation.

It had always been foreseen that the presence in Paris of Jerry Nolinger and his second wife at the same time as Cécile, Tim's mother, would be awkward. Estelle had consulted various friends about how to handle it—the situation arose more and more often in France now too. Madame Aix suggested a common solution. It was a kind of division of labor. Thus Dorothy Sternholz had spoken for Jerry and Terry Nolinger the following night, and had invited some French friends and a few people in the American community. Estelle, she and Dorothy agreed, could deal with Cécile Nolinger and some of Tim's college friends from America. The bridal couple would join Estelle for dinner, but drop in at Dorothy's for coffee afterward.

Anne-Sophie had a shock when, out of some apprehension she could not explain, she tried the dress on and found that it didn't fit at the waist. It was impossible to button the forty little buttons along the side. Estelle heard her scream and came running in. Seeing the problem, and thinking for a moment that Anne-Sophie might be pregnant, Estelle surprised herself by beaming and feeling a grandmotherly joy she had not expected to feel. *"Ma chérie!"*

But it was only the three days in America.

"It must be something they put in the food," Anne-Sophie wailed. "They are very fat, *Maman*. What shall I do?"

They grimly examined the darts and the other side seam, in hopes of finding enough to let out, but there was nothing extra anywhere. Visions of embarrassing piecing brought tears to Anne-Sophie's eyes. The problem with the sleeve over her wounded arm was bad enough; though the arm had resumed almost its normal size, the sleeve had had to be let out.

"Nothing to eat for the next three days, *la pauvre*," Estelle prescribed merrily.

The *maître-chien* came to Cray as he alit from the taxi, and presented his report. "Madame has had a number of visitors, but there have been no hunters," he reported. "There have been no problems. The *monsieur* who was here so often is recognized as a neighbor, and they do not molest him. No hunters have tried to broach the property, no one shooting. Here are the hours and dates of all the activity."

Cray reviewed this report for a long time, reading and rereading it. He thanked the *maître-chien*.

Tim heard Anne-Sophie talking to her friends, singing the praises of America. "No, we didn't get to Las Vegas, but it is a nation of readers. *Je t'assure,* I saw many bookshops, and every single person has a car. A huge one. I bought some *ravissantes* engravings of birds by a *Français*, Jean James Audubon, they are very admired in America. . . ."

At Estelle's *cocktail* everyone remarked how beautiful Anne-Sophie was in her little dark green silk suit. Looking a bit stuffed into it, perhaps, the coat unbuttoned. But how radiant, and the wedding two days away. They looked so happy, she and Tim; she was admired by all his college friends who had flown over—some balding a little, developing paunches, but still young men, with nice wives. They had thought Tim would never take the plunge. The friends admired Anne-Sophie's mother too, so trim and spontaneous, serving such great food, such elegance, the table, the fabulous flowers, the toasts. . . . Jerry Howarth, Graves Mueller, Dick Trent, Peter French were there. Still others would be at the ceremony— everyone he knew in America who could get away tried to organize a little vacation at the same time, a few days in Paris or in cute hotels in Normandy.

The American friends talked to the French couples, Anne-Sophie's friends, who had been invited to Estelle's. All the Franco-American conversations seemed to work. French people were much more friendly than advertised, often stopping you on the street when you were staring at your map, to volunteer information. They had been surprised. Cécile, Tim's mother, they knew already, of course, from summer visits in Michigan during college, the time the five friends got jobs picking blueberries and harvesting tomatoes. A number of Estelle's friends were there, including the academician Cyrille Doroux, which impressed Cécile, though she had never read a word of his esteemed works.

Anne-Sophie ate nothing and took three sips of champagne.

"The thing is," she said to her friends Victoire and Céline, "everyone in America has a private automobile because there are no trains. It is so vast, there is almost no way of getting from here to there. They had to get rid of trains because of a buffalo problem, something like that, the corpses of the buffaloes on the tracks—but this was a long time ago of course, and they just got out of the habit of trains. Hence it is nearly impossible to get to certain places in America. One is called South Dakota—it is romantic, no?"

"You won't believe this," whispered his old friend Dick Trent, the only one of his friends unmarried, "that Frenchwoman over there, the most beautiful girl here—except for Anne-Sophie—her name is Pussy. Yowee! Can you believe that!" He was only in part burlesquing the role of Animal-House American. Tim wondered if he himself was losing his sense of the ridiculous possibilities of Anglo-French *faux-amis*, never having registered the American connotations of Anne-Sophie's friend Phyrne having Pussy as a nickname.

"*Oui,* we had an adorable trip to America, all the Americans speak French, it is quite a surprise," Tim overheard Anne-Sophie saying.

"Anne-Sophie is a great girl," Dick emphasized. "She was telling me about her flea-market thing."

"It's a slightly mysterious thing," Tim said. "It looks like awful junk to me, but she sells it for a fortune."

Estelle, with her gift for seeming hospitable, and knowing most of her guests were American, was making a great show of things she had heard Americans like, like ice cubes. The maid hired for the evening walked among them regularly with ice bucket and tongs, bringing out a sort of rage reaction in Tim, at Estelle but also at the Americans, who accepted the ice cubes and put them into their *kirs champagne* or glasses of Perrier. Whole giant, catastrophic international incidents had probably been started by something like this.

At the princess Dorothy Sternholz's, in the high pink rooms on the rue du Bac, the guests were mostly French tonight, influential people who might enjoy meeting the senior Nolingers, with a few Americans thrown in—the dean of the American Cathedral, the cultural attaché from the embassy, those friends of Dorothy who had the famous garden in Gordes. They had dined downstairs and were now in the salon having coffee when the young couple arrived. Everyone loves a young couple on the brink of the altar, everyone yearns and dreams and confronts his private reservations about their compatibility, or about the institution of marriage itself. Edward Marks nominally counted as Tim's minister, and the ceremony was to be conducted by both him, almost in the role of acolyte, and a Catholic priest in Val-Saint-Rémy. This was one of Madame Aix's most creative ideas, and Anne-Sophie had thought it very suitable. She had also arranged for certain strains of Aaron Copland to be played, thinking fretfully, though, can he really prefer Aaron Copland to Berlioz?

Tim located his father and Terry, surrounded by French guests wearing friendly smiles, in animated talk. Tim was pleased to see them having a good time. He never thought of his father as a conversationalist or as particularly gregarious, but he saw these were qualities he must have had less use for since retirement from his job as a foreign rep for a company with, because of some distant connection, the same name. Tim steered Anne-Sophie over to them, embraced his father and stepmother. Anne-Sophie was warmly greeted, Terry's loud midwestern voice carrying and embarrassing him a little.

"The father is everything one had heard, so amusing and *sage*," sighed someone in French to someone else.

"Well, I do speak a little Turk," his father went back to saying to Madame Wallingforth. "I was for many years in Istanbul."

"Really?" breathed Madame Wallingforth.

"*Richissime,*" whispered Hervé Donend to his friend Pierre-Marie Sarbert.

"*Tiens, ils sont tous richissimes, les Américains.*"

Perhaps it was a worldwide weather pattern; the wind that had brought ice to Oregon, so many thousands of miles away, had brought to Paris a bitter rain, with a heavy snowfall in the Alps. Or perhaps it was a different wind altogether. Tim and Anne-Sophie left the party with Jerry and Terry Nolinger so they could walk them up the rue du Bac toward their hotel, the Duc de Saint-Simon.

"Nice party, Tim. You've found some nice people here," said his father. "I'm just sorry I never learned more French. Though I speak a little Turk."

"I thought they should make more of an effort to speak English, we're guests in their country," Terry complained. "No one talked to me the whole night except the woman whose apartment it was. I guess they all have to live in apartments? It's like New York. Do the very rich ones have houses? Or what would be the equivalent of the New York brownstone in Paris?"

"Uh—they prefer apartments," Tim said, seeing it was going to be a rough few days. "Tomorrow night, the rehearsal dinner at the Crays'—the Crays have a house."

Suddenly Terry screamed. She had caught sight of what appeared to be a live bear staring at them from the foyer of the taxidermist in the building next to the princess's. "My God!" They stopped to stare at the *vitrine* full of foxes, a baby rhino, and other endangered species.

"Imagine living with things like that downstairs." Terry shivered, deeply pitying the princess. They hurried on.

By the time Tim and Anne-Sophie got to their own apartment, they were soaked. "I've had enough of nature," said Anne-Sophie crossly, meaning, probably, "I've had enough of parents" or perhaps "your parents."

In their new apartment their boxes, mostly still unpacked, what with the dogbite and their trip to America, sat reproachfully in the hall. The heat had been off for several days, and the smell of new paint had stiffened the air to an almost toxic level. The aspect of things was mean and empty. They each felt they perhaps ought not to be living there until the wedding, that some operative superstition counselled against it. But it was too late, and they were too wet, to go elsewhere. They stood there bleakly for a minute, arms around each other, and then went to bed without saying much beyond that it had been a nice party. Anne-Sophie did not say she was surprised that his father had so little conversation, nor ask why his stepmother would expect people in a foreign land to speak in her language, and Tim said nothing about the fucking ice cubes.

Lying awake, Anne-Sophie kept strangely remembering a passage in one of her mother's books, probably *Plusieurs Fois*, which had seemed so beautiful at the time and now seemed more baffling than ever. After making love, the heroine's "heart palpitated like the pulpy labia of the star-medusa, when the velvet-covered little bracket fish made its strangely virile thrusts into the delicate pleasure-chamber of the eager creature's very heart." Compared to these lurid descriptions of emotion, her own heart felt flat. It had been—she counted—six days since she and Tim had had sex, and even before that, the velvet surface of love had been strangely showing thin. Why had the manly thrusts become attenuated? Or was it she whose responses were tepid? What was wrong? Whatever it was, it seemed awfully wrong.

It isn't Anne-Sophie, Tim was thinking, it's France, it's a bad fit, France and me. France is evolved, it has no need of me and no place for me. Marriage and it are a mistake and I ought to get out, in a dignified and apologetic but firm way, just say—

Yet how could he? Yet he belonged in America. It was a dilemma worth lying awake brooding about, but Tim had seldom in his life lain awake and did not now.

In Etang-la-Reine, the Crays had been sitting in the kitchen, to be near the Aga stove. The rest of the house was hard to heat. The day was over, and Senhora Alvares was making them some dinner. Serge, sounding uncharacteristically sentimental, asked Clara if she missed him. Of course, she said. But she was startled. He'd never asked anything like this before, maybe because he'd rarely been anywhere without her, not for a long time. She told him about their—that is, her—immediate problem, which she had saved until they could sit down and talk, the decision of the magistrate to find them—that is, her—guilty of defacing a national treasure.

"Do you think I could escape?" she said, her voice becoming tremulous when she thought of the horror of the prison again. "I could get away in the Monday Brothers' plane."

"They're ready with the appeal. There have to be procedures . . ."

Clara had a certain amount of confidence in Serge's influence, even after he was unable to prevent her spending a week in prison, enough confidence to value his reassurances now. Yet, how bitter, just now when she had somehow got in touch with life, to be confined in a place away from life and light, just thrown away, a disposable human being, for no reason. With part of her mind, she just could not believe she could be put in prison, even though it did happen once and furnished her imagination with a very precise knowledge of what it was like there.

"What did you do while I was gone?" Serge asked, mildly.

"Do? I don't know. I was very worried, of course. About Mother, about you, about this court thing." Something inside her quailed, as if he were looking in.

"Yes, I imagined you worrying. It must have been hard not being back there." There was something odd in his voice, but his expression was kindly. It had, truly, been kind of him to go all that way and deal with the Oregon problems. She was surrounded by so much kindness and love, it made tears come to her eyes, or something did—fear and desire, a mortal sense of having spoiled her life at the minute she had begun to care about it. She embarrassed herself by beginning to sob, and excused herself and went up to her room, heart ablaze with a strange, unfocused despair.

56

Rehearsal Afternoon

The caterer came early in the day, hired to relieve Senhora Alvares of the need to prepare the rehearsal dinner for forty that the Crays were giving that night for Anne-Sophie and Tim. The Crays themselves spent the morning with the lawyers from Biggs, Rigby, Denby, Fox, who somberly advised them among other things to immediately retire the Rottweilers, and not to impede any shooting in their woods until further notice; the hunting season in any case was nearly at an end, and a conciliatory stance was essential.

In the early afternoon Clara was obliged to attend the magistrate, to be told officially that she was sentenced to three months in *prison ferme* for she could not prove she did not sell the boiseries, and no one else could be proved to have done so, and she was responsible. Serge put her into the long car hired by Biggs, Rigby, Denby, Fox to carry her to the tribunal, but did not go with her. There was nothing unusual in that per se, since Serge so rarely left the place, though the attending lawyer, Bradley Dunne, thought this behavior cold beyond belief and would try to comfort her himself if he could.

"If we let the locals come shooting today, won't that make a difference? Would they relent about the boiseries?" Serge asked the lawyer.

"The two issues are no longer linked," said Bradley Dunne regretfully. "Once the charges were made and proven, or not disproven, they were out of the mayor's hands."

"Then why do we have to let the hunters in now?" she cried.

"It's still illegal to keep them out. The thing is escalating. Your husband could end up in jail too."

"We ought to have the courage of our convictions. We've been firm until now."

"Yes. With money, people can indulge their convictions," said the cynical Dunne. "But only up to a point."

"Do people—does the ordinary person, I wonder, act according to his convictions more often than not, or does he act against them? When these convictions go against the rules, for instance?" Here she thought not only of the hunting standoff but of making love to Antoine, and of her newfound principle of being true to the heart.

"If principles are optional, what use are they?" said Bradley Dunne.

"And yet we are stuck with them, and believe, yes, we believe in our convictions, by definition. Ha ha, and alas, for some of them are most dysfunctional. . . ." she said.

He thought it quite natural that she be overwrought. He saw that she was frightened, and would have liked to hold her. She looked especially adorable, which would probably have a negative effect on the female *juge*.

Anne-Sophie and Tim had a busy day in front of them. Tim had promised to show some of the American visitors some of the sights of Paris. Anne-Sophie and Estelle had to receive photographers from *Mademoiselle Décor* who wanted in advance to get Anne-Sophie in her going-away dress, the flowers, the table of presents, and other stills that the wedding day itself might be too busy to allow.

Then, Tim and Anne-Sophie had invited their two mothers to lunch. Tim hoped this would go some way toward placating Cécile, who had got the idea that last night's party *chez la princesse* was probably grander than the one she attended at Estelle's, and had made barbed remarks about the glamorous time Terry was having in Paris.

"*Désolée* that *Maman's* efforts weren't up to her standards," Anne-Sophie snapped. Tim correctly took this snapping as a symptom of strain, for he and Anne-Sophie would usually have protected each other, not their respective mothers. He shrugged mildly, but felt that Anne-Sophie ought to be more understanding of Cécile's awkward position as the discarded wife.

Cécile, however, was immensely cheerful at lunch (at Récamier). They all had the ragout of cèpes. "So happy to be here during cèpe season, we don't have them at all in Michigan. People don't gather wild mushrooms much in Michigan. Though wonderful blueberries—*myrtilles*—growing wild not far from my house . . ."

Estelle rose to this food talk, but Tim and Anne-Sophie both were glum and taciturn, making only perfunctory responses and looking at their watches in a way the two mothers founds exceptionally rude, if understandable.

Anne-Sophie, Estelle, and Cécile would drive out to Val-Saint-Rémy later in Anne-Sophie's Mini, install Cécile at the inn, and then help at Anne-Sophie's grandmother's house, where the dinner would be after the wedding tomorrow. Tim had mostly consecrated the afternoon to ferrying various American guests out to Val-Saint-Rémy to the small hotels they had booked, and helping them with arrangements that had broken down. There were hotel problems, "Paris tummy" problems he had not known existed, return ticket problems. Once installed in these hotels, the Americans would be nearby for the ceremony tomorrow and had only to walk over to the Crays' tonight, or, if they didn't have raincoats, come in taxis. It had been civil, most amiable of the Crays to invite everyone who had foregathered, since most of them had come long distances. Cray had planned a sit-down dinner with music and entertainment, a true gala to celebrate Tim and Anne-Sophie's taking the Big Step.

Tim had arranged to pick up Cees and his wife Marta, and two other guests, at six-thirty at the little station. The party was to begin at seven, early for the French and late for all the jet-lagged Americans. The weather did not improve, but this had few implications for the rehearsal dinner, because the main reception rooms in the château were adequate to entertain the large gathering indoors.

"Hello, dear old man," cried Cees, helping the pregnant Marta off the Saint-Lazare train. The other guests had missed the train, but another was expected in fourteen minutes, so the three sat on the platform to wait, and talked.

Cees was smiling oddly, pleased with the droll development he would announce. "The Driad manuscript has been returned to the Morgan Library," he said, as if it were a delicious practical joke on them all. "My office just called me here. It was airmailed from a suburb of Portland, Oregon."

Tim thought about this. Did it mean the manuscript had never left the U.S., or that someone had brought it back to Oregon, presumably in their plane, or that it was a coincidence?

"Delia? But that doesn't make any sense. What about Gabriel? Was Delia his accomplice? Then why didn't she sell it to someone else while he was in custody? Or to Serge? If she meant to just give it back, why let her friend cool his heels in jail in Amsterdam? And what about the murder?"

"The murder, just as it seemed. His colleague killed Boudherbe and stole the half million dollars he was going to pay Gabriel for the manuscript. We are pursuing the connection of Boudherbe to other manuscript thefts of course."

"Ah, and Gabriel hung around the flea market hoping to get a line on the half million 'missing money.' "

"Very natural."

"And Delia?"

"Maybe she was just enjoying her French vacation. I don't know. But regarding jail, we now have no reason to hold the man. From our point of view there's nothing for us to charge him with. We'll probably let him go; let the New York authorities find him if they want him.

"But I wonder, was it really the girl who sent it back?" Cees went on. "It doesn't matter except as a matter of curiosity. There were to be no questions asked about its return. Still I wonder, could it have been Cray himself? Did he buy it from Gabriel, use it, look at it, copy it, whatever, and return it? He always said he would return it if he got it."

"I don't see him spending half a million—or whatever the price turned out to be—and then giving it up secretly. Why would he do that? Anyhow, I think I'd know," Tim said.

"I think we should ask him," Cees said. "Who else could it be? And how are you holding up, my friend? At this time tomorrow you will be married."

"I've begun to think we're making a big mistake," Tim said, hoping by his light tone to indicate he really didn't mean this, though he did. He had a compulsion to mention it, in hopes someone would say something helpful.

"Ha ha, normal enough," said Cees.

*　　*　　*

Estelle looked forward to transacting a matter of practical import at the rehearsal dinner later. One of the reasons she had been interested in the general solvency of Jerry Nolinger was her concern about the cost of the wedding. Though Anne-Sophie and Tim had insisted that, as responsible adults with jobs, they would be paying for everything, still Estelle had taken the traditional view. This, in France, was that the families of bride and groom often split the expense, and now she had been told that this was by no means the situation in America, where she, Estelle, the family of the bride, would be expected to pay it all.

"*La famille de la mariée,*" she had said scornfully. "How primitive. It must be like that in India and Afghanistan too, as an inducement to take female children off their hands."

She knew she should have written to Monsieur Nolinger, but her insecurity about her English had led her to procrastinate, and now here they were. She wished enormously that Tim would offer to bring this subject up with his father, who presumably could with one flourish of the checkbook wipe out the whole mounting debt— the *fleurs* alone more than eight thousand francs, as flowers were the one expense, along with the food of course, she couldn't countenance stinting on. But Tim was too distracted or insensitive to pick up on her hints, and she would have to mention the matter to Monsieur Nolinger herself.

57

The Crays Entertain

People would expect flair from a great *auteur* and *metteur en scène*, and Cray had not disappointed. He had caused the lighting of the twelve sumptuous candelabras, each with eighteen branches, the same that had been used in *Queen Caroline*, and had massed what seemed a half ton of greenery of pine and holly on the chimney breasts and over the doorways, so that the big rooms blazed with candles, and the scent of pine needles gave a festive, nuptial, and seasonal mood that was nearly overwhelming. Guests, arriving by car or on foot from the village, stood dazzled in the entrance hall to take in the scene while Senhora Alvares, in black dress and apron, took their coats.

One of the guests, uninvited, was the mayor, Monsieur Briac.

Some did not notice or understand the drama of this arrival, among them Anne-Sophie. Seeing the number of guests, the lavish decoration, the general air of heightened emotion, she was thinking as they arrived that Monsieur Cray was nice after all, and genuinely fond of Tim. She was also thinking that, in the merriment, she might have trouble speaking alone to Tim.

She had found the perfect wedding present for him. Though he might not yet appreciate the rarity of such things, he would come to when she had explained it—these were a pair of extremely rare faience horses, Delft, from Lampetkan, maybe 1750, the pair rearing up so delicately, their lacy reins intact, not a chip anywhere on them, truly fabulous and sprightly. She did rather well on the price, and they were worth twice as much. A London dealer, seeing them when she had them sitting on her desk, offered her nearly twice what she had paid a few minutes before. Moreover, they would look charming in the Passage de la Visitation. She thought it would be suitable to present them tonight, but she and Tim should be alone; perhaps they could steal away a few minutes after dinner; if not, she'd have to wait until after the dinner tomorrow.

Also, she was not without hope—it had crossed her mind—that there would be some piece of Nolinger family jewelry she would receive to wear tomorrow—the "something old" of the American wedding ritual. But to be honest, looking at the understated style of both Terry and Cécile, the chances looked dim that Nolinger *père* thought much about ornament.

Clara, beautifully dressed in crimson satin as befitted a Jezebel criminal felon, stayed mostly behind the scenes directing last-minute details in the kitchen. Her heart was not in the entertaining. She was still stunned by the intransigent severity of the judge that afternoon, who must have known that though she was legally responsible for it, she didn't steal the panelling. The censorious words and harsh sentence had shocked her even though she was prepared for them.

Bradley Dunne had explained that things were likely to go wrong for an unforeseeable reason that had nothing to do with Clara personally—the new independence of French judges, who were determined not to cooperate with pressure from the executive branch. It seemed the minister of justice had called the prosecutor in and explained why for reasons of state it would not do to inflame and agitate the famous director Cray—one reason being that it would damage the government's efforts to widen Franco-American film coproduction. Then there was the minister's personal friendship with the American ambassador, and there was the general unpleasant resonance in the American community, given the woman's probable innocence, and whatever economic ramifications the unpleasant resonance might have—they had always found foreign investment to diminish at times of strained relations—and so on. Hearing all this had irritated the judiciary, and made it resist the pressure with extra firmness.

Dunne showed Clara the headline: WILL JUDGES SAY SHOVE IT TO THE MINISTRY IN CRAY CASE?

News analysis in the *International Herald Tribune* explained this as a breakthrough show of independence by French magistrates, who had in the past been in sympathy with reasons of state. But now they seemed to be strong enough to insist on the idea of an independent judiciary; so when the prosecutor had recommended letting Clara off, they couldn't.

"If they let you off, they'd be caving in to the government," Bradley Dunne explained to Clara.

Serge, immersed in preparing his fete, had barely commiserated when she got home, had nodded distantly, had even avoided her, as if she were already in jail. Clara had other concerns too. The Persands, as old friends of Estelle and Anne-Sophie, were expected at the dinner, her first meeting with Antoine after their official parting. It would be a sort of test to see how they could bear it. She expected not to be able to bear it, yet she was buoyed by the hope of feeling his love projected invisibly across the crowd of guests. Just to see him would be a little happiness and give her another picture to hold along with the more intimate ones. She would come out when the Persands got there, but for now had the excuse of arrangements behind the old-fashioned baize door of the kitchen.

She was here when her mother called, fretfully, from the Adventist Hospital. "I just told them I'm using the phone, I don't care. You would think no one had ever called Paris, France, from here. They had to get the hospital administrator."

"I'll call them on Monday and get some kind of authorization."

"I don't want to be here on Monday, Clara, I'm not sick. They expect the electricity back on this weekend, I want to go home."

"I don't know, Mother. Serge thinks—the police found—where's Cristal?"

"She's—I don't know, she isn't happy, she wants to come home. I said Tammi could come to our house too."

"But your house, Mother. . . ." Clara sighed. Why was nothing solvable? "Tell Cristal to call me when you see her, okay?"

Tim was eager to tell Cray about the Driad manuscript being returned to its rightful owner, mysterious as that was, and he wanted to watch Cray when he told him. But it was not so easy to draw Cray away. He was completely absorbed by the arrival at the door of Mayor Briac, who had turned up with three other hunters. They were all dressed in breeches and tweed coats and were bearing shotguns, and the mayor carried a brace of pheasants and a dead rabbit. These he handed ceremoniously to Cray, who stood in the doorway of his château greeting the arriving guests. Tim could not at first imagine who invited the mayor. Was it yet another French custom, perhaps some variation of the *droit du seigneur*?

As if his thoughts were read, he heard the mayor say, "It is the custom to thank the proprietor whose game we have shot." He spoke sardonically, without taking off his sporty cap, as he proffered the game to Cray. Cray motioned to the car parker, who already stood in the gravel drive, to take the bloody offering. "Come in," he said to Briac, resisting the provocation with mild courtesy. The men stood their guns against the wall.

Cray, who had at first seemed at a loss, now nodded to the others. "Take the birds to the kitchen, will you?" he said to the car parker. "I wouldn't want my wife to see those." He smiled at the mayor. Now it was the mayor who was at a loss, seemingly disconcerted by the conspiratorial tone of Cray's voice.

"Too soon to cook them, is it? They have to be hung, I understand?"

"A few days," agreed Briac.

"But I can offer the poor fare we have already prepared," Cray said. "Passing the time until dinner, we are just having some champagne, and I insist you join us."

"As you know, we French people set great store by tradition, and . . . Sorry to intrude, I see you are in the middle of something," said Mayor Briac, blinking as, seeing the blazing candles, the people gathering in the salon, smelling the scented air, he came to appreciate his own understatement. "However, I will be glad to thank the lovely Madame Cray as well. We had a splendid day, perhaps the better for not having shot over this way until this late in the season."

Cray picked up the mayor's shotgun and carried it inside with them, as if intending to put it in a safer place. The car parker took charge of the other guns, moving them a foot inside the door.

"The woman wants ten thousand dollars," his father was suddenly muttering at Tim's elbow.

"What?"

"Your bride's mother. My share of the wedding. First I'd heard of it."

"Oh, no, Dad, Anne-Sophie and I are taking care of everything." He knew his father, retired on a pension, with two wives to support, didn't have money to spare, and was sorry to hear it had even been mentioned to him.

"You hear the French are close with a buck—with a franc, ha ha."

"No, really." Tim was shocked to hear the figure, nonetheless. Ten thousand dollars or sixty thousand francs, which must only represent half the cost, assuming Estelle was proposing the two families split the cost. Tim had no idea the thing would rise to twenty thousand dollars. Anne-Sophie had been assuring him matters were going to be done sensibly and modestly. Maybe this was, in the great context of wedding costs, modest? My God.

"I thought it was the bride's family that pays. That's what they told me when I paid for your sister's wedding, I sure remember that."

"I'm not sure how it's done. That is, I think in France they split it."

His father blinked impassively. "It might have been nice to run it by me."

Most of the forty guests were now assembled. More people had been arriving than Tim had realized, on foot from where they were staying in the neighborhood, or by car. There were Antoine and Trudi de Persand, for example, and Madame de Persand his mother; Anne-Sophie's brother, and there were a battery of Anne-Sophie's cousins and girlfriends, here were Jerry Howarth and Graves Mueller and their wives, and Dick Trent.

"Where's Clara?" Cray called. "I have a surprise."

Someone went looking for her. With his vaunted sense of drama, Cray had somehow arranged for a little boy to make his entrance on the line "I have a surprise," with a driver behind him. Lars, their son, a scrubbed-looking boy of eleven, wearing the short pants of an English schoolboy and staring in surprise at the unexpected big crowd of people. Clara, coming into the entrance hall, gave a gasp and rushed toward him. Cray too was there embracing the child. People gathered around Clara and her son, moved by her joy. Tim noticed that Clara waved her hands and fingers at the little boy, who was apparently deaf, but Cray spoke aloud to him. Cray embraced the child again, lifted him up, put him down, and returned to the mayor. The radiant Clara began presenting Lars to the various guests.

"*Bonjour, monsieur,*" said the boy to Tim. He was a fattish boy who looked like Cray, but with his mother's coloring and smile. He spoke in the monotone of someone who had never heard speech.

Clara's heart was wild with gratitude. It was so unexpectedly nice of Serge to see that Lars got home before she had to go to jail. Serge was kindhearted despite his odd, reclusive ways and distant manner, and he loved her. What a bad woman she was.

She had been in the kitchen talking to Senhora Alvares, who had suddenly whispered, "Your husband, senhora, I didn't tell him anything." Clara, momentarily disconcerted by this directness, had only murmured, "Oh, good." Then she was obliged to ask what Serge had been wanting to know. About what she had been doing while he was gone?

"*Sim,* senhora. I told him I hadn't noticed anyone around. He wondered if there was someone short, tall, bald, what color hair? I said there had been a senhor, for only a few moments, wearing a hat."

"Senhora . . . thank you. He should not be asking you."

Her thoughts raced. Why was Serge checking up on her? He had always seemed completely indifferent to what she did.

Cray was talking again to the mayor, and was inspecting the mayor's shotgun, which surely wouldn't be loaded? The champagne was being passed on silver trays by waiters in black jackets. The smells of melted cheese and little sausages *en croute* competed with the Christmasy pine and the scented candles. Tim stood rooted to his spot near Cray, who continued to chat mildly with other guests, his eyes straying often to Clara, impossibly beautiful in dark red and with the radiance of her happiness in seeing Lars, whom she had not expected for a week. Tim absently answered congratulations and the waggish denigrations of marriage people put to him.

"How you holding up, Tim? You'll feel a hell of a lot better when all this is over," his father said, coming up to him again, having had, it was clear from his newly genial tone, more than one glass of champagne.

"I'm wondering if it isn't all a big mistake," Tim said, this observation coming out with more conviction than he'd meant to convey, but not more than he was feeling.

His father took it with a seriousness born of experience.

"Is anything wrong?"

"Jitters."

"Well, remember it's much harder getting out of a marriage than it is to break off beforehand. I oughtta know. Last chance."

"Thanks."

"The important thing is to be true to your instincts," said his father. "Know where you're coming from." Tim wondered when his dad had adopted all this New Age talk.

A string trio played from the little musician's gallery in the dining room as the guests were led in to table. Tim caught up with Anne-Sophie. He had a chance to whisper his news: "The manuscript was returned to the owner, after all that."

"I know." She smiled archly. "It was I who sent it, from the American post office. *C'était moi.*"

It took a second for Tim to register this. "How did you get it? Ah—Gabriel gave it to you. Or Delia?"

"I looked for it in my *grenier* and found it as I expected."

Tim spluttered, his wits failing before the task of explaining this to himself. She hadn't shown it to him, she hadn't mentioned it—what could account for such a lack of trust, of complicity, of consideration? He would have liked to have seen it, at least. "How could you do that?"

"Well, if you'd known about it, you'd have to tell your friend from Amsterdam. They'd keep the poor young man in jail forever, and after all, he didn't steal it, or kill anyone. He'll be disappointed, won't he, when he goes back to look for it?"

"You'll tell Cees. You'll explain to him—"

"You can explain. I'd rather not."

"Plus you sent a half-million-dollar manuscript through the U.S. mail?"

"Well, I wouldn't with the *poste française*, but I'm sure the American post is perfect. Think how clever Americans are with bombs that go down the chimney and so on." Was Anne-Sophie mocking him? He did not know. Tim could not explain his wonder, his dumbfounded sense of talking to a complete stranger.

58

The Rules of the Game

The table was set with greenery and golden bells, symbols both of weddings and Noel, tied with ribbons reading "Anne-Sophie et Tim," and place cards ranging the guests from Cray at the far end, with the mothers Cécile and Estelle on either side of him, to Clara at the far end with the grandmother, Anne-Sophie and Tim on either side of her, a deaf uncle, and then the young American and French friends along the sides. Madame de Persand *mère* sat near her old friend Estelle. No one appeared disappointed with the *plan de table*, Clara's speciality.

Cray drifted with the guests, the gun under his arm, leading the mayor toward the long table, or series of tables unified by one cloth, set for forty people. The shotgun was broken correctly and pointed toward the floor. All the same, Tim wished Cray would give it back to the mayor. But Cray just leaned the gun against the table at his own place and began rearranging the place cards to make room for the mayor and the three others with him, and calling for more chairs. The mayor, it appeared, would go next to Cray, between him and either Cécile or Estelle.

The dinner, punctuated by toasts to fiancés, to the morrow, and of thanks to the Crays, was a simple and good one of clear soup, roast lamb and brown potatoes, and a flaming pudding carried in with musical fanfare on silver trays, for which the lights had to be put out. Then some of Anne-Sophie's friends had prepared a skit—there would be more skits tomorrow night after the actual wedding. Here the pretty young Frenchwomen put on aprons and sang a song they had composed about Anne-Sophie, of which Tim only noted the refrain:

Ma main était bien jouée; nous sommes mariés, nous sommes mariés.

I've played my hand well, we're married.

Dick Trent had clearly lost his heart to Pussy Lautremont. She gave him a flirtatious wink as the singers sat back down.

Escape, escape, thought Tim miserably, unable to stop thinking about the Driad Apocalypse and Anne-Sophie's treachery.

"I have something that I'd like to offer," Cray said. The shotgun, Tim noted, was now laid safely under the table. Cray got up and went to the projector Tim had noticed earlier set up at the back. The blank white wall at the other end of the dining room was animated with black-and-white blurs and flickers, which then resolved into a woman hurrying across a foyer. Cray stopped the film and rewound it for a minute. People left off talking and reorganized their chairs so everyone could see.

"This is a new print of this great classic with the sound track remastered," Cray explained in a loud, public voice. "The sound still isn't good, but good enough, I think."

Tim recognized without being able for an instant to put a name to a newsreel-like scene of men in a variety of overcoats, tweed caps, and country clothes walking many abreast across a thicketed field, shouting and laughing, knocking at branches and shrubs with sticks or throwing rocks ahead of them into the bushes. Many people murmured in recognition.

Immediately it came to him that this was Jean Renoir's great film *La Règle du Jeu*. Rules of the Game. In the scene Cray was showing, these were the beaters, locals driving the game ahead of them toward a party of aristocratic and fashionable hunters. The assembled company at the Crays' murmured expectantly, since everybody liked a movie, and this was a great classic, as Cray had said.

Tim remembered that the characters in the film were at a country house party. The analogy must have come to Cray hosting this party tonight. His purpose was not clear—to make a point about hunting, or simply to entertain his guests? It didn't seem a very nuptial movie. It seemed a damned strange movie to show at a wedding party. Tim watched the mayor and his friends at the same time as he watched the film. Their faces were politely impassive and interested. Cray had disappeared.

Ahead of the beaters, rabbits ran, and small birds flittered up or broke from the heavy copse into glorious untrammeled flight. Even remastered, the sound track was old and thin. This came out when? The forties, Tim imagined. He was no film historian, but he thought before the Second World War, long before his birth, when movies looked like this, and their tinny music sounded as it had whenever film first got sound.

The partridges and hares, with rising panic or innocent instinct, fled before the beaters. The camera lingered on one appealing rabbit, her hesitant hop, warily concerned, and on a frightened squirrel. At the other end of a field stood the members of the marquis's house party, beautiful women in suits with big shoulder pads and smart little hats, men in *tenue* of the field, all of them with shotguns, laughing and chatting to each other as they waited for the quarry to run within range, and there was some personal drama one or two of the characters were discussing—he couldn't remember about that. They talked about it as they waited to shoot, but the sound track was still flawed and hard to understand.

He remembered the next, memorable, shocking sequence, when the birds flew overhead, and the little rabbit made the wrong decision and ran toward the hunters. The smiling, rich, well-off people raised their guns with seeming indifference, much more interested in what they were saying than in the shooting, and picked him off; then slaughtered everything else that moved. Everyone was a wonderful shot. What he had blocked out was the twitching corpses of the rabbits, the flutters of the downed, dying birds—and how the scene went on and on, shot after shot, dying animals one after another shuddering in the leaves. One was the little creature that had looked so brightly at the camera moments before, dead now. The horrifying length of the sequence was worthy of Cray himself, whose reluctance to leave a scene was one of his most characteristic mannerisms, almost a film tic. Behind him, someone— Tim would have said his stepmother Terry—said, "Oh really."

On the screen, the beaters and some of the shooters began to walk across the field picking up the corpses. Cray, back in the room, cut the projector and turned on the lights again. For an eerie moment, they were the company in the film, this was the hall of the little marquis, these were the guests, now dressed in dinner clothes, reviewing an entertainment of which they had been a part that afternoon. An eerie effect, one that surely Cray was aware of.

It was not lost on the mayor. He resisted Cray's gambit, whatever it was. *"Alors?"* he said. "One of the great landmarks of French cinema, thank you, monsieur."

Cray, however, was looking at Clara. Tim followed his eye. Clara had pressed Lars to her bosom, to keep him from seeing the horrid movie scene. She sat, her hand over her mouth, as if the sight of the twitching, dying rabbits had made her sick to her stomach. "Are you all right?" Cray called down the table to her. Without answering, Clara started to rise.

He knows, she was thinking, that was the message of the shooting of the rabbits, he wants to upset or even shoot me, like the sister rabbit whom the filmmakers had so pitilessly brought down. She had seen it in his expression just now. She was not exactly afraid, but Serge had a side of violence, or wished he did, was drawn to it in his own films, and it was an ugly thing to have shown this film tonight.

"In America, is it not, monsieur, they kill people, not rabbits?" said the mayor, who had evidently been composing this insult as a parting shot, and now rose to deliver it with a self-satisfied smile. But the timing was off, and it failed to wound with the force he had hoped.

"It's an allegory of marriage. Think of the rabbits as husbands," Cray said to the table. "All the women are very good shots, ha ha."

The rabbit was really shot, Clara thought, killed for the film.

Someone at Cray's end asked him a question Tim couldn't hear. Raising his voice so as to be heard generally, Cray went on, "No. Now, of course, we wouldn't actually shoot the animals. It wouldn't be allowed, and if you did, the film couldn't be shown. The production people would have to find me some short-acting paralytic agent to give the bunnies, something that would make them twitch but they'd wake up from. Knocking the birds out of the air would be harder." His tone was sardonic.

Yes, he knows, Clara told herself, and into her heart crept not fear but instead the irrational hope that, as he knew, secrecy and forbearance would not be needed, and she could be with Antoine as often as she liked.

* * *

The room suddenly seemed to Tim a stage set not for his own wedding party but for another drama altogether. Was his imagination just disordered about tomorrow, projecting on Cray some rancor he didn't actually feel? For Tim was remembering the rest of the Renoir film. The loyal retainer, husband of the maid, seeing the wife and the lover in the summerhouse, says something like "*Je vais les descendre, tous les deux.*" And eventually he shoots the lover.

Yes, "I'm going to kill them both" was what the character in the film had said.

Despite himself, Tim looked to see where Clara and Anne-Sophie were. It didn't take too much imagination, only a little insider information, to see what was happening, or maybe going to happen here. Cray had some idea, correct or incorrect, about his wife and Antoine de Persand. Since Tim had had the same idea, he reached this conclusion easily. It appeared that Persand also remembered the rest of *Rules of the Game*. Tim noticed him staring pensively at the shotgun, which Cray now picked up from under his chair. This did introduce a general uneasiness, though it looked like he was going to illustrate some cinematic point, and it was unthinkable that the thing would be loaded.

"It is axiomatic in the theater," Cray said. "It is a maxim of Chekhov, that the gun you see in the first act must go off in the third."

This was chilling enough. Still, Tim found it hard to make the next leap. In the aftermath of bloody scenes, people often said, "I couldn't believe it was happening," or "I didn't think he would really do it." The weighing of possibilities and probabilities was delicate. What had a person to lose, to gain? How crazy was he, or how angry? How much did he hate? Tim couldn't guess what Cray was planning to do.

Luckily Serge is not one of those men, thought Clara, thinking of all the tales of murdered Saudi sisters, Sicilian blood feuds, battered women in shelters, lovers gunned down. Still she felt her head grow light. Was there danger to Antoine? But of course there was no danger, this was civilization, France, the twentieth century.

Anyway, he didn't know the name of her lover, even if he believed she had one.

Serge did not think of women as property. Did he? Had no archaic sense of violated manhood. Did he? She thought of the trophy antlers on all the walls of all the local manors. She didn't know how he knew, but she knew he knew.

Antlers, horns, age-old symbols so maddening to men. Why?

"Now, this shotgun is the operative symbol tonight. This is not the first shotgun, I believe, to appear at a wedding, ha ha." Cray looked through the open barrels. An intimation of alarm, not full-blown, rippled around the table, in the form of giggles and "shshsh."

He has often said a man has a right to defend his property, Clara thought. Regarding the newspaper clippings, he was always on the side of people defending their property. She didn't know Serge, really. He would not shoot at her with Lars sitting right here, but she had to expect vengeance, she saw that. He would make no effort to keep her out of prison. With the thought of jail the future clouded, ended. One might as well be dead; yet she would get through it.

These thoughts tumbled through her mind, projections of her guilty feelings. Her mind raced. Senhora Alvares was suddenly at her elbow, drawing Lars away. Clara smiled reassuringly at her child, and sent him out of the room, kissing him and making the little fluttering signs with her hands, her eyes never leaving Cray. He would not shoot me with Lars nearby, she was thinking, but now he can.

"A wedding is, by definition, act one," Serge was saying calmly. At this he put two shells into the barrels and closed the gun with a definitive click. "Though for some of the guests, tonight may be act three of a different drama."

"*Attention, monsieur,*" said the mayor, rising and stepping back.

Cray lifted the gun, aimed over the heads of the guests at one of the splendid gilt chandeliers hanging from the ceiling of the salon beyond, and fired one barrel. The chandelier was revealed to be of papier-mâché; some bits of it were torn by the buckshot and drifted down.

"Ah," Cray said.

Chairs scraped back, people objected, angry voices rose, and laughter too. Some stood and stepped away from the table, but everyone continued to watch with interest, not sure this was not the beginning of a skit or entertainment.

Now he will shoot me, Clara thought. Her body shrank, cringed, in spite of her spirit.

Cray turned back to the table, still holding the shotgun. Tim was on his feet, thinking that he must try to get the gun. Feeling people move toward him, Cray rapidly brought the gun up again, looked down it around the table, until he had Clara in his sights. People screamed. As Tim dived toward him, so did Antoine de Persand, and, surprisingly, Jerry Nolinger, Tim's father, who was nearest of the three to Cray. Cray made no effort to retain the gun, releasing it to Nolinger, and smiling his knowing and sarcastic smile at Persand, whose picturesque dive from eight feet away was seen by everybody.

"I didn't really doubt that it was you," Cray said.

The whole thing was over in seconds. In the sheepish mood of anticlimax, people moved back to the table, trying with concerted insouciance to act as if nothing had happened.

"Sit down, sit down," Cray said to his guests. "Didn't mean to frighten or disturb, go on, go on. Little joke, didn't mean . . . There is dancing." Out of the corner of his eye, Tim noticed Cees returning some object, perhaps a gun, to his pocket.

Not everyone could hear what Cray had said, and it must have appeared to be no more than an incident where the gun-wary Nolingers and Antoine de Persand had moved responsibly to take the weapon from someone unused to guns, someone a little drunk perhaps. But some people took their leave in a few minutes, all the same, including the Persands, the two Mesdames de Persand looking grim. Clara, eyes as transfixed as an animal's at night, had not moved, but now she rose and left the table.

She had seen that Antoine loved her and had risked death.

She walked to the foyer with various departing guests, chatting with her usual poise, with calm conversation, thanking them for coming, bidding them come again. All remarked on her aplomb—she must have had an anxious moment, with the gun, however accidentally, pointed right at her. From the corner of his eye, Tim thought he had seen her put her hand up, futile against being shot.

"Shit, I would have been under the table," said Graves's wife Sue.

Antoine couldn't have known Serge wouldn't fire (or would he have?), thought Clara, and he had wanted to save her, and now perhaps his wife, seeing what Serge believed, would believe the same thing. She was sorry if trouble came down on Antoine. Or was she? She would have to think about this later.

Antoine had not spoken to her the whole evening, not even when they arrived, and not upon leaving. They had left so abruptly, there was no time even for that exchange of looks she had hoped to feed upon: eternal love, eternal desire. Yet he had come tonight, and had bravely sprung at Serge.

So, however, had Tim's father, whom she didn't even know. It was the action of a normally chivalrous man, of anyone brave. Tim Nolinger too had been moving toward Serge. She saw the scene indelibly, she would always see it.

L'Abbé Des Villons saw the Persands out, his arm around Trudi, who he saw would need spiritual guidance and consolation after a scene she too had understood perfectly: Antoine and the neighbor's wife. Madame Suzanne de Persand, livid, would not speak to Antoine.

It is hard to deal with excitement in a foreign language, and one of the aftereffects of the unforeseen moment of drama was that bilingual accord broke down completely. French people spoke to other French people, and the anglophones drew together to talk to each other. Tim and Anne-Sophie persuaded their friends to stay a while longer for the dancing. Anne-Sophie and Tim danced the first dance, but she avoided his eyes.

The Americans especially crowded around Jerry Nolinger, asking for his account of what had crossed through his mind at the moment he moved toward the armed man, et cetera.

"The incredible bravery of Jerry Nolinger," whispered Dorothy Sternholz to Terry Nolinger. "A real American aristocrat."

"It was a stage thing, it was staged," one of the French people said.

Perhaps it was, for Cray did not behave like a dangerous man who had almost succumbed to a murderous impulse, but more like a man with a Hitchcockian mind who had just demonstrated some Aristotelian principle of the drama or cinematic effect. He wandered among the guests with a pleased little smile, inviting them with studied courtesy to have more champagne. He did not look at Clara.

She was sorry he knew, sorry, paradoxically, that now Serge would think less of her honesty, of her character. She felt defiant, but it was more the defiance born of centuries of men controlling women. Can you defy what hasn't expressly been forbidden? Can you have an illicit love affair and also a feeling of perfect rectitude and justification at the same time?

She foresaw that at leisure, perhaps in the night, a decade of small grievances against Serge would find admittance that she hadn't allowed in before, his coldness, distance, the fault of not being that attractive, let's face it, probably people had always wondered how she could stand sleeping with Serge; how had she, anyhow? Thus her heart hardened along the lines dictated by its desires.

It was not lost on those who had followed the contretemps that Cray was angry with his wife, for which there was a common, well-known explanation, especially in cases where the wife is so much younger and better looking than the husband.

"Usually money is an equalizing factor," observed Estelle to Madame Wallingforth. "Cray's money and fame would balance mere biology, but only up to a point."

"He was often very mean to her, I have seen it," said Anne-Sophie. "Once when we were there, he called her the stupidest woman in the world."

"So you think Persand is her lover?" wondered Tim, thinking about Anne-Sophie's role in the Driad manuscript, and that he'd never understand that, or her, or women, or what Persand's secret was, to have lured Clara into his bed, if that indeed was the implication of the little drama, which could also have been simple chivalry.

"I would never say this to Suzanne," said Madame Walling-forth, laughing, to Estelle, "but really, her sons should stay home. Look what happened to Charles-Henri."

"Especially with Americans involved. Their outlook is so un-evolved," said Mayor Briac, who had stayed on, chatting with the ladies and quite enjoying the discomfiture of the Crays and the general confusion.

"Not to say primitive," agreed Monsieur l'Abbé, coming back.

"Out here," said Anne-Sophie to Tim. "I have something for you—my wedding present to you, I wanted to give it you tonight, tomorrow will be so—"

"It's cold out here, it's pouring rain," said Tim. "You haven't got a coat."

"Does a woman feel cold on the eve of her nuptials?" This rather sweet thing was said, however, in a tone of crisp asperity. Once they had stepped out on the terrace, Tim saw that Anne-Sophie was shaking with fury, not cold. He touched her cheek. She turned it away from his hand. They sheltered away from the icy drips off the awning.

She said, enraged, "Going for the gun—how brave of you! But how—how—now the wedding is *raté, gâché,* spoiled, a complete anticlimax, no one will ever remember anything but this appalling scene, of crazed Americans—sorry, but yes, with their guns waving around, and you might have been shot."

"A memorable night?" Tim suggested.

"All revolving around Clara, the darling Clara with her tumultuous bosom, with maddened, jealous, lovesick men all around including the groom—"

"Don't be silly, Anne-Sophie," Tim said, sensing from an irrational note in her voice the extent of the impending storm.

Anne-Sophie mastered herself, remembering full well the maxims of the countess Ribemont with regard to suggesting to men that other women were beautiful or desirable: "Men are infinitely suggestible. Never plant anything in their minds about the beauty of other women. But be sure never to claim another woman is ugly either, for he will not agree with you, and by suggesting plainness you provoke him to her defense. It is a strategic error to mention other women at all."

"*Désolée*," she said, mastering herself, with her sweet smile. "It's just that we don't get married every day. I feel a little that she has breathed on my star. Of course you do not understand."

In fact, Tim didn't. He didn't even understand the expression, and anything seemed trivial compared to a tragedy averted, the onset of painful scenes for the Crays and the Persands, bleak inexplicable passions all around, jail—these all seemed so much more important than Anne-Sophie's feeling slightly upstaged. "Pull yourself together, it'll be fine." It was the wrong thing to say, but his mind wasn't on tact.

"Yes, so brave to stop a bullet for Clara, think how sad, no groom at all, the people all gathered—"

"It doesn't sound so bad to me," Tim said, "though I hadn't quite contemplated death as a way out of this." He meant this more as a sort of joke, and yet they both realized its utter accuracy. Anne-Sophie fixed him with a flinty stare of complete understanding. Tim saw an inscrutable glint in her eye, an implacable hardening.

"What are you talking about?" she asked. She shoved the *cadeau de mariage* at him and stalked back into the party. Tim put the package, beautifully wrapped in bridal silver paper, with his coat, planning to open it later.

If there were those who like Tim were uneasy about what would happen between the Crays, no one gave in to the fear. With the last guests gone, the caterers swarmed around dismantling the tables and bundling the napkins. It was not quite like being alone together. As the candles were put out, the huge room became somber. "Leave one," Clara said. She helped gather the napkins and did not look at Serge until he planted himself in the kitchen door in front of her.

"Did you think I'd shoot you?" he asked.

Her mind raced. "I didn't know." The most prudent answer.

"I might have. I didn't plan to, only to do the little Agatha Christie/Hitchcock number, where the real murderer cracks under the tension. Of course, not murder in this case. Not that I didn't know who your boyfriend was anyway.

"But when I had you in my sights, there was a fraction of a

second—I could see how it could happen, the irresistible impulse, it could happen—"

"I'm sorry, Serge," she said.

"I understand, Clara. You've been upset, you had this ghastly prison experience, Lars—I understand you very well."

Oh God, thought Clara, I'm being forgiven. It was the most difficult moral position she could imagine. Was forgiveness the same as getting permission to go on? It was that he didn't care a whole lot, she suddenly saw. Wounded vanity, maybe, but basically he wanted to get this over, to get on with his movie, his manuscripts. A little warmth of relief crept back into her breast.

"I've always known—you were so young, inexperienced—I always knew you would eventually stray a little if you had any gumption at all. That doesn't make it easier, I'm hurt of course. . . ." He droned on. She got the gist and couldn't hear any more, her ears humming, relief drowning out his words.

"Good night, Serge," she murmured.

"I'll come up with you," he said. Together they looked in at Lars. As she foresaw, he then came into her room. Contritely she loosed her lavish breasts, and laid her nightgown aside, wondering if this was a large or a small price to pay; in any case she was not alone among womankind in paying it to keep her inner reservations in peace, her forward plans unencumbered. Serge made love to her with an attention and passion he had not shown for months. For Clara it was too late, but luckily he didn't notice.

Tim escorted Anne-Sophie, Estelle, and Madame d'Argel back to the Argels' house. He himself was staying at the little hotel where he had put up Dick Trent, just on the square opposite the church. He kissed the ladies decorously.

"Ha ha." Estelle was laughing. "The great moment when he pointed the gun and Antoine de Persand jumped, and the thing was sewn with a white thread."

Anne-Sophie was still steamed. "Stupid theatricals at our wedding party. It's so sordid and out of place. . . ." Fuming on about it. Finally she broke off abruptly, as if stirred by some thought, and said, "I hope you will never want to shoot me, Teem." Now she was smiling lovingly; all the same, he knew what she meant, the hope they would never get to that pass, infidelity, anger. "Good night, Teem, don't forget the registry at eleven."

"Right," he said vaguely, took his leave, and walked across the darkened cobbled square, remembering only now that he had left the wedding present at the Crays' and would have to get it in the morning. As he went down the corridor of the hotel, he could clearly hear whispers and female giggles coming from Dick Trent's room.

59

Wedding Day

Tim was amazed to find that the official helping them with the civil formalities at the city hall was the mayor himself, the longtime adversary of Cray whom they had seen at last night's rehearsal dinner in his hunting costume. The mayor, however, did not acknowledge the connection by any reference to the events of the night before. He gravely showed them where to sign and attest, and indicated that Tim and Anne-Sophie were in fact now married in the eyes of France. It didn't really seem like it, the whole thing had taken only minutes, though they gazed in one another's eyes, kissed, looked around at their parents, grinned stupidly. They were separated almost immediately, in any case, by the need for Anne-Sophie to go and dress for the church.

They kissed goodbye perfunctorily, and Anne-Sophie drove Estelle and Cécile back to Madame d'Argel's. Tim and Graves Mueller, who was his witness, decided to go to a bar-brasserie for a *pression* which turned into several. Tim couldn't help it, his mind kept returning to the horse figurines, wondering why Anne-Sophie would give them to him. He hosted his friends and his parents at the club in Marne-Garches-la-Tour for lunch, and the hours crept toward the ceremonial hour of four.

"Or, as they say, 'sixteen hundred,' which sounds so much like a bombing raid," he complained to the others.

The little eleventh-century Romanesque church of St. Blaise at Val-Saint-Rémy had been added onto in the nineteenth century, with attractive stained glass showing such scenes as the reception of Robert le Pieux, roi de France, by St. Henri, and other scenes from history, all so familiar to Anne-Sophie from the countless times she'd attended this church with her grandmother. Her favorite was Saint Evêque Wolfga. The interior could have been too small and dark for an important wedding, but the big rose window was behind the altar instead of in the transept, so that even with the gray and now stormy weather, enough light was admitted to strike the bride with a flattering pinkish cast, and there was something festive, intimate, and agreeable for a wedding ceremony notwithstanding.

The bells (early eighteenth century) sounded the hour of three-thirty, their ominous—for so they seemed—call to the assembly, and people who had been sheltering in their cars from the icy rain began to move inside.

"*Alors,*" said Madame Wallingforth. "This weather, you know what it is, don't you? The Americans use so much of the world's energy—I heard this on France Inter—they use so much, it creates a kind of suction that destabilizes all the weather patterns, a kind of vortex over the continent of North America that can affect us even over here."

The arrival of Clara Holly Cray alone, without her husband, caused a certain amount of stir, because gossip had travelled fast, and the mayor, among others, had been sitting near enough to Monsieur Cray, the crazy American hunting opponent, to notice who it was Cray had had momentarily in his sights, and to observe the little exchange between him and Persand—the lucky devil. He had repeated the story to his companions as they walked home later. Now Cray had not come to the church. Possible irrevocable estrangement was envisioned and word of it had spread.

"You heard what happened last night at the rehearsal dinner? Her husband threatened to kill her, and three of her lovers wrestled the gun away," whispered Estelle's publisher, Monsieur Lepatre, to Anne-Sophie's colleague Monsieur Lavalle.

"*Three* lovers?"

"The bridegroom, apparently his father as well, and the local squire."

"What a menace to the neighborhood! But if she goes to prison, as I hear she will, at least the local wives can sleep unafraid."

It was even more delicious when Antoine de Persand, old friend of Anne-Sophie's family, arrived with his mother but not his wife, and then did not sit with his mother but on the other side of the church, the ostensible reason being that the bride's side was full. He helped his mother into a pew, then sat down next to Madame Cray with perfect accustomed ease, as though the two belonged together, and though they did not touch or betray any intimacy, Madame Cray's flushed sidelong glance at him made her emotion clear.

People could not guess what Antoine de Persand might have said to the women of his household, but to all appearances, and judging from Trudi's absence, it wasn't a pledge to reform. As he sat down by Clara, their relationship might almost be a settled thing, one of those social facts people accept with a wink, referring to the well-known Wednesdays (or whenever) of two people, married to others, whose irregular love had been sanctified by a kind of community consensus, this being France, Europe, the Old World, and almost the new millennium.

Or they would soon tire of each other, go on to other relationships, other turmoil. Human nature was more like that. But Clara and Antoine, apart from strong sexual appetites, had rather calm, loyal natures, so perhaps they would endure.

A certain consternation developed among the *Mademoiselle Decór* photographers, who had promised to lurk discreetly at one end of the transept, when they discovered that water had begun to trickle in, seemingly through the wall itself, and roll on toward the feet of the congregated people. Tim and Graves stood in the chapel, waiting for the moment they should stand at the altar. Tim felt sick, a normal feeling, his father had assured him. He reached for his handkerchief; he was sweating. He thought again of the horse figurines. What had she been thinking of? He had spent quite a bit on an emerald ring. He cursed himself for this sort of thought.

"Just cold feet," he said to Graves.

"Not surprising, you're standing in the icy water," Graves observed, rather pleased with the joke. But, there being no immediate French counterpart of the expression, "cold feet," the photographers took it literally. In a panic they tried to find something for the people at the altar to stand on.

"Monsieur's feet are cold," Madame Aix whispered anxiously. "The bride will be wearing little shoes, she will get pneumonia if you cannot find at least a mat."

*   *   *

Anne-Sophie, with her mother, maid of honor, and others in her retinue, had finished dressing at her grandmother's house. Anne-Sophie's heart began beating powerfully with the idea this was all a terrible mistake, but her uncle Guy leaned in at the doorway of the bedroom, smiled at the acreage of tulle and flowery scents, and said the car was ready.

A soprano voice from somewhere, the choir loft presumably, began to sing a song by Aaron Copland that chilled Tim with irritation, even as he knew it for the signal for him to do something, come out and stand by the altar. Graves tugged his arm. "Valley of love and delight," sang the voice in a heavy French accent. "Everything is going to come out all right." And, more ominously, "Turn, turn." Turn, turn was the refrain, but it was too late to turn.

The voice receded, the music changed to the *marche nuptiale* of Wagner. Somehow, to the diffuse and, to her ears, funereal organ strains, Anne-Sophie walked down the aisle on the arm of her uncle Guy. Tim and others lurked at the altar, all the Americans seeming by their squirming inattention not to realize this was the processional. They were used to the one called "Here Comes the Bride."

She glanced at the *autel* in the side chapel as she walked along, and what she saw confirmed her feeling of dismay—the painting of Mary and many symbols of virginity, lilies and such, whose message she had unwisely been indifferent to until today. There, also, Mary Magdalene. Did Mary Magdalene regret giving up her former raffish life? Her eyes filled.

She thought of the pilot of the Monday Brothers' plane, of the handsome Gabriel, wherever he was, of Antoine de Persand, and other men she would not now sleep with. She knew she had to summon enough adrenaline to run away; she waited for an infusion either of adrenaline or of certitude, but neither came to relieve her. A kind of potentiality was removed from the world, an inevitable flatness set in. There was Tim, handsome, rather rosy, as from drink, wearing a tense, panicked smile and the unaccustomed gray costume. Above her, from the rose window, Christ beamed benignly, surrounded by angels, no iconography there that would especially alarm Protestants, thank God, but Tim certainly looked to her overborne anyway.

*   *   *

As he stood at the altar watching Anne-Sophie coming toward him down the aisle, Tim's heart quailed, but he saw also that Anne-Sophie was lovely. The people were more numerous on the French side, naturally—a raft of Anne-Sophie's *cousines*, friends, uncles, brother, Estelle in a silverish dress sitting in front, with her mother-in-law and her sister, and Monsieur Doroux the academician. Suzanne de Persand looking unusually grim. Perhaps people's own experience of marriage could be read at such occasions as this, marriage a kind of Rorschach test.

He could also make out the faces in the audience on his side of the aisle, his friends beaming soberly, their wives in hats; other journalist and tennis friends from Paris, Cees and Marta, his parents and stepmother—these last had apparently swallowed their dispute (which arose from Cécile's continuing alimony) and sat in the same row—and a few rows behind them on the aisle, Clara, looking radiant, and next to her, her little boy and—Persand, by God.

The abbé said something quietly to Anne-Sophie and Tim that neither heard clearly, and then aloud to welcome the guests. Several members of the choir sang out, and here Anne-Sophie did take in the words:

> *Dieu vivant, Dieu très haut*
> *Tu es le Dieu d'amour*

The words in French of the Mass had a rather soporific effect, combatting the rising rush of the whole experience, these rival sensations producing something like focus for whole instants at a time. Between them Tim drifted off, not thinking about anything except the wish that it be over, the hope that he might not stumble, that the ring would appear and so on—the normal stage fright, he supposed. He could feel the gazes of the audience, the collective weight of their experience of marriage. He heard Anne-Sophie clear her throat.

The Protestants became restless, waiting for the exchange of vows and of rings, the only part they would recognize of a Mass and in French to boot, though they all agreed it was very beautiful. All knew enough French to concur with the sentiments:

Porter à deux bonheur et misère
Tourner vers le même horizon
Les yeux éclaires d'une même lumière
Chanter une même chanson . . .

Now the salient vows to marry them in the eyes of God, and the definitive words by the priest, the exchange of rings. Father Marks, the Anglican, stepped forward and said in English, "Do you Thomas Ackroyd take this woman Anne-Sophie Laure Marie to be your lawfully wedded wife?" and he croaked, "I do."

He listened for Anne-Sophie to say the same. The rest receded back into French, a language he spoke perfectly but for some reason could no longer understand. They knelt, moved and daunted by the solemnity of the cadences, and by the collective force of the audience's will as it directed its approbation toward them. Tim, feeling the unfamiliar ring, remembered his father always saying, "A gentleman does not wear jewelry." Anne-Sophie, clutching her bouquet, stole a glance at the pretty though smallish emerald and the new gold band on her finger.

When the priest blessed Anne-Sophie and Tim, Clara's eyes filled with tears. She saw she had been leading a shallow life, tense and self-involved, but now, she resolved that would all change. Her short martyrdom in prison for the cause of animals would purge her of vice. She had once been struck by some words of Colette: Vice is bad things done without pleasure. Did that mean that pleasure was virtuous? She thought so. Or did it mean that the bad we do with pleasure is virtuous? That sounded more like the marquis de Sade, or some other of those warped French philosophers. Antoine would know.

"I can't believe it, they're passing the hat!" observed Jerry Nolinger in a whisper during the offertory. "These people don't miss a trick!"

Singing, praying, it still wasn't over. L'Abbé Des Villons gave them communion, even Tim. Some of the older people trundled up to take communion alongside them. Prayer. *Magnificat, Magnificat Magnificat anima mea Dominum.* They were blessed. They were called on once again to sign their names—dear God! This signing alarmed Tim all over again. The strains of Bach, then of Beethoven— the Hymn to Joy? Impossible hypocrisy, why hadn't he reviewed the music? He thought he heard Estelle saying, "There's nothing as depressing as a wedding." They rushed through the congregation, onto the icy damp stones of the porch.

60

The Beginning

If only they could now thank l'Abbé Des Villons, wave goodbye to everybody, submit to being pelted with rice, and be transported to Mallorca by thought waves. Alas, they were only going as far as the Trianon Palace in Versailles this first night, then on for a few days in Bilbao and Lisbon, and there was still the reception to get through with its anxious moments at the end, when those not invited to the dinner afterward would surely show no inclination to leave, thus awkwardly delaying the real festivities. There was the relentless weather and the rising river. Some of the local guests who were also parishioners were asked to stay a few moments to help move the pews to the back of the sanctuary as the water mounted higher in the choir, *Mademoiselle Décor* photographers taking advantage of this hiatus for some posed photos of Anne-Sophie at the church door.

And then there would be the dinner with its excruciating toasts and skits, the departure—happily Tim and Anne-Sophie could take the lead here, but there would still be the thank-yous and exchanges, the intolerable ennui of the interval between the end of the ceremony and the time when the guests would turn up at the cocktail reception at the end of the square, and again as they strayed in to dinner (Pussy Lautremont and Dick Trent, Clara Holly and Antoine de Persand principal among those skipping the cocktail but appearing at the dinner, and at that among the last to arrive).

The dazed bridal couple had now got through most of these events, as far as the dinner. The guests, well served at the reception, were meant to sit down more or less right away when everyone had arrived at Madame d'Argel's house. Eighty people were expected, at eight rented tables set up in the living room and dining room. A little card at each place announced the menu:

*Salade de langoustines et parfait de canard à l'huile de
noix, Brioche tiède*
Navarin d'agneau
Buffet des desserts "à l'américain"
Petits Fours

Local women from the *boulangerie* and the restaurant had
been hired to produce the dinner and serve it. In the kitchen,
scarves tied around their heads, they put the fires on under the
pommes purées and the *sauce*, while the *agneau* simmered in the
ovens.

Antoine de Persand, the squire of the neighborhood, normally
reserved and autocratic, came in a smiling, don't-give-a-damn
mood, with compliments for all, solicitude for his mother, and a
perfectly open regard for Madame Cray, whose place card he was
seen to exchange, moving her from where she had been expected to
sit, with her husband (not there) at Tim's father's table, to his own.
This seemed to some observers to be the last effrontery, considering
Suzanne de Persand was also sitting at that table; it was not correct
to associate your mistress and your mother. Fortunately, Madame
Aix, moving through with a seating chart, saw the error and returned the cards to their predestined places.

Some people, especially the Americans, were disposed to cut
Clara Cray some slack when it became known she would begin
serving a prison sentence in the morning. She had a calm, an almost
saintly demeanor that was puzzling to others, especially the French.

"Considering she goes to prison tomorrow," whispered Anne
Servian Béridot.

"She's the American woman who stole the boiseries of
Madame du Barry," said Carole Simonot.

"That is she? She's a friend of Anne-Sophie?" Marie-Hélène
Pinard inquired.

"*Oui.* More of Teem's, I gather. She and her husband, but it is
she who did it."

"That seems so incredibly wicked. Some Americans are nice,
but they have no idea of history. They only think of money. Frankly
I am surprised Anne-Sophie would have her here."

"Well, she goes to jail, so let that be a lesson to us all," said
Anne Servian Béridot.

"But what is the lesson?" wondered Pussy Lautremont, observing that the handsome Monsieur de Persand appeared to think of the radiant Clara as a heroine, a great woman, as *La Pasionaria* or Marianne herself.

"Oh? Can a woman be a moral agent?" said Estelle, talking to someone else. "I think not. Poor Clara thinks she's going to jail to save animals, but of course she hasn't realized that a woman is a moral receptacle. She receives, enacts, or defies the most conservative strictures her society imposes, but she cannot act or innovate to change them. A woman can only be admired or condemned by their lights. She doesn't seem to know that. At least there have been very few women to act or innovate. Oh, Joan of Arc. How many others can you name?"

The recent kisses of Antoine were still on Clara's lips, stolen on the way over, behind the EDF scaffold in front of the antiquary's. This visceral dissolving sensation was probably happiness. Was happiness a fire you had to keep stoking? Or was it like a painting on the wall, permanently in place? She would have to keep it in memory for three months at least; then it could be renewed, refueled. She was thinking that perhaps she had been right to scorn people who searched for happiness. She had always believed that searching for it led to a degree of self-involvement that was unpleasant and possibly wicked, and was futile. To look for happiness was like looking at the sun during an eclipse. Not only did the sun disappear, but you burned your eyeballs too. Yet here, strangely, unsought, was happiness.

It wasn't that she believed in sacrifice, a dubious virtue that was always urged on women in particular and seemed to give them physical ailments. She remembered the headache she had had. But there was a satisfaction is knowing that by being in prison, she was paying in advance for a future of intended sinning, as often as possible, with Antoine de Persand.

"One of the great happinesses of my calling," the Abbé was saying, raising his glass for the first toast, "is to marry those whom I have seen as little girls, and given to them their first communion, and then to their husbands before God in marriage—and of course to welcome their firstborn, and all the little ones who come after. . . . I remember Anne-Sophie so well, those curls, always with skinned knees. In those days she was riding, and it was so clear she was brilliant at that. But devout, she was always attentive to her duty. And so to Anne-Sophie, entering into this sacred state, and to Thomas, may his heart be prepared for Christ, and to their future unblemished by any hardship, and may they ever harbor a knowledge of their blessings. . . ."

Anne-Sophie had slipped away to her grandmother's bedroom to change into a dress for the departure. A rising note of merriment from downstairs as the dinner guests, well-champagned, were dancing. In her stomach the beginning of a feeling of release, as if she had swallowed one of those Chinese pellets that unfurl in water to become flowers and castles, structures of unforeseeable color and complexity: marriage. She was starting to feel, or to realize she was, married. The fizzy sensation in her stomach came with a qualified feeling of optimism she hadn't been feeling before, or at least a feeling that what was done was done, and if something went wrong with the dinner, *tant pis*. At last she could eat dinner! No wonder she was cheering up.

For since you can't go back, you might as well set your face forward. Tim saw his face, unchanged, in the mirror as he untied the wedding tie and took out the sober stripe he'd brought along earlier. When he came in here, the den, and closed the door, he had found Madame d'Argel, Anne-Sophie's grandmother, hiding behind it, smoking a cigarette. When discovered, her soft old face took on a wild look between glee and panic.

"You're—I know you," she said. "They won't let me smoke."

"Who won't?"

"My daughter-in-law and some others, and the doctor."

"That's a hell of a thing," said Tim. "Stay, I'm just changing my coat. You can smoke. It's my wedding day and I say you can smoke."

As he stepped into the hall, he heard his father's voice. "To Anne-Sophie and Tim," said Jerry Nolinger, plainly uncomfortable at public speaking, but with a great deal of cheer and goodwill showing through, "I hope they will be as happy as the rest of us have been. Happier, actually. Well, I shouldn't put it that way. Even happier, I should say. Well, I mean, of course, as happy as humans can be, and a lucky guy like Tim will have no reason not to be, with such an angel for a bride, and thanks to all of you French friends for making our visit so pleasant here, and, thanks, so let's drink to Anne-Sophie and Tim!"

"Hear hear, hear hear."

He looked around. Anne-Sophie was just coming out of her grandmother's bedroom. Her laughter came directly to his ear over the slightly unintelligible cacophony of English and French that rose to greet them. They sought one another's hands over the shoulders of the guests crowding around them.